Seeds
of
Desire

Robert L. Spooner

OLD RUGGED CROSS PRESS

Copyright © 1994 by Robert L. Spooner
Library of Congress Cataloging in Publication Data:
Spooner, Robert L.
Seeds Of Desire
94-076891
ISBN   1-882270-18-5

Dedicated to my wife Patti and my three boys, without whose patience and sacrifice this book would not have been possible.

Chapter 1

"Oof!"

As I walk through the employee entrance of the Lansing, Michigan, post office, as I have for the last twelve and a half years, my meager five-foot, nine-inch, one-hundred and forty-five pound frame is assaulted by a body half again as large as mine and thrown across the wide hallway by the impact and against the opposite wall.

Under normal circumstances most people would be startled by this sudden collision of bodies off the football field, but for me this is just another everyday common occurrence. In fact, most everything that happens to me is just another everyday common occurrence.

I quickly evaluate the performance of the perpetrator of this violent action against my person.

"Good hit, Joe."

"Yeah, I know."

Joe is about an inch shorter and sixty pounds heavier and loves University of Michigan football, which is a brave thing to do here in the heart of Spartan Country. In fact, Michigan State University has property directly across from the Post Office building.

Most of Joe's extra sixty pounds has settled around his midsection making him look about six months pregnant, and unlike his midsection, the dark hair on the top of his head is beginning to thin.

I go to my locker and stick my jacket on the hook and set my lunch on the top shelf. It's another in a long line of rituals that I go through every day. It's twenty-five minutes after ten, so it's almost time for that all important ritual known as "punching-in".

I guess I've got it better than most, though. I've got good friends and although I'm single, my Mom and Dad live not too far away and, of course, I have my church family.

I guess it's just that sometimes I wish I were doing something a bit more exciting than sorting mail.

We punch in and get to work.

One thing about this kind of job, we can work and still talk to help pass the time. And we will discuss just about anything; there isn't anything that Joe doesn't have an opinion about.

A lot of times we'll argue over subjects just for the sake of arguing. One of us will take a devil's advocate point of view and try to "out-logic" the other.

Much of our ideas for subject matter comes from the front of magazines we happen to be sorting at the time.

"See, Joe, they're doing it to Canada now." I say as I hold up a magazine called *Canadian Mining Journal.* On the cover is an aerial picture of a large Canadian strip mine. "Pretty soon they'll have Canada looking like most of the United States."

Joe looks at the picture on the cover.

"Yep, won't be long now and they'll be strip mining the oceans."

Working at the Post Office isn't so bad, the pay is pretty good, the working conditions are clean, and in fact in the last few years since they've cracked down on some of the waste in management, which resulted in the demotions and even firings of some of the most undesirable supervisors, it's become an okay place to work.

"Five minutes to lunch, Joe. Are you gonna go running with us today?"

Every day now for the last five years I've asked him that same question and each day the answer's the same.

"Nah, I wanna lose some weight first."

"You started riding your bike yet?"

"It's up on its stand ready to go. And today I got as far as actually thinking about riding it."

"That's good Joe, maybe in a few more years you might actually sit on it."

"That's funny, Bob, but it's hard for a fat man to start doing anything. It takes us a little longer to get going."

Although Joe doesn't like being overweight, he does find a lot of humor in it. Some day I think he will lose that excess baggage, simply because he still remembers what it was like to be slim and a star athlete in high school. The only things holding him back are his own lack of will power and his overabundance of impatience.

Joe turns and grabs a box of flats, (that's Post Office jargon for oversized letter mail) and piles a stack on the ledge that feeds the mail into the A.L.F.S.M. (Auto-Feed Laser-scan Flat Sorting Machine)—a fancy name for something that doesn't work as well as some "former" higher-ups would have liked. We gave it a more appropriate name, "The Ollie North": "Ollie" for short. The reason being obvious for anyone who's around for more than five minutes.

KA-CHUNK!! CHUNK! CHUNK! chunk!

"There goes another one Joe, better call a mechanic, it's another inside jam."

Joe walks over to the phone, picks up the receiver and pushes the number six several times. The first time connects him to the public address system. After that an audible tone is heard all over the building.

Beep-beep-beep-beep-beep.

"Mechanic to Ollie number one, inside jam."

A couple of minutes later a mechanic nonchalantly walks over to the machine to where a red jam light is still on. He lifts open a cover on a section of the machine.

"Looks like old Ollie did a number on that one," I say as he pulls out a magazine, or at least what used to be a magazine. "So Jim, when are they going to get rid of this paper shredder?"

"Probably never. They tell me they might try some sort of modification that will cut the number of jams by about three-fourths."

"Oh wonderful," I say sarcastically. "Instead of shredding a thousand letters a week it'll only shred two-hundred and fifty."

Jim turns to go back to the mechanics area, when I remember something I wanted to ask him.

"Hey, Jim!"

He turns, "Yeah!"

"What's it like outside?"

"Good. A little chilly though. I'd say sweatshirt weather."

"Okay, see you in a few minutes."

Jim never seemed the athletic type. He's a tall slim guy who walks with his head bent slightly forward on his long neck. This makes him appear a bit hunched over. I think he leans forward like that because he gets tired of holding up his very prominent nose. I don't tease him much about his nose though, because I figure he's heard just about every "big nose" joke five times over. Even so, he still laughs at Joe's nose jokes. He's a meek kind of guy who never says much even when you talk to him, but you could never find a kinder, more loyal friend than Jim. But back to his athletic ability. When I first talked him into running on our half-hour lunch breaks we would only go a mile and it took us just over seven minutes, which is slow when you're used to running five minute miles. Now we're running five minutes and fifteen seconds, on average, per mile, for two and three quarter miles. Not too shabby for someone who'd never been involved in any sports before.

"You and Jim running tonight?" Joe asks.

"Yep."

"Well maybe by next summer I'll be in good enough shape to join you, if I can just get off my lazy butt and on my bike."

"I'll look forward to it Joe. The more the merrier."

Joe glances up at the clock. "Looks like lunch time, Bob."

It's about a one minute walk from the machine to the locker room where I wash my hands and go to my locker to change into my running clothes. Tonight, because of the cooler temperatures of late fall, I'll be wearing sweat pants and a sweatshirt over my running shorts and T-shirt.

After changing I walk back onto the workroom floor to the time-clocks where I meet Jim, who's already changed.

"Hi, Jim. Ready to go?" I ask as I reset my stopwatch from the night before.

I take my time card, which looks like a credit card, out of its slot next to the time clock. The time clock itself is a small box with a slanted front. On the front are numerous flat square buttons with a three digit number on each. One vertical row of buttons on the left has a pair of letters "O.L." standing for *Out to Lunch*, "B.T." for *Begin Tour* and so on. I push the O.L. button and on the little screen at the top of the box it says, "Out to Lunch, swipe badge." At least it doesn't say things like, "have a nice day" or, "play it safe," which is what the monitors on the weight scales say. I think comments like that are just a shallow, meaningless statement from a source that could care less if you have a good day or a bad day. I slide my card through the horizontal slot beneath the button and set it back in its holder next to the clock. Jim pulls out his card and goes through the same routine. When he's finished we start walking toward the exit.

We walk out the door into the cool fresh air of the night. The slight breeze hits the side of my face, and if I was a little sleepy before, I'm not now.

I move my thumb over the button on the stopwatch as we speed our pace into a trot. The same instant our feet step off the curb onto the employee parking lot, I push the button starting the stopwatch and we break into a full run. It's a pace we hope will get us closer to the five minute per mile mark.

We make the left-hand corner into the drive that leads out of the parking lot and then a right-hand turn that leads past the never-used guard shack out to Collins road which runs north and south in front of the post office building. We make a left onto Collins road heading north, and my legs are feeling good. They don't feel tight and my stride is long and smooth. I feel breathless but that soon disappears as my running lungs take over and my breathing gets in rhythm with my running. We turn left off Collins road onto Dunkel road, up the incline that leads to the overpass over Interstate 496.

I look over to my left and in the clear night sky a three-quarter moon is shining bright. We pass over the bridge into the only un-lighted portion of our course. On the left is a wooded hill, on the other side of which is a large apartment complex. On the right side, across the road, is a wooded area and a small lake called Bear Lake. Bear Lake is a natural wetlands preserve owned by Michigan State University and is used for research. On many nights we've heard animals scurry away into the brush as we've run by.

I hear something crashing through the brush a ways up ahead, and thinking it's another deer I mention it to Jim.

"Watch, there on the left, I think I hear some deer," I pant out, breathing between every third word.

Off in the distance a dark form moves out of the trees on the left.

"There it is Bob."

"Yep. . . Wait, that doesn't look like a deer to me."

We both slow down and then come to a stop as we realize at the same time that there's a person who has run out into the road, has backtracked back to the side of the road and is now kneeling in the tall weeds by the trees. We look at each other, standing there in the dark, barely able to make out each other's facial features.

"What'cha think Jim? Should we keep going, wait, or turn and make a run for it?"

"I don't know." I can tell by the way he said it that he's ready to make a run for it.

"Well, there's two of us and only one of him, and even if he came after us we could probably out-run him."

"Sure, if he doesn't have a gun."

I look back to where he's kneeling.

"I don't think he's seen us."

"I think we should go back."

Jim starts to turn to go back when I grab his arm above his elbow.

"Wait. I think he's looking for something. Maybe we should help him."

"Maybe he's looking for his gun."

"Come on, Jim, he doesn't have a gun."

"Okay, but I'm walking behind you just in case."

We start walking toward him and I'm just about to call to him when we hear something else coming through the trees. I grab Jim by his sweatshirt and jerk him off the side of the road into the weeds.

"Shhh, there's someone else coming," I whisper.

About half way between us and the man searching the weeds, not just one man, but two, come walking quickly out of the trees. The man must have just seen them coming because he jumps up and runs across the road and into the woods toward the lake. As soon as he started running across the road one of the men said to the other, "There he goes," and they start running after him.

Jim and I hide there for a minute or two before either one of us moves. I slowly, half way stand up and stare intently into the shadows looking for any sign of movement.

Jim whispers, "See anything?"

I whisper back, "Nope."

"Let's get out of here," Jim says still whispering.

"Jim, wait, I'll bet those two guys were cops and they were after that guy. Hey maybe he's a drug dealer and he dropped his drugs or maybe his drug money. There could be gobs of money lying in the ditch up there."

"Or it could be just his gun lying up there."

"He didn't have a gun or he would have used it on those guys earlier."

"Maybe he only had one bullet left."

"Oh, quit being a baby, and let's find out what it is."

I stand up the rest of the way. Jim is still crouched all the way down, so I reach down and pull upward on the back of his sweatshirt. Reluctantly he stands up and we jog slowly and cautiously toward the general area where we think he was searching. Not knowing exactly what we're looking for we move our feet from side to side in the weeds, searching more by feel than by sight. Jim kicks something and bends over to pick it up.

"Find it, Jim?"

He holds up an old beat up pop can. "Yeah, I found it, now let's go."

"Come on, Jim, just look a little while longer."

"We're gonna be late for work."

"We've got a couple more minutes before we have to head back."

I move away from the road, up the small hill, toward the trees.

"Maybe he lost it further back this way. Hey, hey, I think I found it."

I bend over and pick up a small, plain white box a little larger than a jeweler's ring box, and heavy enough to be made of lead. I hold it out for Jim to see.

"See, it's not a gun."

"It's probably a bomb."

I pull the top off to look inside only to find styrofoam packing. I put the top back on and walk over to Jim and hand it to him.

"Here, it's not a bomb so it's safe to put in your pocket. Let's head back and we can check it out later when we've got more time."

"Good idea, I don't want to be standing here if those cops come back and see us here and arrest us as accomplices. Besides, this place is starting to give me the creeps."

Jim takes the box, unzips his sweatshirt pocket and starts to put it in, but stops.

"Why do I have to carry this?" He looks at me suspiciously. "What's wrong with this? You think it's a bomb don't you?"

"Don't be dumb. If I thought it was a bomb, I wouldn't be

standing right next to you, and do you think for a moment, if it was a bomb, that guy would come back to look for it if it was gonna blow up? Besides, your pocket zips up, and mine's got a hole in it, remember?"

"Okay, but I'm gonna stay close to you. If I go, you go."

Jim sticks the box into his pocket, zips it up, and we both run probably our fastest three-quarters of a mile back to the post office. As we enter the locker room Jim quickly unzips the pocket, pulls out the box and shoves it at me.

"Here, you blow up your own locker."

"Okay. I'll put it in my locker and we'll look at it after work."

"Well, you can open it without me, and let me know what's in it later . . . if you're still alive."

I put it on the shelf in my locker. "It might be a good idea not to tell anyone about this just yet, Jim."

We quickly change, and rush to the time clock. Back at the flat sorter I start thinking.

Now, I know I asked Jim not to tell anyone about it, but Joe is such a good friend he would hate it if I didn't tell him, and Jim doesn't seem to be all that interested anyway. And Joe is pretty good at giving advice; not as good as me, but pretty good. Maybe if I . . . .

"What's the matter Bob? Are you sick? You haven't said hardly anything since lunch, and that's not like you at all."

"I've been thinking, Joe."

"I guess there's a first time for everything."

"This could be serious, Joe."

"I can be serious."

"Since when?"

"Since now. Try me."

"Okay, but you gotta keep it a secret."

"I promise to keep it a secret."

"Swear?"

"I swear."

"Swear on a stack of Bibles?"

"I swear on a stack of Bibles."

"Cross your heart and hope to die, stick a needle in your eye?"

"Who can't be serious?"

"Sorry. I got carried away."

"Someone should carry you away."

"This really is serious, Joe."

"So, then tell me already."

"Okay, something really weird happened at lunch when Jim and I were out running . . ."

Time goes fast when you've got something to talk about. Just as I finish telling Joe what happened I notice it's only half an hour 'till time to go home.

". . . So now it's sitting in my locker."

"Wow! What an adventure. Lets go see what it is."

"Now?"

"Yeah, now. Why not?"

"Because we might not want anybody else to see it, remember?"

"Oh, yeah."

"After work I'll get it out of my locker and take it home. You can come over if you want and we'll open it there, okay? There's only a half hour to go anyway."

"Do you think those cops caught the guy?"

"I don't know. In fact I was thinking, what if that guy was the cop and those other two guys were the drug dealers?"

Joe looks thoughtful for a moment, then looks at me with a slight smile on his face. "What if it's stolen jewels? You could be rich!"

"I'd probably turn them in to the police. There might be a reward or an insurance company might have a recovery fee."

Joe's face brightens even more. "And if nobody claims it, you could be rich!"

"Or, Jim could be right. It could be a bomb and we could both be blown to smithereens."

"That's just a chance we'll have to take, Bob. You only live once."

We take all the mail off the machines and wheel it out to the dock for dispatch, working right up to punch-out time.

I press the E.T. button for End Tour and slide my card down the slot. I motion with my hand to Joe.

"Come on Joe, if you want in on this."

I almost run to my locker. I stick in my key, turn it and open up the locker door. On the shelf, about eye level is, "the box."

Joe peers over my shoulder into my locker.

"Is that, 'the box?'"

"That's, 'the box.'"

Joe speaks in a hushed, almost reverent tone. "Wow, 'the box.'"

I reach up, grab 'the box' and stuff it into my jacket pocket. Joe follows me outside.

"Are you coming over, Joe?"

"You bet. I wouldn't miss this for anything."

Joe spots Jim over by his car and bellows over to him, "Jim! You goin' over to Bob's this morning?"

As we move within normal talking distance of Jim he replies kind of hesitantly, "Uh, no, I don't think so. Just let me know what's in it, okay?"

Joe goes up to Jim, puts his hand on his shoulder, looks him straight in the eye and says, "But Jim, it'll be an adventure. When was the last time you had a chance to solve a mystery other than reading the Hardy Boys?"

"I don't think so, but, you guys go ahead. If I'm not there you can start without me."

I tap Joe on the shoulder, "Come on, Joe, times a-wastin'. See ya later, Jim."

Joe and I head to our cars. I drive out of the lot and turn right onto Collins Road. It's only eight miles to home but traffic has been getting heavier all the time with the development of the Jolly Road–I-96 corridor. In fact, my house is sort of an overflow of that growth. I turn left on Jolly Road, heading east out of town. The countryside is still very farm-like along this three-mile stretch of road before I get to Hagadorn Road. If it wasn't for Michigan State University owning the land and keeping it from being developed it would probably be all built up with all kinds of commercial and industrial buildings cluttering up the countryside. Like it is from Hagadorn Road all the way to Meridian Road, which is the road I live on.

At the stoplight on the corner of Jolly Road and Okemos Road I look in my mirror and I can see Joe hugging my bumper. I guess Joe doesn't want to miss a single minute of this.

Joe's the kind of guy who loves a mystery and exploring the unknown. I remember him telling me how on vacations, he would go find old abandoned farm houses and just look through them. As Joe would say, "It's an adventure."

The light turns green and I head on down Jolly Road where the businesses give way to the residential. Subdivision after subdivision line both sides of the road with the only break in the monotony being the Okemos Hills Golf Club which runs for a mile along one side of the road looking like a well groomed park.

I look in my rear view mirror and see Joe still right behind me, not that I expected anything different. I smile to myself because of Joe's level of excitement. It's a little bit infectious at times and I sometimes have to stop myself from getting too caught up in it.

I stop at Meridian Road where Jolly Road ends and turn right. On the left are a couple of small horse farms still holding out against the crush of subdivisions. I drive up the I-96 overpass, turn on my left turn signal, and slow down as I come down the other side. On my left is one of the newest subdivisions, where the lots are two acres or more in size and are located within a large wooded area. One of the requirements for building there is to leave as many trees as possible to preserve the "natural beauty" of the area. I turn into the first drive and move slowly down the tree-lined, winding street. It's kind of a ritzy neighborhood, but when you're single and have a good steady job, you can afford some of the nicer things in life, although my house is one of the smaller ones.

I drive all the way to the back of the subdivision to where the road curves right to make the wide loop back out to Meridian Road. On the left is a medium sized stone ranch with dark wood trim. It sits back from the street about a hundred feet, making it partially hidden by the trees. I pull into the driveway that wanders between the many trees up to the two-car attached garage and push the button on my garage door opener. The right-hand door opens and I get out of my car. In the stall next to my car is the diesel utility tractor I use to mow my two and one-half acres of lawn, as well as some of my neighbors' lawns. Extra money is extra money. All my yard tools and mechanics tools are lined neatly along the walls or hanging up.

Joe pulls up right behind me in the driveway, jumps out, and walks quickly up to me with a big grin on his face. I push the buttons on the garage door opener inside the garage and as the door closes, Joe and I go into the house.

Joe and I walk down the short hallway that leads past the kitchen and into the living area. The decor is of a rustic nature, with oak trim and large barn beams running across the ceiling. One end of the room is taken up by a large stone fireplace. The house is actually bigger than I need at the moment, but I planned for the

possibility of a family sometime in the future. Even so, by using
one bedroom as a study and home office area and the other as a
guest room, I do manage to utilize the three bedrooms. The bathroom off the master bedroom I made into a darkroom for my pho-
tography hobby. I even have a secret door behind one wall in the
darkroom that leads to a tiny room where I keep a small safe. The
basement is my all around rec-room where I have every essential
diversion needed for a single man. In one corner is a table-tennis
table, in another the pool table, and in another my set of weights.

Joe and I sit down on the couch.

"You got, 'the box?'" Joe asks.

"Right here."

I reach into my jacket pocket and pull out "the box."

Holding it out in the palm of my hand I say, "The Box." I put
"the box" down on the coffee table in front of me.

Joe and I look at each other and at the same time we say, "The
box."

"Okay, Bob, open it and let's find out what it is."

"Okay, here it goes."

I lean forward to lift the top off the box . . . .

Ding, Dong, Ding, Dong.

"The door bell, Joe."

I quickly grab the box, run to the fireplace and stick it up the
chimney onto a small ledge.

Ding, Dong, Ding, Dong.

"Joe, go to my room and get my gun off the hook behind the
head board on my bed and stay there unless I need you."

Joe hurries to my room and closes the door while I go to the
front door. I look through the peep hole but I can only see a shoulder. Well, here goes nothing, I say to myself. I turn the door knob
and swing the door open.

"Hi, Bob."

"Jim, what are you doing here? I thought you weren't coming
over."

"I changed my mind. Did you open it yet?"

"Not yet."

We walk down the hallway, back into the living room. As I
walk over to the fireplace to get the box I call to Joe. "Oh Joey, its
safe to come out now," I say in a sing-song voice.

I turn to Jim, "Have a seat on the couch there."

I reach up into the chimney and retrieve the box just as Joe emerges from the hallway that leads to the bedrooms.

"It was only Jim. No big deal."

We both walk over to the couch and sit down with Jim. I put the box back down on the coffee table.

"Okay, let's try this again."

I hold the bottom of the box with my right hand and slowly lift the top off with my left. In the box is a styrofoam cube that appears to be in two halves. I pick the box up, turn it upside down onto the palm of my right hand and slowly lift the bottom of the box off the styrofoam cube. The styrofoam is taped on two sides so I sit back a little, carefully peel the tape off, and pull the two halves apart. A gray object inside falls out, lands in my lap and Jim practically jumps off the couch. I pick it up and look at it.

"What do you think it is?"

Joe leans toward it. "It looks like a large gray sugar cube with squiggly lines on it."

Jim nods in agreement. "Yep, that's what it looks like all right."

The small gray cube is about two inches wide, two inches high, and two inches deep. I guess that's why I would call it a cube. Carved into each of its six sides are funny looking squiggly lines and pictures. I rub my finger over its smooth surface. With the exception of a few nicks, even the carved lines have smooth, worn edges.

"Seems to be made out of clay." I pause a moment. "I'll bet this thing is really old."

Joe looks thoughtful.

"Let me see it for a sec."

He turns it over in his hand a couple of times, looking real closely at it.

"You know, some of this looks like the writing on some of those foreign newspapers."

"Yeah," I say. "Sort of like Arabic or something like that."

Joe asks, "Bob, you got a magnifying glass? I'd like to take a closer look at it."

"No, but I've got a close-up lens for my camera. We can look through that. I could even set it up on my copy stand and take pictures of it and enlarge them."

"Great idea Bob, go get it. What an adventure."

I get up and go through my bedroom to the darkroom where I keep all my camera equipment. As I go through the door, on my left are the sinks and next to them are my film developing tank and chemicals. In the corner are paper trays, neatly stacked up with the paper chemicals in front. Along the wall straight ahead is my enlarger, underneath which is a cabinet stocked with 8x10 photographic paper. On my right, on shelves all along the wall, is my camera equipment. Almost anything an amateur photographer would need and wouldn't need. I grab my Canon AE-1 off the shelf and bend to look through the stuff on the shelf below.

"I know it's here someplace," I mutter to myself. Behind a telephoto lens I spot the box that holds my close-up lens, and pull it out. I go back to the living room and sit down, putting my equipment on the coffee table. Jim is looking at the cube, turning it over in his hand. With a half twist I take the normal lens off the camera then put the close-up lens on, an eighty millimeter macro, the latest gadget in the stores this year. I screw the bottom of the camera onto the copy stand, take it over to the small end table by the window and set it down with the camera facing down toward the table top. Joe stands up and comes over to where I'm setting up my equipment.

"I think I gotta get going. Do you think you could make a set of prints for me?"

"Sure, no problem, Joe." I say as I put a plain white cloth on the table under the camera lens.

"Yeah, I think I better go too," Jim says as he gets up off the couch and walks over to hand me the cube. "I have to get some sleep 'cause I got some things to do tonight before work."

I take the cube and place it under the camera. "Okay, Jim. Uh, Jim, do you want some copies too?"

"Umm, you don't have to. I'll just look at Joe's."

"If you change your mind, I can make copies anytime from the negatives," I say as I focus the camera on the cube.

"Okay. See you tonight."

"See ya, Jim."

"Catch ya later Bob."

"Okay, Joe, I'll see if I can find out what language this is, if it is a language, then maybe we can translate it."

"That'd be good. What an adventure."

Joe waves and I wave back and Joe and Jim both leave as I set my shutter speed to achieve the best depth of focus for my aperture setting.

I start taking pictures, turning the cube each time in order to get at least one shot of each of the six sides.

That night in the locker room at work I give Joe a set of 4x5 prints.

"That helps, I can see the details a lot better."

"Yeah, I printed an eight-by-ten of one and it turned out pretty good, so I'm gonna do all of them that size. I didn't have time to find out what the markings are yet. I guess I'll have to do that tomorrow." I pause. "Tell you what Joe, I'll check out the MSU Library and you can check out the library in Lansing."

Joe puts the pictures in his locker and we go punch in. As we're setting up the equipment to put the full flats boxes in, Pam comes up to Joe and I and tells us some news.

"Did you guys see the news tonight?" We both shake our heads indicating that we hadn't. Pam continues, "Some MSU researchers were taking water samples from that lake over there off Dunkel Road when they found a dead body floating near the shore. The police say he died sometime around early morning." Pam looks at me and points her finger. "You and Jim better be careful when you go running 'cause there might be a crazy person out there. The police said he was mutilated really bad and they think it could be some sort of satanic thing."

"Thanks, Pam, but a Christian can outrun a Satanist any day."

"You guys just be careful anyway, okay?"

"Okay, Mom."

Pam goes to label the boxes and Joe and I look at each other, then Joe looks around to make sure nobody's listening.

"Bob?"

"Yeah?"

"Do you think it's the same guy those two were chasing?"

"Might be. Maybe Pam knows more about it, like who he was."

"I'll ask her." Joe goes over and starts helping Pam put labels in the boxes. A little later Joe comes back.

"Find out anything Joe?"

"A little. Pam says he was a professor at MSU but there was no reason for him to be at Bear Lake."

"Why not? It's MSU property."

"Pam doesn't remember. There might be more in tomorrow's paper. Are you gonna tell Jim?"

"I don't think so. He's a little nervous about the whole thing as it is."

Joe and I spend most of the rest of the night exploring our options. Should we or should we not go to the police and if we go to the police should we tell them about the cube?

At lunch Jim and I, being fair-weather runners, stay in because of a steady rain outside. Joe, on the other hand, makes his usual trip to Quality Dairy, a nearby convenience store, for a large snack and a newspaper.

After lunch Joe comes to tell me what was in the paper.

"Well, Joe, what'd you find out?"

"The guy was a professor of archeology and he had just returned from the Middle East, they didn't say where, and let's see, what else? Oh, yeah, and he lived in those townhouses just off of Jolly Road. The police say they don't have any suspects and they're looking for any information from anybody who might have seen something."

"So what do ya think Joe? Think it's time to go to the police?"

"I don't know, Bob. You might be able to help catch those two guys but if this is part of a satanic ritual then there would be eleven more members of the coven out there after you, since covens come in groups of thirteen."

"Think we oughta, kinda, sorta, maybe, like, lay low for a little while longer with this?"

"Yep."

"I guess we could still try to find out what's on the cube in the meantime."

"My thoughts exactly, Bob. We might even be able to crack the case for the cops. What an adventure."

"Hey, Joe. You wouldn't happen to know what time the library opens would you?"

Chapter 2

As I drive to the library I wonder if it'll be open, because a lot of things on campus aren't open this early in the morning. Oh well, only one way to find out.

I climb the steps to the library, a large glass and brick building with vines running up the narrow brick walls that break the solidness of the glass. I start to reach for the door, only to be met by a sign taped to the window of the door. It reads; "CLOSED SATURDAY OCT. 29TH THRU SUNDAY NOV. 6TH FOR REMODELING. DUE TO WATER DAMAGE.

"Terrific," I say out loud as I turn to go back down the steps. Probably the first time it's been closed in twenty years. So what now? Maybe I've got something at home, maybe if it's Greek or Hebrew, I can translate it using my analytical concordance to the Bible. After all, it does have both the Greek and Hebrew alphabets listed in it.

I drive home a little discouraged. I really was hoping to find something at the library. I get home, go straight to my study and scan the many books on my wall. It's amazing how many books a person can accumulate in just a few years when they teach a high school Sunday school class. Those kids can come up with some of the most off-the-wall questions on just about any subject imaginable, and that's when I have to have reliable sources handy with which to answer their questions.

I pull out a large, hardcover book and put it on my desk. Then I go to the darkroom, get the photos of the cube and bring them back to my desk. Just as I get settled in my chair the doorbell rings. Ding-dong.

A little startled, I quickly stick the photos inside the front cover of the concordance and put it back on the shelf. Here I go again. I hurry out of the room, down the hall and into the foyer. I look through the peep hole. Last time I did this it was only Jim. I breath a sigh of relief as I open the door to greet my neighbor from just around the corner, Doctor George Myerson, a veterinarian.

Doc Holiday (we call him that because he's always complaining about how he seems to be called in for an emergency almost every holiday) is an older gentleman with mostly white hair, what's left of it, and a little less than average in height and mental faculties. Now I'm not saying he's dumb, not by any means. In fact he's quite the opposite, but he is showing signs of senility. But seeing him here, now, I knew he didn't forget what I forgot yesterday.

"You forgot to mow my lawn yesterday."

"Yeah, I know. I got busy with a project. Tell ya what I'll do. I'll change my clothes and run right over and get it done this morning."

"Good. That'll be perfect, thanks."

"No problem, Doc. This'll probably be the last time it'll need mowing till next spring anyway."

Doc gives a little nod of agreement, turns to go and without looking back gives a little wave of his hand.

"See you in a few minutes, Bob."

"Okay, Doc."

I close the door and head to my room to change. Well, I guess that takes care of working on my little project for today.

I know that after the mowing's done I still need to get some sleep and I have to study tomorrow's Sunday school lesson. By the time I get that done I might have just enough time to make the rest of those enlargements of the cube I promised Joe.

I hop on my lawn tractor and head on over to the Doctor's house. It's a large, two story, white frame house with a small balcony at each of the two front upstairs bedrooms. The front yard has three large, mature maple trees and a horseshoe-shaped drive flanked on each side by a four-foot high hedge.

As I pull into the driveway I can see Dr. Myerson standing on the front porch waiting for me. I stop in front of him and pull back on the throttle handle to idle down the engine.

"Yeah. Doc?"

"I was wondering if you could do me a favor. There's something scratching the siding just outside my bedroom. I think it's a branch from that tree there."

Doc Myerson points up toward where it looks as if a large branch has grown to the point where it's touching the siding near his bedroom patio. I can see scrape marks where the wind has pushed the ends of the branches back and forth across the siding.

"Oh, shoot, no problem Doc, but I gotta tell you I won't be able to get to it 'till prob'ly Monday."

"Oh . . . well, that will be okay, Bob. I'm going to be out of town for a few days to attend a convention/seminar in Cincinnati. I've got to keep up on all the latest do-dads in veterinary science, you know. Oh, gosh, that reminds me. Can you feed Samson while I'm gone and just sort of check up on him now and then? I know I can trust you, and Samson knows you. I just don't feel comfortable leaving him with those strangers at the kennel."

"When are you leaving?"

He looks at his watch.

"In about five minutes. You know where the key is don't you?" He doesn't expect or give time for an answer. "Thank you, Bob. See you in a few days."

He spins on his heels and is in the house before I can say, "But . . ."

I just resign myself to the fact that I've volunteered to feed the Doctor's dog, and throttle up the tractor to begin mowing the lawn.

"Ahh."

I lay back on my bed, looking forward to a good night's sleep.

I'm suddenly awakened by the sound of the phone ringing. I lift my head and squint through my heavy eyelids at the green luminous numbers on my radio alarm. It reads 5:10 a.m. Who in the world is calling at this time of the morning?

I fumble for the phone on my nightstand in the dim light, almost knocking it onto the floor.

"Hello?" I say in a hoarse voice, just barely getting it out.

"Hi Bob, this is Joe. I'm at work."

"You woke me up just to tell me that?"

"No, Bob, listen. Jim just got beat up."

"What?" I'm suddenly wide awake now. "Is he Okay?"

"Yeah pretty much. He's got some cuts and bruises and his nose is swollen. He's hoping it's not broken."

"What happened, Joe?"

"Well, according to Jim he was running around that bend where you found the cube when two hooded men jumped out of the weeds alongside the road, one in front and one in back of him. He said they grabbed him, and blindfolded him and took him to an apartment. He doesn't remember which one. Anyway, they made him sit in a chair and they started asking him all kinds of questions about a map or directions to someplace or something like that. Jim told them he didn't know what they were talking about, but he figures that it had something to do with the cube. When Jim acted dumb they started threatening him, asking him if he'd like to see his next birthday and if he'd still like going around the block if he were in a wheelchair. Jim said that didn't scare him too much until they said something about ending up like that professor in the lake."

I'm sitting on the side of the bed now, wiping the sleep out of my eyes. "Joe, did he say anything to them about me?"

"No, but they knew that Jim was running with somebody else that night and they wanted to know who, so they started punching him out so he'd tell."

"Where's Jim now?"

"He's right here, but his mouth is kinda swollen so it's hard for him to talk."

"How'd he get away then?"

"When they were slapping him up it moved the blindfold up enough so he could just see under it, so he was able to see one of them. These guys must have been dumb or something 'cause they didn't tie him up or lock the door or nothin'. Anyway, something outside the window distracted one of them and Jim just jumped up, shoved the one guy out of the way and ran out the door, cut across the field next to the freeway, jumped the fence, ran across the freeway and came in through the back dock." Joe pauses. "What's that Jim? Uh huh. Jim says they got his wallet."

"That means they know where he lives, Joe. You're gonna have to sneak Jim out in your car somehow."

"Jim wants you to go to the police with him."

"Yeah, it's probably best, considering what's happened. Is he gonna stay with you? I still wanna go to church. We can go to see the cops in the afternoon, and I'll bring the cube."

I hear Joe's muffled voice as he pulls the phone away from his mouth and talks to Jim.

"Jim says that'll be okay. You can pick him up at my house."

"Okay. Uh, tell Jim I'm sorry I got him into this mess and I'll see him this afternoon. Catch ya later, Joe."

"Bye, Bob, see you later."

I hang up the phone and lay back in bed, my mind going a mile a minute. My first thought is to check all my doors and windows to make sure they're locked, but I realize I'm still okay. They only know about Jim so I'm still safe.

But what if Jim had my name in his wallet? This thought makes me get up and check all my doors and windows and get my gun closer to where I can reach it real quick. I get back in bed and struggle to get some sleep. Finally I drift off into a troubled sleep.

Startled by a noise I sit up quickly and call out, "Who's there?" There's no answer but I hear a shuffling noise in the hallway. "If there's somebody out there you better speak up 'cause I've got a gun!"

I reach over to the night stand to grab the gun but it's not where I left it. I glance toward the door and there's the large form of a man in the doorway. More frantic, I search with both hands all over the nightstand, knocking the phone onto the floor and shoving the radio alarm up against the wall. It's not there.

"What are you looking for?" the person in the doorway says menacingly.

Not answering him I roll off the bed onto the floor, searching desperately around the side of the bed and the nightstand.

"Have you found it yet? Maybe I can help." He laughs a sinister laugh and flips on the light switch. I turn quickly around to see a large man standing almost directly over me pointing my gun at my head.

"Is this what you're looking for?"

I sit on the floor feeling defeated when Joe gets pushed into the room by another man. "Get over there with your friend." He gives Joe another push. "Move it!"

The guy with the gun motions with it toward the bed. "Both of you on the bed."

We both climb on the bed and kneel in the middle. I whisper to Joe, "What happened?"

"They caught us leaving the building and on the way here they threw Jim out of the car going sixty-five miles an hour."

"Both of you shut up!" the man with the gun says. "Now where is it?" He looks straight at me.

"Where's what?"

"Don't play cute, skinny. I'll blow that smart mouth of yours right off your face. Now where is the cube?"

"Which cube do you want? I've got lots of different ones. I've got ice cubes, and a Rubics cube, and cube roots and . . ."

The man fires a shot into the ceiling. "Knock it off or you'll get the next one."

"You do and I'll never tell you where it's at."

"Well then maybe you'll change your mind if we start with your fat friend here." He points the gun at Joe and looks at me. "Well?"

"Okay, okay! It's in the chimney. I'll get it for you."

"You stay!" He points the gun back at me. "He'll get it." He motions with his head to the other guy still standing near the doorway.

A little later the other guy calls back from the living room "I got it!"

"Well," the man with the gun says, "I guess we don't need you guys for anything else tonight." He points the gun at Joe and shoots him in the forehead. Joe slumps down and falls face down on the bed. In an instant I grab a pillow and swing it down on the gun in his hand as he starts to point it at me. The gun goes off and there's a sharp pain in my right leg. I yell and grab my leg and suddenly the room is dark, and everybody's gone.

"Wow, what a dream."

I'm still holding my leg which still has the dull pain that's left over from the muscle cramp I had gotten. Wait 'till I tell Joe about this one. I look at the clock and see that it's almost time to get up anyway so I get myself around and head for church.

I've been going to church most all my life. In my early years I was brought up in a church that was more of a social club than a place to worship and learn. Sure there were sermons on Sunday mornings, but they were more on social issues rather than spiritual growth. As a teenager I began to feel something was missing, that there had to be some greater purpose in life, so after I moved from home I began to search.

I knew the Bible held the key, so I began reading, not fast, just two or three chapters a day. At first the reading was a little difficult but as I kept reading it got easier. It's like listening to someone with an accent—the more you listen to them, the easier they are to understand.

From my reading I searched for a church that most closely followed the teachings of the Bible. The church I go to is not a large church; we run about a hundred in Sunday School, but it is friendly and close-knit.

I sit through the sermon drifting in and out of what the preacher is saying as my mind keeps going back to Jim. I only catch enough to know he's talking about original sin and everybody's need for salvation.

"God, in his infinite wisdom, drove man from the Garden of Eden," I hear him say. "Why? Why would it be necessary to get Adam and Eve out of the Garden after they've already eaten the fruit of the tree of knowledge of good and evil? Turn with me in your Bibles to Genesis, Chapter three. We begin reading at verse twenty-two.

> *And the Lord God said, 'Behold, the man is become as one of us, to know good and evil and now, lest he put forth his hand, and take also of the tree of life, and eat, and live forever. Therefore the Lord God sent him forth from the garden of Eden, to till the ground from whence he was taken.*
>
> *'So he drove out the man; and he placed at the east of the garden of Eden Cherubims, and a flaming sword which turned every way, to keep the way of the tree of life.'*

"Imagine now, if you can, what would have happened had Adam and Eve eaten of the tree of life. How it would be to walk around in a sin and disease-ridden body that is rotting away with cancer or some other disease. You feel all the pain but you never die. That's the way it will be in the Lake of Fire on Judgment Day if you're not saved, if you're not born again. Your body will be burning with fire but it will not be consumed. Like the burning bush Moses saw. You will feel the pain but you will not die. But there's hope. Trust in Jesus, repent of your sins and ask Jesus to be Lord of your life, and then you can spend eternity with Jesus in Heaven. Let's go to the Lord in prayer."

During the prayer my mind wanders again as I think about the evil that's been done to Jim, not to mention that poor professor. How evil does man have to get before God will intervene? As evil as the world is now, I simply can't imagine how bad it must have been in the time of Noah for God to finally get fed up and flood the world.

"Amen." I hear the preacher finishing up. "Let's all stand and sing a hymn of invitation. What number Brother Steve?"

The song leader, a smallish man with glasses calls out the number. "Two-twelve. Two-hundred and twelve."

The preacher responds with the name of the song, *Just As I Am.*

During the song the preacher invites those who want to get saved, those who need prayer or those who want to pray for someone else, to come forward.

There's a prayer for dismissal and everybody files through the door, each person shaking the preacher's hand as they leave. Some joke with him or tell him some news about themselves or their families. When I get up to him I grasp his hand to shake it and lean forward to quietly whisper to him, "Are you going to be home later this afternoon?"

"Uh, yes, I think so."

"Can I call you? There might be something I'd like to talk to you about."

"Sure, Bob, no problem. Anytime."

"Thanks, Pastor. Talk to you later."

I walk out of the church building and break into a trot in the parking lot. I have only one purpose in mind now. I have to get home, get the cube, pick up Jim and get him and the cube safely to the police station.

I pull up in front of Joe's duplex and wait a couple of minutes for them to come out. What's taking them so long? They knew I was coming over right after church. After a couple of more minutes I decide to go up to the door. Maybe they slept in or they're not paying attention, goofin' off. I reach out to ring the door bell, when the door swings a quarter of the way open and a large arm reaches out and jerks me into the house.

There are no lights on and the blinds and drapes are shut, so it takes a little while for my eyes to adjust to the light, or lack of it. When they do, I see Joe standing in front of me.

"What are you doing, Joe? You didn't forget I was coming over right after church did you?" I glance quickly around the room. "And where's Jim?"

"He's in the kitchen finishing his sandwich, and no, we didn't forget. We didn't want anybody to see you hanging around out there."

"Why? Have those guys been around looking for Jim?"

"No, but they could be."

"Come on, Joe. You're too paranoid. You don't see me hiding out in dark houses, do you?"

I remember my own insecurity last night and kind of smile to myself. Who am I to talk about paranoia?

"Come on Joe, you big baby. Lets get this over with."

We walk through the swinging door that leads to the kitchen. Jim is standing at the counter with his cheeks puffed out like a chipmunk from the sandwich he's just polishing off. With his voice muffled by the food in his mouth and a grin on his face he says, "Ha, Mop."

"Hi, Jim, I see getting beat up doesn't affect your appetite."

Jim grins again and stuffs another quarter of the sandwich into his mouth.

Joe goes over to the counter and picks up a piece of bread and a butter knife, "You want a sandwich Bob?"

"Yeah, I guess. Probably won't get a chance to eat again until I get home from the police station."

"Which one you and Jim going to?" Joe asks as he starts fixing a bologna and cheese sandwich.

"I figured downtown since the city police are probably the ones investigating the professor's murder." I lean back against the refrigerator and look at Jim eating his sandwich. His face is bruised, his lower lip on one side still looks a little swollen and his eyes look a bit puffy.

"You mad at me, Jim?"

"For what?"

"For getting you beat up."

"Why? Did you tell those two guys to pound the life outta my face?"

"No."

"Then why should I be mad at you?"

"Thanks, Jim."

Jim just grins and stuffs the last of his sandwich into his mouth. Joe hands me my sandwich. "Thanks, Joe."

"You're welcome." He turns to Jim. "Hey, Jim, you want another sandwich?"

Jim, still chewing on his mouthful, grins again and nods his head. Joe points to the bread.

"There you go, Jim. Help yourself. I'm glad you guys are getting this taken care of today, 'cause I don't think I could afford to keep Jim around for more than a couple days."

I finish my sandwich and drink a glass of milk. Meanwhile, Jim's finishing his third sandwich.

I look at my watch, "Ready to go, Jim?'

"Yep."

Jim gulps down the last of his milk and grabs a handful of cookies. Jim notices Joe and I looking at each other. "For the road," he says as he walks by and pops a cookie in his mouth.

We all head back to the living room where Jim is putting his jacket on and sticking his cookies into his pocket. I zip my jacket up and head for the door.

"Wait," Jim says. "Let's see if the coast is clear first."

Jim goes over to the window and pulls one side of the blinds away from the window so he can just peek out.

I grab the doorknob and open the door. "Looks clear to me, Jim. What do you think, Joe?"

Joe walks over to the open door and stands on the cement slab porch next to me. "I don't know, Bob. Looks partly cloudy to me."

"Real funny, you guys. I'd like to see how you guys would act if you got your faces pulverized. But it does look safe. Let's go."

Jim pushes between us, runs to my car and hops in.

"Looks like he's ready to go, Joe. See ya later."

"Yeah. See ya, Bob. Good luck."

"I don't believe in luck, but thanks anyway, Joe." I walk out to the car where Jim is waiting.

When I get in the car Jim asks, "Did you bring the cube?"

"Yeah. I've got it right here in my jacket pocket."

"I was just wondering if you'd bring it."

I start the car and pull away from the curb. "I figured I didn't have much choice. The police will need it for evidence."

Jim sticks another cookie in his mouth and we sit in silence for a minute.

"Jim?"

"Yeah?"

Did you get a good look at this guy?"

"Yep."

"That's good 'cause they'll probably want to make a police sketch of him."

Jim puts another cookie in his mouth and looks out the window.

"Jim?"

"Yeah?"

"How'd they know to grab you?"

"They said they saw us running away from where we found the cube and just waited for us to go jogging again."

"But how'd they know we had the cube?"

"Before they killed the professor he told them where he dropped it and when they couldn't find it, they naturally figured we had it and then just waited for someone to come running by that same spot at four-thirty in the morning."

"So they didn't really see us, did they?"

"Nope, and I acted dumb like I didn't know what they were talking about, so maybe they'll think they got the wrong guy."

"Except that really doesn't matter 'cause they know you saw one of them and you can connect them to a murder. I don't think they're gonna let you go that easy."

"I don't think so either."

Jim tosses another cookie into his mouth.

"Uh, Jim?"

"Yeah?"

"Do you eat more when you're nervous?"

"Yeah, sometimes. How'd you know?"

"Just a good guess."

Chapter 3

We turn left onto Michigan Avenue. Up ahead, looking like it's sitting in the middle of the road, is the state capitol building with its big white dome.

"Shouldn't be too difficult to find a parking space downtown on a Sunday afternoon, eh Jim?"

"Yeah, might even be able to almost park right in front of the station." Jim pauses. "You don't think those guys would be waiting for us at the police station do you?"

"If they were they would have done it earlier, thinking you'd go to the cops right away, but it's been almost ten hours since you got away. Nobody'd hang around the police station that long. It'd look suspicious. They're more likely waiting for you to show up at your apartment, since they know where you live."

We pull into a space with a parking meter just a few spaces from the front of the police station, which used to be city hall.

We get out of the car and walk up the sidewalk past the steps that lead to the old entrance to the police station, but is now for police officers only. The sun goes under a cloud and suddenly it feels a lot chillier.

"Looks like it's gonna rain again, Jim."

"Yep. Weatherman says forty percent chance this afternoon, sixty percent tonight."

We round the corner of the part of the building that's closest to the street.

"I guess that means you're not going running tonight."

Jim smiles, "Prob'ly not."

The rest of the station sits back farther from the street than the other buildings on the block. It looks more like an office building than a police station with its large reflective windows that cover its entire outside walls.

We walk up the steps to the thick glass doors.

"You ready, Jim?"

I grab the door handle and wait for Jim's reply.

"I hope so."

I pull the door open for Jim and he goes in first. We enter into a large lobby area. To the left are small offices with large windows. Going up half of the right side wall are the escalators leading to and from the second floor. The other half of the wall gives way to a wide hallway which has on one side an information desk and on the other the two elevators. Directly in front of us is an island area of decorative trees and shrubs encircled by benches, and beyond that, against the far brown marble wall, is a long counter on which are three computer terminals. Behind the counter is more counter space with drawers underneath, and standing there is a police woman.

This part of the building used to be city hall and the district court, but the courts moved to larger quarters, city hall stayed, and the police department moved into the available space.

The doors didn't used to be open on weekends but demands made it a necessity. Even with budget pressures, increased police manpower has become mandatory.

We walk up to the counter and wait for the police woman to notice us. She has her back to us and is flipping through some papers. Jim looks around a little nervously.

"Nervous, Jim?"

"A little, I guess."

The police woman hears us and glances around quickly. "Oh, I'm sorry. I didn't see you come in. Is there something I can help you gentlemen with?"

"Uh, yeah, um, I'm Bob . . ."

Jim tugs at my shirt sleeve with a lot of quick, short jerks.

"Wait, wait."

"What, Jim?" I ask, a little annoyed.

"Come over here." He points to the area by the elevators.

"Why?"

"Because."

Impatiently, Jim practically pulls me off my feet in the direction of the corner.

"Excuse us a minute," I say over my shoulder as I'm drug away.

As soon as we're around the corner I turn to look at Jim who's not even looking at me, but over my shoulder.

"Okay, Jim, what's the problem? You're not chickening out on me are you?"

All this time Jim is making quick glances at me and then back over my shoulder.

"Bob, look over there in that far room."

His voice is shaky as he points in the direction of a glass enclosed room on the other side of the building. In the room are three men in conservative-type business suits.

"See the big one on the left, closest to the door?"

"Yeah, the one with the moustache?"

"Yeah, well, he's the one I saw in the apartment last night, he's one of the guys that beat me up."

"Well, what's he doing here?"

"I don't know, Bob, but I'm not sticking around to ask him."

"Maybe not, but we could get one of these cops here to arrest him and ask him for us."

Keeping an eye on the man to make sure he doesn't get away, I start back to the counter where the police woman has gone back to her papers. When the man pulls his jacket back to hike up his pants, I stop dead in my tracks, turn quickly around and head back to Jim.

"Jim, Jim, he's a cop!"

"What do you mean a cop?"

"I mean he's a cop; as in, police; as in, we're in trouble."

"How do you know he's a cop?" Jim starts to look worried.

"I saw his gun, and his badge was hooked on his belt."

"We gotta get outta here, now!"

"I'm with you, but we gotta try to get out without him seeing us."

We wait until the guy's back is completely turned toward us before we begin to walk quickly toward the door, both of us keeping an eye on the guy in the room. Jim leads the way, but I'm right behind him with my hand on his back in order to both prod Jim along and to keep from running into things, since I'm not watching where I'm going at all.

Suddenly my feet are tangled up in Jim's legs, and there's a horrendous crash as we both fall in a twisted mass over the cylindrical butt can that Jim ran into right next to the door.

I regain my bearings, but as I try to get up I slip on the white sand that has spilled out over the tile floor. I land on top of Jim's chest.

"Oompf. I think he's seen us Bob."

"How could he help but notice?" I grab hold of the door handle and pull myself up. "A person would have to be deaf."

I pull open the door and Jim crawls out the door on all fours. As soon as Jim gets outside, off the sandy tile floor, he jumps up and starts running for the car. I follow right behind Jim, but about six steps from the building I stop and stick my hands into my jacket pocket.

"Jim! I dropped the cube! I'm going back for it!"

Jim calls back from the corner of the building next door, "Leave it! Let's get out of here!"

Jim's advice falls on deaf ears though because I'm already going in the door. I get inside and as the door closes behind me, I notice a small group of people have gathered across the room from me and several have already started across the lobby, led by the big cop. I must have startled him by coming back because he stops just a few feet away and we both just sort of stare at each other for what seems like a very long time.

I try to remain calm, "Uh, hi, um . . . ." I force a little smile. "I, uh . . . ." I scan the floor real quick and spot the cube about two feet off to my right. "I, uh . . ." then speaking real quickly, "dropped something." I bend over quickly, snatch the cube up and run out the door. I never look back all the way to the car, all the time thinking that he could be right behind me pulling out his gun and getting ready to start blasting away.

I jump into the car and toss the cube to Jim, who's already in the car and slouched down in the seat about as far as a person could get without digging into the upholstery. As I turn the key in the ignition I look up and see the big cop coming around the corner of the building, followed by a couple of uniformed cops and another plain clothes cop.

The instant the car starts, I slam it into reverse and shove the accelerator to the floor. Jim slides off his seat and onto the floor frantically grasping for a handhold as the car accelerates backward, tires screaming. With almost reckless abandon the car careens down the middle of the four lane road. I drive backward for about half a block until, at the first street I come to, I slam on the brakes and put the car in drive all in one motion. With tires squealing again, I turn left down Washington.

"If they don't kill me, you will." Jim climbs back up into his seat.

"You really should put your seat belt on Jim, you could get hurt."

"That's the best idea you've had yet."

Jim looks behind us out the back window. "Nobody following us yet, Bob."

"I backed away from them so I know they didn't get my license number, but they did get a good look at me and my car."

"What are we gonna do now?"

"Go back to Joe's, I guess."

I turn off Washington, which is a major street, onto a neighborhood side street and slow down. I weave my way through town on these small streets, avoiding as much as possible the heavier traveled ones, all the way to Joe's. Instead of parking out at the curb though, I pull into Joe's driveway and park right behind Joe's Jeep Cherokee.

Joe runs out to meet us. "That was quick. How'd it go?"

Jim gets out of the car and walks past Joe toward the house. "It didn't."

Joe looks confused. "Why? What happened?"

"One of the guys that beat Jim up is a cop."

"Really? What'd you guys do then?"

"I'll tell you in a minute, but first, how much stuff do we have to move so there's enough room in your garage for me to hide my car?"

"Not much, just a few things."

We go into the garage by way of the service entrance. As a kid I called it, "the people door." What greeted me was a sight to behold. Immediately to my left and directly in front of the large overhead garage door were four, well actually maybe three and a half, push mowers in varying degrees of condition.

"Do any of these things work, Joe?"

"Yeah, I think this one does." He points to one of the rustier looking ones. "I used parts from these others to keep it going."

Piled up behind the mowers are about six or seven full garbage bags.

"Hey, Joe, did they cancel your trash pickup on you?"

"No, those are empty coke cans. I just haven't quite made it to the store to get my deposit yet. So, tell me Bob, what happened?"

We start cleaning as I bring Joe up to date on our predicament.

". . . So that's why we gotta hide my car in your garage."

I pick up the remnants of an old electric motor. "What do you want me to do with this?"

"Just toss it in the corner over there with the washing machine parts."

Joe picks up a barbell with about sixty pounds of weights on it. Strewn around it are more weights.

"Haven't used these in a while. Gonna have to get back into it."

Joe sets the barbell over next to the wall, or at least as close to the wall as he can get it.

"Hey, Bob?"

"Yeah?"

"Where you guys gonna stay?"

"Well, I kinda thought we could stay with you, uh, temporarily that is. Until we figure out what to do next."

"I was afraid you were gonna say that."

Just then Jim comes through the garage door that leads to the kitchen with a handful of cookies and a large glass of milk. "You guys need some help?"

Joe turns around in time to see Jim pop a cookie into his mouth.

"Yeah, you could get some more of those cookies for us, if there's any left."

"Yeah, there's a few left."

"Okay," I say. "I'll have a couple too, but we gotta hurry and get this cleared out. I'm a little nervous about my car being out where everybody can see it."

I stop to pick up a pile of old newspapers when the headlines of another crime catches my eye. "Hey Joe?"

"Yeah?"

"You still got papers from the last couple days?"

"Yeah, they're in the house. Why?"

"I just thought maybe we could find out who's in charge of the investigation and go directly to him."

Jim comes back with two handfuls of cookies and gives a handful to me.

"Thanks, Jim."

Joe put his hands on his hips and pretends to be disgusted.

"They're my cookies."

"Okay. Thanks, Joe."

"You're welcome."

Jim gives the other handful to Joe. "Thanks for bringing me my cookies, Jim."

"You're welcome, Joe."

We munch on our cookies for a couple minutes, then Joe, in a serious tone, makes a suggestion. "Hey Bob, instead of trying to find the detective in the paper, wouldn't it be easier to just call the police from like a pay phone so they can't trace it and just ask for the person in charge?"

"Good idea, Joe. You go ahead and call and Jim and I will finish cleaning up here."

Joe pushes a two-wheeled mower off to one side. "Okay, see you guys later."

Joe starts to leave when I remember my car is parked behind his.

"Hey, Joe! I think I'm in your way." I reach into my pocket, pull out my keys and toss them toward Joe. Halfway there, Jim dashes in between us and with one hand snatches the keys out of mid-flight. Then, imitating a sports announcer and moving in slow motion, Jim describes his imaginary football exploit.

"He's intercepted the ball. He's going in for a sure touch-down. The crowd is going crazy. There's no one that can stop him."

Then Joe, from Jim's blind side, slams into him and drives him into an old mattress that's leaning against the wall. The sound of tools that used to be hanging on the wall behind the mattress can be heard clattering to the floor.

"No one but me, that is."

Everybody laughs and Jim willingly gives up the car keys to Joe. Joe leaves and Jim and I start cleaning again.

"Hey, Jim. Look at this."

Next to the wall opposite the mattress is a ten-speed bike up on a training stand. With the exception of a couple of recent hand prints on the frame and stand, it has a thick layer of dust all over it.

I look at Jim and smile.

"Okay, Bob. What are you thinking? I know that look."

"Oh, I just thought we could help Joe out by cleaning this off and moving it into the house so he can use it. What d'ya think?"

"I think he'll be forever grateful that we would be thinking so much of his well being."

"I think I saw an oil can someplace."

"I'll get a rag."

Jim goes in the house to find a rag while I scrounge for the oil can I thought I saw. Jim comes back with a hand towel.

"I couldn't find any old rags so I guess this'll have to do."

We clean it up and oil it and carry it into Joe's living room, setting it down in the middle of the room.

"There," I say with satisfaction. "Now Joe's got no more excuses not to use it."

We hear the sound of a car pulling into the driveway. Jim goes to the window and peeks out. "It's Joe."

"Quick! Lets get back to the garage."

We both hurry back to the garage and move a few more large items. I give a quick look around the floor. "That should be enough room for my car."

Joe walks in through the service door into the garage.

"Wow, I hardly recognize this place. There hasn't been this much room since I moved in three years ago. Oh, uh, by the way, the man in charge is Detective Mitchell Taylor."

I wait a second expecting Joe to tell us more, but he doesn't.

"Well?" I gesture with my hand in a rolling motion.

"Well what?"

"Didn't they say anything else?"

"No."

"You mean they weren't curious to know why you wanted to know?"

"Nope. Maybe they just thought I was a reporter or something, 'cause they just gave me his name. I said 'Thanks' and hung up. That was it."

"Well good. Let's get my car in here and we can go call him. Where's my keys Joe?"

"I left them in your car."

I open the large overhead garage door while Joe and Jim go

into the house. I pull the car into the newly cleared space. We cleaned just enough of an area because when I open my car door to get out, I'm barely able to squeeze my skinny body out. I slide sideways along the side of the car until I get outside the garage where I grab hold of the overhead door and pull it down with a thud against the cement floor.

Joe sticks his head out the front door.

"Hey, Bob, you better get in here. There's something you gotta see."

Joe sounded urgent so I dash around to the door.

"What's up?"

"Just get in here and take a look."

As we walk through the house into the kitchen, Joe explains to me what's happened.

"Jim was sitting at the counter looking at the cube when he noticed that a corner of it was cracked and when he handed it to me so I could see it, the corner fell off."

When we walk into the kitchen Jim is holding the cube, looking intently at the broken corner.

Joe continues, "Look what's inside, underneath the clay."

Jim hands me the cube and I sit down on a bar stool next to him and turn it over in my hand. I expose a ragged looking corner to the best light possible.

Joe moves in close to look over my shoulder. "See it?"

"Do you think this is what it looks like it is?"

Jim interjects, "Why else would they want it so bad?"

Underneath the layer of clay is something shiny, metallic looking and the color of gold. With the cube in the palm of my hand I move my hand up and down.

"How much do you guys think this weighs?"

Joe stretches out his hand. "Let me see it again."

I hand him the cube and Joe moves it up and down in the palm of his hand. Joe thinks for a moment and goes through the motion again, pauses, and hands it back to me.

"I'd say maybe just over two pounds, maybe two and a quarter at most."

"What do you think, Jim?"

I hand the cube to Jim and he goes through the same routine. He hands the cube back and I put it down on the counter.

"Well, Jim?"

Jim thinks for a moment, "I don't know. Let me see it again."

I pick the cube up again and hand it to Jim who goes through the same routine and hands the cube back to me. I put it back on the counter.

I question him again. "Well, Jim? What's it weigh?"

Jim tilts his head to one side a little, staring at the cube. Joe's looking a little impatient and I pick up on Jim's little game.

"You wanna see it again, Jim?"

"Yeah."

I pick up the cube again and hand it to Jim . . . again, who goes through the same routine . . . again, and hands the cube back to me . . . again. I can tell Joe is beginning to get irritated as I put the cube down on the counter again.

"Well, whataya' think, Jim?" I can hardly hold back a smile as Jim pauses to contemplate.

"Well, Jim?"

Joe, a little perturbed, interjects, "Yeah. Well, Jim?"

"I think, um, I think it weighs about, umm."

"You wanna see it again?"

"Yep."

I start to reach for the cube when Joe blurts, "All right you guys, knock it off. I know what you're trying to do and it's not gonna work."

"It's already worked."

"Has not."

"Has too."

"Has not."

"Has too."

"Has not."

"Has too."

"Not."

"Has."

"Not."

"Has."

"Not."

"Jim, did it work?" I ask.

Jim's grinning real big. "Yep."

"Did not."

"He seems irritated to me, Jim."

"Me, too."

"It's just your guys imagination. I'm not irritated."

"Whatever you say, Joe. So Jim, how much do you think this thing weighs?"

"Well, I don't know, Bob. Maybe you oughta let me see it again."

"Okay, Jim. Now you're starting to get on my nerves. And if that happens, Joe and I will just have to rearrange your body a little."

"Okay, okay. I'd say I agree with Joe. It's a little over two pounds."

"So, Joe, how much is gold going for these days?"

"How should I know. I'm not into that yuppie stuff, but I'll bet I can find it in the paper."

Joe turns and goes to the living room to find today's newspaper, leaving Jim and I in the kitchen.

"Well, Bob, I guess now we know why they killed that professor. To get the gold."

"Could be, Jim. Could be."

Joe comes back with the paper in his hand.

"I couldn't find today's paper but I got yesterday's. I figure that'll be close enough."

Joe opens the paper and turns to the precious metals listings.

"Ah, here it is. Gold; five-hundred and twenty-six dollars and seventeen cents an ounce, up three dollars and twenty-seven cents at yesterday's close. Let's see, at five-hundred and twenty-six dollars for, say, thirty-two ounces. That comes to, oh, about," Joe draws numbers in the air, "carry the one, sixteen. It comes to about sixteen-thousand, eight-hundred and thirty-two dollars."

Jim scratches his head. "Why would someone kill a person for only sixteen-thousand dollars?"

"People have killed for less. Right, Joe?"

"Yeah. I remember a little while back when a guy robbed another guy for five dollars and then shot him."

"Well what if we just let them have the cube. You know, just leave it where they can find it. Maybe they'll leave us alone. Maybe . . ."

Joe interrupts, "Maybe you know too much about a certain murder."

"Oh, yeah, I forgot."

Joe laughs, "Yeah, I know. Just a minor detail, right, Jim?"

"I think it was just wishful thinking on my part."

I pick up the cube, "I wonder if this thing's gonna fall apart anymore."

I turn the cube over slowly in my hand, inspecting it closely for any more cracks or chips. Joe moves closer then points to one side of the cube.

"There's a big crack on this side, Bob."

I turn the cube around. Starting at the corner that already has the chip out of it and running jaggedly across the face of the cube to the far corner, is a crack that is fairly wide at the chipped corner, narrowing to being just barely noticeable at the other corner.

I put the cube gently back down on the counter. "I guess we'd better not mess with it very much anymore. It might fall apart on us."

Jim's muffled voice comes from across the kitchen. "So what if it does. They're after the gold anyway, aren't they?"

I look up from the cube and Jim's got his head in an open cupboard scanning the food. "Maybe and maybe not."

"Yeah, maybe not, Jim," Joe says as he walks over to Jim and closes the cupboard door. "Remember, Bob said it looked kinda old, so it could be worth more as an artifact than the gold that's in it. It could be priceless."

Jim wanders over to another cupboard door and opens it. "Then maybe we oughta make it worth less by smashing it into little pieces."

"That won't help your situation any, Jim." Joe closes the cupboard door. "In fact, if worse comes to worse, you might be able to use it as a bargaining chip to buy you some time for a getaway."

"Okay, so I won't smash it." Jim walks over to the refrigerator. "But I'd like to." He opens the door and sticks his head in.

I laugh. "You hungry, Jim?"

"Yeah a little."

I reach into my back pocket for my wallet. "Tell you what, let's order some pizza. I'll buy this time. Sound good to you guys?"

Jim pulls his head out of the refrigerator and Joe quickly closes the door.

"Sounds good to me, Bob. How 'bout you, Jim?"

Jim looks back at the closed refrigerator door and then at Joe. "Yeah, okay. I guess."

"You guys go ahead and order. I gotta use the bathroom. I can stand just about anything on mine except anchovies and pineapple." I hold a couple twenty dollar bills out to Joe. "Order some Pepsi or Coke, too. Whatever they've got."

I get up from my stool and follow Jim and Joe into the living room. As I walk down the hallway toward the bathroom, I can hear Jim and Joe discussing what they want on the pizzas, agreeing only on the absolute necessity of extra cheese.

I come back to the living room and Joe's on the phone ordering the pizza. I look around the room and don't see Jim. My guess is he's in the kitchen looking for something to tide him over until the pizza comes. Joe hangs up the phone.

"Where's Jim? Feeding his face again?"

"No, he's in the bedroom taking a nap."

"But the pizza's gonna be here in about twenty minutes. Couldn't he wait?"

"He said to wake him up when it gets here. He figured a little sleep is better than nothing."

I look at my watch. It says four-ten. In less than two hours it'll be time for church. "Church. Joe, can I borrow your phone for a minute? I just remembered I was gonna call my pastor."

"Sure, go ahead. You gonna tell him about everything?"

"I don't know. I think for now I'll just see if he's got some good books on ancient languages. Maybe while we're trying to figure out what to do next we can translate that thing." I pick up the phone and check for a dial tone. "You got a phone book around here some place, Joe?"

"Yeah, it's right there under the couch on your end."

I bend down and feel with my hand for it. I grab hold of it, slide it out and flip through the pages looking for my pastor's number.

Joe goes over to his large overstuffed chair, picks up the television remote control and turns on the TV. "I'll keep it down so it won't bother you."

"Thanks, Joe." I push the buttons on the receiver of the phone. After a couple of rings I look toward the TV and notice there's a local news program on. Sort of an imitation of *Meet the Press*. I let the phone ring four or five more times and hang up.

"I guess he already left for the nursing home."

Joe looks up from the TV. "Do you have church members there?"

"No. Every Sunday afternoon at four-thirty he conducts a short worship service for the old folks there."

"That's kinda neat."

I sit down on the couch next to Joe's chair and look at the TV. The next thing I know, I swallow my spit wrong as I stand up and point frantically at the television set. All the time I'm trying to choke out a few intelligible words.

"Thaaa . . ." I cough hard a couple of times to clear my throat. "That's him, Joe! That's the cop at the station!"

"You mean the one that beat up Jim?"

"Yeah. Quick, turn it up."

Joe quickly picks the remote control up off the end table next to him and points it at the TV, pressing the volume button.

As the volume gets louder I can begin to make out what's being said. The lady interviewer looks intently at the man sitting in the chair next to hers. "Now, moving away from the subject of the drug problem here in the city, Detective Taylor, I understand the department is asking for some help from the citizens in the Lansing area in solving the cities latest murders."

"Yes, that's right. The latest victim was a graduate student at MSU assisting the late Professor John Royston, who was also murdered just this last week."

"Do you believe the two murders are related?"

"There are many similarities. Both were brutally beaten and the bodies mutilated, just to name a couple."

The lady interviewer leans forward slightly. "Rumor has it these murders are the work of a Satanic cult. Is there any substance to this rumor?"

"That is one avenue we're pursuing, but I can't give you a definite yes or no on that just yet."

"Do you have any suspects or leads yet?"

"Well, we believe there were at least two people involved. We have a witness that can place two people on foot, running away from the professor's murder scene at about the time of the murder."

"Then you have a description?"

"Well, actually we can go one better than that. We have the name and home address of one of the suspects and a description of the other."

"Then you expect an arrest soon?"

"Well . . ." Taylor pauses and gives a crooked little smile. ". . . you see, it's kind of strange and a little embarrassing. Earlier this afternoon the two suspects walked right into the downtown head-quarters, and before anyone noticed and could react, they vandalized some furniture in the lobby, ran out the door and sped off in a late model red Chrysler sports car."

"You mean to say they walked in right under your noses? Why would they do that? Why take that risk?"

"Well, laying aside the possibility of occult influences, some psychotic killers have been known to taunt authorities, daring the establishment to catch them. They may do things like call into radio stations or send letters to newspapers. For some it's a need for publicity, for people to pay attention, and for others it's a subconscious call for help. They want someone to catch them and stop them because they know what they've done is horribly wrong."

"Do you think this is the case here?"

"Perhaps and perhaps not. All the evidence isn't in yet."

"We're going to have to break for a commercial message at this point, but when we come back Detective Taylor is going to provide us with the name and picture of one suspect and an artist's conception of the other. Stay tuned. You may have the opportunity to solve a murder and claim the five-thousand dollar reward for their apprehension. We'll be right back."

As the television switches to a window commercial Joe and I just stare at each other not believing what we just heard. "Bob, he's framing you and Jim for those murders, and that Detective Taylor is the guy who's supposed to be in charge of the investigation."

"I don't think Jim is going to like this turn of events, Joe. I know I don't."

"That's an understatement."

"What are we gonna do now, Joe? We can't go to the police at all now. Somehow, we've got to clear ourselves. Somehow, we've got to get some evidence against this guy. We could tell them there wasn't enough time for us to run out there, perform a ritualistic killing and then run all the way back to work and still have no blood on our clothes."

"I don't think that'll work, Bob. They could say you guys drove your car, parked it a little way from the murder scene, ran to meet your buddies who are already there, killed him, ran back to your car, changed your clothes, drove back to work, and ran back into the building. All in half an hour."

"You're right. Then we'll have to get some evidence against him."

"But how? And what kind of evidence?"

"I don't know, Joe, I just don't know. I'm gonna wake Jim up. He's gotta know about this."

I start to get up off the couch when there's a loud knock on the front door. Joe and I both freeze, not moving a muscle. We look at each other and Joe has a frantic look on his face. He's probably seeing the same look on my face, but just before complete panic sets in, Joe's face relaxes and he lets out a sigh.

"It's the pizza, Bob."

There's another knock, as I go to the door. When I open it, there stands the pizza delivery man.

"Hi. Pizza for Maderna?"

"Well, close." I say. "He's over there." I point in Joe's direction and Joe waves. "But I'm paying for it."

"That'll be twenty-three dollars and ninety-six cents."

I reach for my wallet when I realize I'm being had.

"Okay, Joe, where's the money I gave you for the pizza?"

Joe stands up, reaches into his front pants pocket and pulls out a couple of wadded up bills.

"Shoot, for a minute there I thought I was gonna make me forty dollars profit."

"No such luck, Joe."

Joe hands me the money which I in turn hand to the pizza guy.

"So, Bob, think we oughta get Jim now?"

"That's up to you." The pizza guy hands me my change which I stuff into my front pants pocket. "If you don't he'll wake up hungry." The guy hands me the pizzas and a two liter bottle of soft drink. "And you know what that'll do to your refrigerator."

Joe heads for the bedroom while I close the door with my foot and head over to the coffee table in front of the couch, where I set the goodies down.

"You better hurry, Joe. The show's about to come back on!"

The program's theme song begins to play as I flip the lid open on the first box of pizza. As I lift a large slice from the box Joe hurries back from the bedroom, swoops down with one hand picking up an entire pizza box, and plops himself into his chair. Jim follows, his hair disheveled, rubbing his half open eyes.

"What's this about us being on TV?"

Joe and I both turn toward Jim, "Shh!"

I point to the pizza, "Stick some in your mouth and watch this."

The lady commentator comes on the screen. She's sitting on a low bar stool type chair with arms, holding a clipboard.

"We're glad to have you back. If you're just joining our show, our special guest this afternoon is Detective Mitchell Taylor of the Lansing Police Department. We've been discussing the recent incredible rise in violent crime in the Lansing area, mainly due to the drug gangs, and now there seems to be a bizarre twist in which there may be satanism involved in two very recent ritualistic type murders. Now, as promised, we are going to show you, the public, a picture of one of the main suspects in these murders. The police are asking your help in finding these dangerous men. Detective Taylor will give more details as we show the picture. Detective Taylor?"

I glance at Jim who's sitting next to me, his eyes are glued to the TV set. He's got a mouthful of pizza but he's hardly chewing, which is unusual for Jim. I look back at the TV. A picture of Jim flashes onto the screen and Detective Taylor begins talking.

"This is a picture of one of two prime suspects in the brutal murders of Dr. John Royston and a graduate student at MSU, Richard Symons. He's approximately six-foot tall with a slim build, about one hundred and fifty pounds, and in his late twenties. If you see this man do not approach him. He is considered extremely dangerous."

"To a refrigerator," Joe says laughingly.

"Shh!" Jim says. "Stick some more pizza in your mouth and listen."

Detective Taylor continues, "The suspect's name is Jim

Kemplar, and he was last seen leaving the Lansing Police Station in a red Chrysler sports car with a second person driving."

The lady interviewer interrupts, "You said you had a description of the second suspect. Is he the person driving the car?"

"Yes. The second suspect is described as being approximately five-foot nine, one-hundred and forty pounds. He has dark brown curly hair, brown eyes and a moustache."

An artist's conception comes on the screen. It looks a little like me but it still could be a lot of other people, too.

"Both suspects wore blue jeans."

"What should someone do if they see either one of these suspects?"

"Call the police immediately and do not approach them. They are armed and considered extremely dangerous."

Joe looks over at Jim and I. "Dangerous? Maybe if you guys don't take a shower for a couple of weeks. Then, I might consider you guys dangerous."

The lady interviewer begins closing the show. "We're just about out of time for today's show. We'd like to thank Detective Taylor and the Lansing Police Department for their cooperation. This is Rhonda Reynolds saying so-long until next week when we join councilwoman Mary Johnson on *Lansing This Week.*"

Looking at the TV screen but not really seeing what's on it, I say to no one in particular, "We've got to somehow connect that detective to the murders, and that stupid cube has got to be the key."

I look at Joe and he nods in agreement. I turn toward Jim and he's just sitting there, staring at the floor. The things that must be racing through his mind. His entire way of life has been turned upside down and by no fault of his own. Forgetting for a moment that I'm in it as deep as Jim, I suddenly find myself getting angry at the injustice of it all. Jim's done absolutely nothing wrong and this poor excuse of a human being is trying to crucify him just to have a scapegoat and to get his hands on that cube.

I stand up suddenly, slapping Jim on the leg. "I'm not gonna let him get away with it, Jim! We're gonna get to the bottom of this and Joe's gonna help! Right, Joe?"

Joe, a little bit surprised by my outburst stutters, "Oh . . . us, yeah, uh, right."

I virtually run to the kitchen and snatch up the cube. I feel some of the cube crumble and fall out between my fingers and I hurry back into the living room where Joe is still munching on some pizza and Jim is staring a hole in the TV set.

"Come on, you guys. We've got some detective work of our own to do! I think Jim should stay here out of sight." Joe doesn't move. "Joe?"

"Here."

"Can you drive me to my church? I think my pastor might have the books we need to translate this thing. Services are probably starting about now."

"Yeah, sure, I guess I can handle that." Joe begins to get excited again. "All right, a real mystery to solve. Just like the Hardy Boys. You know, I've got every one of their books."

"Yeah I know, you've told me before."

"I have?"

"Yep." I look over at Jim and he hasn't moved. "You okay, Jim?" Jim blinks once and nods his head slowly. "Good," I say. "Have some more pizza and you'll be fine." I give a sweeping motion with my hand to Joe. "Joe and I will be back in a couple hours or so."

Joe groans a little as he lifts himself out of his chair. He starts to follow me toward the door but turns around and with quick short steps he retrieves the bottle of Pepsi on the lamp table next to his chair. "Pepperoni makes me thirsty."

"Where did you find this, Bob?"

I sort of stall with the answer to my pastor's question as he looks down his nose through his reading glasses at the cube, which he's slowly turning over in his hands.

Pastor Dr. Martin Greenhoe's office at the church is a fairly modest room. On the wall to our left is a rather large window that looks out on a small courtyard. The window takes up virtually the entire space on the wall except for a couple of religious posters on each side. Behind the pastor, covering the entire wall, is a bookcase full of books and on the wall to our right are various pictures of his family and friends, under which are his filing cabinets, typewriter table, and a copy machine.

"It's a long story, Brother Martin."

"I've got some time." The pastor leans forward a little to get an even closer look at one side. "Interesting."

He rolls his chair back toward the book shelf and reaches up to pull down a large hardcover book. As he scoots back to his desk he looks up at me.

"You're in some kind of trouble, aren't you, Bob?"

"Well, sort of, I guess. Maybe a little."

Joe snickers a little. "That's an understatement."

I give Joe a dirty look but he just leans back in his chair and smiles.

Without looking up from the cube Brother Martin pulls a pen from his inside suit jacket pocket, slides a pad of paper from near the phone on his desk, and begins copying some of the symbols on one side of the cube.

"Now, Bob, you were about to tell me how you came to possess this unique artifact." He still doesn't look up but is intently copying each detail.

"I sort of found it alongside the road."

"Bob," he looks up from his work, sets his pen down, leans back in his chair, speaking softly, "I've known you for a number of years now and if you say you found this by the side of the road then I believe you. However," he leans forward a little. "Things like this are not your everyday ordinary roadside litter. There's more to it than that, now isn't there?"

"Well, yeah."

"You said it was a long story, so let's hear it from the beginning."

Brother Martin picks up his pen again and resumes his work while I begin relating the details of the last few days. By the time I'm finished more than half an hour has passed and Brother Martin has six and a half pages of strange symbols arranged in neat rows.

"You have quite a large chunk missing from this one corner here, but we may have enough here to maybe get an idea what this is all about."

Joe sits up a little. "You can read that stuff?"

"Well, no, but with this book I'll be able to." The pastor flips open the book to the table of contents. "What we have here, gentlemen, is a very early form of cuneiform writing." He points to the first page.

Joe looks puzzled. "Coon-a-what?"

"Cuneiform, Joe." I remember some of the studying I did for Sunday school class. "It's writing that uses a combination of pictures to form words. Right, Brother Martin?"

"Well, basically you're right. The earliest cuneiform writings were pictures that meant exactly what they looked like. That's what we have here. However . . ."

"However?" I figure I'm wrong in my definition.

"However, this second page . . ." He slides the top page off, ". . . is a later form which incorporates sound-like pictures."

"Sound-like pictures?" Joe asks.

"Yes. Take for instance two pictures, one of a thin man and one of a king. It doesn't mean the thin man is the king's slave and the king doesn't feed him well. The thin man would simply stand for thin, and the king for what he is, king. Now put them together as one word."

Joe pipes in, "It's a thin king."

"Not quite. I said one word. Do you have a guess, Bob?"

I shake my head.

"It's one word, two syllables." He pauses and looks at each of us, waiting for an answer. Getting none he says, "Thinking." He smiles at the thought of teaching us something new. "So you could have a picture of a king, then a thin man and a king together. The sentence then would be, 'The king is thinking.'"

Joe's getting a little anxious and with not as much patience as the rest of us he blurts, "That's neat, but what does the cube say?"

"Well, fellows, that's going to take some time, at least for these first two pages. You see, each of the sides of this cube is a different language and each language is progressively newer." He picks up all the pages but one, the page that is only one-third full. "With this last one being Hebrew, and that's the one with the most missing. Too bad, too. It's also the easiest for me to translate."

"How long will it take?" I ask.

"That is hard to say." He spreads all the pages out on his desk and leans back in his chair rubbing his chin. "Ohhh . . . I'd say somewhere between four and five hours. If I get right at it, that would put me approximately around the one-in-the-morning mark. Would you fellows like to stick around or shall I give you a call when I'm finished?"

"I think Joe and I should get back to Jim. He wasn't looking too good when we left."

"Yeah," Joe says. "I think he even stopped eating and that even worries me somewhat."

I point to the cube. "Are you gonna need that for anything, Brother Martin?"

"No, you may take it with you if you wish, I've everything I need written down."

Joe and I get up from our chairs and go to the door. "Bye Brother Martin, and thanks."

"Sure, Bob. No problem. Nice meeting you, Joe. Oh, and by the way, Bob has told me you haven't found yourself a church yet. We're open every Sunday and also Wednesday night."

"I know," Joe says a little embarrassed. "But I've been just sort of putting it off, letting little things get in the way. But I really do know I should be in church. Maybe next week. I've already got plans for Wednesday."

"Okay, see you in church next Sunday then. You fellows stay out of trouble now, or should I say, stay out of more trouble."

"Okay, and thanks again for taking the time for this," I say with a little wave.

"Like I said, no problem. Now you fellows scoot on out of here so I can get busy. I don't want to be up all night on this."

Joe and I leave and head to Joe's place. When we arrive the house is dark except for a faint light flickering in the living room.

"He must be watching TV." Joe says as he sticks his key into the front door lock.

When we walk in Jim turns around on the couch to look at us. "Hi guys. How'd it go?"

His face is lighted on one side by the glow of the television set. Joe flips on the light switch and the room is flooded with light chasing away all the dreary shadows.

"Well," Joe says, "I can see you're feeling better." He walks over near the couch where Jim is sitting, bends over, and picks up an almost empty potato chip bag.

"Yep, that's the Jim we all remember." I walk over to Joe, take the bag of chips from him, and begin munching on them.

Joe gives me a funny look. "Care for some, Joe?" I hold the bag out for him but not before taking a huge handful for myself.

"Maybe just a couple," Joe says sarcastically as he grabs the bag and sits down in his chair.

"Sooo . . . . How'd it go? Did you find anything out?" Jim still looks longingly at the potato chips.

I sit down in the middle of the couch next to Jim. "Not yet, but my pastor, Dr. Greenhoe, is working on it. He said he'd let us know when he's done. So for now we just sit and wait."

"When's he gonna be done?"

"He said around one this morning. Was there anything more on the news about us?"

"They just flashed my name and picture on the screen again for the whole world to see. Oh, one thing, though. They had a new and improved composite drawing of you. It looks almost just like you now."

Joe laughs, "Are you sure you weren't watching *The Twilight Zone?*"

"Not funny, Joe. Somebody at work is bound to put the two of us together and call the police."

"Speaking of which," Joe says as he gets out of his chair, "what are you going to do about work?"

"Well I definitely can't call in sick and I can't show up, so I guess for now I'm out of a job."

Joe goes to the kitchen and comes back with a large glass of ice water. "I think you guys are gonna have to leave the country. Hide out in Canada or something. It's getting way too dangerous for you here and I can't hide you here forever. One of the first places they're going to look is at your friends and relatives."

"He's right, Jim. Joe's going to have to sneak us across the border."

"Me? Why me?"

"Because they know us and they know our cars. How much money do you have Jim?"

Jim pulls his keys out of his pocket and turns his pockets inside out. "That's it. Everything I have is either in my wallet or at home."

"And you can bet they'll be watching his home, Bob."

"Well I've got about a hundred and fifty in cash on me and probably another hundred at home and if I can get to an automatic teller machine I could get another two hundred and fifty. You could do that, Joe, if I give you my p.i.n. number."

"Okay, and while I'm doing that you guys can look in my spare bedroom. I've got a bunch of camping stuff in there. You could hide out in the Canadian wilderness. Nobody'll find you there."

I jot my p.i.n. number down on a piece of paper and I hand Joe both it and my teller card and he heads for the door. As he's leaving I hear him say, "What an adventure."

After the door closes behind Joe, Jim turns toward me looking a little apprehensive. "Bob, I don't know if we should run away like this. Won't it make us look more guilty?"

"We already look plenty guilty, Jim. A little more isn't going to hurt."

"But I've never been camping before. I'm the kind of guy who takes a secondary road off the freeway and I feel like I'm in the wilderness."

"Don't worry, Jim. My folks used to take me camping all the time, and not in one of those motor homes, either. We camped in tents. Why, with just a few supplies we could live for months at a time without ever having to see a store."

"But this is already late fall. Isn't it going to be cold up there? How are we gonna stay warm in a flimsy little tent?"

"Come on, Jim, let's see what Joe has and I'll tell you how we're gonna do it."

We walk down the hallway past Joe's room to the spare bedroom. When I open the door a sight greets me that doesn't surprise me at all. In fact it is very reminiscent of the sight that greeted me when I walked into Joe's garage.

"Wow, what a mess!" Jim exclaims.

There's a skinny path that meanders through the room with two branches. One leads to the closet. That's the one we want.

"Joe said the stuff was in the closet, so let's start there, Jim."

We start rummaging through his closet pulling out anything that looks like it could go on a camping trip.

"So Bob, how are we going to do this now?"

"I figure a couple of weeks is all the time we'll have to spend in a tent. By then, if I can get a hold of a chain saw and axe, we should have a small but cozy log hut built. Complete with a fireplace."

"You know how to do all that?"

"I saw a guy do it on public television once and I cut my own wood for my fireplace, so how tough could it be?"

I pull out a couple of sleeping bags from a corner of the closet.

"Wow, Jim. These are good ones. These will keep us warm in below zero weather easy. We won't have to keep the fire burning as hot and that'll save on wood."

We start hauling things out to the living room. I find a piece of paper and begin taking inventory.

"What're you doing that for, Bob?"

"So I know what we've got and what we still need. We may have to stop on the way up and buy whatever we don't have."

Spread out all over the floor is a wide assortment of camping and outdoor equipment. I begin listing them: a four-man nylon tent, two sleeping bags, two air mattresses, a Coleman lantern, a Coleman stove, one backpack . . . .

"Gonna need another backpack, Jim, just in case."

"Just in case what?"

"Just in case somebody finds us and we have to move to another place in the wilderness. Now let's see." I point to each item with my pen and then write it down. "One set metal camping pans, one set metal dishes, one set plastic cups, one flashlight. Check to see if it works Jim. If it does we'll need just one more."

Jim picks it up and pushes the switch on. A dim glow shows on the lens of the flashlight.

"Looks like it just needs some new batteries."

"Okay. One flashlight and extra batteries." I write it down in the column with the backpack.

Just then Joe comes back through the front door, stops, and looks around at the mess in the middle of the floor.

"Looks like you guys found everything okay."

"Did you have any problems with the money machine?"

"Nope, just spit out the money like it was yours. Of course it wouldn't spit it out as if it was mine 'cause I think I'm overdrawn again."

Joe hands me a small handful of crisp twenty dollar bills and a ten. I fold them once and stick them in my back pants pocket opposite my wallet. I turn back toward the mess on the floor to resume my inventory.

"What are you doing?"

"I'm making a list of what we've got and what we need."

"What do we need so far, Bob?"

"Just another backpack, another flashlight and some extra batteries, but I'm sure we'll need more before we're done."

Jim sets the flashlight down after taking the old batteries out and screwing it back together. "I know what we really need. We need a survival book."

"You mean you guys didn't find it in there?" Joe gives a little smile.

I look at Joe. "If you mean did we find it in your closet, the answer is no. We were fortunate just to find this stuff in that mess and still get out alive."

"Well no wonder you didn't find it. It's in one of the boxes of books in the middle of the room."

"Oh well, silly us. We should have known that's where it was even if we knew it existed in the first place," I say with a sarcastic edge. "How come it's not on your bookshelf?"

"I just haven't gotten around to unpacking those books from the last time I moved." Joe puts his hand on my shoulder, "Come on, help me find it."

We all walk back into the spare room. I look around again at the piles of boxes and numerous other articles. "You amaze me, Joe. Don't you ever throw anything away?"

"Banana peels and egg shells." Joe scans the room a few seconds, then fixes his eyes on a pile of boxes just ahead and to our left. "I think it's in one of those boxes."

"At least this time Jim and I have a guide for this safari."

Jim walks over to the pile in question and opens up the top box. The box is crammed full of hardcover books, paperback books and small pamphlets. "Are all these boxes like this?"

"Welcome to my library."

Chapter 4

For the next hour and a half the three of us search through dozens of boxes, each filled with the widest assortment of topics imaginable—from religion to *The Hardy Boys*.

Jim gets up and stretches backward with his hands on the back of his hips trying to get out some kinks in his back. "I need a break. I'm gonna get a drink of water."

As soon as Jim leaves I get up myself. "Yeah a drink sounds good to me too, Joe. You want some? I'll bring it back for you."

"Nah, just make sure Jim doesn't get into the leftovers again."

I laugh, "You got it."

As I leave I hear Joe mutter something about the book having to be here someplace. I shake my head and wonder how with a group like this we're gonna survive, let alone clear our names. When I get to the kitchen Jim is standing at the counter. Next to him is a plate of cold chicken and he is in the process of chowing down on a thigh.

"At it again, eh, Jim?" Then speaking louder so Joe can hear, "So Jim, how do you like the chicken?"

A voice from the other room comes back, "If somebody doesn't stay out of my food, they're gonna find themselves up to their neck in floor."

I laugh as Jim takes three quick bites of his piece of chicken and hurriedly sticks the plate back in the refrigerator. I walk over to the cupboard and pull out a glass. "I thought you came in here for a glass of water, Jim."

"I did."

"Joe must have a lot of iron in his water."

"Why do you say that?"

"'Cause that was the stiffest looking water I saw you munching on."

Jim grins his big grin then gets a cup himself. We're standing next to the sink drinking our water when Joe comes in holding up a book about shoulder high and waving it a little with a twisting of his wrist.

"Guess what I found?"

"Your sanity?" I hold out my hand. "Let me see it, Joe."

He hands me the shiny-covered paperback book. On the cover is a picture of two hikers, a man and a woman with backpacks, standing on a large rock overlooking a lake in the valley below.

I read the title out loud. "*Wilderness Survival Made Easy*. The title sounds promising."

Jim looks over my shoulder. "I like the part where it says 'Easy.'"

I flip the book over to read the blurb on the back cover. "'This book by Thomas Thorn will give every reader the basic knowledge he or she requires to survive on their own in the wildest of country. Everything from building shelters and gathering food, to making your own clothes and tools. A must read for the serious wilderness adventurer.' Hmm, Thomas Thorn, eh. If we were to meet this guy in person, I guess he would be a Thorn in the flesh."

Joe gives a little moan. "Another Bob joke. Oh, and by the way, Jim, you've got some extra crispy on the corner of your mouth there."

Jim grins and wipes his mouth with his sleeve in one grand sweeping motion. Just then the phone rings and Joe goes to answer it in the living room, but just before he leaves the kitchen he turns around and looks at me.

"While I'm gone see if you can't keep Jim out of the food."

With that said he turns and leaves. I fill up a cup with water and hand it to Jim, "Here, have some more water."

"Bob," Joe calls from the other room, "It's your pastor!"

I hurry to the living room, my heart pounding with expectation. Joe hands me the phone.

"Hello?"

"Bob?"

"Yes. Are you done already?"

"Well, yes and no. I've gotten everything but the missing section."

"Well? Can you tell me what you do have?"

"I'd rather all three of you fellows meet me at my office as soon as possible. It is extremely imperative that all three of you be here."

"Why?"

"Please, just do as I ask and bring the cube with you."

"Okay, but I don't . . ."

"No more questions now. Save them for when you get here. See you in a few minutes."

I hear a "click" in my ear as Brother Martin hangs up and then the dial tone. A little stunned by all this, I hand the phone to Joe for him to hang up.

"Well?" he asks, "what'd he say? Did he find out what it says?"

I reply softly, "He says we have to go see him and he'll tell us what it says then."

"Why?"

"I don't know, he wouldn't say, but he wants all three of us there."

"Why?"

I get a little impatient with Joe. "He wouldn't tell me. He said he'd answer my questions when we got there."

"It sounds suspicious to me, Bob. It could be a trap."

"No, I don't hardly think so. My pastor wouldn't do that."

A voice comes from behind me. "Yeah, Bob. What if it is a trap?"

I turn around and Jim is leaning against the doorway to the kitchen with the survival book hanging by his side in one hand.

"I still don't think so. I know Brother Martin pretty good and I think he would die first before betraying anyone."

Joe walks over to the window and peeks out, "I don't know, Bob, it just seems awful strange to me."

Jim walks to the middle of the living room and drops the book onto one of the sleeping bags with a plop. "It sounds strange to me, too, Bob."

I look at each one of them and decide it's not worth arguing the point. They just don't know Brother Martin like I do.

"Okay, you guys do what you want, but I'm going over to the church to find out what the cube says, with or without you. It doesn't matter to me either way." I swipe my jacket from the back of the couch. "Either of you guys coming with me?" I put my arms through the sleeves and head for the door when Joe turns quickly away from the window.

"Wait, Bob! I'm coming with you. Just let me get my jacket first. I'd just as soon drive my own car anyway."

I'd forgotten that I couldn't be out in my car. I'd be picked up in a second. "Oh . . . yeah, I forgot."

Joe goes to his room to get his jacket. When he comes back he has two jackets in his hands and as he comes within five feet of Jim he throws one at him. The jacket smacks against Jim's chest and half his face with one sleeve wrapping around the back of his head.

"Come on, Jim. The preacher said he wanted to see all three of us."

"But I thought you said it sounded suspicious."

"I did, but this time I'm gonna trust Bob's feelings. Just this one time. After all, he does know his pastor better than we do. Besides that, it'll be an adventure."

As we all step outside we're greeted by a slight cold north breeze and a heavy mist, heavy enough to begin putting puddles on the sidewalk. I can hear the faint sound of drops of water falling from the leaves on the trees.

On the way there I notice that Joe is checking his rear view mirror almost continually.

"Are you afraid we're being followed Joe?"

"Can't be too careful."

The rest of the way to the church nobody says a word, each of us absorbed in our own thoughts.

By the time we get there it's raining fairly hard, making it hard to see out the windows, even if they weren't a little fogged already.

Joe gets out and stands next to the car with the door still open. He takes a quick look around and proclaims, "Looks all clear."

"I told you, Joe."

I open my door and run to the door of the church, my feet splashing through a couple of puddles. Behind me I hear two car doors slam and Joe and Jim follow right behind me through the door.

When we enter the pastor's office, he's leaning back in his chair with a bunch of papers in his hands.

"Ah, very good. You all made it. Sit down, please."

Joe and Jim sit in the two chairs that are available and I grab a chair that's just outside the door and drag it into the office.

"Could you shut the door please Bob?"

I know this is going to be serious because Brother Martin never closes the door to his office unless it's important and confidential, even if there isn't anybody in the church who would be able to overhear. It's just his way of doing things.

I pull the door closed and sit down. Brother Martin leans forward, putting the papers face up on his desk.

"Now, before I tell you fellows what I've discovered, I need to know a few things."

"Like what?" Jim asks tensing up a bit.

Meanwhile, Joe is leaning as far forward as he can and stretching his neck to it's limits trying to get a look at what's on those papers. If he moves any more he'll slide off the edge of his chair.

"Like your family background," He says as he flips the papers face down.

Joe slumps back into his chair, realizing he was caught in the act.

"Jim, you first. Tell me what nationality you are please."

"American."

"No, no, Jim," Brother Martin says laughingly. "From what country did your ancestors come from?"

"Oh, that. They came from Germany at the beginning of World War Two."

"What is your last name again Jim?"

"Kemplar."

"Well that certainly is a German name."

"Okay, Joe, how about you?"

"I'm Italian."

"Oh, are you Catholic then?"

"Used to be. I got saved about three years ago. I've been to a Mennonite church a couple of times a couple years ago.

"Both your parents were Italian?"

"Yep."

"Hmm . . ." Brother Martin looks a little puzzled as he strokes his chin. "Let's get back to you again, Jim. What is your mother's maiden name?"

"Schwartz."

"Ah, now we're getting somewhere. Did your father happen to mention a name change before or after the war started?"

"Yeah, how'd you know?"

"It was a pretty common practice among eastern European Jews before and during the war. They did it to avoid persecution or to escape the country or even the concentration camps."

"You mean I'm Jewish?"

Joe laughs, "That explains why you're so tight with your money."

"Yes Jim, all indications point in that direction."

"But my folks never said anything, I mean they mentioned that our name changed but they never said what it was before."

"Maybe your parents felt it was best to spare you the kind of persecution they received. So, now you, Joe. Have you had any name changes in your family history?"

"Nope, none at all."

"How can you be so sure?"

"My grandmother had a genealogy done on our family and we're all Italian as far back as records were found. Somewhere around eleven-hundred A.D."

"Well, Bob, I guess that leaves you."

"Leaves me for what? I haven't volunteered for anything yet."

"On the contrary, depending on how you answer my next few questions will determine whether or not you have already volunteered. Now then, I know you've told me that you're adopted, but do you have any idea who your real parents are, or what nationality?"

"No, they never told me. I don't think they even know themselves."

"I hope you don't get too upset with me but I took the liberty of calling your mother and explaining a bit of your situation. But my primary purpose in calling her was to glean some information from her."

"My mother, shoot! I should have called her. She must have been worried sick."

"Actually, she wasn't. Truth is, she didn't even know about it. She and your father have been out of town all weekend, away from the radio and television."

"That's good, at least she heard it from you instead of the police or the news. So was she able to help you any?"

"Oh, by all means. She was a great help. On the day you were born your mother and father were called by the adoption agency saying there was a newborn baby boy available for adoption and asking if they would like to come and see him. Well, your parents were thrilled so they hurried off to the hospital. When they got there a nurse brought you to them wrapped in a blanket. Your mother said she fell in love with you the moment she saw you.

But then she noticed something that disturbed her. When she pulled the blanket away from your face a little, she saw the blue hospital bracelet on your little wrist. It said, "Baby Levitt." The nurse must have noticed it too because she quickly pulled the blanket back over the arm and made some excuse about feeding time and scurried off with you back to the nursery. Anyway, the next time your mother saw you, you had another wrist band on and it said, "Baby Doe."

"You mean I could be Jewish, too? Just like Jim?"

"I know this is a lot for you to comprehend at this time, but I feel circumstances necessitate it. After I talked to your mother I knew I couldn't get ahold of anyone in county records on a Sunday night so I began looking up all the Levitts in the phone book on the off chance there may be relatives still in the area. There are only three and on my second try I was successful."

"You mean I have real live relatives living right here in Lansing?"

"Just one, your Grandmother."

"So what happened?" I get kind of a queasy feeling in my stomach, "I mean . . ." I swallow, ". . . why did my parents give me up for adoption?"

"They didn't have a choice, Bob."

"Why not?"

"You see, your parents were on their way to the hospital to have you when a pickup truck ran a stop sign, hitting the driver's side of your parent's car. Your father was killed instantly and your mother was very badly injured. They rushed your mother to the hospital where you were born. Your mother remained alive for several hours afterward, long enough to give you a name and for the hospital to put a wrist band on you. A few hours later she died of a massive brain hemorrhage.

By the way, I asked your adoptive mother if it would be acceptable to tell you about all this."

"What did she say? I mean other than yes."

"She felt you were old enough to handle it, and under the circumstances she thought you should know."

"You mean just in case we don't make it out of this alive."

"Well, yes, that too. There is one thing she thought you ought to know."

"What's that?"

"Your full name originally given to you by your mother before she died. Would you like to know it, or would you rather not? It's up to you."

"Yeah, I think I'd like to know."

"Benjamin Michael Levitt."

"I guess we can call you Benny from now on, Bob," Joe says jokingly.

"It is finally nice to know where I come from, but I'm still Bob and I probably always will be Bob. I don't think this is going to change me any."

"Okay, so now you fellows are wondering what all this has to do with the writing on the cube."

Joe, who's been slouching, straightens up. "Yeah, I was kind of wondering when we'd get around to that."

"Now you know me, Bob, that I'm not one that is given to flights of fancy and before I take on any project, I check it out thoroughly. You know, I must 'prove the spirits' so to speak and that is what I had to do with this. Just by the mere fact that all three of you are Christians with two of you being of Jewish ancestry and the other of Italian descent makes the odds of this being merely coincidental almost astronomical. And to top it all off, I'm ready to hazard a guess that both you, Bob, and you, Jim, are virgins."

Jim and I look at each other a bit taken aback. Jim's face is beginning to turn red. Joe, on the other hand, is trying desperately to subdue an almost uncontrollable laugh.

"Well, I know you are, Bob. At least a couple months ago you were because we talked about it then. Nothing's happened since then, has it?"

"No."

"Am I correct about you, Jim?"

Jim looks sheepishly at Joe.

"There's nothing to be ashamed of Jim. In fact I applaud you both."

Jim nods his head. "Yeah, I am."

Joe starts to get a little excited and I'm bewildered. Joe finally can't contain himself, "That's really wild! How'd you know about Jim?"

Brother Martin just leans back and shakes his head. "This is almost too farfetched to be true, and yet . . . here it is, more proof than I could ask for."

"Proof of what?" Joe asks getting a little antsy.

"Proof, my dear fellow, that this is the seed of desire."

"Seed of desire?"

"Allow me to start at the beginning. There is an old legend about Gilgamesh, king of ancient Babylon. The story we have now goes something like this; King Gilgamesh heard that Noah, who had survived the flood with his family, had been given eternal life from God. So Gilgamesh went to see Noah in order to obtain eternal life for himself. Noah told him he had to first accomplish three deeds. The story speaks of Gilgamesh following a cavern for eleven hours, only to come out at the sea. Naturally, Gilgamesh failed in his attempt to accomplish even one of the deeds and went back to Babylon where he decided he would live eternally through his works and writings."

"That's a really neat story, Brother Martin, but what's it got to do with the cube?"

"Do you have the cube with you, Bob?"

"Yeah, right here." I pull the cube out of my jacket pocket and put it on the desk where it crumbles a little more. "It's becoming almost like a growth on my body."

"Now about the cube. As you well know, most legends are based on some fact with a lot of embellishment in between."

Brother Martin picks up the cube and begins picking at the clay, breaking off small chunks as he continues to talk. "According to the writing on the cube, Noah did not receive eternal life in the sense that his body would live forever. We know this by the fact that the Bible records his death. But, he did get something from God that had to do with eternal life. I wish I could save these writings because each one was written by a different prophet, from Noah all the way to King David. However what is underneath is far more important."

Brother Martin slams the cube down on his desk and chunks of clay fly in all directions. He slams it down a second time and again clay is sent flying. With his hand he then pushes most of the loose clay fragments into a small pile. In his other hand is a shiny, gold colored cube, and like the previous clay cube, it has lines and pictures on it.

"Yes, yes, yes." Now even Brother Martin is getting excited. "Do you fellows see these pictures and these lines here?" He goes on, not really expecting an answer from us. "These are directions to someplace, a map if you prefer, exactly where I have not as yet figured out. Noah called this cube 'the seed of his desire,' meaning Gilgamesh. It planted in his mind a desire for eternal life, however, Noah would not give just anyone the map unless they met three criteria first. Hence the legend of the three deeds. The first was that there had to be a group of three men. The second was two of the three were to be virgins, and the third was that the one person who was not a virgin was to be a descendant from the city of the seven hills."

"I know that one!" Joe pipes in. "That's Rome."

"Exactly, Joe."

Sometimes I'm a little slow but eventually I usually catch on. "I get it now Brother Martin. Jim and I are the two virgins and Joe is the guy from the seven hills, but I don't understand one thing."

"What is that, Bob?"

"What does Jim and I being Jewish have to do with anything?"

"I was just getting to that. You see, Gilgamesh didn't just go home to be content with the rest of his life and forget about his failure. After he got back he became very despondent and vowed that he or his descendants would achieve the secret of eternal life by any method at their disposal. So Noah, being warned by God, encased the cube in a thick layer of clay and wrote this story on two of it's sides. In later years, as the cube was handed down from prophet to prophet, more specifics were added to the requirements. These were added so as to keep the Babylonians from faking or hiring people with the first prerequisites."

Joe's curiosity is piqued. "Well? What are the other ones?"

"Oh, they are nothing special, Joe, other than the two virgins having to be Jewish, the rest are mainly physical descriptions."

"Like what? I'd like to know."

"I'd like to know, too, Brother Martin."

"You fellows are sure?"

All three of us nod our heads but I begin to get the feeling Brother Martin was trying to spare some feelings.

"Okay, one of the Jewish virgins is to be slim with curly hair."

"That's Bob," Joe says.

"The other Jewish virgin is to be tall with a . . ." Brother Martin clears his throat as he searches for the proper words, ". . . a prominent nose."

"That's Jim," Joe blurts. "He's got a big nose. What else? This is really neat."

"Well, the Roman is to be a rather robust sort with very little patience. Sorry, Joe, but you wanted to know."

"That's you, Joe," I say. "You're the robustest one here."

"I'll ro-bust your body." Joe quips.

Quietly, almost inaudibly, Jim says something.

Brother Martin hears him but doesn't quite understand what he said. "Pardon me, Jim. Could you repeat that again, please?"

Jim clears his throat a little. "There's more, isn't there? Can you tell us what it is?"

"Oh sure, Jim, but you're not going to be very pleased with this one."

Joe sits back in his chair, sitting cross-legged with one ankle across his other knee and folding his arms across his chest in a defiant manner. "Go ahead, Doc. We're all men here. We can take it."

"Very well, then. I will quote directly from my translation." Brother Martin shuffles through his small pile of papers. "Ah, here it is. 'They three will be hated of all men as killers of men, though they be innocent of all.'"

"We're already accused of murder, Brother Martin. Why should that bother us?"

As soon as I ask the question I suddenly get this feeling in the pit of my stomach that I'm not going to like the answer.

"There are actually two reasons. First it says you will be hated by 'all' men. The 'all' in this context indicates that popular opinion will be against you on an international scale, and second it says,

'They three.' That means Joe, who thus far has not been implicated, will be."

Joe's arms, which had remained folded, drop into his lap.

"Oh, thanks a lot, guys. This really makes my day."

"There is one other problem."

Joe looks even more dejected. "Oh terrific, more good news."

I try to calm him down a bit by reminding him of his earlier proclamation. "Come on, Joe, we're all men here. We can take it. What is it, Brother Martin?"

"There is something you three must do, according to the cube."

"What?" I ask.

"That is what the problem is. I don't know. That is the part of the cube that was missing when you brought it to me. I need to know if any of you fellows by any chance can recall what was on that missing part or can bring me the missing fragments."

There's silence for a while as we try to picture in our minds what the cube looked like before it was chipped. I finally break the silence.

"I can't remember it, and the last time I saw the missing pieces they were scattered all over the floor at the police station."

"Well I guess it was a bit much to expect anyone to remember something as obscure as . . ."

Joe suddenly perks up and interrupts Brother Martin with more excitement than usual in his voice. "Wait! I got it! I've got pictures of the cube in my locker at work!"

"That's right, Joe, and I've got eight-by-ten enlargements at home."

Brother Martin then brings a sense of reason back into the room. "That is all well and good, gentlemen, but are we in a position to retrieve them? Joe, you said your pictures are in your locker at work. Is there any time you would be able to get in and out without being seen?"

"That'd be really tough, 'cause there's always people there. Besides, I called in sick tonight so I can't be caught wandering around there."

"It sounds to me as if that would be most unwise, but not because you called in sick. As I recall, you mentioned leaving Jim's car in the parking lot. Not only will they be watching the car to see if he comes back for it, but they will also be there questioning your co-workers. Bob, how about your place?"

"It's pretty well secluded. Even during the day it's hard to see my house through all the trees."

"So you think someone could get in and out without being seen without too much trouble?"

"Yeah, probably."

"Okay, Bob. It's settled then. You and Joe go to your house for the pictures while Jim and I wait here for you."

Just as we're about to leave, the pastor's phone rings.

"Hold on a moment please, gentlemen. It's one of our spies checking in."

Brother Martin gives a little wink and picks up the phone in the middle of a ring.

"Hello? . . . Uhuh . . . Uhuh . . ." There's a long pause. "Okay, well listen, keep your eyes and ears open." There's another pause. "No, don't call until they leave and pay close attention to how fast and, if you can, which direction they go. I'll be praying for God's guidance for you." Brother Martin hangs up the phone, leans forward putting his forearms on his desk and folding his hands. He looks down at his hands for a short period. The three of us just sort of stand in the doorway quietly, thinking he might be praying. He slowly lifts his eyes and looks at us.

"That was Brother Mark, Bob. He says the police are at the post office questioning your fellow workers. When they questioned Brother Mark, he said the questions seemed to center around who Jim's friends are. I've asked him to call back when the police leave. Now, Bob, if you and Joe are not back when I get the call I will call your house, letting the phone ring only twice. That will be your signal that the police will probably be heading toward either Joe's house or yours or both. Both of you hurry, now. You're burning precious minutes."

I pat Joe on the shoulder. "We'll be back before you know it, Jim." As I turn and begin running down the hallway out of the church I yell to Joe, "Come on, Joe. You heard the preacher. Time's a-wastin'!"

When we get in Joe's car, I turn to Joe. "Joe, if they come to your house they're gonna find my car in your garage. We're gonna have to move it."

"Where?"

"Well I've kinda been thinking about that, and since we gotta go there anyway . . ."

"Your house?"

"Yeah, why not? That way they have no idea where I'm at and I don't incriminate anybody else. Whadaya think?"

"I like it. Let's go for it."

"Only one thing though, Joe."

"What's that?"

"You're gonna have to give me a ride back, but you better not park in my driveway. You know, just in case the cops arrive before I can get out of there."

"Where do you want me to pick you up then?"

"I don't know. Let me think a minute."

"Don't hurt yourself."

"It's you that's gonna get hurt if you don't shut-up." I run a few options through my head. "Okay, how about this? Do you remember where Doc Holiday, the veterinarian, lives?"

"Isn't he just a couple houses up the street from you?"

"Yeah, that's the place. So, what you gotta do is park in his driveway facing out, for a quick getaway. After I get what I need from the house I'll run around through my neighbors' back yards and meet up with you there in the driveway. Oh, and don't worry about the good doctor. He said he was going to be gone for a week at some convention or seminar or some such thing. I'm supposed to be feeding his dog."

Joe grabs the wheel a little tighter and gives a little shudder. "What an adventure Bob. What an adventure. I just got goose bumps thinking about it."

"Well, don't get too excited, Joe, this could get really dangerous."

"Yeah, I know, but it's still exciting."

"Yeah, it does tend to get your heart pumpin' pretty good."

We're both quiet for a couple minutes as we travel the near-deserted neighborhood side streets of Lansing. The only signs of life are the occasional glow of lights from inside a house, and of course the drug dealers that hang out at several street corners. I remember when the problem was prostitution. There's still a light rain falling so about every twenty seconds Joe's wipers swish across in front of us and then slap back into position. Finally Joe breaks the silence.

"I uh, was just thinking, Bob."

"Joe," I put my hand on his shoulder. "It's good to try new things once in a while."

"Yeah, it is. Maybe you should try it sometime. Anyway, I was thinking that if the cops are talking to everybody at work, it's a sure bet I'm gonna be tops on their list of people to come see."

"Yeah, that's a pretty good assumption."

"Well, what I was thinking was maybe I could take a couple minutes and load all that camping stuff into the back here. That way if the cops come by they won't see all that stuff in the middle of the floor."

"Good idea Joe, but don't take too long. I don't wanna be hanging around my neighborhood too long without a ride."

"Don't worry, it won't take me much more than five minutes or so."

"It's the 'or so' I'm worried about."

About that time we pull up to the front of Joe's place. Joe drives past his driveway a little then backs in onto his lawn, right up to his front porch. Joe pushes a button on his dash that unlatches the rear gate. There's an audible "click" and both Joe and I hop out of the car. I wait by the door as Joe lifts the gate on his Cherokee.

"Come on, Joe, unlock this door. I haven't got all night, you know."

Joe walks up, digging in his pocket for his keys.

"Oops, left them in the ignition."

"Not a good idea to do that, Joe. Some desperate murderer might steal it and use it for his getaway."

Joe comes back with the keys and unlocks the door. He flips on the lights and I head for the garage. A cool, musty, oily smell greets me when I enter the garage. I open the overhead door and instead of trying to squeeze around to the driver's side door, I get in on the passenger side, and slide over to get behind the wheel.

At the end of the driveway I stop and look carefully both ways, watching more for patrol cars than for regular traffic. Trying not to attract any attention, I dim my lights and drive the speed limit. I know my time is limited, but to speed would only invite trouble. I scan the radio dial for a good station but become frustrated for the lack of something to fit my mood. I twist the switch off with a quick snap of the wrist and drive in silence.

It's stopped raining with just a few big drops hitting my windshield as they fall from the large trees that line both sides of the street.

I have to start planning now how I'm going to do this. First, I can't turn on the house lights—that could attract attention. If I can make my way to the darkroom, I can use my small penlight to find what I need. I think I left it on the shelf above the enlarger. At least if I shut the door to the darkroom I can turn the light on in there. Oh yeah, and I can't forget the negatives. I'm not so sure it'd be a good idea to let the cops get ahold of those.

I spot some headlights in my rear view mirror and immediately my heart begins to pound. I strain, trying to see if there are any lights on the top of the car, but there is too much glare from the headlights. I quickly check my speed. I'm only going about twenty-seven miles-per-hour but I slow down a little anyway, just in case.

Maybe if I go around the block I'll know for sure if I'm being followed. I turn on my right blinker and turn at the next street. I'm about halfway down the block when the car turns onto the same street. I signal for another right turn, but as I approach the street I see the big yellow sign, "DEAD END." I quickly switch my signal to a left hand turn and almost at the same time make the turn. Once again, about halfway down the block, the headlights from the car reflect off my rear view mirror, putting a rectangular spot of light across my face.

My hands become sticky on the wheel as they begin to sweat. I try to calm myself down. Okay, just relax now, Bob. Maybe it's coincidence.

I signal for another left turn and glance in my mirror just in time to see the car turn into a driveway.

"Whew." I breath a big sigh of relief and almost miss my turn. Now it's time to get moving again. I lost some precious time back there.

I get back on my original course again. Once out of town I take some of the more secluded roads to Meridian Road. I end up coming from the opposite direction I normally would.

I hope I've beat them here.

I pull into the south entrance of the subdivision. This is the newer part and the street has not yet been paved. I feel as though I'm going to wake up the entire countryside as my tires crunch and rumble over the gravel. I can barely make out the dark skeletons of two unfinished homes that are just going up. As I come around the bend toward my home, I slow down a little more and turn on my brights. I scan my yard, as much as I can see from the road, for movement or unwelcome vehicles of the law enforcement persuasion. Except for a couple of rabbits that scamper into the backyard, it seems to be all clear.

I pull up toward my garage and push my garage door opener. The garage door opens and light spills out onto the concrete apron. As I get closer my car activates the motion sensor on my outdoor flood lights and suddenly the entire front yard is lit up almost like daylight.

Terrific, let's just let the whole neighborhood know I'm here.

I pull into the garage and the door closes behind me. I wonder if Joe's at my neighbor's house waiting for me yet. I run around the back of my car and into the house. Groping down the dark hallway I stumble over my basketball shoes I left there a few days ago. At least I think they were my basketball shoes. Finding the corner of the wall, I head down the hall toward the bedroom. There's some light shining through the window of my study from the floodlights outside. Using that light I quickly make it to my bedroom.

The floodlights should be going out any second now.

"Ouch! Dang." I bang my knee on the corner of my waterbed. Finally, I make it to my darkroom, close the door behind me and flip on the light switch. Squinting into the suddenly bright room, I make hasty steps to the shelf above my enlarger.

Yep, there's my little flashlight. I give it a quick test.

"Good". I whisper as the light faithfully comes on.

I turn it back off because I don't know how good the battery is, and stick it in my jacket pocket. I quickly turn my attention to looking for the negatives. I remember that after I made the enlargements I put the strips of five negatives each into plastic sleeves that are notebook-sized. Each page in turn holds a thirty-six exposure roll of film.

Sure enough, looking to my right, next to the enlarger, is the plastic page with the negatives.

It's a good thing I was in a hurry and didn't file them yet. It would have taken me a couple minutes longer to find them in my negative file.

I pick it up and notice a negative strip is missing, but a quick check of the negative holder in the enlarger reveals that I'd forgotten to put it away. I slide it out and into the remaining empty slot. Folding it up accordion style, I unzip my jacket a little and stick it in my shirt pocket. Turning back toward the door I reach into my jacket pocket and pull out my flashlight. I know the floodlights have already turned themselves off, so as I turn the light off in the darkroom, I turn my flashlight on and then open the door. Making my way quickly but carefully through the bedroom, I keep the flashlight pointed low, not only to keep from tripping over things, but so I won't shine the windows should anyone be driving past. I spot my running shoes on the floor and stop to pick them up.

These will be more comfortable and I'll be able to move a little quicker in these.

I go back to my bed, and sitting on the edge, I change out of my dress shoes into my running shoes in the dim light of the flashlight.

"Ahh, much better."

The shoes feel cool on my feet after having those other ones on since early this morning, or should I say yesterday morning. It's been eighteen hours since I got ready for church.

I hop off the bed and practically bounce all the way into the study. I'm in my element now, and it's no wonder. In a few more hours it'll be my usual time for running and my body knows it.

Sweeping the light across my bookshelf, I scan for the large blue book with the gold lettering.

Ah hah, got it.

I pull it out, plop it on the desk and whip the cover open. The phone rings and I freeze in my tracks. It rings a second time. My heart is in my throat as I find myself praying for it to ring again. I wait. It's not ringing. I've gotta get out of here. But first I think I'll make it a little more difficult for them to maneuver around here.

Pictures in hand I run down the hall, flip on the basement lights and run down the basement steps to the main breaker box, where I pull the main breaker. The basement goes dark so out comes the flashlight again. On the way back to the stairs I pull anything I can get my hands on out onto the floor.

I've got an idea: soap. I grab the gallon of liquid laundry detergent off a shelf in the laundry room and as I go up the steps I pour the whole container out behind me. When it's empty I just simply give it a toss down the steps.

I notice then that I'm bending the pictures all up. Shoot, I'd better get a photo mailer for these. I remember having some of those large manila envelopes with the cardboard inside for support on a shelf in the darkroom. In fact I think it's on the same shelf that my flashlight was on.

I hurry back to the darkroom, this time avoiding my basketball shoes and the corner of my bed. Of course, it helps a little when you've got a bit of light to see by. Shining my light on the shelf I look for the envelopes, but they're not there.

Where are those stupid things?

I check the shelf just above. Not there either.

Where did I put them? I can't be spending all night looking for them. One other possibility—they might be under the sink. If they're not there I'll just have to do without.

I open the doors under the sink and, lo and behold, there they are. After opening the flap on one of them, I start to slide the pictures in. As they slide in and hit the bottom of the envelope with a "thunk," I feel, and hear, a low rumble. It's the sound of a vehicle, probably a car, coming up the driveway.

"Oh, Lord."

Chapter 5

I run out of the darkroom, through the bedroom, and into the hallway where, through the doorway of the study, I can see the headlights of a car shining on the garage door.

I stop in my tracks. Well the front door is out. I listen carefully for the doors to shut. No sound. Then the headlights go out and the engine stops.

A light suddenly shines in through the study window and I duck back into the bedroom, shutting off my light. I knew I should have closed those blinds. The light goes away and I hear footsteps heading up the front porch steps. Maybe I can make it to the back door. I start to make my move when I hear someone run past the bedroom windows, first on the side facing the road and then around the corner of the house through the side yard past the other window.

Dang, he's gone to cover the back door. So let's see, there's one at the front door and one at the back, so that leaves the windows. I move slowly and quietly toward the side yard window and start to unlock it when another car pulls up the driveway. I lock the window back up again as I hear more foot steps running around outside.

Shoot, shoot, shoot. Now what?

I hear some faint voices from outside.

One says, "You cover the south side, and I'll get the north."

"You got it," the other one says.

As soon as they're in position I know they're gonna break in. They're on every side so I guess the only way to go is either up, or down. So . . . I guess I'll go up. I move toward the open darkroom door and my one chance for escape when I hear a voice come over a bullhorn in the driveway .

"This is the police! Put your weapons down and come out with your hands behind your head!"

What weapons? I don't have any weapons. Just my gun behind

my bed, and I'm not dumb enough to try to use it against this many cops.

"You have thirty seconds to comply!"

You can give me thirty years and I still won't come out, 'cause that's probably what I'll get, thirty years to life.

I crawl through the doorway, shut it, and then lock it. That should slow them down a little. Going over to the counter with the enlarger, I open the bottom cupboard doors and push several stacks of eight-by-ten photographic paper over to one side. There in front of me is the two-foot by two-foot door that leads to the small room where I keep my safe. I grab hold of the latch that holds the door closed, turn it, and give the door a small push. It opens easily and I turn around to go in feet first, pulling the cupboard door closed after me.

"This is your last warning! Come out or we're coming in!"

Must be my thirty seconds are up. I scoot back about another half foot and my feet touch the back wall of the room.

The room is long and narrow, being only about three feet wide and five feet long. The walls and ceiling were never finished so all the studs and ceiling joists still show. It was always meant as a secret room for my valuables.

"Wham!" There's a loud noise at the front door. Here they come. I turn on my side and bend my knees, scooting back into the room a little farther. There's another loud bang on the door. One more like that and they'll be in. I slide the photographic paper back in front of the door, scoot the rest of the way into the room and close the door. There's a third bang and a crash as the front door gives way.

"We're in!"

With these words I hear the crashing of glass from almost every part of the house. They're coming in the windows. I stand up and take a quick look around with the flashlight. Using the commotion around me as a cover, I push the safe over against the door. The safe weighs over a hundred pounds empty, but it moves easily on the casters I never seemed to get around to taking off. I tip the safe half way over and wait. At about the same time as one of the policemen kicks the bathroom door open, I tip the safe onto its side.

"The lights aren't working!"

The voice of the one in charge echoes through the house, "Don, you and Greg get to the basement and find the fuse box and get us some lights in here! We don't want to be shooting each other in the dark! Everyone else hold your positions!"

"Come on, Greg, let's get it."

I stand up on the safe and push the ceiling insulation up and out of the way.

"Whoa!" Thud! Thump, thump, thud! "Ow!"

"Don, are you okay?"

"Dang, I think I broke my arm!"

"Sir! Don is down with a possible broken arm!"

"Is it a compound?"

"No, sir!"

"Get Don up here and I'll call an ambulance when we get this place secured. Which rooms have not been searched?"

One of the men in the bathroom answers back, "Just the master bedroom at this end of the house!"

"Okay, that also leaves the basement and the living room!" He uses the bullhorn again. "I want a man at each of the basement windows and at each of the bedroom windows."

While the orders are being shouted, I toss the pictures through the hole in the ceiling and pull myself up between the ceiling joists into the attic. I look to see where the pictures landed and push the insulation back into place.

"Any extra men I want to see in here with me, on the double!"

I pick up the pictures and with my toes I feel for each succeeding ceiling joist as I slowly, and as quickly as I can, work my way through the attic to the back side of the house. Now I have to pray they search the basement first. I'm just thankful it's not summertime. I would dehydrate in five minutes up here.

I hear more footsteps inside the house, maybe two or three more men. Then one trots down the hallway to join the other two outside my bedroom door.

That means there's probably two or three men plus the guy in charge at the basement steps. I've gotta be ready the instant they clear this area, which I hope they do soon. I reach into my pants pocket and pull out my keys, holding them tightly so they won't rattle.

Next to my head is a triangular attic vent screwed to the side of the wall. I find my locker key and separate it from the others on the key ring. Holding the rest of the keys tightly in the palm of my hand, I stick the round end of the locker key into the head of one of the screws and slowly, one by one, I begin to take the screws out of the vent. I have to be very careful, though, not to shine my flashlight out the vent. I decide it's too risky to have it on at all, so I turn it off and begin doing it by feel, turning the light on only long enough to locate the next screw.

The voices below, inside the house, become muffled and the words become unintelligible. They're either talking quieter or they're making their way into the basement or both.

I lift myself up a little to stretch my legs and also to try and get a peek at the ground below between the vent slats.

Dang, can't see a thing. Better get back to work. I've only got a couple more screws to go. I take a deep breath and let it out slowly as I twist out the last screw the rest of the way with my fingers.

It sounds awful quiet down there. I wonder what they're doing.

I take my key and start prying at the flange around the vent. By slowly working the vent away from the studs, I'm able to fit my fingers behind it.

Now I wait. I put my keys back in my pocket, sit down and stretch my legs again. They feel stiff and one foot is half asleep and feels tingly from the lack of circulation.

I hope I don't end up pulling a muscle or something when I make my run for it, and . . . I hope all these cops haven't scared Joe off.

I hear a hum and then someone from the basement yells, "The basement is secure and we now have power!"

I look out through the vent slats just in time to see the lights from the basement come shining out through the windows, making small patches of light on the ground below. Then the kitchen and dining room lights come on, illuminating more of the back yard in a dim yellow glow.

The officer in charge must be in the kitchen almost right below me 'cause I hear him in an almost normal voice give orders to the two men in the backyard stationed at the basement windows.

"You men go to the southwest corner and support the men already there."

My prayers have been answered. Now I just wait for my signal.

I slide my fingers of both hands under the two lower corners of the vent's flange and grasp it firmly.

Crash! They smash the bedroom door open and at the same time I jerk the vent toward me. It comes out easier than I thought it would and I almost lose my balance. I just barely catch a roof support with one hand.

At the same instant I hear the sound of gunfire and crashing glass. I pull myself up and halfway out of the hole.

"Hold your fire! Hold your fire! It was only your reflections in a mirror, you idiots!"

That's a good way to gain the respect of your employees.

I take a quick look around and turn to sit in the hole. Putting my hands on each side of the peak of the roof, I pull myself up until I'm standing with my feet on the bottom of the triangular hole. I can see both side yards and down my driveway. On the left I can see there are at least four policemen and on the right three cars. I put the palms of my hands flat against the roof of the house. The shingles are cool, damp, and rough, like course sandpaper. I turn my elbows up and push, lifting my feet off their perch. Then, swinging my right leg up and over the edge of the roof, I roll onto the side of the roof sloping away from the four policemen and toward the garage. I peek over the top of the roof to double-check the position of the policemen.

Yep, still there.

I scoot back down a little, then getting into a crouched position, I begin to slowly waddle down the roof toward the back side of the garage roof. I'm about halfway down when another car comes up the driveway, a station wagon. The lights on its top flashing red and blue, it creates a circus-like atmosphere. I lay flat on the roof hoping not to be spotted. Hopefully they'll be too interested in what's going on inside to look around outside, especially up here.

As soon as the car pulls up alongside one of the other police cars, the motion activated flood lights come on pouring light into the faces of the policemen as they get out of the car.

Now's my chance.

I get back into my crouch position and begin waddling down the roof again, keeping an eye on the new arrivals. One of them goes around to the back of the car and opens up the back. Just as I'm about to go behind the peak of the garage I see a German shepherd jump out of the back of the car.

My feet slip out from under me as I try to stop and I fall backwards onto my hands, sliding on them a few inches. My hands sting from being scraped along the rough shingles.

I crane my neck to catch a glimpse of where the dog is going, but they're already gone. I'm gonna have to hope they've taken him inside.

Up into my crouch again, I wipe my hands on my pant legs, and waddle down to the edge of the garage roof. Taking a quick look around, I wait for them to make their assault on my darkroom. And I wait, and I wait. It seems like forever when . . . .

Bang! Bang! Crash!

Right after the first "bang," I launch myself off the roof, and just about the same time as the second bang, I hit the ground and roll several times.

I get up and get my bearings and make sure I'm still in one piece. Nope, nothing broken. Now to lead that dog on a merry little chase.

I head straight for the wooded area behind my house. During the past summer I spent some of my free time cutting a winding path through the woods. It goes in behind my house and comes out behind the local veterinarian's house. When I wasn't in a hurry I would enjoy the leisurely walk on my way to do a project for the Doctor.

I can just barely make out where the path enters the woods in the dim light from the house. As soon as I enter the woods, though, it becomes pitch black, and before I can get my trusty little penlight out I get whacked in the face by a small branch.

"Ouch." I say it quietly, even though I'd like to say it much louder.

I pull out my flashlight and look to see if I'm still on the path. In front of me is the narrow, slightly worn path just wide enough for one person to get through at a time.

The light from the flashlight was fine for close up work, but for running through the woods in the dark, it's the pits. With all the twists and turns I have to slow down to a fast walk.

I wonder if this is such a good idea. With that dog of theirs they'll be able to catch up with me in no time at all.

I catch a glimpse of a large tree to my right; just a large black form.

I've got an idea.

I walk off the path under a low hanging limb from the tree. I go about ten more yards, then I turn around and backtrack until I'm under the limb again. Jumping up, I grab hold of the limb and pull myself up until I'm sitting on the limb, straddling it like a horse. I pull myself down the limb to the trunk of the tree, step onto a limb next to it, then over to another limb so that now I'm on the other side of the tree. I crawl out onto that limb until I think it won't hold my weight anymore, and jump.

The path is just a few yards to my left, but I don't want to get back on it, not just yet. You know, just in case the dog runs a little past where I turned off and accidentally picks up my scent on the trail again. After about thirty feet of fighting my way through the brush, I get back onto the trail once again with, I might add, only a couple of extra scratches to my credit.

With the help of that dog they've probably found and gotten into my secret room by now.

Walking in my little light with darkness all around, I feel like I'm in another world,(not the soap opera), in another time. If it weren't for the realization that this world will soon be invaded, I would feel comfortable just staying here, it's so peaceful.

My feet start to feel damp as the water from the wet grass and weeds soaks through my shoes and into my socks.

I catch sight of the yard light in the back of the Doctor's home. Just a little way to go now.

When I get a little closer I pick up my pace to where I can start jogging and even turn off the flashlight. As I come out of the woods the yard light makes the backyard look an eery greenish color. Even the Doctor's immaculate white house looks a dingy green.

I sprint up to the back door and Samson begins barking. "Shhh, Samson," I say in a loud whisper. "It's me."

I dig into my pocket and get my keys. Finding the Doctor's house key, I unlock the door and enter the kitchen of the house. Samson jumps up on me and I rub him behind his ears and pat his shoulders.

"How ya doin', Sam? Are you hungry boy?"

Even in my hurry I feel the need to fulfill my obligation to the

Doctor to feed his dog. I get out the bag of dog food, rip it open and just lay it in the middle of the floor.

"There you go, Sam. That should hold you until your master gets back. I'll bet you're thirsty, too."

I go to the closet and get a mop bucket and fill it with water, setting it in a corner.

"There, now you keep those bad people outside as long as you can, okay?"

I look around the kitchen. The only light is a fluorescent bulb above the sink that the Doctor leaves on as a night light to discourage intruders. I see something that gives me an idea. I remember seeing this in a movie once.

I start looking through the cupboards for the spices. "Ah, here they are. I want . . ." I move a few spices around until I find the one I want. "This."

I pull out a black can with gold writing on it. It says, "Watkins Black Pepper."

"Time for me to go, Sam. Maybe I'll see you again sometime."

I move quickly out of the kitchen, through the dining room, down the hallway, to the main staircase near the front door that leads upstairs. I go halfway up the stairs and begin sprinkling the pepper all over each of the steps the rest of the way up and then part way down the hallway toward the bedrooms.

Running down the hallway, I toss the pepper can into a waste basket just inside the bathroom door and make a left into the master bedroom. I unlock the slide-by patio door, push it open, and walk quickly to the railing. Looking down through what's left of the leaves of the big maple tree, I can see the top of Joe's Cherokee.

Awright, Joey! I go back to the slide-by and close it. No need giving them any clues as to which direction I went.

I go to the side railing, and balancing on the top of the railing with my feet and leaning against the side of the house with my right forearm, the pictures still in my hand, I grab hold of the tree limb.

I sure am glad I didn't get around to trimming this thing.

I climb onto the limb and work my way down to the trunk. By the time I'm done with all this climbing around I'll be perfect for playing the part of Tarzan. I climb down the tree to its lowest branches where I give the pictures a little toss to the ground. Now I shouldn't touch the ground or they'll realize I've gotten a ride. I'd just as soon keep them guessing 'till I'm well away from here. I move out on a limb that hangs directly over Joe's jeep. I let myself down slowly until my toes touch the top of the jeep.

I can hear the radio playing inside as I crawl toward the front. When I get to the front I plaster my face against the driver's side of the windshield.

A startled Joe almost hits his head on the top of the jeep. He quickly rolls down his window. "What are you doing up there? You almost made me pee my pants."

I move over to the side window and hang my head over the side. "Keeping my feet off the ground."

"Why?"

"So the tracking dog can't follow me."

"Tracking dog?"

"Yeah, you know, a large furry animal with four legs that likes to gnaw on arms and legs."

"I know what they are."

"Then why'd you ask?"

"Never mind. It's just that they've got enough cops here now they could surround the whole county. What do they need a tracking dog for?"

"Really? There's that many? When I left the house there were maybe only a dozen or so."

"Well, there's more now. So can we get out of here now?"

"Yeah, but first you gotta open the door for me and get the pictures. They're on the ground by the tree right there." I point toward the big maple tree.

Joe slides over to the passenger side, opens the door and jumps out of the jeep. "The things I do for you," he mutters.

While Joe goes to retrieve the pictures, I slide off the top into the jeep and close the door. When Joe comes back he tosses the pictures onto my lap and hops into his seat, closing the door behind him in one motion.

"Your dome light's not working Joe."

"I know, I had to pee really bad and I didn't want the light coming on when I opened the door, so I took the bulb out."

"Good thinkin', Joe."

"Yeah, I know."

With headlights off we move slowly down the driveway to the

edge of the road. Through the trees we can see some of the police lights dancing through the branches. Then, just as we're about to pull out into the street, I see the headlights of a car heading our way from the direction of my house.

"Wait, Joe."

"I know, I see it."

Joe backs up into the driveway a little way and turns off the ignition.

A car zips by at a rate well above the posted speed limit of twenty-five mph, but even at that speed and in the darkness of night, I couldn't help but recognize the car.

"Joe!" I take a breath before continuing.

I startle him and he looks quickly around thinking we've been discovered.

"What?"

"That was my car. What are they doing with my car?"

"I don't think it matters much now. You can't drive it around anymore anyway. Besides, they're probably only taking it in to gather evidence."

"Yeah, you're probably right."

"Of course I am."

Just then two police cars speed past with their lights flashing.

"They're in an awful hurry, Bob. You think they got another call or something?"

"Prob'ly or something, Joe. My guess is they're trying to cut me off somewhere on the other side of the woods. So we best get going while they're off the beaten path."

Joe starts his Cherokee up and we head back to the end of the driveway again.

"All clear my way, Joe."

"Mine, too."

We pull out into the road and travel another hundred feet or so when I look back toward the direction of my house.

"Looks okay, Joe."

"Good, I can't see the potholes like this."

"This is a new road, Joe. There aren't any potholes.

"Oh, well I can't see the possums."

Joe turns his headlights on and we pick up some speed, going just over the speed limit. When we get to the main road we can see a couple more police cars turning onto the next road down after the other entrance to the subdivision.

"Looks a little busy to the left, Bob. Better go Jolly Road back." As he pulls out onto Meridian Road again he asks, "So, what took you so long back there? Five more minutes and I was gonna leave without you."

"Well I'm kinda surprised you waited as long as you did. What with all those cop cars driving by."

I keep looking back, watching for cop cars.

"Joe laughs, What an adventure."

"Yeah, maybe so, but that adventure was a little too adventuresome for my taste. If it weren't for the fact that I don't believe in luck, I would say I was lucky to get out of there, but since I don't believe in luck, I won't say it."

"Well, let's see just how well the luck you don't believe in holds up."

"Why?"

"We just passed a county cop sitting in that drive back there."

Joe looks in his rear view mirror and I turn around to look out the back window in time to see a car pulling out onto the road.

"Looks like your non-existent luck is running out."

"Not yet, just drive normal. They might not be following us."

I look back again and I'm greeted by a blinding light as a spotlight is turned on us.

"Okay, Bob. Two choices: pull over or make a run for it."

I look back again and I can see the lights on top flashing. I take a quick look ahead and hit on an idea.

"Well, Bob?"

"Pull over, Joe. I think I've got a plan."

"What is it?"

"You don't want to know, but when it happens just tell them you'll get them."

"Why?"

"You'll know why. Believe me, you'll know why."

"I don't like the sound of that."

"Just pull over and I'll take care of the rest."

Joe slows down and pulls off onto the shoulder of the road, just opposite the golf course. The instant he stops I open my door, jump out and quietly close the door behind me. I can imagine the look on Joe's face and it makes me smile.

Like most police cars, this one pulls up behind Joe slightly to the left and a little more on the road than Joe. I move about halfway to the back of the Cherokee, keeping my head below window level.

After what seems like hours, I hear the car door open, then slam shut. I bend way over with my hands on the ground and look under the Cherokee. I feel the blood rush to my head. I watch the legs of the cop walk up to the driver side. As soon as the feet stop I begin to slowly and quietly work my way around to the back of the Cherokee. The night is quiet and I can hear everything that is being said, even above the sound of the two vehicle's idling engines.

"What's the trouble, officer? I wasn't speeding, was I?"

"No, we're . . ." The voice is that of a female and the tone of the voice suddenly changes to one of familiarity. "Joe? Joe Maderna? Well, I'll be." There's a short pause. "You don't recognize me, do you?"

"Well I might if you'd get that dang flashlight out of my face."

"Oh, sorry, Joe. It's me, Terri. Terri Sigetty. I used to work at the post office a few years ago."

"Oh, yeah. Terri. I remember you. You left to go to the police academy. I see you made it to be a policeman."

"Policewoman. Do you still give the women at the P.O. a hard time with your male chauvinist pig attitudes?"

"Sure do. I wouldn't have it any other way."

Good, Joe. Keep her talking. I work my way to the back of the patrol car. I kind of hate to do this to Terri, she was always nice to most everybody when she worked at the post office. Quite often she would bring in bags of candy to pass around. Joe could always get her fired up though by getting her into discussions about a woman's proper place.

"You still working at the P.O.?"

"Yep."

"How is everyone doing?"

"Oh, pretty good. So why'd you stop me? I wasn't doing anything wrong was I?"

From the back of the patrol car I walk quickly on the quieter road surface up to the driver side door.

"Oh, no, no. I just got a call to stop all traffic coming from

Meridian Road. In fact it has to do with your friends, Bob Reslock and Jim Kemplar."

"What about them?"

"You mean you haven't heard?"

"I've heard some."

"Well, I couldn't believe it when I first heard about it. I mean they just don't seem the type."

"They aren't."

Thank you, Joe. I reach for the patrol car door handle and begin to lift it slowly so as not to make any noise.

"I didn't think so either, Joe, until I saw some of the evidence against them. I don't think there's a jury in the world that wouldn't convict them."

I pull the door open and jump in, pulling the door closed quietly behind me. I leave the door slightly ajar just because she might hear the click of the door as the door latch catches. I take a quick look around at my new environment.

Okay, let's see, automatic on the floor. Good, I won't have to get used to a clutch again. What I didn't notice before but I do now is the almost constant chatter coming from the radio. No time to pay any attention to that now, though.

I shove the shift lever into drive and floor it. I can hear one rear wheel spewing gravel all over while the other wheel screams on the pavement, stripping a good ten-thousand miles of tread from it.

I swerve out into the left lane around Terri and around Joe's Cherokee. I can see Terri standing there with eyes wide and mouth open. Poor Terri.

I straighten the car out, getting back on the right side of the road, and continue accelerating.

I wonder if Joe took my hint.

Looking in the rear view mirror I can't tell if Joe is following me since I've already gone over a hill. Turning my attention back to the road ahead, I'm amazed at how fast I'm going past the homes alongside the road. I look at the speedometer.

"Eighty-five?"

I take my feet off the accelerator a little and slow down to about seventy. I can't slow down too much because I don't know how long it will take Terri to find a phone.

I come down the hill toward the light at Okemos road. On the left is a Dunkin Donuts. I'll wait for Joe there. I pull into the parking lot, park in a space to the left of the building and turn everything off, including the overhead lights.

Hmm, that's strange. I look around. No cops at a donut shop. Must be they've got something to do tonight.

I take the keys out of the ignition, get out of the car and toss them into a nearby dumpster. There, that takes one car out of the picture. Well, at least for a little while anyway.

I close the door and begin trotting toward the road when I see Joe coming down the hill toward me. I run out to and across the road waving my arms over my head so he can see me. As he slows down I stick my thumb out like a hitchhiker. Joe stops and I hop in.

"You're not a dangerous criminal on the run from the law are you?" Joe asks as he takes off again. "I don't pick up dangerous hitch-hikers."

"Me? Dangerous? Only if I don't take a bath for a week. So, uh, what did Terri say when you took off after me?"

"Not much, but I didn't give her much time to say very much. I just said 'I'll get him!' and she said 'But . . .' but I just took off before she could finish."

We turn the corner onto Okemos road to get on the freeway and I look over at the donut shop and see several faces at the windows staring at us as we go by.

"I may have attracted a little attention with that police car, Joe."

"Why do you say that?"

"There were some people in the donut shop back there watching us real close."

We get on the on-ramp to the freeway and Joe begins to question me about what happened back at my house.

"So what happened back there at your house?"

"Well, while I was getting this stupid envelope for these pictures," I hold up the envelope and plop it back down on my lap, "the police came and surrounded the house."

"How'd you get out, then?"

"Divine intervention?"

"Prob'ly. I doubt you'd be talented enough to get out without it."

"Thanks for the big self-confidence builder, Joe."

"You're not supposed to have confidence in self. You're supposed to have confidence in God. I've been put here on this planet to tear down this monster called self-esteem, alias ego, alias pride, and make people see that they can do nothing unless God lets them, that we are nothing but scum, just maggots on a big pile of poop called Earth. When all is said and done . . ."

"Okay! Okay! So I misspoke myself. It was just a figure of speech. What I meant to say was that God gives me certain talents and abilities that I use in conjunction with the wisdom that He gives me to get me out of the situations like the one I was in."

"Well, did He give you any certain talents, abilities or wisdom to get us out of this mess we're still in?"

"Maybe, maybe not. I'm not tellin'. So, do you want to hear how I . . . pardon me, how God helped me get out of my house or not?"

"Well, since you put it that way, okay."

"Basically I got up in the attic, pulled the vent out, crawled out onto the roof, and jumped off the back of the garage roof."

"That seems simple enough. Even I could have prob'ly done that."

"Yeah, maybe, except for one thing."

"What's that?"

"You never would have fit through the attic vent opening."

"Maybe not but I'll bet I could make you fit into that ashtray."

Off in the distance I can see the lights of the Post Office.

"Maybe it would have been easier to get the pictures out of your locker, Joe. Especially since all the police are at my house."

"Not all the police. I can think of one that has a long walk if they want her at your house."

"Yeah, poor Terri."

"Well, I just hope your pastor appreciates all the trouble I've gone through to get those pictures."

"All the trouble *you've* gone through? What about *me*?"

"Okay, I guess you helped out a little, but don't let it go to your head."

Chapter 6

Back at the church I take the pictures out of the envelope and set them down on the desk in front of Brother Martin.

"I'm glad you fellows made it back safely. Did you run into any trouble?"

Joe, in a it-happens-all-the-time tone replies, "Not much. Bob just went into the house, got the pictures, snuck out through thirty policemen who had surrounded the house and stole a police car while I distracted the policewoman. What could have gone wrong?"

Brother Martin shuffles through the small pile of pictures and pulls out one in particular. "There we are."

He turns around, pulls his large ancient language dictionary off the shelf, brushes the other pictures off to one side with a sweep of his hand, and opens the book.

I move around the desk to stand slightly behind and to one side to sort of look over his shoulder. "You don't mind do you?"

"Oh no, of course not." Brother Martin looks up at Jim and Joe. "If you like, you gentlemen may observe also."

At that Joe practically leaps forward to the desk, followed closely by Jim.

"Now, let's see." Brother Martin reaches into his top drawer and pulls out his sheets of paper with the other translations. "Where was I?"

Joe reaches back, putting the instep of his foot on a chair, sliding it up behind him. He sits down, putting his elbows on the desk and his chin in his hands.

Brother Martin flips through the book. Jim decides he wants a chair also, and steps over, picks one up and carries it over next to Joe. Jim sits in the chair leaning forward a little letting his arms dangle down between his knees.

I turn my attention back to Brother Martin. He evidently has found what he wanted as he looks at the photograph and then quickly flips back and forth through the book, every so often giving a little "Uh huh," or a "Hmm." This goes on for about five minutes without anything being written down.

Joe, with his usual impatience, breaks the silence. "Did it take you this long with the other parts?"

"Actually, no. It took longer to do the other ones. Many of these words I already know, but what I have to be extremely careful of are the verb tenses. I need to double check those."

"If you've translated the word into English, why do you have to recheck it?"

"Quite often with these ancient languages you have words within a sentence that will change the entire meaning of another word in the sentence, and they are not always next to each other, and the verb tenses are important so that we know if what they are talking about, in their context of time, has already happened, is happening now, meaning when this was written, or will happen in the future. Which could be our present time. I hope that is clear as mud now."

Joe nods his head, "Yeah, I think I understand that, but if it's been so easy to translate, how come you haven't written anything down yet?"

At this point I jump to my pastor's defense. "He prob'ly has his reasons, Joe. Don't you, Brother Martin."

"As a matter of fact I do, my impatient friends, but I can't tell you. Not yet anyway. I can tell you this, you must take this cube with you."

"Who has to take the cube, and take it where?" Joe asks.

"Why, all three of you. You three will work as a team, or should I say you *must* work as a team, but as to where, I don't know yet. However, I'm not finished yet and I believe the answer to that final question is hidden within these final phrases. So, if you fellows will allow me."

Brother Martin goes back to his work, but Joe still seems a bit edgy. Since there's really nothing for me to see, I step back from the desk a little and lean against the bookshelf. I close my eyes for a moment and realize just how tired I am. I look at my watch. A couple more hours and I will have been up for almost twenty-four hours, and I still don't have any idea when or even where I'll get any sleep. Then there's poor Joe; he must be running on fumes because he worked the night before. If he got up about three or four o'clock Saturday afternoon, that would mean he has been up for almost thirty-eight . . . no, thirty-six hours. Unless he took a short nap this morning, well actually yesterday morning. Would you listen to me rattle on to myself. I must really be tired. Next thing I know I'll be talking to myself out loud.

I'm jarred out of the conversation with myself by Brother Martin, who actually begins talking out loud to himself.

"Now wait just a moment, this can't be right." He leans back to think a moment then goes back to the book. He runs his finger down the page.

"It's got to be the ancient town of Elam, or maybe Edom." His finger stops about three-quarters of the way down the page, then he looks intently at the photograph and then back at the book. He repeats this process a couple more times and then shakes his head.

"No, not Elam. So then it's got to be Edom." He moves his finger back up the page, then turns back a page in the book. Looking at the lower right hand corner, he then begins the ritual of alternating his attention between the book and the photograph.

Brother Martin shakes his head again. "Not Edom, either. I can't believe it, though. It would definitely be a miracle. I have to double-check this again."

Joe can't stand it anymore. "What is it? What have you found?" Joe's voice is almost beyond anxious and heading toward hysteria.

"Just one moment, gentlemen. I have to be extremely positive that I am correct about this." Brother Martin looks back and forth between the book and the photograph several more times, each time following it with an "Uh huh" or an "Okay." Finally he stops, picks up the cube and leans back in his chair, looking closely at the cube. Without looking back he says, "Bob, could you hand me that atlas just behind you there?"

'Sure." I turn around and at the end of the shelf, about shoulder level, is a black, hardbound book with gold embossed lettering that says, *Atlas of the World*. I pull it down and hand it to Brother Martin, who in turn lays it down on his desk, setting the cube down just to the left of the book.

"Well, fellows, if I were a gypsy telling you your fortunes, I would be saying to you, 'You are about to go on a long journey.'"

Brother Martin flips open the atlas and turns to the pages showing the entire world.

Quietly, Jim asks, "A journey to where?"

"Where? I do not know where yet, but I do know the name of the place where you must go. It is called Eden."

"Eden?" I say. "Isn't that a tiny little town just south of here? You know, near Mason."

"No, no Bob. The Garden of Eden."

"Oh, come on." Joe sounds skeptical now. "You mean we're risking our lives in order to go to the Garden of Eden? That's impossible, it would have been destroyed in the flood."

Brother Martin, in his usual calming voice, replies to the skepticism. "True, but what I believe you have to do is take this cube to the site where the Garden of Eden used to be."

"Well then how do we do that since professional archaeologists can't agree on even the general area where it used to be."

"Ah, true again, but we have an advantage that they don't. We have a map." He holds the cube up with the tips of his fingers and rotates it slightly by the twisting of his wrist. "You see the reason nobody could accurately locate the position of the Garden is because they failed to take into account the magnitude of geologic changes that took place because of the flood. Almost everything changed. Mountains were washed away, rivers changed their courses, or even disappeared, and plains and plateaus had great gorges cut through them."

Joe's still not satisfied. "So what good is a map if nothing is the same as when the thing was made?"

"*A* map like that would not be any good, but two maps, one showing what it was like after the flood and the other showing what it was like before the flood, is a different story altogether, and that is exactly what we have here."

Suddenly, out of nowhere, Jim straightens up and practically yells, which is totally out of character for Jim.

"Map!"

"What is it, Jim?" Brother Martin asks.

"Map!"

"We heard that already, Jim," I say. "What about it?"

"Map, map, map."

"Whack his head Joe, I think something's stuck."

"No, you guys, the map. That's what that guy that beat me up wanted. He wanted to know where the map was, remember? I told you guys about it."

"This is not good news, gentlemen."

"Why?" Joe and I say in unison.

"It means that this evil fellow has or has had access to all the information contained on the clay portion of the cube. The only thing he lacks are the maps, and if his past behavior is any indication at all, he will stop at nothing to get his hands on this."

"So what do we do now, Brother Martin?"

"I think paramount in importance is to find a place for you fellows to stay for a while and get some sleep. Frankly, if I may say so, all three of you gentlemen look like the walking dead. Meanwhile, I am going to try to pinpoint the location of the Garden."

Brother Martin stands up and stretches, making his large frame even more imposing. He pushes his chair out of the way with his leg and leans over to pick up the phone. "I think I will try to contact the Morgans."

"Isn't it a little early?" Jim asks. "It's only five a.m."

Brother Martin and I both laugh. Joe looks puzzled. "What's so funny? It is early."

"You'd have to know Floyd and Millie to understand," I reply. "First of all they've probably both been up for almost half an hour already. In fact, Brother Martin will be fortunate if he catches Floyd before he goes out the door to do the chores."

Brother Martin has already dialed the phone and is waiting for an answer as I continue to tell Joe and Jim about Floyd and Millie Morgan.

"Actually, Joe, you will probably envy their lifestyle."

"Why's that?"

"Floyd inherited their three-hundred-acre dairy farm from his parents who inherited it from their's, and I know you've always wanted to be a farmer."

"How many cows do they have?"

"I don't know exactly, but I herd there's a lot of them."

"Funny, Bob."

Brother Martin interrupts as he hangs up the phone. "Mildred wanted to know if you "boys" have had any breakfast yet, and she says that you "boys" are welcome to stay as long as you want."

"Breakfast, Brother Martin?"

"Yes sir, Bob. Breakfast."

"Boy are you guys in for a treat. We are talking good old fashioned homemade everything here. Jim, this is one time you won't be able to eat any more and Joe, you might just as well wait to go on that diet."

"You fellows go on now, they're expecting you. Bob, it would be a good idea if you took this with you."

Brother Martin picks up the cube and hands it to me.

"Don't you still need it?"

"I've already got all the information from it that I need and I have these photographs, and you know as well as I do that it won't take the police very long to come and question me. I certainly don't want them waltzing in here with that shiny object sitting on my desk. Now you know the way there, don't you, Bob?"

"Sure do."

"Excellent, now get a move on. I have work to do here."

The three of us begin to leave and Jim calls back, "Thank you, sir."

"You are welcome, but please feel free to call me Pastor, or if you prefer, Brother Martin, or even Mister Greenhoe. Sir is for business people or children. That goes for you too, Joe."

"Okay . . . Brother Martin."

With that we leave Brother Martin's office closing the door behind us. As we walk down the hallway toward the back door, Joe comments, "Your pastor's a really neat guy Bob. I think when this is all over with and things get back to normal again, I'll start coming here for church."

"I'll believe it when I see it, Joe."

"Well, this time I promise."

"Okay, but I'm not gonna hold my breath."

We walk outside and there's a light drizzle coming down again, just starting to put a thin film of wetness on the surface of the parking lot.

Joe pulls the keys to the Cherokee out of his pocket and asks, "Anybody know what the weather's supposed to be like today?"

"Joe," I say, "I really don't care what the weather's gonna be like today. I just wanna get something to eat and then sleep for a couple days straight."

"Me too," Jim adds.

Joe unlocks the doors and since the back is crammed full of camping gear, we all climb into the front seat. I feel a little squashed in between Joe and Jim.

"It's a good thing you didn't get bucket seats, Joe. I don't think I could handle sitting on an emergency brake lever."

"Funny, Bob."

Joe starts the engine and immediately turns on the radio to the information station.

"I still want to know what the weather's gonna be like."

Puzzled by his insistence, I have to ask. "Why Joe?"

"Well . . ." Joe acts a little embarrassed like his answer may be a little silly. " . . . because . . . because if it's nice they might let me help harvest a field or something like that."

"Don't worry, Joe, we're probably gonna be there a few days. At least until Brother Martin finds out exactly where we're gonna go and then can make arrangements to get us there."

Jim leans forward in his seat a little and looks at me. "How do you know that's what he's gonna do?"

"Just because he's that kind of a person. Just look what he's done for us so far. That's one thing about Brother Martin, once he really believes in something, he goes all out and covers all the ground. He goes for the gold. He leaves no stone unturned. He's untiring. He's unrelenting. When the going gets tough, he gets going. He runs for the prize. He fights the good fight. Once he gets started, there's no turning back . . ."

Joe interrupts, "That's all well and good, Bob, but there's a couple things I need to know."

"Like what?"

"Like, can we count on him for anything?"

"Like, maybe. If we're lucky. And like, if there was any such thing as luck, which I don't believe in anyway and like, what was the other thing you need to know?"

"Like, where are we going? Like, you may know the way to these people's house but you're not driving and I am and like, I don't know the way to these people's house. So, like, can you tell me which way to turn here?"

"Like, head toward Grand Ledge. That's a little town west of Lansing. You do know where Grand Ledge is, don't you?"

"Like, I know, you know."

"Like, I know you know I know, but do you know, you know?"

"Like, I know I know, you know."

"Look, you guys, could you not know something and stop liking everything for a while?"

Joe and I look at each other and smile. Then like a precision team we say together, "Like, you know, why?"

"Because you're driving me crazy, that's why."

"Hey, Joe."

"What, Bob?"

"To change the subject, I just thought of something else the Morgan's have on their farm that you're gonna like."

"What's that?"

"Floyd has a team of draft horses that he takes around to horse pulling contests."

"Neat."

"Yeah, but not only that, he trains them by having them actually plow some of his fields with an old two bottom trailer plow. He says they can plow almost as fast as his tractor."

"Wow, just like the old days. Just like *Little House on the Prairie* and Mr. Ingalls."

"Shut up a second, you guys!" Jim sounds urgent. "I think there's something on the radio about us."

Joe leans forward and turns up the volume. The man is speaking in a deep, matter-of-fact voice.

"Once again, in a late breaking news story, there has been a multiple slaying in Meridian Township. It has been reported that one of the victims is an Ingham County sheriff's deputy. The number of other victims remains sketchy but are believed to all be members of one family."

Joe butts in. "I thought you said this was about us?"

"Shhh! Listen Joe!" Jim says insistently.

"Police sources say that before the deputy died, she was able to identify the assailants involved. Named were Bob Reslock and Jim Kemplar who are still wanted as suspects in the murders of Professor Royston and his assistant, Richard Symons. But in an added twist, she has added a third name to the list of suspects being sought, that of Joseph Maderna. These three men are described as armed and very dangerous. Citizens are being advised not to approach these men under any circumstances, but to contact the authorities immediately. We will have more on this tragic event as the facts are made available. Stay tuned to this station for complete updates on this and other fast breaking news of the day."

Joe reaches over and violently snaps the radio off. "Terrific, now I'm a murderer just like you guys."

"Joe," I say, "maybe we should keep the radio on. It may be to our advantage to know what's going on, and I think we oughta get off this main street and onto some side streets. If they think we killed a cop they're gonna be setting up road blocks all over the place."

"If I turn onto St. Joseph here we can get onto some really back-roadsy type areas. I think there's even some gravel roads still left out in that area."

Joe comes up to a light and pulls into the left turn lane.

"Joe, you don't think that cop that was killed was Terri, do you?"

"I don't know, but it would be just about 'the' perfect frame up. You were spotted leaving her police car at the donut shop and getting into my car, so basically we were the last ones to see her alive."

"Except for maybe that family that was killed," Jim says.

"And the killer or killers." I lean forward to turn the radio back on. "Do you guys think that family was killed because maybe Terri made a phone call from their house?"

"That's entirely possible," Joe replies. "You know, for a stinkin', low-life, rebellious, non-submissive, wench of a women's libber, she was kind of an all right person, I mean for a woman."

"Yeah, Joe. She did have a pleasant personality most of the time. She was kind of enjoyable to talk to."

"You're right, Bob, she was a fun person to be around. You know, if she hadn't been so much of a libber, I probably could have liked her a lot. She also wouldn't be dead right now."

Joe's voice sounds a little choked, like he's close to tears. I've only seen Joe cry once and that was during a rerun of a *Highway to Heaven* episode.

I try to get philosophical with him. "Joe, she didn't kill herself, and you didn't kill her, and I didn't kill her, and Jim didn't kill her. But I do think I know who did kill her."

"You mean that detective guy?"

"Yep. I think we all need to realize who's behind all this and try not to blame each other or ourselves for anything that's happened."

"Or going to happen," Joe adds.

"There's only one thing we should remember, though."

"What's that?"

"We still don't know for sure that it was Terri that was killed. They never said."

"Chances are it is, though."

I feel Jim's leg pushing against mine, squashing me against Joe even more. I look at Jim and he's fishing around between his legs for something.

"What are you doing, Jim?"

"I dropped some candy."

"Candy? You've got candy? What kind? Let me see."

Jim tries to keep the small yellow bag away from me.

"It looks like M&M's with peanuts, Joe."

"M&M's with peanuts! That's my favorite. Get some for me too, Bob."

"Okay, okay, I'll give you guys some."

Jim pours out all the candy into his hand and hands me two.

"There, that's for you and Joe."

But before I can protest, he pops all the rest of the M&M's into his mouth. Then he holds up his hand with his fingers spread apart, and mumbles, "Melts in your mouth, not in your hands."

I hand Joe his one M&M.

"Thanks, Jim, " he says. "Your generosity to a starving fellow human being is beyond words."

"You're welcome."

We come to a stop sign and Joe asks, "Which way now, Bob?"

"Um, left. We'll go south a couple of miles and then turn back to the west again. Uh, that's to the right."

"I know my directions."

"I'm just making sure. I wouldn't want you taking a wrong turn somewhere and getting us lost."

"Lost? Shoot, I never get lost."

"Never?"

"Never."

"Then what do you call that time you, me, Jim and Randy were going to that campground near South Haven and we ended up at Gary, Indiana?"

"I wasn't lost. I'd never seen Gary before and I wanted to see if it smelled as bad as everyone says it does."

"Then how come on the way back toward the campground we ended up near Kalamazoo?"

"I wasn't lost then, either. I knew exactly where I was."

"Yeah, right after you saw the sign that said, *Kalamazoo, 12 miles.*"

"So I like to take the scenic route, so what's the big deal?"

"Maybe so, but Randy didn't seem to enjoy your unguided scenic tours."

"Speaking of Randy," Joe says, "I stopped in to see him the other day."

"Really? How's he doing these days?"

"Pretty good. He only limps a little now, but he still uses a cane, and he's kind of blimped out some more."

"Probably from eating his profits."

Jim finally enters the conversation.

"How's his coffee and donut shop doing?"

"Not too bad, I guess. He clears just about what he was making at the post office before he had to quit because of his injury."

"You know, Joe, I know that you and Jim tried to warn him and I did, too. You'd think that after getting a severe sprained ankle at least once a year, and after breaking each one of his ankles once and breaking his foot once, he would have quit playing basketball. But I guess it took blowing his knee out while trying to cut to the basket to finally sideline, as Red would say, 'the knuckle head.' I guess my point is this; why wouldn't he listen to the warnings from his friends and from his own body?"

"I don't know exactly, but maybe it's the same thing that keeps people from accepting Jesus and getting saved."

"You mean pride?"

"Yep. Of course that is Satan's sin. He refuses to submit to God's authority and thinks that he himself is equal with God and with a little more effort he can be higher than God. He also refuses to listen to the warnings of God that are written in the Bible. The prophesies about what his ultimate end will be. He thinks he can change all that by himself."

"Yep, a lot of people are like that too."

I notice that we're coming to the road we need to turn onto.

"Take a right at this next road, Joe. Their house is about a mile and a half on the right hand side. It sits pretty far back from the road so you really can't see it at night, but they have a mailbox shaped like a barn, a little red barn."

We turn off the smooth, well-paved road onto the washboard surface of the one and a half lane dirt road. The surface is punctuated by potholes filled with water from the last couple days of rain, making it hard to tell how deep they are. The road is made rather ominous by the large trees that hug the sides of the road and by the frequent sharp curves that we are warned of by the black and yellow signs that seem to glow in the darkness as they are hit by the light from our headlights.

"Shoot, Bob, this dang road is getting my car dirty."

"The only reason your car is as clean as it is is because you left it out in the rain. In fact, if I were a betting man, I would be willing to bet that you haven't had this thing in a car wash more than a couple times in the two years or so you've had it."

"No way."

"Yes, way. Who do you think is right Jim? Jim?"

There's no answer so I look over at Jim. His head is bent over toward the window and his eyes are closed.

"He's asleep, Joe."

"You probably bored him to death."

"Me? You're the one that got into that deep theological discussion about pride, and . . . there's the drive!"

We skid past the drive a little as Joe hits the brakes and Jim flies forward, almost hitting his head on the dashboard.

Jim rubs his eyes. "It's a good thing I was wearing my seat belt. Are we there?"

Joe puts the car in reverse and backs up a few feet. "Yeah, Jim, we're there."

We pull into a driveway that resembles something more like a wagon trail. There are two parallel tracks worn several inches deep with a wide mound of short weeds running down the center between them. On each side of the drive is a wire fence with one strand of barbed wire stretching all along the top.

As we come around a right hand bend in the drive, the headlights hit the white siding of a large, two story, wood-framed house. All across the front is a large wooden porch.

The side door porch light is already on and as we stop near the steps, the screen door swings open with a loud squeak as it stretches out the old spring closer.

Jim gets out and I follow right behind him. No sooner does Joe get out and close his door that we hear the welcoming voice of Millie Morgan. "Hello, boys. Now you boys hurry and wash up, breakfast is waiting."

Millie is a short woman, her head barely making it to my shoulders, with gray hair and a pleasant smile.

Joe and Jim go in through the door first.

"The wash room is right down the hallway there on the left."

Millie turns to me and gives me a big hug and pulls me down to kiss my cheek.

"And how is my Bobby?"

"I'm fine, Millie. Just tired."

"Just tired, Bobby? You're not just a tad bit hungry also?" She gives me a little wink and smiles.

"I'm always hungry when I come to visit you, Millie."

Millie laughs and pushes me a little with her hand on my back. "Now you git along now, Bobby, and wash up, or there may not be anything left if'n your friends git to it first."

Whenever you enter Millie's kitchen the first thing you notice is the smell of something cooking, and this morning is no exception. The first aroma is that of pancakes. As I walk through the kitchen I detect the slight smell of blueberry muffins. The sound of bacon and frying eggs pervades the air.

I reach the bathroom door and Joe and Jim are engaged in a contest where they're pushing each other to see who can get to the breakfast table first. The two of them are grunting and laughing as they each are trying to push the other back into the bathroom while at the same time get out into the hallway.

I smile. "Would you guys grow up." Then I just put my hands out in front of me about chest high and blast my way between them, pushing them to either side.

Jim, being a little quicker, beats Joe out the door.

"Well, Joe, I guess as the saying goes, 'To the quicker go the spoils.'"

"Yeah, right," Joe says disgustedly as he leaves.

I go over to the sink and turn on the water to wash my hands. I don't know what it is about the sound of running water, but almost every time it seems to send a message to my bladder that it's time to unload.

So I quickly dry my hands and move into position at the bowl. If I know Millie, I don't have to worry about whether I get anything to eat. In fact, in just a few more seconds, Joe's going to be yelling at me to hurry up. With that thought in mind I purposely begin to take a little extra time washing my hands again.

"What are you doing in there? You only have to wash your hands, not take a bath!"

"I'll be there in a minute, Joe!"

I practically let my hands air dry before I finish wiping them on a hand towel. Then I slowly saunter back into the kitchen.

"There you are," Joe says. "We thought we were going to have to call the paramedics to come get you out."

"What's your hurry, Joe, you've never waited for me to start eating before. You either, Jim. Are you guys sick?"

Just then Millie comes back inside with a basket of fresh eggs. "Oh good, there you are, Bobby. All you boys are together now. Bobby, would you ask the blessing on the food?"

"Sure." I say it with confidence, but inside I feel a little uncomfortable. Praying out loud in a group has always given me a kind of stage fright and even with such a small group of close friends, this instance is no exception. I clear my throat a little and start with my usual beginning. It helps me get started and usually once I can get going I can start to feel a bit more at ease and the words then seem to flow on their own.

"Dear Lord, we thank you for this day that you've given us and for all the blessings we've received." Well that takes care of the introduction, and that's all it takes to get me on a roll. "We thank you for keeping us safe. We ask that you be with each of our families through these trying times, that you comfort them and keep them safe. We also ask that you be with the families of those who have been needlessly killed recently, and that you comfort them also. We ask now that you give us the wisdom and the abilities needed to carry out whatever your will is for us. Thank you for the bountiful food you have provided for us. We ask that you bless it to the nourishment of our bodies and our bodies to your service. In Jesus' name we ask it, amen."

"Whew, Bob," Joe says wiping his brow of mock sweat. "I

thought we were going to have to scrape mold off our food before you got done with your sermon. Whatever happened to 'God is great, God is good, let us thank him for our food?'"

Millie brings over a platter heaped high with pancakes. "Never you mind, Joseph. It was a very nice prayer, Bobby."

"Thank you, Millie." I stick my tongue out at Joe and he sticks his out at me.

Millie puts the platter down in the middle of the small white wooden kitchen table and the three of us attack the pile of pancakes with forks and fingers. Before we even get our syrup on them, Millie comes around to each of us with a large frying pan of scrambled eggs, scooping it out and creating a large pile on our plates. As we're taking our first bites of the pancakes, we suddenly find five or six strips of bacon on our plates nestled in between the eggs and pancakes.

"How many blueberry muffins would each of you boys like?" Millie stands with her hands on her hips. I know that asking for anything less than two would hurt her feelings so I lead the way.

"Three for me, Millie. You too, Joe?"

Joe looks up from his plate of food which he is trying his best to devour. When he sees me, I'm nodding my head up and down, coaching him.

"Uh, yeah. Three will be fine."

Millie turns and looks down at Jim who, as usual, has a mouth full of food.

"How many shall I get you, James?"

Jim swallows the lump of food in his mouth.

"Five please, Mrs. Morgan."

"Please, call me Millie, and your blueberry muffins are coming right up."

I lean over toward Jim. "You just made her day," I whisper.

Just as we're finishing up our breakfast, Millie begins clearing off the dirty dishes. "I understand you boys have had a long night. Bobby, you know where the guest room is, why don't you show your friends where to get some sleep."

"Okay, guys, this way. Oh, and Millie, everything was delicious as usual."

"Yeah," Jim says putting his hand on his belly with a contented look on his face. "I couldn't eat another bite."

Joe has an exaggerated surprised look on his face. "I never

thought I'd ever hear that coming from Jim. In fact, I thought it was almost impossible. But I have to admit one thing, I don't think I've ever seen so much food in one little kitchen."

"This way, guys."

I open a narrow door, that could be mistaken for a closet, to reveal a narrow, blue carpeted stairway leading up into darkness.

"Shall we go see our new home for the next few days?" I flip on a light switch and the stairway becomes a lighted tunnel.

The guest room has two beds and is located over the back portion of the house. It's actually a finished attic, so the ceiling slants with the slope of the roof.

Joe looks around and sees there are only two single beds. "So . . . uh, who gets to sleep on the floor?"

"I figured we'd take turns." I pull three coins out of my pocket and hand Jim and Joe each one of the coins. "Okay, we'll flip for it. Odd man get's the floor."

We don't have to flip for that," Joe says. "We already know Jim's the odd one here."

I put my coin on the top of my thumb nail. "Ready? Now."

We all toss our coins into the air. Jim tosses his a little high and it hits the ceiling, bouncing away from him and onto the hardwood floor. Joe and I catch ours.

"What do you have, Joe?"

"Heads."

"I've got tails. What's yours, Jim?"

"I don't know, it rolled under the bed."

Jim's down on his knees on the floor with his head stuck under the bed and his butt up in the air.

"I got it."

A nickel comes sliding out from under the bed like a hockey puck and Joe tries to step on it to keep it from going down the stairs. He misses.

Joe takes off down the stairway after it. "Whatever it comes up, it counts."

I take off right behind him.

"Don't touch it, Joe, just leave it right where it lands." With all three of us coming down the stairs we sound like a small stampede.

The coin finally settles at the bottom of the stairway, in the middle of the hallway. Joe has his eye on the coin as he comes down the stairs, but just as he gets almost close enough to see whether it's heads or tails, somebody picks it up and holds it out to Joe.

"Hey!" Joe says rather annoyed at the interference.

I come up beside Joe and he's just standing there, mouth open, and speechless. Standing in front of him is a petite Oriental girl with long, black shiny hair. Her tan is still dark after a long summer of working outside in the garden. Her unblemished face is graced with a gentleness that can only be described as angelic. She is beautiful by anyone's standards.

I take the coin from her. "Thank you, Mi-Ling."

"You are welcome, Bob."

Her voice is sweet and whispery and the words come out very precise with a strong Japanese accent.

"Let me introduce you to my friends. This is Joe next to me here, and that's Jim behind us there."

Joe manages to lift his hand weakly up to shoulder height and lets it drop back limply to his side.

"Hi, happy to see you."

"Guys, this is Mi-Ling."

Jim smiles and gives a nod of his head.

Mi-Ling starts toward the kitchen.

"Oh, Mi-Ling, did you happen to notice how the coin was facing when you picked it up?"

"I see the building. You call it . . . tails?"

"Yes, we call it tails. Thank you, Mi-Ling."

"You are welcome."

"Tails. You get the floor Joe."

"Okay," Joe says as if in a trance. He watches Mi-Ling go into the kitchen without moving a muscle.

"Hey, Jim, I think Joey's in love. Here, grab an arm and help me get him back upstairs."

Joe snaps out of his daze as soon as we start to pull on his arms. "Don't touch me. I'm perfectly capable of walking on my own."

"Maybe so, but just a minute ago you seemed to have a little trouble talking."

"You're gonna have trouble talking with swollen lips."

Back upstairs Joe begins to quiz me about Mi-Ling.

"Who is that girl, Bob?"

"She's Mi-Ling. Don't you remember? I introduced you to her just a little while ago."

"You know what I mean. How come you didn't tell me about her?"

I pull the covers back on one of the beds.

"I didn't know you wanted me to fill you in on every new person we have come to church."

"She goes to your church?"

"You bet."

"For how long?"

"Oh, for about two hours Sunday mornings, two hours Sunday nights and one hour on Wednesday nights."

"Nooo. How long has she been coming to your church?"

I sit on the bed and begin to take my shoes off. Joe continues to stand over me.

"Since the beginning of summer."

"And you knew about her all this time?"

"Yep, and so did everyone else in the church. See, you should have come to church when I invited you."

"How old is she?"

"Twenty-four."

"Is she married?"

"That should have been your first question."

"Yeah, but is she married?"

"Nope."

"Boyfriend?"

"Nope."

Joe's face really lights up but it's quickly replaced by a serious, questioning look.

"What's wrong with her?"

"Nothing, she's only been in the United States for a few months and her English is only just now getting good enough so that she can carry on a conversation, and then on top of all that she is extremely shy. Now let me get some sleep. I'm bushed."

I slide under the blankets and lay back on the clean-feeling sheets. I take a deep breath and let out an audible sigh.

Looking up at the ceiling I ask Jim, "How's your bed, Jim?" No answer. "Jim?"

"He's bit the dust already."

"And I'd like to too, so good night, Joe." I turn on my side with my back toward Joe, leaving him standing between the two beds.

"Wait a minute, I don't have anything to sleep on."

"You have the floor."

"It's a hardwood floor and I don't even have any blankets."

"Oh well, that's life."

We hear someone coming up the steps. I look toward the stairwell in time to see Millie's head rise above the railing. In her arms are a pile of blankets and a foam pad.

"Here comes your bed, Joe."

"Well," Millie says. "I see James has found his bed to be quite comfy. Here you go, Joseph. It looks as if these are yours."

She hands him the blankets and foam pad and turns to leave.

"You boys sleep well now. Lunch will be at noon."

I look at my watch before I take it off and put it on the lamp stand next to the bed.

"It's almost seven, Joe, so we should get about five hours of sleep."

"Five hours will be good."

Joe lays out the foam and his blankets on the floor and finds a pillow in the pile. He lies down and all is quiet and restful for the first time in a long time.

"Bob?"

"What, Joe?"

"Do you think that someone like Mi-Ling would go for someone like me?"

"Maybe, you're not so bad looking and your personality's pretty okay, too."

"Thanks, Bob."

"You're welcome, Joe."

Ahh, silence once again. I can hear the faint noise of dishes being done in the kitchen below, and I start to drift off to sleep.

"Bob?"

"What, Joe?" I say it a little exasperatedly.

"Would she like me better if I lost some weight?"

"Go to sleep, Joe."

Chapter 7

I'm awakened out of a blissful unconsciousness, otherwise known as sleep, by the sound of heavy footsteps coming up the stairs and across the hardwood floor. I pry my eyelids open and see dirty blue coveralls. I look up higher on the tall thin frame of the man standing next to the bed and look into the face of a man who has stood the test of time and hard work.

Surprisingly for his age, sixty-nine years in all, his hair retains most of its youthful black color and fullness, with only the slightest evidence of a higher forehead.

Then in a voice loud enough to wake the dead, which we are very close to being, he booms, "You boys gonna sleep the day away? Life's too short to be spending a beautiful fall day lying in bed. Besides, it's high noon and Millie's got the grub on the table. Best not keep the little woman waitin'."

I hear some groans from Jim and Joe as they begin to stir. I move my arm to throw off my blanket and let out a groan myself as every muscle in my arm aches.

"I oughta hire you boys out on Halloween spookin' houses."

Floyd turns, clomps across the room in his work boots and disappears down the stairs.

He must have come in the house without Millie seeing him because she never lets him through the door without first making him take those 'stinky' barn boots off.

I try to move again and I can feel every muscle in my body. I sit up on the side of the bed and give one long groan.

"A little sore, Bob?" Joe asks.

"You would be too if you were climbing around in attics, on roofs, and through trees and running around in the woods in the dark and stealing police cars all night."

"Not me. I'm a man. I could take it."

"Then take this." I grab my pillow and smack him on the side of the head with it. Before Joe can recover, I roll over to the other side of the bed. "Sore or not, I'm still quicker than you."

Joe starts to come after me but I hustle down the steps and into the bathroom, locking the door behind me.

Sitting at the table with Joe, Jim and Floyd, waiting for lunch to be served, I rub my hand along the bottom of my chin. The prickly stubble pokes at the palm of my hand.

"Joe, you're the expert on the Amish, are there any Amish in the U.P. or Canada?"

Joe has always admired the Amish lifestyle. The simple un-cluttered lives that they lead. That's one of the reasons he wants to be a farmer. Maybe not as simple as the Amish but still uncluttered by some of the needless trappings of society.

"There really aren't any in the U.P., but there are a few in Quebec and maybe some in the agricultural belt further west."

"What about Mennonites?"

"Oh there's some in the U.P. and quite a few in the area of Canada just east of Lake Huron and Detroit. There's quite a lot of farming that goes on there. But those are mostly the Old Order Mennonites. They're almost as conservative as the Amish."

"Do they wear the Amish type beards?"

"Not too many, no. Why?"

"I was just thinking maybe we should all grow beards to sort of help disguise ourselves, and if we end up in Canada we could sort of stick close to the Amish communities so we'd blend in a little better with the local people."

"I don't think that'll be a problem. A lot of Canadians have beards during the winter."

"Even the women?"

"I've seen some pretty hairy women."

"If they're hairy, how can they be pretty."

Floyd chuckles a little. "Beauty is in the eye of the beholder, my boy."

"Speaking of beauty, Floyd, I think Joe was a bit smitten by the sight of Mi-Ling this morning."

"No, I wasn't." Joe's face begins to turn a deep red.

"Yes, you were, Joe. When you saw her you just stood there like a vision of God had passed before your eyes."

"You're exaggerating."

"No I'm not, you were definitely smitten."

"Was not."

"Were too."

"Was not."

"Were too."

"Was not."

"Were too."

"Was not."

"Were too, and I've got a witness. Jim, what do you say?"

Jim swallows down a mouthful of food. "Smitten," he says and goes back to eating.

"See, told you so."

"So I think she's kinda cute. Is there a law against it?"

"Just 'kinda cute' Joe?"

"Well . . . maybe a lot of cute, but that's all."

"Joseph my boy," Floyd says with a grin, "she's a whole lot of cute in my book, so you don't have to be embarrassed about sayin' so."

There's a bump at the door and Millie, who has her hands in pie crust dough, asks for help. "Oh goodness, that's Mi-Ling with the corn. Could somebody get the door for her?"

In a flash Joe is out of his chair, across the floor and opening the door.

"Smitten," Floyd says shaking his head.

"Twitterpated," Jim says without looking up from his plate.

"Twitterpated?" Floyd looks puzzled.

"Yeah." Jim stops eating for a moment and looks at Floyd. "You know, on Bambi. That's what they called it when Flower, Thumper and Bambi fell in love."

"You still watch that Jim?" I laugh. "I haven't seen that movie since I was a kid."

"I got the video so my nephews would have something to do when they come to my apartment, Bob." Jim puts a strong emphasis on my name.

"Well, boys," Floyd slides his chair back from the table and quickly wipes his mouth with a napkin, then lets it drop on his plate. "Since the fields are still too wet to get out in them this afternoon, I've got a little project for us. So, if you're done with lunch, follow me."

We all get up from the table, Jim a little slower than me. Joe is still talking to Mi-Ling.

"Come on, Joe, Floyd wants us outside for something."

"What?"

"I don't know what, just come on."

Joe says good-bye to Mi-Ling and follows us out the door.

"Joe, we're gonna have to git this outta sight," Floyd says patting the fender of Joe's Cherokee. "And I've got just the spot. Follow me."

We continue on down the drive as it curves past the house and about a hundred yards until we enter in through the big open doors of the barn.

All along the right side of the barn, piled halfway up to the roof, is a huge stack of straw bales, and on the left side, again, all along the wall only stacked within feet of the roof, are bales of hay.

Floyd points to the hay. "This is where we hide her. You boys start making a path through the middle of the hay bales about ten feet wide and go back, oh . . . about twenty feet. You can stack the bales you pull out over there against the back wall."

Jim whispers to me, "That's gotta be about a hundred of 'em."

But Floyd still has excellent hearing.

"I figgered two-hundred-fifty, give or take."

I slap Jim on the back. "Sounds like an all day job, Jim."

"It's just good clean exercise," Joe says as he peels his jacket off. He tosses it to one side and grabs the first bale. "It's best to just get started guys. It's not gonna get done by just staring at it."

"We could try," Jim says grudgingly.

But he takes off his jacket anyway and I hand Jim my jacket.

"Since you're going that way."

Jim puts our jackets down on top of Joe's and the three of us begin the long, arduous task of moving a mountain, one bale at a time.

"Hey, Joe."

"Hey, what?"

"What would you call a Catholic clergyman if you found him sitting at the top of all this hay?"

"I don't know, what?"

"A high priest of bale."

Jim laughs.

"Don't encourage him, Jim."

"Hey, Joe. What do you call the priest's dog?"

"What?"

"Bale wolf."

With that Joe throws a bale of hay down at me. It bounces off a couple of bales and comes apart, sending loose pieces of hay in all directions.

I stick out my tongue. "Missed me."

Joe starts to come down after me but he suddenly stops, picks up a bale of hay and in a real macho type manner, carries it down. I look to see what caused this sudden change of behavior and find my suspicions to be correct.

"Hi, Mi-Ling."

"Hi, guys. Hi, Joe." She walks over to Joe with a tray of four glasses. "Do you want lemonade? I make it myself."

"Yes, please. I'm really thirsty from all this hard work."

Jim and I look at each other with surprised expressions on our faces. I mouth the word *please?*.

Jim just shrugs, and takes his glass of lemonade from the tray.

From then on, about every hour on the hour, Mi-Ling shows up with a fresh supply of lemonade, and each time she and Joe spend a few more minutes talking. But even with Joe's twenty minute breaks we're making good progress and it takes us until six that afternoon to get it done.

Joe tosses the last bale on the new pile. "There, that's a big enough hole, isn't it?"

"Let me check."

I pace off both the width and the length of the opening we've dug into the side of the stack of bales. "Eleven by twenty-two, give or take a foot."

Joe sits down on a bale of hay and wipes his forehead with his sleeve.

"Sounds good to me."

"Me, too," Jim says leaning against one of the large wood barn supports.

"Me, too."

I turn to see Floyd standing in the doorway and behind him, coming up the drive, is Mi-Ling carrying her load of glasses.

"Well," I say, "it's a good thing we're done, 'cause Joe's gonna be worthless for a good half hour now."

"Why is that?" Floyd asks.

I just smile. "You'll see."

"Hi, I bring cold water. Sorry, lemonade is gone."

"That's okay, Mi-Ling. I love ice water."

I walk over to Floyd and nudge him with my elbow. "That's not the only thing he loves," I say quietly.

"I see."

Floyd walks over to the opening in the hay bales. "Okay, Joe, get your truck and park it right smack dab in the middle of this opening you boys have made. Then we can all get some supper."

All during supper Joe is preoccupied with Mi-Ling and vice-versa. Jim on the other hand is preoccupied with the fried chicken and anything else on the table that's digestible. So I talk to Floyd about the more pressing issues that are confronting us.

"Did you watch the Michigan State game Saturday? I didn't get a chance to 'cause I promised to help my neighbor."

"Nope, I don't watch TV no more, but I did listen to it, an' it was a doozie of a game, Bob. State won it with a touchdown with just thirty seconds left on the clock."

"What was the final score?"

"Twenty-eight to twenty-six. The lead went back and forth the whole game."

Millie interrupts our conversation. "Bobby." Her voice is quiet and serious. "I got a phone call from Brother Martin this afternoon."

"Did he have some good news?"

"He just wanted you boys to work on a list of things that you need."

"Well I can think of something right now, clothes. I've been wearing these things since yesterday afternoon."

"Make a list and put down your sizes."

"They're not gonna buy all new stuff are they?"

"To tell you the truth," Floyd says leaning back into a slouch and rubbing his full belly, "I don't think there's too many people hankerin' to cross that big yellow police ribbon they got stretched clear around your house just to get your clothes."

"But we can't afford new stuff."

"You don't have to, Bobby," Millie says wiping her hands on

her apron. "It's all being taken care of." Millie smiles and goes to get her dinner off the counter.

"What do you mean, 'it's all being taken care of?'"

Millie returns with her plate and sits down next to Floyd. "Well, the way the phone's been ringing off the hook today, I would say that you boys should not concern yourselves with what you'll wear or eat or even where you'll be able to stay. The church and our sister churches are behind you all the way. Isn't that right, Floyd?"

"You betcha. 'Ask and ye shall receive.'"

"Come on, Millie, how much support do we really have?"

"Well there is our church, a church in Flint and a church in Kalamazoo. Four or five other Michigan churches are waiting for Brother Martin to offer them proof of your calling."

"You know, I still can't get used to that idea. I've never really thought of myself as called to do anything . . . except maybe to teach. I mean, I'm just plain old Bob, nobody special. I'm not a Moses or anything like that and neither is Joe or Jim."

"It's funny you should mention Moses." Floyd sits up and puts his elbows on the table with his forearms laying across in front of him on the table top. "You see, he kinda said the same thing about not being anybody special and all and look what God helped him do."

"Yeah I know, but this is different, this is me, not Moses."

The phone rings and Floyd gets up to get it. "You just go ahead and finish your supper, Millie, I'll get it."

Floyd walks over to the old rotary dial wall phone and picks up the receiver on the third ring. "Hello."

I try to listen in over Joe and Mi-Ling's conversation.

"Howdy Brother Martin, what's new? . . . Uh huh . . . Uh huh . . . Oh . . . Oh, I see . . ." With each response Floyd becomes more serious. "No that'll be okay . . . When do you think . . . Any more news from the other churches? . . . Uh huh . . . Oh really? Good . . . okay, I'll tell 'em . . . okay . . . Uh huh . . . I guess I'll just have to dig the old black and white out of the basement. It's a good thing I didn't toss the blamed thing out . . . okay, I'll wait for your call. God bless your efforts, Brother Martin. Bye now."

Floyd hangs up the phone and rubs his chin for a moment. "Okay, boys, listen up. As you might have already figgered, that was Brother Martin. First off, we are not to call him, he will call us."

"That's not like him, Floyd," Millie says sounding a little concerned. "He's always made it known that anybody can call him anytime, day or night. What's wrong, Floyd? What would cause him to act that way?"

"If'n you'd stop yer jabberin' for a minute woman, I'll tell you." Floyd says it with a smile on his face, but Millie also knows he means it.

"This afternoon Brother Martin had a visit from some police detectives who asked a lot of questions about Bob's personal life, like who his friends are, what places he likes to go, and what things he likes to do. They also searched the church."

"Did they find anything?" Joe asks.

I notice that Mi-Ling has her hand on Joe's shoulder. I guess she's beginning to really like Joe.

"No, but Brother Martin did after they left. After what you boys had told him about those detectives he felt there was something untrustworthy about them, so after they left, he searched his office and sure enough, he found one of them little microphone jobs stuck under his desk."

"What'd he do with it?" I ask.

"Nothing, he just left it. He didn't want them to think he's on to their shenanigans. He's gonna be keeping in touch with us by calling from a different church member's home each time."

Joe reaches up and puts his hand on Mi-Ling's hand. "Did he say anything about the map?"

"No, but he did say something about having some information just about ready for you. But if you boys need maps, we got us a whole slew of 'em right here we can let you use."

"That's okay, Floyd," I say. "We appreciate the offer but this is a special kind of a map. It's not found in stores. Along the sides of roads maybe, but not stores."

"Oh, so that's that thing that everybody's after eh? So the blamed thing's a map. Who'd a guessed. When I saw it up there on the night table this morning it looked like just a fancy paperweight."

"Yeah, it's hard to believe such a little thing could cause so much trouble. So what else did Brother Martin have to say?"

"Let's see . . ." Floyd rubs his chin again. "I know there was something else."

Millie gets up from the table. "Well, while you're thinking

about what it is, we can all have a piece of pie. Mi-Ling, can you help me please?"

"Yes, Ma'am." She says it in a very polite and cheerful voice.

Joe's face just beams with pride as he leans over to me and whispers so no one else can hear, "She's really something, isn't she, Bob?"

I shrug my shoulders to pick on him just a little. "I suppose, if you like that kind of girl."

"You mean because she's Oriental? I didn't know you were prejudiced."

"I'm not, and I didn't mean because she's Oriental."

"Then just what did you mean? Is there something wrong with her you haven't told me about yet?" Joe wrenches his head around. "Oh man, there is something wrong with her, isn't there. Otherwise you would have been dating her. How could I have been so dumb."

"Settle down, Joe. When I said, 'if you like that kind of girl,' I meant a girl who's pretty, intelligent, kind, thoughtful, hard working, sensitive, and single. That's all I meant by it."

"You mean there's nothing wrong with her?"

"Nope."

"You stink."

Joe wads up a napkin and throws it at me. I laugh as it hits me in the chest.

Millie brings a couple of small plates, with a large piece of pie on each, over to the table. "My gracious, boys, you would think there were a bunch of children in here the way you two are carryin' on. Now here, occupy yourselves with these."

She sets one plate in front of me and the other in front of Floyd, while Mi-Ling brings a plate each for Joe and Jim.

With my fork in hand, I dive into my piece of apple pie, but Floyd is just looking off into space still rubbing his chin.

Millie comes back to the table with her pie and sits down next to Floyd. "Come on Floyd, eat your pie. It'll come to you soon enough."

"Yeah, prob'ly." Floyd leans forward shaking his head and picks up his fork. "I must be getting old, boys. Was a time I had a mind like a sponge. I could remember everything."

Uh oh, he's gonna go into his l-o-o-o-n-g story about how when he was a kid he was able to remember the names of all the cows and other animals on the farm. I need to change the subject quick, or we'll be here for twenty minutes listening to all the details.

"Why I remember when I was, oh, about four years old or so . . .

"Uh, Floyd, before you get started with your story, do you have some paper and something to write with? We've gotta make out our list of things we need."

"Oh, sure thing. I've got some by the phone. I'll be right back." Floyd gets up, goes to a drawer under the counter by the phone and pulls out several pens and pencils and a pad of paper. When he comes back over he puts everything in a pile in the middle of the table and sits back down. "Ah, now, where was I?"

"Does anybody know what the weather's supposed to be like tomorrow? I haven't heard any weather or news since yesterday."

Jim scrapes the last crumb of pie crust off his plate and looks up making strange faces as he cleans his teeth with his tongue. "You heard it this morning on the way here."

Joe laughs. "How would you know. You were sawing logs so loud on the way here we could hardly hear the radio."

"I don't snore, and besides, the news came on before I fell asleep."

Floyd practically jumps out of his seat. "That's it! The news! Brother Martin wanted us to keep up on the latest news. Something about new developments. Anyway, I was a gonna bring up the old black and white set from out of the basement." Floyd stabs the last bite of his pie with his fork and shoves it in his mouth with a look of achievement on his face. "Well, best go find that TV set."

Floyd walks out of the kitchen into the hallway and disappears through a doorway next to the one that leads upstairs.

"There can't be too many new developments," Joe says pushing his empty plate away from him. "After all, we've been here all day staying out of trouble."

"Yeah, I haven't stolen a police car in over twelve hours."

There's silence in the room as the thought of what may have happened to Terri comes to mind.

"Do you really think it was Terri that got killed?" Joe asks looking at me.

"It wouldn't surprise me. I actually can't imagine it being anyone else."

We hear the noise of what sounds like a pile of junk falling come from the basement.

Millie rushes to the basement door and calls down the steps, "Are you all right, Floyd?"

"Yeah, I'm fine Millie. I just had to move some old shutters out of the way to get to the TV set. One of these days I'm just gonna have to clean this place up."

Millie turns and comes back into the kitchen with a smile on her face. "He's been promising to do that for the last twenty years."

"Here you go guys." I shove one pencil each toward Jim and Joe. "Let's get started with our wish lists." I tear a piece of paper off the pad for each of us.

We spend the next fifteen minutes or so with our lists while Floyd spends his time cleaning the dust and grime off the television and fidgeting with the controls. Finally, he gets it to the point where he's satisfied with the picture. Floyd steps back with his hands on his hips. "There," he says. "The blamed thing still works after all these years in the cellar." Floyd steps to one side to let everyone see his handiwork.

Joe points at the television set. "Where's the color?"

"There ain't any on this. It's a black and white set."

"Wow, how old is it? I didn't think there were anymore of those around."

"When did we get this, Millie?"

"August twenty-fourth, nineteen-sixty-seven. I remember because it was given to us by Gordon two days before he left for Vietnam. I'm surprised at you, Floyd." Millie sounds upset at him now. "I would have thought you would have remembered that."

Floyd defends himself. "I do remember. I just don't remember dates. I remember everything about that day, even what Gordy was wearing. He had on his blue bell-bottom jeans and his blue and white paisley shirt, and those stupid looking shoes with the thick soles."

"What's Gordon doing now?" Joe asks.

While Joe's asking his question I'm shaking my head vigorously, hoping to make him stop.

Floyd and Millie look at each other to see who would answer the question.

"Joe," I whisper. "He was killed in action."

I must have whispered too loudly, though.

"It's okay, Bob," Floyd says in a calm, quiet voice. "Millie 'n' me know that one day we'll see Gordy again and that he's in heaven, better off than we are here."

"That's right, boys, so don't you fret any about Floyd and I. We will join Gordon soon enough and what a family reunion that will be."

"Amen to that." Floyd smiles and starts flipping through some stations on the TV set. Floyd stops at a local station. "There, now we just wait for the news."

"Floyd," I say, "this isn't a radio. The news won't be on again until eleven."

"At night?"

"Yes, Floyd, three hours from now."

Floyd looks at the clock on the wall. "It's almost eight o'clock Millie. I didn't realize it was gettin' so late. It's best we be gettin' ready for bed. Gotta be up with the chickens you know."

Joe laughs a little. "You really go to bed this early?"

"Sure do. Makes for a short night when you've got chores to do at five-thirty."

Millie interrupts pointing with her finger at the television. "Floyd, turn it up! There's something on the set!"

We all look at the TV set. On the screen is an anchorman with the station logo behind him. Floyd turns it up.

"This is Newsbreak. Brought to you by your greater Lansing Chevy dealers."

"I thought you boys said the news wasn't on 'till eleven."

"It isn't, Floyd," I say trying to hurriedly explain before I miss anything on the TV. "This is just a news commercial. It only lasts about half a minute."

"Oh." Floyd acknowledges his understanding by slowly nodding his head and looking back at the television.

"Good evening. I'm Michael Harrison, and this is Newsbreak. Police are still looking for the three men suspected in the latest rash of killings that are believed to be the worst in Lansing's history.

The trio's latest victim was an eight-year-old girl who was run down as she walked down the sidewalk on her way home from school. Victoria Ann Newberry was pronounced dead at the scene. Witnesses say the red sports car with three men in it seemed to aim right for her and then sped off. This makes the seventh victim in this killing spree.

We will have more details on this and other stories of interest at eleven. This has been Newsbreak."

The television goes to a Chevy commercial. Everyone in the room is completely still. Some are still staring at the television but not seeing what's on the screen. Others just look at each other in disbelief.

I finally break the silence as the torrent of emotions within me begins to swell. All the frustrations, and all the injustice, and all the cruelty. "I can't believe it. They used my car to kill a little girl."

Everyone else is still quiet.

"That does it!" I pound my fist against the table. "I'm taking that stupid cube and I'm gonna give it to the police and I'll take my chances with the justice system. No more people are gonna die because of it!"

I start to get up out of my chair but I feel a firm hand on my shoulder and it pushes me back down into my seat. Surprised, I turn to see Floyd standing over me.

"You're not gonna do no such thing."

"And why not? Why should I sit here and let that guy kill eight-year-old girls?"

"Because if you give him that thing up there, a lot more than seven people will die."

"How?"

"I can't say."

"Why not?"

"Well . . . 'cause."

"'Cause why?"

"Just 'cause I can't, that's all."

"But why can't you?"

Floyd looks to Millie for help and as usual she comes through for him.

"Because Brother Martin told us not to."

"Did he tell you why you can't tell us?"

"Yes."

"Well then why can't you tell us why you can't tell us?"

"He just simply felt there were some things you boys shouldn't know right away, at least not until he gets everything straight in his own mind. But I think it's all right to tell you this much, he said it is very important that the cube does not fall into the hands of anyone who cannot be completely trusted. It could mean the end of almost all that we hold dear."

Joe's been exceptionally quiet up to this point I guess because I was asking the same questions he was wanting to ask, but now he needed to ask one. "Does that thing have some sort of special powers or something?"

The question comes out more as excitement than just inquisitiveness.

"I'm afraid, Joseph, that that is the question we can't answer at this time and I don't know if we ever will."

"I don't think it has any special powers, Joe." I say. "Remember Brother Martin said it was a map, so if anything, the place we have to find might have some sort of special powers."

Suddenly Jim sits up in his chair. "There's something on TV again."

Everyone turns around to look. On the screen are the words "Special Report."

"Quick, turn it up, Floyd." I point to the television. Floyd steps over and turns a knob and the volume increases.

". . . to bring you this special news report. At seven forty-seven p.m. eastern standard time, Pope Paul John died of respiratory failure due to pneumonia, which he has been battling for almost two months. He was fifty-six. His career was short, lasting only fourteen months, many of which were spent in and out of the hospital. There were high hopes for the Pontiff when he was first elected. He was one of the youngest Popes ever elected and full of energy and drive. Shortly after assuming his position he vowed to correct some problems he said were 'festering' in the church and holding the church back spiritually, but before he could realize any part of that dream, he became ill. It would be an illness from which he would never fully recover.

"In a moment we will be going live to Lansing, Michigan, where our reporter will be talking to Cardinal Nain Olyba Blived who will be enroute to the Vatican to vote for the next Pope, and is in fact himself considered to be a top contender to succeed the late Pope Paul John. If he should become Pope, he would be the first from the western hemisphere."

Floyd reaches over with a disgusted look on his face and flips the television off.

"Hey." Joe says. "Why'd you do that?"

"Oh we don't need to watch that, it don't have nothin' to do with you boys. Besides, I don't trust that Cardinal Blived much."

"Why not?" I ask.

"I saw him at the county fair one time." There's a short pause, as if he's not sure he wants to continue, but he does. "The man has shifty eyes."

"Really?" Joe says. "I wanna see. Turn the TV back on so I can see his shifty eyes."

"Well okay, but you'll see that he really does."

Floyd turns the TV back on. This time the picture brightens up a little faster since the tubes are still warm. There's a tall man with rugged features talking. He pulls the collar up on his trench coat to protect himself from the cool fall breeze and I can see the white rectangle on his neck to signify that he is indeed a Catholic clergyman. His hair is dark and wind-blown, and although he has a smile on his face and his voice is deep yet soft, I find myself fascinated by his eyes. Myself I wouldn't call them shifty, but I would call them dark and cold.

"Yes," he says. "The passing of this great man of God is a terrible tragedy indeed. We in the clergy had been counting on him to bring a new spiritual life into the church. It is unfortunate that his dreams, and ours, were cut so short.

"Perhaps now we can only pray that his successor will be able to pick up the torch left behind and carry it the full distance."

"Do you have any idea as to who might be that person to carry the torch?" The reporter prods.

"I am sorry, but in my position I cannot divulge my preferences, either before or after the vote."

"Then can you say . . ."

"I'm sorry, no more questions. I have a plane to catch." The Cardinal waves to the small crowd of reporters and he and his entourage move toward the gate. The camera follows their movement as the reporter continues to talk.

"We've been speaking to Cardinal Nain Olyba Blived about the death of Pope Paul John as he prepares to leave for the Vatican in Rome. One of the statements he made . . ."

Suddenly I don't hear what the reporter is saying any more as I recognize a face in the Cardinal's group, and my attention is riveted to the screen. He pushes his way up to the Cardinal and whispers in his ear. The Cardinal nods his head and whispers back to Detective Taylor. The detective puts his hand on Cardinal Blived's shoulder and then leaves.

"Did you guys see him, too?"

"You saw the guy, Bob?" Jim asks.

"Yeah, he was talking to that Cardinal."

"Good, I was hoping I wasn't just seeing things."

"I thought he looked familiar," Joe adds. "That was that detective wasn't it? So what was he doing with the Cardinal?"

"Maybe he's protecting him from you, Jim and me."

"Or more likely," Joe adds, "he's gonna assassinate the Cardinal and then somehow blame us for it."

Everyone has lost interest in the television as a commercial comes on, so Floyd turns it off. Floyd turns and I see a stern look on his face.

"What is it, Floyd?"

"I think they're in cahoots with each other."

"What makes you say that?"

"Didn't you notice, Bob?"

"Notice what?"

"They both got shifty eyes."

Everyone starts laughing but Floyd looks a little incredulous. "What's so funny?"

"Well I for one don't think that's a very foolproof way of telling what a person is like," Joe says. "Besides, he may have been there looking for us in case we're trying to skip out by plane."

"Yeah, well I still think they're in cahoots."

I lean my hand on my chin. "You know, Joe," I say thoughtfully, "it's probably a good sign. If they're looking for us at the airport, it means they have absolutely no idea where we are."

"Well that certainly makes me feel better, knowing that even though we're wanted for a bunch of murders we didn't even commit, they can't find us just yet."

"It is all right, Joe," Mi-Ling says trying to settle Joe down a little. "Everything will be . . ." She searches for the right word. "Okee-dokee?"

"That's right, Mi-Ling," Millie says.

"Okee-dokee." Mi-Ling smiles with a little added confidence.

The three of us spend the next few hours talking about any number of things while waiting for the eleven o'clock news. Meanwhile Mi-Ling has gone home and Floyd and Millie have gone to bed.

I turn the TV on but I'm careful not to turn the volume up too loud so as not to disturb Floyd and Millie.

"Well," I say as I turn and sit back down in my chair at the table. "I wonder what new and hideous crimes we've committed in the last couple hours."

Joe turns his chair around backwards crossing his arms on the back of the chair and laying his chin on his arms.

"Probably something like jaywalking or spitting on the sidewalk."

"This is Live Action News," the announcer says. "With Leo Stephens and Joan Frazee bringing the news. Phil Parrish with sports, and meteorologist Michael Pryor.

"Hi, I'm Leo Stephens. Heading tonight's news stories is the death of Pope Paul John. At seven forty-seven p.m. eastern standard time, Pope Paul John died of respiratory failure due to pneumonia, which he has been battling for almost two months. He was fifty-six. His career was short, lasting only . . ."

"This is a rerun," Joe says. "I wanna hear some new stuff about us."

"Maybe they'll run that interview with the Cardinal again," I say. "Can either of you guys read lips?"

They both shake their heads.

"Me neither. Too bad we don't have closed captioned."

"Why don't we just write the station for a transcript of everything that anybody said at the airport all day?"

Joe's being sarcastic so I play dumb.

"I don't think they'd be able to do that, Joe. Besides, they would be able to find us by looking at the return address. But it was a nice try at a good idea."

"Shut up."

"But it . . ."

"Just shut up."

"Okay, now shh. I think we might be on next."

"I'm Joan Frazee. In other news, police are still searching for the three suspects believed to be responsible for the deaths of as many as seven area residents. The latest victim of the murder spree is eight-year-old Victoria Newberry, who was run down while on her way home from school. Police recovered the car suspected in the hit and run two hours later, partially submerged in the Grand River in a remote area south of Lansing. Police also have recovered from the car a twenty-two caliber revolver believed to have been used in the murders of thirty-three-year-old Ingham County sheriffs deputy Terri Sigetty and a family of three in Meridian Township. Both car and weapon are being dusted for fingerprints and the gun will have ballistics testing done to determine if it is indeed responsible for the murders of four people.

"We caught up to the detective in charge of the investigation at Capitol City Airport. We have this report from Michael Harrison."

The news goes to a taped interview from several hours earlier. The reporter and Detective Taylor are standing on the sidewalk just outside the front doors of the terminal building.

"I'm here with Detective Mitchell Taylor at Capitol City Airport. Officer Taylor, can you tell us what is being done to capture these men and why you have been so unsuccessful up to this point?"

"To answer your last question first, we believe that they are being helped by a person or persons unknown. We would like to warn whoever is harboring these fugitives that there are severe penalties involved in helping fugitives. As to your first question, the Governor has given me the authority to set up a twenty man task force using officers of my choosing from any of the law enforcement agencies within the state. That includes any city, county or state police officers I deem qualified for this special task. Also, if they should leave the state, we have been promised the cooperation of the F.B.I."

"How soon then do you expect an apprehension?"

"That's hard to say exactly, but we can't see them being able to hide from us for more than a couple of days. If somebody is hiding them we will still find them. It's only a matter of time and time is what's on our side."

"Thank you, Detective Taylor. This is Michael Harrison coming to you from Capitol City Airport."

"That was a taped interview with the detective in charge of the investigation of the murders of seven area residents. Once again, the police are asking that if you see or know where any of these fugitives are . . ."

All three of our pictures are on the screen and I hear Joe give a low groan.

". . . you are asked not to approach them, but to call your local law enforcement agency at once. These men are armed and considered extremely dangerous. A five-thousand dollar reward is being offered for information leading to the arrest of these men. Leo?"

"Thank you, Joan. In Dewitt township a fire . . ."

I turn the television off and turn to find them both looking at me. I'm still at a total loss for words as all the recent information is swirling around in my head, so I just calmly shrug my shoulders, pull a cup out of the dish drainer by the sink and start filling it with water.

"Well?" Joe asks.

"Well what?"

"Aren't you gonna say anything? It is your fault we're in this mess you know."

"What do you mean 'my fault'?"

"If you hadn't picked up that stupid cube, none of us would be in this mess."

"Well how was I supposed to know all this was gonna happen? I'm not a psychic, you know. Besides, who was it that kept saying, 'What an adventure. What an adventure. What an adventure'?" I say it in a mocking sort of tone.

"You still should have ditched that thing at the first sign of trouble."

"As I recall, Joe, we discussed that and we both agreed to wait."

I can feel myself beginning to lose my cool, so before I do, I know I need to leave the room. Before I'm able to leave though, Joe gets to say one more thing.

"All the same, Bob, if you cared anything at all for your friends, you never would have gotten us involved."

"Forget it, Joe, just forget it," I say as I leave the room and go upstairs to my bed.

I lay back on my bed with my hands behind my head and stare at the ceiling. Maybe I was wrong. Maybe I shouldn't have gotten anybody else involved. I wonder if there was any way at all I could have seen this coming and gotten out of it.

I run the events of the last few days over in my mind. Everything happened so fast, and Jim and I did try to get it to the police, and that didn't work. Then again, if we truly are chosen for some sort of mission for God, then He's gonna make it impossible for us to back out on it. Joe's wrong. I did what I could with what I knew at the time.

I feel a little better having come to that conclusion, but there's no use me trying to tell Joe he's wrong. Especially if he's already in a foul mood.

Just then I hear footsteps coming slowly up the stairs. I turn my head to look and it's Joe. He's looking a little more subdued.

"Hi Bob, um . . . I'm sorry. I know you did your best trying to get the cube to the police and you had no way of knowing the police were corrupt. So I'm sorry I blew up at you. I guess I'm still just a little bit tired and a lot angry at the world."

"That's okay, Joe. I think we're all physically and mentally worn out by all this. I'm actually kind of surprised we haven't really tried to kill each other before this."

"So what do we do now?"

"I guess we wait for Brother Martin."

The next morning we're up before dawn and at work putting bales of hay back in front of Joe's Jeep Cherokee. We make a wall four bales thick and about seven feet high across the opening.

"Well, it looks like you all are ready to put the top on it."

We turn around to see Floyd standing just inside the door.

"We were just talking about how we were going to do that," Joe says. "We couldn't figure out how to make the bales stick together in midair. Jim said we should just pile it on top."

"Oh heavens, no. The weight would crush the top of your truck, Joe."

"See," Joe says punching Jim in the arm. "It's a good thing for you Bob and me talked you out of that idea."

"Follow me, boys."

"I remember that movie," I say.

"Shut up, Bob," Joe says pushing me in the direction Floyd is heading. "Uh, what is it exactly we're gonna do?"

"Well boys, as I recollect, I've got me some old two-by-tens and a coupl'a barn beams in the old tool shed. We'll just lay them there little buggers across the bales and then finish it off with the pile on top. It'll be as if nothing were there."

The two-by-tens weren't too heavy, but for Floyd to call the barn beams 'little buggers' was a gross understatement. Back in the barn all four of us are struggling to lift one of those 'little buggers' over our heads so we can set it on top of the bales.

A sliver jabs me in the shoulder as I rest it there to get a better grip.

"Ouch!"

I twist the beam which causes a chain reaction as first Joe loses his grip then Floyd lets it go and it becomes too heavy for Jim. The beam hits the floor with a thud as we all jump back away from it in case it rolls toward our feet. I hear giggling and turn to see Millie and Mi-Ling.

"What's so dang funny, woman?" Floyd says.

"You all remind me of the Three Stooges."

Joe points at me. "It was Bob's fault, he twisted the beam."

"I couldn't help it. I got stabbed in the shoulder by a sliver. I might even be bleeding." I pull my shirt collar away from my shoulder. "But do you care? Noo, all you care about is who's to blame. I could be lying here bleeding to death and you'd be standing there pointing your finger at me saying, 'He did it, he did it, it was his fault.'"

"Like I said," Millie says, "just like the Three Stooges."

"What is, Three Stooges?"

Millie laughs. "You're looking at them."

"I not understand." Mi-Ling looks confused. "I see four and you say three."

"Never mind, I'll explain it to you in the house. Now, would you boys like something to drink?"

For the first time I notice Millie and Mi-Ling have a cup in each hand.

"I do." I hurry over to Millie and take a cup from her. I figure I'll be nice and let Joe get his cup from Mi-Ling.

It only takes us one try each to get the beams in place and another three hours to stack up the hay on top. We all step back and wipe the sweat from our brows.

Joe puts his hands on his hips and looks in my direction. "So now what do we do?"

"What are you looking at me for? I don't have the slightest idea."

"I do."

The voice comes from behind us and Joe jerks around startled. Jim and I turn around and it's Floyd again.

"Hi, Floyd," I say. "We're finished."

Joe isn't as calm. "Why are you always sneaking up behind us all the time?"

Floyd laughs, "You city boys are all alike, high-strung."

"That's you all right, Joe," I say. "High-strung."

"I'm not either high-strung."

"You are too."

"Am not."

"Are too."

"Am not."

"Are too."

"Not."

"Are."

"Not."

Each time we go faster and now we're both saying it at the same time until we both sound like Alvin and the Chipmunks.

Floyd's just chuckling. "Millie was right, you boys act just like the Three Stooges."

"Anyway, Floyd," I say, "is there anything else we need to do?"

"Nope. I just need to add one final little touch to our project."

Floyd pulls out a small plastic container and begins to sprinkle a liquid onto the bales of hay.

"What's that?" Joe asks.

"You'll find out right shortly my boy."

Floyd's right. Within seconds the three of us are making tracks out of the barn holding our noses as the pungent odor of skunk attacks our nostrils.

"I guess that answers your question," Jim says grinning.

A few seconds later Floyd walks out of the barn. "There, that oughta keep people from nosing around in there." Floyd holds up the empty container. "Bought this for huntin'. Never got around to usin' it, though. I never remembered it 'till I got clear out in the woods, and there ain't no way I'm a gonna come traipsin' clear back to the house just so's I can smell bad."

We stand around for a couple minutes just "shootin' the breeze" as Floyd would say, when Millie yells from the back door of the house, "Bobby! Telephone! It's Brother Martin!"

I take off on a dead run and leap onto the back porch without hitting a single step. Millie steps to one side holding the door open for me. I only slow down enough to navigate around the kitchen table.

"Hello?" I say breathlessly.

"Hello, Bob, this is Brother Martin. I just called to let you know that Brother Steve and I are bringing your things out to you this afternoon. Now what I want you boys to do is to find a place as far away from the house as you can and still be able to keep an eye on it. Don't worry, it's only a precautionary step just in the event that we happen to be followed. When you see us drive in, wait one hour before coming back to the house. Can you remember all that, Bob?"

"Yeah sure, but . . ."

"Good, see you in about three hours, or should I say you'll see me."

"But . . ."

I wanted to ask him what's been going on in the outside world but he's already hung up, leaving me holding a phone listening to a dial tone.

I hear footsteps clomping up the back steps and I look to see Joe, Jim and Floyd walk in the door. I begin to tell Joe what Brother Martin said before Joe has a chance to ask.

"Brother Martin and Brother Steve are bringing some stuff for us in about three hours. He wants us guys to hide for about an hour after they get here in case somebody follows them. We need a place where we can watch the house from a safe distance. Can you find us one, Floyd?"

"Yeah, I think I got just the spot. Come on I'll show you where it's at."

We all start to leave when Millie blocks the doorway, her hands on her hips. "Not until you boys have some lunch first. Now you four get yourselves cleaned up."

After lunch we follow Floyd out behind the house. We travel between the rows of brown sweet corn stalks in the garden until we come out on the other side. From there we take a wagon path that takes us up a gradual grade past the cow pasture. After walking for a couple minutes we stop at an electric fence where Floyd unhooks part of it from a post. A single wire with an insulated handle at the hook end.

"Come on in, boys."

We all go through the opening and Floyd hooks the wire back on the post. "Don't want old George gettin' out."

"Old George?" Joe asks.

"Oh don't worry about old George, he's just a feisty old bull I put out to pasture years ago. I didn't have the heart to get rid of him after all the years of service he put in for me. Matter of fact, most of my herd is his. Besides, I got him fenced up in the corner over yonder."

I look in the direction Floyd is pointing, which happens to be the same direction we are heading, and see the gray, weather aged wooden fence Floyd is talking about. In the center is a group of trees and a large pile of field stone in amongst those trees. Beyond the fenced corral is a large wooded area.

"Watch this," Floyd says with a smile as we approach the fence. "Hey, George! Come on out here! You got some visitors here that want to meet you!"

Just about the time we get to the fence I see something large emerge slowly from behind the rock pile and trees.

"There you are you old geezer. Get your tired old butt over here."

The old bull moves slowly and methodically toward us, not speeding up or slowing down, his head moving from side to side with each step, as if it takes nearly all his strength to move each leg under his massive body.

He sticks his head over the fence and snorts twice, each time jerking his head up and down. Jim stumbles backward a little.

"Don't worry, Jim," Floyd says. "He just wants what he knows I've got in my pocket here for him."

Floyd pulls his hand out of his coverall pocket and holds out a handful of dry cat food, palm open. Old George practically inhales it.

"He just loves this stuff," Floyd says, patting George on the forehead with his other hand.

"Can I touch him?" Joe asks. "I've never been this close to a bull before."

"Sure, Joe. Go ahead."

Joe slowly sticks his hand out. "I always thought bulls were supposed to be mean."

"Oh, they are—"

Joe jerks his hand back.

". . . when they're younger and when they're with a heifer."

"Oh," Joe says, and sticks his hand back out.

"Joe!" I yell

"What!" He jerks his hand back again.

"Oh nothing. I just wanted to see how good your reflexes are."

"How come George didn't move when Bob yelled?" Jim asks.

"Well, I guess it's 'cause he's a little hard of hearing," Floyd replies.

Joe's skeptical. "Then how come he came when you called?"

"Oh, I just do that out of habit. He prob'ly smelled us even before I called."

By now Joe already has his hand on George's head and is stroking his forehead.

"Okay, boys, I want all three of you to stand here and let old George get to know you real good for the next ten minutes or so." Floyd reaches into his pocket and begins handing out cat food to each of us. "After that, you should be able to go in without any trouble."

Jim's face turns white. "Go in where?"

"Why, in there, behind that there pile of rocks. You can see the entire house and yard from there without bein' seen yourselves. So if there's any trouble down there, you boys got yourselves a good quarter-mile head start. Good luck, boys."

Floyd walks back down the hill toward the house.

Joe pulls his hand back away from George again. "Just what did he mean by that comment?"

"I don't know, Joe," I say holding a handful of cat food out to George. "But I think it'd be a good idea to get real friendly with George, real fast."

Suddenly there's three hands, each piled high with cat food, stuck under old George's nose. George finishes off Jim's handful first.

Jim wipes his hand on his pants. "You guys think he knows me pretty good now?"

"There's one way to find out," I say. "So who wants to go in first? Not it."

"Not it." Joe says quickly. "Well, I guess you're it, Jim."

"Uh uh, no way. If I go in there, you guys are going with me."

George gets done with Joe's handful and Joe wipes his hand on his pants also.

"Okay, as soon as he gets done with Bob's cat food, we all go in at the same time, agreed?"

"Okay," I say.

Jim nods his head signifying his agreement.

I stroke George's forehead while he eats. As soon as he's done I wipe my hand on the back of Joe's jacket. Joe starts to turn around to get me.

"Wait, Joe. Don't make any quick moves. You might startle George here."

"Don't worry, Bob, I'll strangle you slowly." Joe wraps his hands around my neck and mockingly shakes me.

"Okay, okay, that's enough. We best get ourselves hidden. In fact, you big babies, I'll even go first."

I go about five feet down the fence and climb up and over it so I'm standing inside the fenced in area. Old George just watches me, turning only his head.

"Come on, George!" I say rather loudly.

I start at a leisurely pace toward the rock pile. I look back and George slowly turns and begins following me, walking at the same pace as when Floyd called him over.

"Come on, you guys. What are you waiting for?"

Joe and Jim must think they're fairly safe now because they both climb over the fence, all the time paying more attention to old George than to where they're going. Neither one of them gain any ground on George. I guess they'd just as soon keep a safe distance.

What Joe and Jim don't know, though, is that George, even if he wanted to, can't move any faster, and also that I've been over here several times before, so George knows me as a friend.

We settle down on the back side of the rock pile, sitting high enough to see the house. George bothers us for a while, nudging us with his nose, until he realizes he's not going to get anymore cat food, and becomes content to nibble on his small pile of hay next to a large beat up old water pan.

I point to the water pan. "If you get thirsty, Joe, there's some water right over there. That is, if you don't mind sharing."

Jim, who's been sitting a little further away, picks up a large, flat rock, sets it down a little closer and sits on the rock. I suddenly get a whiff of some barnyard smell.

"Whew! Who stinks?"

"Don't look at me," Joe says. "I took a shower this morning."

"It's not that kind of a smell, Joe. Either one of you guys ate some beans or one of you wasn't watching where you were going. Look at your shoes."

Joe looks at the bottom of each of his shoes.

"Nope, not mine."

Jim turns on the rock a little so he can steady himself better. A couple seconds later, without saying a word, he gets up, walks into a grassy area and begins scraping his right foot along the ground.

I hear a loud snort from over my left shoulder and there's a look in old George's eyes I'd never seen before.

"Jim!" I yell. "Stop! George thinks you're being aggressive toward him!"

Too late. George starts toward Jim at a pace faster than he's gone in years. Jim doesn't waste any time as he sprints around to the other side of the rock pile. However, George still has him in his sights and follows right behind. Meanwhile, Joe has clamored up to the top of the rock pile, not wishing to be any part of this.

For the next five minutes Jim and George circle round and round the rock pile until, finally, old George's age catches up to him and he stops to rest. He stares at Jim for a short while and then figures it's not worth the effort and just ambles over to his water dish to quench his thirst.

Jim climbs up the rock pile and joins Joe there.

"I don't want you up here, you're not safe."

"I wouldn't worry about it any more, Joe," I say. "I think he's gotten it out of his system."

"Quick," Joe says with an anxious tone in his voice. "There's a car pulling in. Everybody down."

I stand up to look over the rocks as Joe and Jim scramble down. It looks like Brother Steve's car. "Yep, it looks like them all right."

"Don't you think you oughta get down, Bob?"

"Not to worry, Joey. I can barely make out their car from here. To them my head would be just another rock."

"And with good reason."

"Yeah, well if you laid on your back on the top of the rock pile, they would mistake you for the Rock of Gibralter."

"So, if they took . . ."

I interrupt Joe in the middle of his next insult. "Yep, it's Brother Martin and Brother Steve."

I scan down the driveway and as much of the road as I can see, at least the parts that aren't obscured by the house, barn, and trees.

"Were they followed?" Jim asks.

"I don't see anybody else, but we should do like Brother Martin said and hang around here for about an hour."

The three of us watch quietly as the car is quickly unloaded, each person carrying armloads of things into the house. I don't think I've ever seen Brother Martin move this fast.

Within minutes they're done. They stand near the front of the car for a couple more minutes and then they leave.

I watch the road for a while for any signs of unwelcome company and seeing none, I make myself comfortable on my rock.

"You know, this would make a good hiding place for this." I reach into my jacket pocket and pull out the cube. "Then we can come and get it whenever we need it again."

I pick up several rocks to make a small depression. Then I take a large rock that's flat on both sides and set it next to the hole. I take the cube, put it in the hole and place the flat rock over the top. Then I take a variety of smaller rocks and pile them around and on top of the flat rock.

"There," I say brushing the dirt off my hands. "I guess we wait another fifty minutes or so and head back. So . . . what do you guys wanna talk about?"

Jim must feel that George is no longer a threat because he moves back down the rock pile and sits on his flat rock again. Staring off into the woods he asks, "What do you guys think will happen to us if we get caught?"

"They'd prob'ly put us on trial for murder and we'd be sent away for life if we're convicted," Joe answers.

Without looking up from my feet I reply, "I don't think we'd ever make it to trial. Somehow, they'd make it look like we all committed suicide in some sort of pact or something."

"Or some inmate would be paid off to kill us for them," Joe adds.

"Yeah, Jim, there's just too many ways to get rid of people like us when there's such a corrupt person in a high position like that. Oh, and speaking of getting rid of people, Joe, I had this really wild dream the other morning. I'm sorry to say you and Jim both bit the dust in it."

"Oh yeah," Joe says. "And just how did this happen?"

"Well, I guess the bad guys caught you two and on the way to my house, Jim wouldn't cooperate so they threw him out of the car going sixty-five. I guess you could say that you literally did bite the dust, Jim. Anyway, they brought Joe into my room at gunpoint and made both of us kneel on the bed. Then they threatened to shoot Joe if I didn't tell them where the cube was."

"Did you?" Joe asks.

"Yep, but when they got it they shot you in the head. Then I grabbed a pillow and hit the gun with it and got shot in the leg."

"Oh, thanks a lot. Why didn't you think of that before I got shot?"

"I figured you were okay 'cause you didn't get shot in a vital spot."

With that Joe gives me a shove and I slip off my rock and hit my rear end on another rock.

"Ow." It hurts a little but not enough that I can't sit back on my rock again.

"There, how's your vital spot feel?"

I look at Jim and he's just grinning like crazy.

"What are you grinnin' about?"

I give Jim a shove and his rock tips, dumping him over. Jim stands up and Joe points at him.

"Yuckola, Jim. What did you roll in?"

"Where?"

Jim looks frantically around at himself trying to see what was on him.

"Just kidding, Jim."

I look back over the rocks at the tranquil farm scene down below. I see Mi-Ling go into the house.

"Hey Joe, Mi-Ling's here."

Joe scrambles up the rocks.

"Where?"

"I don't mean 'here' here, I mean I just saw her go in the house."

"Oh."

I look at my watch and figure it's close enough. "Well guys, I don't see anything out of the ordinary, other than you two, so I guess we can head on back to the house."

That's what Joe was wanting to hear. Instead of going around the rock pile, he climbs up and over it and starts jogging toward the house.

"Come on, Jim, he doesn't have a very big lead. Let's beat him back to the house."

Jim and I sprint around the rock pile. Old George looks up only long enough to acknowledge the fact that we're leaving and then goes back to eating. Up ahead Joe's already over the fence and heading for the electric fence. He looks back and notices us coming full tilt, so he picks up his pace. Instead of unhooking the electric fence, Joe ducks under it and is on his way.

Jim and I reach the old wooden fence at about the same time. I put my hands on the top rail and vault over the top. Jim tries to do the same but he catches his foot on the top of the fence and tumbles, his spaghetti arms and legs flailing through the air until he hits the ground with a thud. The sight is more than I can take and I begin laughing hysterically. So much so that I can't run anymore. In fact, it's all I can do to be able to remain standing.

"It's not funny, Bob, I could've got hurt."

I catch my breath a little. "But you didn't."

"But I could've."

"But it was funny and it made me laugh and that's all that counts."

"Would you be laughing if I got hurt?" Jim brushes himself off.

"Only at first. Then I'd help you and after you're all fixed up, then I'd laugh some more."

"But what if I got hurt and later I died?"

"Well I guess I wouldn't laugh at all . . . at least not until after the funeral."

I laugh and take off running because I know Jim is really wanting to punch me.

I reach the electric fence and roll under it instead of ducking under it as Joe did. As soon as I'm on my feet I can see that I'm not going to be able to catch up to Joe since he's almost to the garden, but I still have to outrun Jim.

Just as I reach the edge of the sweet corn, Joe comes flying back out of the corn and head on into me. The impact stops Joe dead in his tracks and sends me flying about three feet back in the direction I'd just come from. I sit up and shake the thousand points of light out of my head. "What are you . . ."

Joe quickly clamps his hand over my mouth so I can't finish my sentence.

"Shh. There's some cars coming up the drive. Where's Jim?"

Joe pulls his hand away so I can answer.

"Back up there."

We both look up the path and Jim is running full speed toward us. Joe and I begin waving at him and trying to signal to him to get down. He doesn't see us but he must have seen the cars because he dives headlong onto the ground doing a great head first slide. Good enough to steal second base in any baseball game.

When he comes to a stop Joe and I, bent at the waist, run up to him.

"Who are they, Joe?" Jim whispers.

"I don't know but I didn't want to take any chances."

We hear several car doors slam and someone says, "You men come with me to check the house and you others check the barn and other out buildings."

I've heard that voice before, only at that time I was in an attic.

"We've gotta get back to the rock pile."

Joe protests. "But they might see us going up the hill."

"They'll see us anyway if we stay here. After we get the cube we can cut through the woods. On the other side of the river, about a quarter of a mile, there's a road."

"Then what?" Joe asks.

"I don't know. I guess we'll have to cross that bridge when we come to it. We really don't have any other choice."

"Well we're wasting time sittin' here. Let's go."

"Stay low," I say.

We start out bent over but when we figure we're higher than the top of the sweet corn we straighten up and start running as fast as we can and hope they don't look in our direction.

Suddenly there's the sound of a shotgun blast that comes from the direction of the barn and we all dive to the ground.

"Anybody hit?" I ask.

Joe pats his body. "Nope. I'm all here."

"Jim?"

Jim spits some dirt out of his mouth. "Yeah, I'm okay."

I look in the direction of the barn and there behind the barn, waving his shotgun in the air, is Floyd. I wave back and he makes a motion with his gun like it's a paddle. I get his message and wave an acknowledgment back.

"Come on, you guys. Floyd's the one who fired the shot. He's creating a diversion for our getaway."

As soon as we get up and start running again, there's another shotgun blast. Jim and I begin to put a little distance between us and Joe.

"Bob, Joe's getting behind."

"Don't worry, he'll catch up when we stop to get the cube." We roll under the electric fence and when I get back on my feet I notice Joe's only about ten yards behind.

There's another blast from Floyd's shotgun and I chance a look back. Floyd is still behind the barn and the police are lying flat on the ground in front of the barn.

We sprint across the open meadow and hop over the fence. The sound of our running or more likely the vibrations on the ground from our running, has attracted the attention of old George and he comes slowly out from behind the rock pile.

"Hi, George," I say as I rush past him.

I reach the spot where I hid the cube and begin tossing rocks off onto the ground. Jim stands beside me and a few seconds later Joe joins us.

"What's he doing?" Joe asks breathlessly.

"I don't know," is Jim's reply.

"I'm getting the cube, you dummies."

"Not you," Joe says. "We're talking about Floyd."

I grab the cube and stand up to see what they're talking about. Floyd has climbed over the barnyard fence and is standing with his back to the barn in the middle of a field of tall weeds. He has his gun raised as if he's about to shoot at something in the weeds.

"I don't know. The only time I've ever seen him go out there is to shoot woodchucks."

Moving around to the back corner of the barn are several policemen with their guns drawn.

"He's not gonna try to hold them off with a shotgun out there in the middle of that field is he?" Joe asks.

"I don't think so," I say. "Floyd is up to something, 'cause he's smarter than that. Come on, let's go. He's doing this to buy us some time and we're wasting it."

We take off running to the back of the corral, climb over the fence and under the electric fence, the two of which are at this point only a few feet apart. A couple of steps later we're into the woods. Jim and I slow down enough for Joe to keep up and I use the time to explain what we're going to do next. Especially since Joe's already asking. "Where . . . we . . . going . . . now?" He heaves between each breath.

"Down to the river to catch a boat. Floyd has a canoe down there. He signaled for us to use it."

"How . . . far . . . is . . . it?" Joe pants again.

"Oh not far. Only a couple miles or so."

"What!?" Joe comes to a complete stop. "No way . . . am I gonna . . . be able to . . . run that . . . far."

Jim and I stop and look at Joe. He's bent over with his hands on his knees breathing heavily.

"I was just kidding, Joe. Come on, it's only a couple hundred yards from here and it's all down hill. In fact, we'll let you set the pace. That is as long as it's faster than a crawl."

It's a lot easier running through Floyd's woods than the ones behind my house. The cows he lets graze in here keep the brush from growing up and keep the low branches trimmed very nicely. All we have to do is run around the rocks, stumps and mature trees. The carpet of fallen leaves crunch under our feet as we run.

We come to what Floyd calls 'the river' but is actually somewhere in size between a small stream and a large creek. I don't know what its official name is but I'm sure there's a sign on a road some-where for it.

The stream meanders around for about ten miles and eventu-ally empties into the Grand River. Floyd told me several times that he's canoed it a few times and only got stuck five or six times where he had to get out and carry or push the canoe.

I look at the stream which is slightly higher than normal be-cause of the rainy season, so maybe we won't get stuck as often as Floyd.

Just a few yards from us, under a blue plastic tarpaulin, is an aluminum canoe sitting upside down atop several cement blocks.

"Here's our transportation, guys," I say as I start untying the ropes of the tarp from the cement blocks. "Help me get this tarp off."

Joe and Jim grab a rope and untie theirs and I start on another one. "The paddles and life jackets should be in the canoe already."

We flip the canoe over and the paddles clatter to the bottom of the canoe. Joe and I carry the canoe to the edge of the water and I slide it two-thirds of the way out into the stream.

"Who wants to paddle first?" I ask.

"You guys go ahead," Jim says. "I've never been canoeing."

"Really?" Joe says. "You don't know what you've been missing. There's nothing like being out in God's great creation, alone with your thoughts, without the noise of some sort of engine droning in your ears."

"It's even better if you don't have the droning of Joe's mouth in your ears, Jim. But then, I guess we gotta take the bad with the good."

I climb into the canoe and pull a paddle out from under the seat. I lay it across my legs as Jim stumbles into the canoe, rocking it unsteadily back and forth.

"Sit down, Jim, before you dump both of us into the water."

"I'm trying."

"Trying to what? To dump us in or to sit?"

"To sit."

Jim wobbles a little more and settles onto the bottom of the canoe in the middle. Joe pushes the canoe out a little farther, grabs a handful of leaves and scatters them over our tracks. Joe rolls up the tarp and hands it to Jim, then climbs in himself. He pulls the other paddle out and sticks it into the dirt on shore and pushes us out into the stream.

We coast out a little way and I stick my paddle out to push off a tree root on the opposite shore. This gets us pointed downstream.

"We probably shouldn't paddle for a while, Joe, so we don't accidentally bang our paddles against the side of the canoe."

"Yeah, I'll just use my paddle as a rudder."

"How fast do you think we're going?" Jim asks.

Joe replies, "I'd say about three miles an hour."

"That seems about right to me, too," I say.

"So how long will it take us to get to the Grand River?"

"Well, Floyd told me one time that it's about ten miles, but we'll be going about five or six miles an hour when we start paddling, so it'll take us only a couple hours."

"What then?" Joe asks.

"Beats me. This was Floyd's idea, not mine."

We coast for about ten minutes before we start paddling. The shadows are long as the sun is nearing the end of its course for the day. Each time we approach a house that's close to the stream, we quit paddling and coast on by. Hopefully we won't disturb any household pets that would draw attention to our presence.

The stream is deep enough that we don't scrape bottom too often, however we are doing a lot of ducking and moving of branches that hang low over the water.

Occasionally we see an otter slide into the water and disappear, however Joe insists that they're actually not otters, but river rats.

"Really?" Jim says. "Rats really get that big?"

"You've lived in the city most of your life, Jim," Joe says. "Haven't you ever seen sewer rats?"

"I lived in the suburbs."

"Well Joe, I think you're wrong. Those were otters. They were too small to be river rats and besides, the tails weren't anything like a rat's tail."

It's really beginning to get dark, making it hard to see the branches and anything that might be in the river. I get whacked in the face by a small branch.

"Ow!" I emphasize it but not very loud. "We're gonna have to slow down, Joe. I can't see very good any more."

"Maybe you should get your eyes checked." Joe continues paddling.

"Maybe you should get your brain checked. Here, Jim." I hand Jim my paddle. "Slide this under the seats, I'm gonna hold my hands out so I can feel for oncoming branches, since Joe doesn't seem to want to do the intelligent thing."

"Okay, okay, I'll slow down, you big baby."

Joe quits paddling and uses his paddle only as a rudder.

"Happy now?" Joe says

"My body thanks you, Joe."

We go like this for a while longer but as it gets darker it becomes difficult to tell where the stream turns.

"What we need," Joe says, "is a full moon."

"Any moon at all would be nice, but it looks like it's clouding up again."

Suddenly we come to a stop with a thump as we run into the bank. I'm almost thrown forward out of the canoe, but I catch one side with my hand and settle back into my seat.

"You're supposed to be telling me which way to turn, Bob, not star gazing."

"Well if I could see which way to turn, I'd tell you which way to turn. Hand me my paddle again, Jim."

I take the paddle from Jim and push us off the bank. I stare into the darkness as if putting more effort into it will cause more light to shine on everything.

"I think we gotta go left, Joe."

"Left it is."

I push off with my paddle, and we go a little farther and run into something else.

"I think we hit a tree Joe, and I think it's all the way across the stream. We're gonna have to get out and lift the canoe across."

"Or, we could go to the bank and carry it around on dry land," Joe says.

"I like that idea better, too," Jim says squirming a little in the boat. "My butt hurts. Do you think we could just stop for a little while and stretch our legs?"

"I could handle that. Joe, what do you think?"

"Okay by me."

"I think the bank's not as steep to the left there, Joe."

We swing the canoe around to the left and run it aground on the bank. I climb out and pull the canoe farther onto the shore, then Jim gets out and we both pull it almost all the way on to dry land.

Just as Joe stands up and begins to slide the paddle onto the bottom of the canoe, a bright spotlight lights up the canoe and everything around it for several yards.

"Hit the dirt!" Joe yells.

He didn't have to tell us. Jim and I are already doing belly flops in different directions. Joe flies over the side of the canoe and takes cover behind it.

"Bob!" A voice calls from the direction of the spotlight.

It sounds familiar, but I can't quite place it. My heart is pounding so hard I'm surprised I heard it at all. I turn my head hoping I can hear it better if I point one ear in the direction of the voice.

"Bob!" The voice calls again. "It's us, Brother Martin and Brother Steve! Hurry up and get in the car!"

I jump up and start running toward the light. "Come on you guys, the cavalry's here."

With the spotlight lighting our way, we climb the steep embankment up to a bridge which crosses the stream. When I reach the road Brother Martin grasps my hand tightly, then pulls me to him and gives me a big bear hug.

"Thank God, you're safe. Quick, into the car, gentlemen. We've been sitting on the road long enough. We don't wish to press our luck too much longer."

I turn to Joe and whisper, "I didn't even know our luck had wrinkles in it."

"Just get in the car, Bob."

The three of us climb into the back seat of the car and somehow I end up in the middle again. Steve jumps into the driver's side and Brother Martin slides into the front passenger seat.

"How'd you guys find us?" I ask.

Brother Martin turns in his seat to respond. "Millie called us to tell us you would be canoeing down the river. We were unable to retrieve your things from the house so we picked up a few things from the store to help you out. They are in the trunk."

"Good," Joe says. "I can't wait to get out of these stinky old clothes."

I laugh. "We can't wait for you to get out of them either." I pause then direct a question to Brother Martin. "So where are we going now Brother Martin?"

"It's a long shot, but Brother Steve says he seems to remember a member of the Flint church mentioning that he knows someone who owns a plane. If we can get you safely there, we will have you fellows well on your way."

"On our way where?" Joe asks.

"Why, on your way to Israel, where else?"

"I'll turn on the scanner," Brother Steve says. "We'll be able to get a fair idea where the road blocks are being set up."

Joe ponders the idea of going to Israel for a while before he says anything. "You know, I've always wanted to go to Israel. To walk where Jesus walked and to see the land that the prophets saw. There's just something about the thought that gives me butterflies."

"I rather envy you fellows in that respect," Brother Martin says. "That is one place I have always wanted to go, also. While going to school I had studied about it and saw the pictures and even watched several videos, but there is absolutely no substitute for actually being there."

Brother Martin's voice has a faraway sound to it now as he continues. "To feel the ground under your feet, to smell the things that are common only to that region and to hear the sounds of the country. To actually be surrounded by the environment and be a part of it, instead of watching it go by."

I feel like I should ask him to come along, but I'm not sure if that would complicate things more than they already are.

"Why don't you come with us?" Jim asks.

"Oh I'd love to, son, but I would just slow you fellows down. Besides, I've got a congregation that I am responsible for right here in Michigan. You fellows have your calling and I have mine. I am just satisfied that I could have been a part of yours."

None of us are paying much attention to the static filled voices coming from the scanner except for Brother Steve.

"We're going to have to go a little further west before we start north, so we can swing around the outside of the police perimeter roadblocks that are being set up."

"You do what you think best." Brother Martin says. "You have the controls. Well, fellows, it looks as though it is going to take us a little longer than expected, but we will get you there in fine fashion."

Running the events of the last few hours over in my mind, I feel a little disturbed by what has happened.

"Brother Martin?"

"Yes, Bob."

"How'd the police know we were there?"

"We do not really know. Brother Steve and I were discussing that very question while we waited for you fellows at the bridge. Either they were tipped off or they followed us. Whichever the case may be, we are all here now and we are all safe."

"What about Floyd and Millie?"

"And Mi-Ling?" Joe adds.

"I do not know, but I am sure they are all right. Floyd called Millie from the barn and told her the situation and approximately how far down river you would get by nightfall. Millie then called us. It would seem he was pretty much on the mark."

I stare out the window and watch the scenery go by. I see the nice homes as we drive by. The soft yellow glow from the lights within make me long for the peace and security I once knew. In fact, I would love to have back my same old dull routine.

Brother Steve stops the car at an intersection. "Brother Martin, could you hand me the map in my glove compartment there?"

"Sure."

"We're in unfamiliar territory now and I don't think now is the time for us to be getting lost."

"Here you go."

Brother Martin hands him the map and Brother Steve opens it, blocking out any kind of view out the front window. "Okay, we're right here, so I guess we've got to go this way."

I watch Brother Steve as he traces a side road with his finger, until it gets to a road on the map marked in red.

"There. We can probably safely pick up highway twenty-one just east of St. Johns here." With that declaration, he folds the map up haphazardly and hands it to Brother Martin to finish the job.

"I never could fold those things," Steve says as he checks for traffic and makes a right turn.

Joe leans forward a little to speak into Brother Steve's ear. "Where exactly are we headed?"

"There's a private air strip just west of Flint. If Josh Neuman got my message, he'll be waiting for us there with a plane all set to go."

Brother Steve has always amazed me. He's one of those guys who knows somebody, who knows somebody else, who knows somebody that's a good friend of somebody else. He could always get good deals on things. I even asked him one time how he got free roundtrip plane tickets to Orlando and he just sort of smiled a sly little smile and said, "I've got my connections."

"I don't think I know a Josh Neuman at the Flint church," Brother Martin says. "Is he a new member?"

"Not exactly. Herb Snyder knows him."

"Oh yes, good old Herb. I've talked to Herb on a couple of occasions at revivals. I hear he is being considered for a vacant deacon position."

"That's right. He told me that when I talked to him on the phone this afternoon. Personally, I don't think he'll have any problem getting ordained."

I think I met Herb once, but at the moment I can't seem to picture him in my mind. Like many other people I've met from the other churches in the association that I've only seen once or twice a year, I might remember them, but they don't remember me or vice-versa. It does make for awkward moments, however I guess it is an excellent way for God to keep us humble.

"I have to go to the bathroom."

Joe reaches around behind my head and slaps Jim on the back of his head.

"We can't take you anywhere, Jim," Joe says.

Brother Steve gives a quick glance at Jim and then back at the road ahead. "We'll be getting to St. Johns shortly, we can stop someplace there, but not for very long. We'll be running a high risk of being spotted. Once we're past there, we should be pretty well in the clear."

"You think you can hold it that long?" Joe asks.

"Maybe. . . maybe not."

"Listen, Jim," I say. "Why don't you and I switch places so that if it turns out to be 'maybe not,' you can be sitting nice and close to Joe."

"Okay."

I start to stand up to let Jim slide over next to Joe but Joe grabs me by the shoulder and shoves me back down into the seat.

"No you don't. I'm not havin' no dam burst next to me."

A little while later we pull into a gas station near downtown St. Johns. St. Johns is a fair-sized town with a population of about ten thousand, just off the freeway. It's big claim to fame is their annual mint festival each summer.

The gas station itself is not much to look at. The selling of gasoline seems to be more of a sideline to the auto repair shop inside the garage rather than the major income like that of most of the other name brand stations in the area.

As soon as the car stops Jim hops out and runs around to the side of the building that has two dingy blue doors. Over each is a sign that used to be white with black lettering but now is grey with black lettering.

"Does anybody else need to go?" Brother Martin asks. "Better go now because it will definitely be a while before we will want to stop again."

I don't really feel the need but it might be a good idea to empty the old bladder anyway. "Yeah, I'd better go too, just in case."

"Me too," Joe says a little reluctantly, almost like it's too much effort to move.

Joe's probably done more running today than he's done in the last few years, and his groaning as he climbs out of the car testifies to that fact.

"Ohh . . . my legs." Joe looks around at his surroundings. "Geez, do you think we could find a grungier place? I can't wait to see the bathroom. It's a good thing I don't have to take a dump, 'cause there's no telling what kinds of little creatures are crawling around in there."

We get to the bathroom door and Joe tries to open it. "It's locked." Joe bangs on the door. "Come on, Jim, there's people out here with needs too, ya know."

"Maybe a bunch of those little crawly creatures of yours has taken Jim hostage."

"They aren't my crawly creatures, they were left by somebody else."

"They're yours if you sit in there. Instant adoption."

The door squeaks open and Jim steps out quickly letting the

air escape from his lungs in a rush and then pants quickly to replenish the oxygen in his system.

Jim doesn't have to explain his behavior in any way, shape or form as the stench of ammonia and other by products hits our noses and causes me to take a couple steps back away from the door.

"Whew." Joe says. "I don't have to go that bad."

"Me neither. I haven't smelled anything that bad since Morton Murphy was fired. I thought these things were supposed to be inspected by the health department or something."

"Me, too . . . Hey, where's Jim going?"

I look in the direction Joe is looking, and see that Jim is going into the station.

"I don't know, but we'd better find out."

Joe and I hurry in through the front door of the station in time to see Jim stuff something into his jacket pocket as he turns away from the candy machine.

"Hi, guys."

"Getting a little snack, Jim?" Joe asks.

Jim pulls the package back out of his pocket. "Just some pumpkin seeds." Jim holds it out for us to see and then sticks it back in his pocket.

"They're too salty for me," I say. "I always end up drinking about a gallon of water."

"You might like these, Bob." Jim pulls the package out of his pocket again. "See? They're unsalted."

"That's good, Jim, but I still prefer M&M's with peanuts."

I go over to the candy machine and push a couple of quarters into the slot. I select the button to get some M&M's and the yellow package drops to the bottom of the machine. I grab the package and turn to find Joe still standing there. Jim has already gone out to the car.

"You gonna get something, Joe?"

"If you lend me fifty cents I will."

"You don't have any money?"

"I told you that the other day at my house when we ordered pizza, remember?"

"Oh yeah, how could I forget."

I dig into my pocket and pull out the rest of my change, an assortment of nickels, dimes, and pennies.

"You're in luck, Joe. I've got just enough."

"I thought you didn't believe in luck."

"I don't, it was just a figure of speech."

"But if you don't believe in something then why say it?"

"For the same reason people who don't believe in God say, 'Thank God it's Friday,' or something happens and they say, 'Oh my God.'"

"But did you stop to think that if you say things like, 'You're in luck,' aren't you actually endorsing the idea that there might be such a thing?"

"And if you keep this up, did you stop to think that I might not loan you fifty cents?"

I hand Joe the change and he buys a bag of mini pretzels which he immediately rips open and begins to munch on.

"Come on, Joe, we best be getting back to the car."

Just as we're going out the door, Brother Martin meets us.

"What is taking you fellows? We should not have been stopped here this long. We are still too close to the Lansing area."

"He's right, Joe, come on."

I start running back to the car. Joe tries to run too, but his legs are too sore. So with each step it hurts.

"Ouch, ooch, ouch, ouch, ooch, ow, ow, ooch."

"Your pace leaves much to be desired, Joe," I say as I stop at the car and look back. "In fact, Brother Martin is walking and still keeping up with you."

"I guess I should have started riding my bike a little sooner."

"A little sooner? If you'd ridden it at all it would've helped."

"Well, I meant to ride it."

Brother Martin gets into the conversation just as we're about to climb into the car. "A lot of people have meant to get saved and waited until it was too late. It is best not to put things off because you may never know when it will be too late."

We climb into the car and Brother Martin continues. "But getting back to your problem, Joe, you really could use a little exercise, if you do not mind me saying so."

"Well I would have been exercising all along, but the Bible says it's a waste of time."

I know what's coming next and I know that this time Joe is going to come up short with his side of the discussion.

"How so, Joseph?"

"Well, doesn't the Bible say that bodily exercise profits little? So if it doesn't do us any good, why do it?"

"Joseph, I must say your reasoning would be flawless but for one thing."

"What's that?"

"A flaw in your reasoning."

"What flaw?"

"Remember what the scripture says, 'Bodily exercise profits little but righteousness delivers from death.' The key word is 'little.' It doesn't say none at all. In fact there is another verse that says that by reason of strength you might be able to add an extra five years to your life and that can be very important. If by your being around an extra five years you can lead even just one more person to the Lord, it would be worth it. Also, exercise can give you more energy for your daily activities and keep you more alert. However, the Bible also says to do all things in moderation. The Lord should always come first, so unless your profession is in a professional sport where you would be required to exercise many hours a day, I would say no more than an hour a day is sufficient. Anything more is excessive and takes away from more needful activities."

Joe's quiet for a moment so I take the opportunity to rub it in somewhat.

"I guess he's got you there, huh Joe?" I say, jabbing him in the ribs with my elbow.

"I knew all that already. I just wanted to see if anybody else did."

Chapter 8

As we pull into the driveway a porch light goes on, lighting up the front of a small, light blue ranch home. We're still out in the country and I can only see a couple lights far off in the distance indicating where the next nearest place where inquisitive eyes might be found.

Joe, as usual, is the first one to speak. "Where's the airport? I thought we were gonna get to catch a plane."

"We are," Steve says sounding rather short with Joe and a little annoyed. "The runway's behind the house. Everybody stay here while I check to see if everything's all set to go."

Brother Steve walks quickly up to the door and rings the doorbell. After a short wait he's greeted by a well-dressed man in what appears to be a three piece business suit. He's taller than Brother Steve, but then most everybody is. With dark straight hair cut in a conservative style, I figure he must be the owner of the plane. Probably some top executive-type for a big company.

I suddenly notice that their movements have become slightly animated as if something has them both a little agitated. Finally, Brother Steve just drops his hands to his side as if to say, 'I give up,' and begins to walk back to the car.

"I think something's wrong."

"Why do you say that, Bob?" Brother Martin asks.

"Brother Steve looks like he's upset."

Brother Steve walks up to Brother Martin's car door and Brother Martin rolls down the window. "Is everything okay, Brother Steve?"

"Yeah, but it looks as if I'm going along with you three guys on the plane trip."

"Is it necessary?"

"Yeah, I guess there's some F.A.A. rule about all international flights having to have both a pilot and a co-pilot. Otherwise we'll be in trouble either before or after we land."

"So are you gonna be our co-pilot?" Jim asks.

"You guessed it."

I'd heard that Brother Steve had been in the Gulf war as a Navy pilot, but I didn't know he had kept his pilots license up to date. He never talked much about his war experiences but I'd heard he was one of the best.

"Well gentlemen, let's get you inside and out of sight until it's time for your departure," Brother Martin says as he opens the car door and climbs out. "I'll get your clothes out of the trunk so you can finally get out of those nasty old clothes of yours."

We climb out of the car and start for the house as Brother Martin goes to the back of the car to open the trunk.

Brother Steve walks ahead of us but as we approach the house, he veers to the left of the house. I figure he's going to take care of some other business so I keep heading for the front door.

Brother Steve glances back and apparently it's important that we not go in as he practically yells at us, "No! You can't . . . I mean we're not going in the house." He calms down some. "We'll be leaving in just a few minutes and Phil wants us to wait with the plane."

I look at Joe and Jim a little perplexed, but also understanding the circumstances. I also realize that Brother Steve has always been a bit high-strung. I shrug my shoulders and follow Brother Steve to the door of a large, gray aluminum pole barn.

Brother Steve opens the door and flips on the light switch. I step inside onto the hard packed dirt floor and take a look around as Joe and Jim follow me in.

The first thing that catches my eye is a gleaming white, two engine prop plane with blue markings and black lettering, sitting in the middle of the floor. There's not much else in the building except for a work bench in one corner and some tools hung on a sheet of pegboard nearby. At the other end of the building are two large doors that roll to each side, allowing room for the plane to go through. Along the wall opposite us is a stack of large boxes and that's about it for everything in the building.

"Wow," I hear Jim say.

"She is a beaut, isn't she?"

We all turn around at the sound of a different voice. Standing in the door is the man I saw talking to Brother Steve at the house, wearing a big friendly smile.

"You must be Phil," Joe says.

"That's right, my boy. Phil Appleton's the name, and I'm very glad to meet you boys." He shakes each of our hands. "I'll be your pilot on this little intercontinental jaunt, so if you have any questions, feel free to ask."

Just then Brother Martin stumbles in carrying two full grocery bags, just barely squeezing himself and his load through the door. He bumps friendly Phil a little and for just an instant, the smile on Phil's face disappears. Quickly regaining his composure, Phil takes one of the bags from Brother Martin.

"Here, let me help you with this." Phil peeks in the bag. "And what do we have here?"

"It's a couple changes of clothes for these three gentlemen," Brother Martin says, responding to Phil's question and coming back with one of his own. "Is there someplace where they can change?"

"If they wish privacy, no. However, there's plenty of room right here in the hanger."

"Well, I guess if you fellows aren't too modest, this will have to do." Brother Martin hands me a bag and Phil hands the other bag to Joe.

It's not that I'm all that embarrassed about changing around guys I know, but I do get uncomfortable around people I don't know.

"Nothing personal guys, but I'm gonna rearrange those boxes over there and change in privacy," I say looking at Phil. "They say that one in ten guys are homosexual and I see five guys in front of me." I look at each of them suspiciously. "That means that one of you is half a homosexual."

"You mean bisexual?" Joe adds.

"Yes, I'm afraid so."

"Who do you think it is?"

"Well, I know it's not me."

"Not it," Joe says.

"Not it," Jim says quickly.

Brother Martin just smiles and looks at Brother Steve and Phil, who look a bit taken aback.

"Well fellows, I think it's time I should head back." Brother

Martin turns to Brother Steve. "Give me a call when you get back if you need a ride back home. I'll put some gas in your car on the way back just in case your better half needs to go anywhere."

"I probably won't be needing a ride when I return but thanks for offering."

"You fellows be careful now and remember, God is on your side and as you all know, 'If God be for us . . .'"

The three of us join in, "Who can be against us."

"I guess you do all know. Well, okay then, I'll be praying for you."

"Bye, Brother Martin," I say. "And thanks for everything."

"Yeah, thanks," Joe says.

"Me too," Jim says.

Brother Martin waves and disappears out the door. I notice Phil looking us over and Phil notices me noticing.

"I'm sorry," he says shaking his head. "It's just that you guys don't look or act like mass murderers to me." He says it in a rather mocking tone.

"Maybe it's because we're not," Joe says defensively.

"Oh, hey, it's none of my business anyway. I just owe somebody a big favor and with this we'll be even."

I suddenly notice he's not smiling anymore and I get the feeling he's not entirely thrilled about having us around.

"Come on, you guys," I say to Joe and Jim. "Let's go change so we'll be ready to leave when Phil is."

"That's a good idea," Phil says. "The longer you hang around here, the greater the chance of getting discovered."

The three of us walk over to where the boxes are stacked. I put the bag of clothes down and begin moving the boxes into a semi-circle, straining somewhat with each one.

"These are kinda heavy," I say groaning a little as I lift another one off the stack and move it into position on the new stack. "I wonder what's in these."

There are no markings on the outside of the cardboard boxes and they're sealed extremely well with packing tape.

Joe peeks around the boxes kind of sneakily and then begins to pry at the tape with his fingers.

"What are you doing, Joe?" I say in a slightly frantic whisper.

"I just want to see what's in here," he says calmly.

I smack Joe's hand away from the tape. "Knock it off, Joe. It's not our stuff."

"I'm not gonna take anything, I just wanna look at it."

"Well what if it's blood samples from A.I.D.S. patients or something like that?"

Joe takes a quick step back. "Maybe you're right. I guess it isn't our stuff to be messing around with."

Jim pulls a pair of new blue jeans out of the bag and looks at the tag. "Who wears thirty, thirty-twos?"

I grab the jeans from Jim. "Those are mine."

Jim pulls out another pair, looks at the tag and hands them to Joe. "These must be yours. They're a little short and roomy for me."

"I detect a bit of a slam there, Joey. Are you going to take that from him?"

"Only for now, but sometime when he least expects it, something will happen that will make him regret the day that he slammed Joseph Maderna."

I look at Jim and he's just grinning like crazy. "Wow, Joe, you've really got him scared now. Maybe if you threaten him a little more he might laugh himself into submission."

"Shut up, and just give me my clothes."

We finish changing and take a look at ourselves.

"Whoever did the shopping did a pretty good job. Don't you guys think?" I say finishing tying my shoes and checking out the length of my pants.

"Yeah," Jim says. "Except for maybe Joe's shirt there."

I look at Joe and notice his shirt sleeves hang down to his knuckles. "I guess you could always roll your sleeves up a little. That wouldn't look too bad would it?"

We come out from behind the boxes and there's nobody around.

"They must've gone to the house," Joe says rolling up his sleeve. "Say, how come Steve can go to the house and we can't?"

"Maybe it's because we're the ones wanted for murder. Maybe Phil's wife can't be trusted to keep a secret."

"How do you know he's married?"

"I don't, but maybe he is and maybe she can't be trusted. Or maybe he wants us out here so that if the cops catch us, Phil can say he didn't know we were here and that we were trying to steal his plane. That way he wouldn't be arrested for aiding and abetting fugitives. Anyway, help me move these boxes back."

"Okay," Joe says. "As long as you stop talking for just a little while."

We take a couple minutes to move the boxes back up against the wall where they were.

"Hey guys," I say. "I've got a joke for you."

"Uh oh, here we go again," Joe says rolling his eyes.

"The Lone Ranger and Tonto ride into town and go into the saloon . . ."

Joe interrupts. "I've heard this one before."

"No, you haven't. This is a different one."

"Okay, go ahead then. Let's get this over with."

"Let's see, where was I? Oh yeah, the Lone Ranger and Tonto ride into town and go into the saloon. After a couple hours, they come back out and discover that somebody's stolen the Lone Ranger's horse, Silver. So the Lone Ranger and Tonto start walking down the street looking for clues when the clumsiest man in town bumps into a lady carrying groceries and then trips over his own feet. The Lone Ranger stops and tells Tonto, 'That's him. That's the man who stole Silver and he's got him down in his gold mine pulling the ore out in the carts.' Tonto looks at the Lone Ranger in amazement. 'How you know all that Kemosabee?' 'Why don't you know Tonto?' The Lone Ranger says. 'I thought everyone knew, that every clod has a Silver mining.'"

"I knew it was gonna be another one of those jokes," Joe says as Jim chuckles. "And you're not helping, Jim. You just encourage those jokes of his."

"Come on, Joe, that one was better than most of the other ones. At least it makes Jim laugh."

"Well that's a real good standard to go by. Jim laughs at disaster movies."

"He's just got a keen sense of humor."

"Sick is more like it."

"Well, I'd just like to see you make up a better joke. 'Cause I'll bet you can't."

"Bet I can."

"Then go ahead. See if you can do it. Come on, Joe, we're

waiting." I pause a couple seconds. "Well? Where's the joke? I thought you said you could make one better?"

"I can't with you yakking in my ear."

"So now you're making excuses."

"I'm not making excuses. Just give me a little time and I'll come up with one and it will blow your sorry little jokes out of the water."

"Will not."

"Will too."

"Will not."

"Will."

"Won't."

"Will."

"Won't."

"I'm beginning to think I've got the Three Stooges for passengers."

I spin around and see Phil standing near the front of the plane. He's changed his clothes and now looks like a World War Two pilot.

"How long have you been standing there?" Joe asks.

"Long enough to doubt my sanity in taking you guys on my plane."

"That'd be fine with me," Joe says.

"What do you mean by that, Joe?" I ask, being perplexed by his statement.

"I mean that I don't particularly care much for flying."

He says it rather quietly as if he were hiding it from the world.

"I didn't know you were scared of flying, Joe."

"I didn't say I was scared, I said I didn't care for it very much."

"You mean you've flown before?"

"I've taken a tour on an old B-52 bomber once."

"Well there's nothing to be scared of, Joe. Just sit back and relax."

"I'm not scared."

"Whatever you say, Joe."

"If you guys are done with this meaningless discussion of yours, I came in to tell you we'll be leaving in about half an hour."

Without smiling, Phil walks over to the stack of boxes and inspects them quickly. Evidently passing inspection, he picks one up and carries it to the plane.

I whisper to Joe with my one hand cupped to the side of my mouth. "See, Joe, it's a good thing I stopped you from snooping in those boxes."

"Yeah, yeah. Even a broken clock is right twice a day."

"So what do you guys want to do for half an hour?" I ask, looking around at our barren surroundings.

"We could talk about religion," Joe says with a grin.

Talking about religion and coming up with hypothetical situations is something Joe loves to do. I remember one time he asked me, "What if you were married and had a sixteen-year-old daughter and she started dating this long-haired guy wearing earrings, smoking and swearing. What would you do?"

I replied, "I would tell her she would have to stop seeing him and give her the reasons why."

Then Joe said, "But what if she said she was gonna date him anyway and there was nothing you could do to stop her. What would you do then?"

And I replied, "Then I would have to tell her that if she couldn't live by my rules while living under my roof, she would have to find another place to live."

Then he says, "But then what if she says she's not moving anywhere and you can't make her move out and she's still going to see her boyfriend?"

At this point in the conversation I would say anything just to end his "what ifs." In this particular case I simply said, "I'd shoot her and her boyfriend and then plead temporary insanity."

Joe leans back against the boxes with his feet slightly spread, looking thoughtful.

"Well Joe?" I ask. "What's the topic for discussion this time?"

"What do you think about the Pope dying?"

"What do you mean, exactly?"

"Well, I think the circumstances are a little fishy."

"How do you figure? He'd been sick for quite a while before he died."

"Maybe so, but he was fairly young for a Pope and he was in excellent shape before he became Pope. In fact, I'll bet if you were to check it out, you'd probably find out that he became ill right after he made his famous 'I'm going to clean God's house' speech."

"Is this another one of your conspiracy theories?"

"No, I just think that there are some circumstances involved here that make his death rather suspicious."

"Such as?"

"Such as, why didn't they let that specialist look at him? They had no reason not to. He was a Catholic in good standing and recognized as an expert in pneumonia and pneumonia related illnesses."

"Didn't they say that the Vatican doctors were sufficiently qualified to handle the problem?"

"They may have said that, but what would it have hurt to get another opinion? I think the Vatican doctors were in on it."

"Where do you get all this stuff, Joe?"

"Oh, mostly out of stuff I read."

"Oh, yeah," I say nodding my head. "All those little religious newspapers and pamphlets you're always sending away for. Some of that stuff is pretty fanatical, isn't it?"

"Yeah, some of it is, but even in that you can find little tidbits of useful information."

"Yeah, but how can you trust any of it?"

"Actually I don't, but I do try to check into some of their theories, just to see what I can find, and a couple times I've found out they were right."

"Like what?" I say skeptically, sticking my hands into my back pockets.

In my left pocket I feel my wallet but in my right pocket where I normally don't put anything. I'm surprised when I feel a stiff piece of paper stuck down in it.

"Like the time . . ."

I pull the piece of paper out of my pocket.

". . . What's that?" Joe forgets all about our previous conversation.

The piece of paper turns out to be a plain white business envelope folded in half.

"I don't know, I just found it in my pocket." I unfold it and there's handwriting on the front, but it's not an address.

"What's it say?" Jim asks looking over my shoulder.

"It's for me," I say. "It says I'm supposed to open this only when we get to Israel and then only the three of us are to know what it says inside."

"Who's it from?" Joe asks.

"Brother Martin," I say a little quieter, feeling that maybe somebody might be listening that shouldn't be.

"Listen, I'm gonna put this back in my pocket and we better not mention it anymore until it's time to open it, okay?"

I look at Jim and he nods his head in agreement. I look at Joe, but he's looking longingly at the envelope in my hand.

"Okay, Joe?"

"Yeah, I guess," he says grudgingly. "But I still don't know why we can't read it now."

"Maybe God wants to teach you patience," Jim says.

"He can teach me later. Right now I want to know what's in that envelope."

"Well maybe there isn't any 'later' time that God can teach you patience," I say. "Because if you touch that envelope you'll have all eternity to learn patience."

"Okay, okay, I'll wait, but I'm not gonna like it."

I'm not either, Joe. I'm not either. I'm half tempted to find a corner and try to read it through the envelope. After all, he said we couldn't open it and I wouldn't be. But I better not. I know what Brother Martin meant, and besides that, if I get caught I'd never hear the end of it from Joe.

I hear a noise coming from the direction of the plane like that of a heavy door being opened. I look in that direction and Phil has the door to the plane open and is putting the box inside. The door itself is located about two-thirds of the way to the back of the plane and is almost oval in shape. After putting the box inside the plane, Phil walks to the end of the building, unlatches the doors and slides one of the doors open.

While he's doing that the three of us just stand and watch.

"I don't think I like him much," Joe says quietly.

"I was just thinking the same thing." I'm a little surprised that I wasn't the only one thinking along those same lines. "His friendliness seems kinda hollow, you know, forced. And did you see the way he reacted to Brother Martin?"

"I did," Jim says.

"Well, it's not like I don't trust him to take us on the plane . . ." I glance in his direction to make sure he can't overhear our conversation. He's opening the other door so I continue. ". . . it's just that he seems so phony. It's almost like being lied to. If he doesn't like us he should just say so. All this fake small talk is just hypocritical."

"Do you think he's a Christian?" Joe asks.

"In what way do you mean? Do you mean does he have ties to a religious organization with claims of holding to the teachings of Jesus or do you mean does he have a personal relationship with Jesus Christ as Lord and Savior?"

"In this case I guess it'd be good if he were either one."

"Actually, I don't know."

"Then why'd you bother asking what kind of Christian I thought he was?"

"Just to bug you, I guess. But maybe I could ask Brother Steve. He seems to know him better than us."

There's the sound of a small engine coming from outside the hanger and with the three of us still a bit nervous about being discovered, we all move to a position where the boxes could hide us.

I kind of figure it's Phil, but my heart doesn't slow down or my breathing start again until Phil comes around the corner on a large garden tractor, not much different than the one I left back at home.

Phil swings the tractor around and backs it up to within about five feet of the tail of the plane, and turns the tractor off. "Get your stuff on board," he says walking past the front of the plane toward the work bench. "And don't forget anything 'cause once we're on the runway we're not coming back."

"Shoot," Joe says. "What are we gonna forget? Everything we've got now is what's left in these two grocery bags."

I pick up both bags, one in each hand, by their top edge. "Then I guess we'd better get all our worldly possessions on the plane, Joe."

I carry the bags to the open plane door and set them inside and give them a little push further in. I check out the inside of the plane real quick, noticing that the back part of the plane looks like it would be for hauling cargo. There are no seats and except for the box that Phil had just placed in there and our two bags, it's basically empty.

I do, however, take note of a door toward the front of the plane that I imagine is the door leading to the cockpit.

"See anything interesting?"

My heart jumps into my throat and I turn quickly at the sound of Phil's voice behind me. He's standing a couple of feet from me holding what looks like some sort of heavy metal towing bar which he will probably be using to pull the plane from the hanger.

"Uh . . . no . . . Uh, I was just looking. You got an awful lot of room in there."

"Yeah, it serves my purposes."

I try to make a little conversation. "How much can it carry?"

"More than I'd ever need it for."

I'm getting the impression that unless Phil wants to initiate the conversation, he doesn't want to be bothered. I simply respond with a weak "Oh," and Phil walks away to hook the plane to the tractor.

Left standing alone by the plane, I look in Joe's and Jim's direction, and Joe mouths the word, *Well?* I just shrug my shoulders and walk slowly back over to them.

"Well?" Joe says out loud this time. "What'd he say?"

"Not much. I just asked him how much the plane could carry, and all he gave me were vague answers."

"I don't like him."

"Come on, Joe, you don't even know him very well yet. Why don't you like him?"

"Okay, maybe 'don't like' isn't what I meant. How about, 'don't trust?' Maybe you could talk to Steve and get him to fly us."

"Won't work, Joe. Remember, Brother Steve said there has to be a co-pilot."

"What if one of us pretended to be the co-pilot?"

"And what if someone wanted to see our pilot's license? Besides, Phil owns the plane."

For once Joe can't come up with another 'what if.'

"Okay, so we're stuck with him, but I still don't trust him."

"No one says you have to, Joe. If it makes you feel any better, I don't really trust him either."

Phil calls to us, "Okay, you guys, it's time to get aboard."

We all hurry toward the plane and Phil meets us at the door and climbs in first. I follow next, keeping my head low so as not to bump my head on the ceiling. As we move toward the front of the plane the ceiling gets a little higher but not much.

"I'm glad we don't have to stand up for this trip," Joe says putting his hand on his lower back. "My back's already sore and it's only been a few seconds."

Phil stops at the door to the cockpit and turns. He looks past me and Joe and his expression changes to something that tells me to back away. I start to take a step back but Phil pushes past me and then Joe. I almost lose my balance but catch a rib on the ceiling of the plane with my hand.

"These stay back here!" Phil grabs the two bags of clothes out of Jim's arms and tosses them down into a corner. "I don't need any extra flying debris hitting my head or getting in my way in case of a forced landing."

None of us moves a muscle or says a word. Phil gives each of us a cold look and returns to the door of the cockpit. The first thing I notice as I step into the cockpit is that it, too, is extremely cramped. There are a total of six seats, three on each side. The four back seats are small with no headrests, while the two front seats, which are for the pilot and co-pilot, are larger, softer and have headrests.

"Find yourselves a place to sit and park it," Phil says bluntly, sliding sideways between the front seats.

Joe mouths Phil's words with exaggerated contortions of his face and I find myself struggling to keep from laughing out loud.

Of course, it wouldn't be the first time Joe, or for that matter, a few other people have gotten me in trouble for something I didn't do. Even back in elementary school, I think it was the third grade, this kid standing next to me lofted a snowball into a group of girls and the next thing I know I'm on my way to the principle's office.

Phil sits down in the left hand seat and begins flipping some switches. I hear an engine start up outside but it's not the plane's, it's the tractor.

I sit down in the seat directly behind the co-pilot's seat and Joe sits behind me. I watch Jim as he starts to sit in the seat right behind Phil but quickly changes his mind and sits in the next seat back, across from Joe.

I lean back and whisper to Joe, "I don't blame him."

"I don't, either."

I notice Jim fastening his seat belt. I guess I'd better do the same. I find the two ends and snap them together. It's not spring loaded so I have to adjust it by pulling on the end of the strap.

I hear Joe moving around restlessly behind me.

"What's the matter, Joe?"

"Aren't there any shoulder harnesses?"

"I don't think so."

"Well what if we have to eject? Wouldn't we fall out of our seats if we eject?"

"I don't think these seats eject, Joe."

"Then I want a parachute to put on. Where are they?"

"There aren't any," Phil says without turning around.

"Then what if something goes wrong with the plane?"

"You bend over with your head between your knees and your hands behind your head and I bring it in the best I can. Now if that's not good enough, you can leave right now. Either way I still get paid."

I can tell Joe's about ready to take him up on his offer. My only hope is to head this off by changing the subject. "I thought you said you were doing this as a favor."

"Same difference. Nobody could pay me enough to take you guys anywhere. Just sitting and putting up with your mindless chatter has already gone past the point of what I'm getting paid."

Well, that didn't work. The look on Joe's face says he's just about had enough. I'm going to have to try reason.

"Joe," I say quietly. "We've got to go on this plane. Where else are you gonna go? Out there the cops will eventually find you and it'll probably be the wrong ones, and you'll be dead."

"I'll take my chances."

Uh oh, that didn't work either and that leaves only one alternative. When reason and logic fail you have to hit him where it hurts the most . . . "Oh, I get it. You're scared. Just a big, fat, butterball chicken." . . . his pride.

"I'm not either."

"You are too . . . chicken." I stick my hands under my armpits and flap my arms like a bird.

"I'm not either. I'm . . . I've just never been on a plane before. I'm just anxious, that's all."

Joe puts his seat belt back on that he'd taken off and sits defiantly, stiff backed, with his arms crossed across his chest.

I feel the plane give a slight jerk. The tractor outside throttles up and we begin to move slowly backward toward the pen doors.

My heart begins to pound and I tell myself I'm just anxious,

I'm just anxious. There's no reason to be nervous and I know there's no way I could be scared.

I loosen my stranglehold on the sides of my seat and take some slow deep breaths, and the color returns to my fingertips. Now that I think about it, I've never flown before either. Unless I count that time I was riding a dirt bike through a field and hit a stump. I told Glenn he should have gotten insurance on his bike. I wonder if he ever got insurance on his new one. Probably not, 'cause he never let me ride it.

The plane stops again and the tractor throttles down. Phil is still busy going over his checklist and Joe and Jim are both staring out their windows. The tractor throttles up again and now I can see it with Brother Steve driving. It disappears around the corner of the building and into the blackness of the night. A few seconds later though, he comes trotting back around the building and into the light that is coming through the large open doors.

Suddenly the engine on the right wing, which I'm closest to, stirs to life, followed closely by the other engine on the left wing. I'm sure that if I were outside the noise would be deafening, but the body of the plane seems to be doing a good job of muffling the sound. It's a little reminiscent of the whirring of the three blades on my big mower deck back home.

What I wouldn't give to be mowing my lawn right now, even in the dark. Just to have my life back to normal would be great. I would probably even enjoy doing my dishes. Well . . . maybe not.

There's the sound of a thud in the back, then the door to the cockpit opens and in walks Brother Steve.

"You guys all settled in?"

We all nod our heads and Brother Steve moves past us between all the seats and settles into the co-pilot's seat, pulling his shoulder harness across his chest and fastening it into place.

"Okay, let's go," he says. "Everything's all set." As the engines rev and we begin to taxi out to the runway Brother Steve turns and looks around his seat at me. "Once we're in the air I'm gonna take the controls while Phil shows you where you can stash that thing in your pocket. There's about a fifty-fifty chance that we could be searched by Canadian customs for contraband and they just might consider it smuggling if a two pound cube of gold comes into their country undeclared. Wait just a second now while I get a few things you're going to need."

Brother Steve's head disappears as he faces the front again. I look out the window and the only thing I can see is what is lit up by the flashing lights on the plane and the landing lights lighting up the runway ahead. We pick up speed with the engines roaring at full throttle. I take a quick look back to see how Joe is doing. His eyes are closed tight and he's stiff in the seat, but other than that he's doing all right.

"Hey, Joe," I say. "Isn't this fun?"

"If you say so," he says without opening his eyes.

As we lift into the air in a steep climb I glance over in Jim's direction, surprised by what I see. Jim is just as relaxed as can be, enjoying every moment of it. He's even opened his package of pumpkin seeds and is slowly munching on them.

It almost seems Joe and Jim have switched personalities. But I've seen this same sort of thing happen before, in varying degrees of course, where in times of stress or emergency situations, the person who has a macho type personality will disintegrate into confusion or panic much more readily than a more timid person. It's not something I can explain or even understand, but it is something I have observed.

"Here you go," Brother Steve says handing me a handful of small booklets and plastic cards. "There are your new identities. Each of you gets a passport, a new driver's license, social security number and a credit card. Please memorize your social security number. If you are asked, it will be more convincing if you know it by heart. Oh, and you'll have to stop calling each other by your real names. Get in the habit now of saying and responding to your new ones."

"Who's is who's?"

"That's easy, your passport and driver's license both have your pictures."

"Oh yeah, duh."

I shuffle through the stuff in my hands and pick out the driver's license with my picture on it. The name on it stuns me a little and I just stare at it. It says Benjamin Levitt. I look slowly up at Brother Steve.

"Who picked out the names?"

"Brother Martin, why?"

"Oh . . . uh, no reason. I just wondered why I got this particular name."

"I guess Brother Martin just felt that since we're going to Israel, having a couple Jews on board would help smooth things along and since you and Jim look the part most, he decided to give you the Jewish names. Don't take it personal, okay?"

I smile. "Oh it's okay, I'm not prejudiced against Jews. Are you, Jim?"

He grins. "Nope."

I pull out my passport and my social security card and put all the items in my jacket pocket.

"Okay, Jim, let's see who you are now." I see Jim's license and read his name. "Stephen Goldbloom. Isn't that gonna get confusing if both of you are called Steve?"

"Not really, 'cause my new name is Tony MacIntosh, and you're gonna have to drop the 'brother' in reference to anybody. It doesn't sound Jewish."

"Okay, Bro . . . I mean Tony. Here you go, Jim, uh, Steve." I hand Jim all his stuff and look at the ones that are left. "And the winner of a new identity is . . . Mario Carloni!"

"Mario Carloni? What kind of name is that? Let me see that." I hand Joe the documents and he snatches them out of my hand. Joe stares at them shaking his head. "Geez, it makes me sound like some sort of Mafia Don or something."

I laugh at Joe. "Maybe you can make us a deal we can't refuse."

"Maybe I ought to."

We spend the next couple of hours with our own thoughts. I study my papers and go over everyone's new names in my head. Every so often I look out the window into the darkness below. Through a rare break in the clouds I catch a glimpse of a cluster of lights on the ground. Probably the street lights of a sleepy little Canadian town.

"Okay, I got one!" Joe blurts out, making my heart skip a beat.

I turn around. "Got one what, Joe?"

Steve calls out from the front, "Mario! His name is Mario."

"Oh . . . yeah, Mario. Got one what, Mario?"

"A joke."

"Really?" I say, exaggerating my surprise. "Okay, let's hear it."

"Don't act so surprised. It's gonna be better than any of yours. Now let's see, how'd it start?"

"Don't ask us, it's your joke."

"Shh! Don't mess me up. Oh, yeah. One day Norman and Jane Klegg took their two children, John and Sarah, for an afternoon drive in the country, but suddenly tragedy struck. As they were going through an intersection a milk truck ran the stop sign and all four of them were killed. Their bodies were taken to the local funeral home to be prepared for burial. Now the guy who normally would handle everything was going out of town for a couple days so he had to leave it in the hands of his young apprentice, George. 'Now George' he says, 'I'll be back in a couple days. I hope you can handle it. After all, this is your first time doing it solo.' 'No problem,' George says. 'You've taught me well.' So a couple days later the head mortician returns the day of the funeral and walks into the chapel. He's taken by surprise at what he sees. 'Oh George, George, George. How could you do this?' 'Do what?' George asks. 'What's wrong?' The head mortician just shakes his head. 'Why George, I thought everyone knew that . . . you should never put all your Kleggs in one casket.'"

The joke was pretty good, but there's no way I'm going to let Joe know that. "You call that a joke? Even calling it a joke is a joke."

Of course Joe knows I'm just picking at him. So here comes the challenge. I knew that if he ever took up my dare the contest would be on.

"Okay, then, you make up one and I'll make up one and then we'll ask Jim—Steve to tell us which one is better, okay?"

"Fine with me."

There is silence for a while as Joe and I go into deep thought, trying to come up with something on the punny side.

"How about this?" Joe says breaking the stalemate. "This guy from a zoo went to Africa to collect some new animals. When he got there he met a native who informed him that the regular guide had fallen ill and that he would be his guide. The zookeeper got a little concerned, though, because the regular guide was supposed to supply the cages and he didn't see any. But the new guide told him not to worry because before the regular guide got sick he left the cages on a big rock just over the next hill. Relieved by this news the zookeeper sings out, 'Oh, good. A . . . Rock of cages left for me.' Pretty good, huh?"

"Not bad, but give me a minute and I'll come up with one."

"So what do you think?" Joe asks Jim.

"I liked it okay."

"Just okay? It was better than okay. At least it was better than any of the ones that . . . um . . . Ben-Bob here has come up with so far."

"Quit badgering the judge or you'll be disqualified. Just give me a minute here, I'm working on one right now. Just let me run it through once in my head."

"That shouldn't take long," Joe says. "There's plenty of running room up there."

"Shh, I've almost got it." I pause for a few seconds, making sure my punch-line fits the story. "Okay, I'm ready. A man was walking through the woods one day when he noticed an old sign on the ground. He picked it up and read it. It said, 'Toxic Dump Site, Keep Out.' Immediately he dropped the sign and ran out of there as fast as he could. Which just proves the old saying . . . Waste makes haste."

Jim's laugh is about the same as that for Joe's joke.

"Well?" Joe asks. "Mine was better, wasn't it?"

"They both were pretty good. I'd have to say that . . . it was a tie."

"That guy should be in politics," I hear Phil say up front.

"Come on, Jim," Joe says. "You know mine was better, just admit it."

"Well if you ask me," Phil says dryly, "all of them were pretty stupid and especially annoying."

Joe screws up his face and mimics Phil's words.

I lean back close to Joe and say quietly, "Remind me not to invite Phil to any parties."

I try to think of some more jokes but find myself nodding off every so often. Finally I just give in and lean back in my seat, dozing off into an uncomfortable sleep. Sure wish I had a bed.

Chapter 9

"Okay, this may be a little tricky." Phil's voice wakes me and I find my neck is stuck in a left hand tilt. "But we're gonna need some fuel sooner or later."

I move my head in a circular motion trying to get the stiffness out. I look out the window and in the light of the plane a fairly heavy snow shower seems to be going on.

I toss out a question for anyone to answer. "Where are we?"

"Somewhere over Greenland," Joe answers.

"What happened to Canada?"

"We managed a good tail wind so I estimated the extra fuel savings would get us to this small airfield near the southwest coast of Greenland," comes Phil's answer. "Now let me concentrate. They don't have any fancy equipment here and I'll just be able to see the runway lights."

"Wonderful," Joe mumbles.

I stare out the window toward the ground, straining for a glimpse of the runway lights that are supposed to be down there, as if my being able to see them might in some way help Phil safely land the plane.

"There she is," Phil says rather matter-of-factly.

I still don't see the lights but I guess it doesn't matter just so long as Phil can.

The plane bumps the ground sharply and bounces back into the air. Phil brings it back down again, this time a little smoother, but when Phil touches the brakes we begin to slide a little sideways. Phil quickly lets off the brakes to straighten the plane. When that is finally accomplished he begins pumping the brakes.

"Just as I thought," he says. "It's a bit icy out there."

Finally we slow down to what might be considered a safe speed and after a while we taxi to a stop, but where? The snow seems to be coming down harder and I can't make out anything distinguishable through the snow that at first was going almost straight down, but is now streaking almost horizontally past my window. Gusts of wind begin to shake the plane. I feel like a bug stuck inside a kid's toy.

"Looks like we landed just in time," Steve says.

"Yep, that cross wind would have ripped us out of the sky if we'd come in a minute later," comes the reply from the pilot's seat. "We're all pretty lucky today."

I turn around and look at Joe with a smile. "No such thing as luck, eh Mario?"

"I don't believe in it, do you, Steve?"

Jim answers, "Nope."

Annoyed, Phil shoots back, "Well, it was just dumb luck and you guys aren't going to convince me otherwise. Now, before our 'luck' runs out, let's get this plane tied down and out of this weather." Phil climbs out of his seat, flips a couple toggle switches and moves past us like a man with a mission.

As soon as he disappears through the door Steve gets up and as he walks past, he leaves us with a warning. "You guys better be careful. Phil's known for his short temper."

Steve doesn't wait for any response. I guess he figures we got the message.

I unfasten my seat belt and stand up, as much as I can, anyway, and head for the door. Joe and Jim quickly follow my lead as a strong gust of wind tips one side of the plane a few inches. It also strengthens my resolve to move my feet at a more accelerated pace. In other words, I think it would be a good idea to beat feet out of there.

I hadn't thought about it before, but as I step outside I quickly conclude that my unzipped spring jacket is going to be insufficient protection against the sub-zero gale force winds that in a split second have ripped all the heat in my body away from me.

I zip my jacket up, for all the good that'll do, and look for shelter. Phil is by one of the wheels with a tie-down, wearing a parka he must have had stashed in the plane somewhere.

Joe and Jim huddle up close to me.

"Where to now, guys?" I yell over the sound of the wind.

Joe squints through the snow. "There!" He points and starts running.

Jim and I blindly follow Joe's lead, but it doesn't take long and I can see what caught Joe's attention. Hanging out over the middle of a door is a single light, blurred by the snow swirling around it. I can't let Joe slow me down, so I sprint past him to the door. All I can think about is the warmth waiting for me beyond this gray metal door. With a quick twist of the door knob I give the door a shove. It doesn't move. It must open outward. I tug on the door. It doesn't budge. Joe and Jim arrive each sliding to a stop at the door.

"It's locked!" I yell.

"Bang on it!" Joe yells back.

But he doesn't wait for me, Joe takes his fist and pounds four or five times on the door. We wait. I'm running in place to keep my circulation going.

"Bang on it again J . . . Mario!" I yell again.

Joe pounds on the door again and we wait again.

"Let's get back to the plane!" Joe yells. "We're gonna freeze to death out here!"

Just as we're about to turn and head for the plane Jim reaches between us and pushes a button next to the door.

"This is no time to be ringing the doorbell, Steve!" Joe hollers. "If they didn't hear my pounding, they're certainly not gonna hear a doorbell! Come on!"

Joe grab's Jim's arm to pull him away when the door swings open. Standing in the greenish fluorescent light coming from inside the building is a short stocky man, with disheveled gray hair and reading glasses hanging on the end of his nose. He's motioning for us to come in.

"Come in! Come in! It's much too cold for you to be out in this weather!" He looks the three of us over with a questioning look on his face and adds, "Especially dressed like that!" The door is closed behind us and he continues to talk loudly. "Come, you must be cold!" He turns and we follow him through what looks like an indoor scrap yard.

Joe, being the diplomat that he is, asks, "How come you didn't answer when we banged on your door?"

The old man doesn't respond.

"Good going, Joe . . ." I clasp my hand over my mouth. "I mean Mario, you prob'ly made him mad now."

I tap the man on the shoulder and he turns around. "Mario

didn't mean anything by it, you were probably busy and couldn't hear us. He apologizes, don't you, Mario?"

I jab Joe with my elbow.

"Oh . . . uh . . . yeah, I'm sorry."

The old man just smiles and turns around again. "Come!" he says. "I will explain!"

In the corner of the huge warehouse is a small cement block office with one door, one window looking into the warehouse and one window with a view outside. The windows aren't more than two foot square in size. The old man opens the door and warm air flows from inside.

"Come into my office!"

Joe, who's standing next to him, covers the ear that is just inches from the old man.

Much quieter, the old man apologizes. "Oh I'm sorry, am I too loud again? You see, about ten years ago my hearing started to go. Now I'm practically deaf. I guess it's from all the noise in my metal shop. So, if you wish to talk to me you'll either have to yell or write it down, I don't understand sign language. But I'll give you boys credit for one thing, some people knock on that door for a long time before they finally push that doorbell." He points to a bare red light bulb over a cluttered heavy wooden desk. I would say it could be oak but it's difficult to tell beneath what looks like years of built up grease and dirt. "Yessir, you push that button an' this light flashes, otherwise you could stand out there forever an' I'd never hear you."

Jim's looking mighty proud of himself, thinking he's saved our lives. I jab him in the side with my elbow. "Wipe that smirk off your face. You just accidentally found that doorbell."

"Clear off a chair boys an' make yourselves comfy. Care for some coffee to warm your innards?"

I'm not a coffee drinker so I shake my head, however Joe and Jim both nod their heads.

"Excellent."

The old man goes to his desk where sitting at one end is an old instant coffee maker. Until he had mentioned it I hadn't even noticed that there were chairs in the room and when he said "clear off a chair," he really meant "clear off a chair."

I start clearing off a gray padded metal chair but I'm not exactly sure its original color was gray. After moving a couple boxes full of papers and manila folders, I wipe my fingers across the seat to make sure it's clean enough to sit on. Must be the boxes kept the dust off because my fingers come up fairly clean.

"Hey, Mario," I say. "This place must really make you homesick."

The office seems to be the only heated area in the building and that heat is supplied by a small electric space heater sitting atop a four drawer filing cabinet.

Joe holds up a fist. "I'll make you sick and it won't be for home. How does intensive care sound?"

"You use that tired old line all the time. When are you gonna come up with something new and original?"

"Maybe when you come up with some new and original insults."

"That was new and original, this is the first time I've ever been in a place that even came close to looking like your place."

"Well I admit that my house isn't as neat and orderly as yours, but I'm not obsessed with cleaning like you."

"I'm not obsessed, I just like to be organized."

The old man turns around with two coffee mugs in his hands. I can see the steam rise out of them and disappear several inches above the cup.

"I hope you boys like it black," he says handing one to Jim. "Won't get anymore sugar or cream in 'till day after tomorrow."

He hands the other cup to Joe and then stands with his hands on his hips looking at each of us in turn, taking his time with each. We look at each other and just shrug our shoulders.

"You guys see a pencil and paper anywhere?" I ask. "Maybe I can ask him if there's something wrong."

We all scan the room, but before we're successful in our search, the old man breaks his silence.

"May I ask you boys a question?"

We all nod our heads.

"Are any of you Christians?"

Not really knowing where he's coming from with his question, I hesitate a moment before I slowly nod my head. I didn't see them, but Joe and Jim must have done the same, at least judging by the old man's reaction.

"Really? All three of you?" A big grin spreads across his face and his whole countenance lights up. "Wait just a moment," he says excitedly.

He goes to his middle desk drawer and opens it. His body is blocking my view so I can't see what he's getting out of it. Either this guy likes Christians and is going to give us something or he hates Christians and he's getting ready to let us have it. I cringe a little as he turns.

"There," he says putting the ear plug of his hearing aid in his left ear. "Now I can at least hear out of this one ear." He taps on the hearing aid with his finger. "I only wear this thing when there's someone around I wish to talk to or when I listen to the radio for weather or news. Hearing aid batteries are a might scarce in this neck of the woods."

He shoves some stuff on his desk toward the back and sits on the spot he's just cleared. "So you boys are Christians eh? Don't run into many in these parts. Of course I don't run into many people period, and the ones I do aren't exactly what you'd call people of high moral standards. You boys been Christians long? I'm going on forty-one years come February. How 'bout you?"

He looks directly at Joe.

"Uh . . . three years."

"Ah, just a babe, and you?" He looks at Jim. Jim holds up two fingers.

"I've got my hearing aid in son, you can go ahead an' talk to me. Now is it two days, two weeks, two months, or two years? You're too young for it to be two decades."

"Years."

"You won't get much more of an answer than that," I say. "He's not much of a talker."

"So we got two baby Christians here. Are you number three?"

"It depends. Do you consider ten years as being new?"

"Nope, not new, but you may or may not have grown up during those ten years."

"Well, I hope I have."

"Oh, by the way, I've been awfully rude. My name's Clifton Hawley, but you can call me Clif. What's you boys' names?"

I volunteer to do the introductions.

"The tall one over there, he's Steve . . ." Suddenly I can't think of Jim's new last name. To cover, I go on to Joe and go only with first name introductions. ". . . and this is Mario . . ." I can feel my face going flush. I try to calm down to get my face back to normal. ". . . and I'm Ben."

"You boys got last names? You can tell a lot about a person by their family names. There's a lot of family history in your names if you bother to look. Like for instance my Great Grandfather Hawley was a Baptist preacher and my Great Grandfather Cook on my mother's side, he was what you would call a pack rat. He made his living by taking things that other people threw out, fixing them, and reselling them. So as you can see, I picked up some traits from both of them; I'm Baptist and I fix things. So let's have your last names."

"Mine's Levitt."

"Mine's Goldbloom."

Joe still doesn't like his new name so he hesitates to give it.

"Come on son. Uh . . . Mario was it? Your name is nothing to be ashamed of unless you've done something to make it that way."

"Carloni," Joe says grudgingly with his eyes to the floor clutching his coffee cup in both hands.

"Ah, two Jewish Christians and a Gentile Christian." Clif looks at Jim and I. "Were either of you practicing Jews at the time of your conversion?"

We shake our heads.

"How about you, Mario? I gather by the name that you are very much Italian and therefore my guess is you were born into Roman Catholicism."

Joe begins to loosen up a little, feeling less threatened by Clif's friendliness.

"Yeah, I was born a Catholic but my family really didn't practice it much. You know, the usual. We'd go to mass three or four times a year, mostly for Christmas and Easter. Then of course there was baptisms and confirmations, weddings and funerals. Other than that we rarely saw the inside of a church."

"Then you were one of the fortunate ones to have the true understanding of God's salvation in some way presented to you."

"Yep."

"I must say, it is refreshing to have you three here. Normally about all that comes through here are a bit on the seedy side, and if what comes through here is any indication of what the rest of the world is like, then I expect the Lord to return any day now."

There's a rush of cold air as Phil and Steve enter the room.

"Whew! It's cold as hell out there," Phil says taking his gloves off and wringing his hands together.

Joe and I look at each other and smile. We're both thinking the same thing. If it were "cold as hell" outside, it wouldn't be snowing or even raining for that matter.

Phil unzips his parka. "You got any more of that go juice?"

"Sure do. Help yourself. There's some cups on that shelf over there." Clif points to a small shelf on the wall near the door. "Now where were we?" Clif turns his attention back to us. "Oh yeah, we were discussing the soon return of the Lord. Are you boys pre-trib, mid-trib, or post-trib?"

"I'm pre-trib and I think Mario and Steve are, too. Aren't you?" I double-check to make sure. I know I've discussed it with Joe before but I'm not too sure about where Jim stands on the subject.

They both nod.

"Good, me too."

"What's all this trib stuff?"

I get the feeling that Phil hates not being in on or understanding what's going on based on the edge to his voice.

Clif replies to Phil's question. "It's short for tribulation, and the pre, mid, and post is when the rapture would come during the tribulation period. We believe the rapture will happen before the tribulation."

"Oh, well that makes it all clear as mud. So now tell me what the hell a tribulation and a rapture is."

"Basically, you're close. The tribulation period is a time of judgment upon the earth when you will think you are in hell, however you're not even close with the rapture. That's where all the saved people are changed, physically, in an instant and meet Jesus in the sky."

Phil laughs mockingly. "And you really believe this stuff? I mean, come on. Do you really expect me to believe that some dude who's been dead for two thousand years is going to come flying through the air, change a bunch of people into supermen who just fly through the air to be with him? That's all quite a stretch of the imagination, don't you think?"

Clif calmly looks Phil in the eye. "Not at all. I have absolutely no problem believing that there is nothing that God cannot do. How anyone could put limits on a limitless God who spoke the universe into existence is beyond me. I find it more difficult to believe we came from monkeys."

"Well, I just think the Bible is only a fascinating collection of fictional stories put together by men who are trying to justify their own existence and position of power, bilking millions of people out of their hard-earned money by promising something better in the hereafter, or good health and wealth in the here and now."

"You sound bitter. I'll bet you had a rough life, but you shouldn't take it out on God. It is the sins of others and the consequences of your own sins that lead to your problems."

"Well then let me ask you this. If your God is such a loving God, then why doesn't he just fix it so there's no more hunger or suffering or death? I mean, if he's so almighty powerful and loving, why doesn't he just fix it?"

"He has."

"What do you mean, he has?"

"Two thousand years ago God came down in the form of a man, Jesus Christ, and died on a cross to pay for the sins of the whole world, past, present, and future. Then he rose again, conquering death so that anyone who believes that Jesus is the Christ the son of God and that God has raised him from the dead, he will be saved. That means that after your body dies, your spirit, your soul will be free from hunger, suffering and death for all eternity in a new, perfect body."

"Well, maybe I'd believe it if he did all that here and now. Show me a miracle and then I'll believe, but not any of those fake faith healing things you see on TV, you know, part the Red Sea or something like that, then I'll believe."

Clif shakes his head slowly. "I'm afraid that when something like that happens, it will be too late."

"Well, it's not going to happen so I'm not even going to worry about it." Phil puts his coffee cup down on the desk next to Clif. "Thanks for the coffee. I better go check on the plane. If this squall has almost passed, I can refuel and we can be out of here in half an hour."

I shudder from the cold air rushing in as Phil makes his exit. Steve is staring down into his coffee mug.

"How'd you meet this guy, Steve? I mean, Tony." I've slipped again and this time it's too obvious for me to cover up.

Steve tries to turn attention away from the slip by pretending it never happened. "I really don't know him that well, like I told a mutual friend of ours. I met him through somebody I know in Flint."

I glance sideways out of the corner of my eyes to see Clif's reaction. He's got a look of suspicion on his face as his eyes dart back and forth between Steve and I.

"All right," he finally says. "You don't have to tell me your real names. That's your business, but the names you gave me really aren't yours, are they?"

The four of us look at each other. Finally, I shrug my shoulders, and shake my head.

"Is everything else you've told me a lie also?"

I've been called a liar only a few times in my life and most of them were false accusations. Even before I became a Christian I prided myself on being able to tell the truth, even if it got me into a little hot water. I always found it more advantageous to have people believe everything I say rather than being able to fool a few people once in a while and then, when it really matters, having no one believe you. It's a lesson I learned from the story *The Boy Who Cried Wolf*. It simply made sense to me. So naturally I emphatically say, "No! Everything except our names have been the truth." Suddenly a thought comes to me. "And actually, for me, even the name that I told you is my actual name. It's the name I had before I was adopted."

"Ahem." Steve clears his throat . . . loudly. "I think you've probably already said more than you should have, Ben. How do you know you can trust this guy?"

"I'm surprised at you, Steve." I purposely use his real name to prove that I do trust Clif. "You, of all people, should be the first to trust another Christian, even with your life."

"How do you know he's a true Christian, though?"

"I just use the Biblical test."

"And what is that?"

"Well first there's their fruits. The Bible says you will know them by their fruits. Does Clif display the fruits of the Spirit? I've only known him a short while and he's already displayed several.

Now the other is the Bible says that no one can call Jesus Lord but by the Spirit of the Lord. I'm paraphrasing, but that's basically what it says and I distinctly remember him calling Jesus 'Lord.' But there was also one other thing I noticed. Clif is the one who steered the conversation into a religious direction. An unsaved person would have evaded the subject at almost any cost."

I look at Clif and he's got a big smile on his face and is slowly nodding his head.

"That's very perceptive of you. How long did you say you've been saved?"

"Ten years."

"I must congratulate you, then. You certainly haven't been wasting those ten years. You've obviously done some Bible study. Do you teach?"

"Yeah, senior high Sunday school . . . well at least I used to."

"Why don't you any more?"

"That's . . ."

Steve interrupts, believing I may give out too much information. "Bob?"

"Don't worry, Steve, he's not a threat to us or anybody else, except for maybe Satan. Besides, I thought my name was Benjamin."

"It is. What'd I say?"

"Bob."

"I guess I was thinking about a guy named Bob and it just slipped out."

"Come on, Steve, let's not play games with Clif. In a little while we'll be out of here and about the only thing Clif will be able to do is pray for us. So I say we come clean."

"Okay," Steve says grudgingly. "It's your necks."

What would normally have taken me five minutes to tell, ends up taking me twenty minutes. It seems that after every two sentences, Joe would jump in to add a few extra details he's afraid I would forget.

"Well," Clif says, letting out a sigh, "it seems you boys are really in a fix, but tell me, why didn't you go to another government agency. Like the state police or the F.B.I.?"

"Yeah," Joe says. "Maybe we can still do that."

"That wouldn't be a good idea," Steve says rather matter-of-factly.

"And why not?"

"Because . . . well we didn't want to worry you guys but . . ."

"But what?"

"We, meaning Dr. Martin and I, came across some information that that detective is only the tip of the iceberg and that he's acting on orders from higher up."

"And what's that supposed to mean?" Joe asks.

"It means that there is a very powerful organization out there that wants that little item Bob's been carrying around really bad."

"You mean like the Mafia?" Jim asks.

I poke Joe in his side. "Yeah, maybe it's your cousins."

"I hardly think so, and don't do that," Joe says referring to the poke in his side.

"Now don't go jumping to any conclusions, you guys," Steve says seriously. "I can't tell you for sure who or what they are, but I'm sure we'll find out soon enough."

"Why do you say that?" I ask wrinkling my forehead into a quizzical look. "If the police are having trouble tracking us down, how is anybody else going to find us?"

"In case you haven't figured it out yet, they are part of the police and not just the local department in Lansing. They're also in the F.B.I. and the C.I.A. and even Interpol. They even have more people as CEO's of companies than any organization on earth."

Joe and I look at each other, then Joe looks at Steve suspiciously. "How do you know all this? If you have this much information about the organization, then I would think you'd know the name of it too, wouldn't you?"

"Well uh, actually all this information was given to me by Dr. Martin and he didn't tell me where he got it and he said he didn't know the name of the organization but that he'd keep digging 'till he did."

Clif slides off the desk, picking up a coffee cup. "You boys definitely need praying for. Take heart, though. The Bible says, 'All things work for good to them that believe.' And just do what I do when it seems you're at a dead end or don't know what to do next. You simply pause, look to heaven and say, 'Jesus is Lord.' I always find that this clears my mind of all my fears and doubts and allows the Holy Spirit to work through me to solve the problem." Clif goes to the coffee pot.

"Jesus is Lord," Joe says reflectively. "I like that. I'm gonna have to try that sometime."

"We'll probably all be saying it a lot before this is over." I finish my statement just as the door swings open and Phil reenters the room.

"The wind and snow is letting up. We'll be able to leave this God forsaken place in about ten minutes. Be on board the plane and in your seats in about five."

With that said, Phil turns back out the door pulling it closed behind him with a bit more force than would normally be necessary.

Steve puts his coffee cup down on the desk where Clif was sitting. "I'd better go see if Phil needs any help getting things around. I'll see you guys in five minutes."

Clif extends his hand. "It was nice meeting you, Steve. I pray that things go well for you."

Steve seems taken aback for an instant by Clif's outstretched hand. Steve does, however, extend his hand and Clif gives it a hearty shake.

"Uh, yes, it was good meeting you, too."

They let go their hands and for an instant Steve just stands there staring Clif in the face with a blank expression on his own. Then Steve quickly turns and hurries out the door.

Clif walks slowly over to his desk, pushes Steve's coffee cup to one side and sits back down on the same spot.

"Your friend . . ." he says looking more at me than at the others, and pausing to think. "Your friend, Bob, seems to be disturbed about something."

"Yeah, I kind of noticed that myself. What do you think it is?"

"I think he knows more than he's telling you."

"He might. I've got a letter that I'm not supposed to open until we get to Israel. He might know what's in it."

"That sounds probable. But just the same, you boys be careful with Phil around. He has a bad spirit and I'm not sure he can be trusted."

"We already figured that one out," Joe says with a smile.

I stand up and put my hands behind my head and give my torso a twist, feeling a number of vertebrae pop in succession up my back.

"We better get going before Phil comes ranting and raving for us. It's been real good meeting you, Clif."

I reach out to shake Clif's hand. He grabs hold of it with both hands and pulls me to him, giving me a big bear hug. Putting his hands on each of my shoulders he holds me at arms length.

"May God bless you and your goings."

"Thank you, Clif."

Clif lets me go and proceeds to hug Joe and Jim also.

With our goodbyes said, the three of us make our way back through the indoor junkyard and out the door toward the plane. There's still a light snow in the air but the previous gale force winds have been reduced to the point where it is barely noticeable. Steve is on a step ladder brushing snow off the plane's windows and Phil is in the process of returning the fuel hose to its proper place on a fuel truck.

Phil passes us as he heads back to the building. "You guys go ahead and get on the plane while I go pay Clif and get a receipt."

I feel the cold wetness of the new fallen snow as some of it melts on the nylon uppers of my running shoes. I know now that my feet probably won't get warm again for the rest of the day.

Joe nudges me and looks behind us to see where Phil is before he speaks. "You better check to see if the cube is still safely tucked away."

"Good idea."

The thought of getting to Israel and finding the cube gone causes me to pick up my walking pace.

In the plane it's warmer but not much. At least I'm out of the cold breeze. I go to the fire extinguisher and twist off the top. I look inside and still safe inside is the cube.

"You're more trouble than you're worth. I oughta just toss you out over the ocean and forget you ever existed."

"He's talking to fire extinguishers now, Jim."

I look up at Joe who's laughing. I stick the top back on the fire extinguisher. "It's more interesting than talking to you." I hang the extinguisher on it's hook and go to the front of the plane. Settling back into my seat, I look out the window. The sky is beginning to turn a light gray in the direction that I assume is where the sun is coming up.

"So what do you think, Bob?" Joe says as he pokes his head

through the door and plops into his seat with a grunt. "Should we use our real names or should we continue to lie and use our aliases?"

"First of all, you guys would be the ones bearing false witness, not me. My name really is Benjamin Levitt. So I can go by either name and not be telling a lie, but I was wondering about that earlier and I thought maybe we could pass it off as hyphenated nicknames. You know, like Jim-Steve, or Mario-Joe, or Ben-Bob."

"Yeah," Joe says. "That'll work 'cause your name is Robert but we've always called you Bob as a nickname, so it is your name and yet it isn't."

"I don't get it," a bewildered Jim says.

Joe turns in his seat toward Jim and with his elbows on his knees, he begins to explain. "Okay, what is your name?"

"Jim."

"Okay, now what is your name on your birth certificate?"

"James Harold Kemplar."

"Harold?" Joe laughs.

"It's my uncle's name."

"Okay, okay, um, so James is your name on your birth certificate, right?"

"Yeah."

"So then did you lie when I asked you what your name was and you said Jim?"

"No."

"Did you lie when you said your name was James?"

"Nooo . . . Oh, I get it now. Your name is whatever people call you and you answer to."

"By Joe, I think he's got it." I say.

I hear what sounds like a truck approaching and look out my window. A large dump truck with a snow blade on the front stops next to the plane. The person inside rolls down the window as Phil steps up on the running board. After nodding his head a couple of times Phil jumps back down so I can see who's in the truck. It's Clif.

"You know what, guys?" I say still watching Clif as he rolls up his window and takes off, throwing a plume of snow high into the air. "I think Clif is the only one here running this whole airport."

"Yeah," Joe says. "I kinda noticed that when I never saw anyone else and Phil was using the self-serve gas truck."

Phil glides past us, and putting on his headset and sitting down at the same time, he begins flipping switches and checking gauges.

"We'll be outa here in about five minutes." Phil seems to be hurrying through his checklist. "Maybe less if I can help it. I just hope that old man can clear that runway as fast as he says he can."

"Why?" Joe asks.

"That squall we just had was the leading edge of a large storm system. If we don't get out of here in the next ten minutes we'll be stuck here for another three or four days with that crazy old man."

Steve comes through the doorway closing the door behind him. "The wings didn't have much ice on them, just near the engines where it was warm enough to melt some snow. I sprayed some de-icer on it anyway, just in case."

"Good man," Phil says handing Steve his headset. "The old man only needs to make another pass out and back and we'll be set to go."

I look down at my feet and wiggle my numbing toes inside my wet shoes and socks. I might be better off to take my shoes and socks off. Maybe there's a dry pair of socks in our clothes bags. I unbuckle my seat belt and get up to open the door when Phil snaps at me.

"Where do you think you're going?"

I freeze. "I was . . ."

"It doesn't matter anyway 'cause you don't have time to do anything so just set your butt back down in that seat!"

I look at Jim who just shrugs his shoulders. I figure my toes will survive, which I might not if I get Phil any madder so, reluctantly, I drop back into my seat and buckle up again.

Phil starts each of the engines in turn, the blades causing a snowstorm of their own behind them. Out the front window I can see the lights from Clif's snowplow heading our way, the snow being flung high into the air and off to the side.

Joe notices too. "Clif must be going pretty fast. You see that snow fly?"

"Yeah," I say. "The way he's moving you'd think he was a county employee with a mailbox in his sights."

Only seconds pass and Clif whips past the front of the plane, backs up once and clears off a little mound of snow from the plane's path. Then with a sound of his horn, which now is barely audible above the noise of the engines, Clif drives away.

I feel a little sadness knowing this is the last time I'll see Clif. For as short a time as I spent with him I felt very comfortable with him, and I guess I'll always consider him a friend. Maybe I can get his address and write to him when this is all over and let him know how it turned out.

The plane begins to move and Joe goes into his white-knuckled takeoff posture.

"I hate this," he says with his teeth clenched.

"Relax, Joe," I say. "We'll be in the air in a few minutes and it'll be all over."

"That's what I'm afraid of."

Phil talks loudly over his shoulder. "You guys are gonna have to be quiet back there. I'm going to need a lot of concentration on this takeoff. There could be some slick spots and I'd hate to lose control before we get off the ground."

Joe leans forward so only I can hear him. "Better before than after we get off the ground."

"Good thinking, Joe. You want me to suggest that to Phil?"

"Maybe later. I think he's busy right now."

Phil guns the engines to about half throttle and Joe pushes himself against the back of his seat, his eyes closed tight.

Joe's not going to be much of a conversationalist for the next few minutes, so I might as well watch the scenery go by, that is, what I can see of it.

It's still rather dark outside but I'm beginning to make out the dark outlines of some of the larger objects, such as buildings and trucks.

The plane skids a little on a patch of ice then jerks as it makes good contact with the pavement again.

"Yep," Phil says. "It's gonna be a little tricky all right."

I say a short prayer to myself and then leave it all in God's hands.

Phil revs the engines to full power and we begin picking up speed until first the nose rises off the ground and then, at a steep angle, we ascend toward the gray-blue sky.

After cruising along in silence for a while, I lean forward and tap Steve on the shoulder. He takes his headphones off and looks around the back of his seat.

"Yes?"

"I was just wondering where our next stop would be."

"A small airfield in the north of France."

"France, wow, that means after that we oughta be able to make it the rest of the way to Israel."

"Uh . . . not really. We'll be leaving Phil and this plane in France. We're gonna have to take a commercial flight into Israel. Well not me, just you three. I get to go back home and see if I'm under arrest for helping fugitives escape."

"Well, I hope not. I'd hate to see anybody else get hurt because of us."

"Thanks for your concern Bob, but I think I'll be okay."

"I hope you're right."

Joe taps me on my shoulder. "Ask him if we'll be able to find out if everyone's all right back home when we land. I'd make the phone call real short."

"You're worried about Mi-Ling aren't you?"

"Yeah, she went in the house just before the police arrived."

"I know how you feel, Joe. I'm wondering about Floyd and Millie myself. What do you think, Steve? Would it be all right to check on them?"

"I'd like to say yes, but I can't. Long distance calls are too easily traced, and I'm not convinced that that Detective Taylor wouldn't go halfway around the world to catch you guys."

"Yeah, you're probably right. Maybe we could send a postcard instead," Joe says half jokingly, disappointed that he won't get to talk to Mi-Ling.

We catch up on plenty of sleep the rest of the way to France. Even Phil is able to take a break once as Steve takes over the controls.

Chapter 10

I think it must have been the change in the sound of the engines, or more likely a change in air pressure, but whichever it was I wake up to find us descending through a cloud bank. When we come out I can see a couple small villages down below with their red tile roofs, but what is really striking is the golden color reflecting off the straw stubble in the many wheat fields that spread across the landscape. I wonder how much prettier it must have been before the wheat was harvested. The land itself looks fairly flat but seems to drop off in the distance like a huge plateau.

I tap Steve on his shoulder. "Is this France?"

"Sure is, and we'll be landing real soon."

Phil turns his head for just a second. "You three have your papers ready, there'll probably be customs agents waiting for us. It's a rural landing strip but they know we're coming."

Phil wasn't kidding when he said it was rural. We land in an open field where there aren't even any markings for a landing strip. They must ruin a lot of wheat during the growing season. We bump along on the washboard surface and I'm glad I don't have a headache.

"Oh, my head," Joe groans, his voice vibrating with each bump. "This is not helping my headache."

We finally come to rest about fifty yards from a group of three cars and a small panel truck.

Phil gets out of his seat the instant he kills the engines and before we can even begin to unbuckle our seat belts.

"You guys sit tight for the time being. Just hand me your papers and I'll see if I can't get you okayed."

Phil snatches up each of our papers and heads out the door. Outside about six men have gathered in a group by the panel truck.

Half look like they're wearing business suits while the other three look like they're dressed to do some work, each in their blue coveralls.

Phil walks past the plane carrying the large box he had put on board before we left Michigan. I can see our papers sitting atop the box.

As Phil approaches the cars one of the men in a business suit signals to the guys in their coveralls, and one of them runs to Phil and takes the box from him. Phil keeps our papers and goes to the well-dressed men where they hold a conversation. Meanwhile, the worker takes the box to the truck, where one of the other guys has opened the back, and puts the box inside. They quickly close the doors, with one of them still in the back, and the other two jump in the front and they drive off.

For a while everyone's eyes are on the truck as it pulls onto a dirt road and disappears over a hill, leaving behind it a trail of dust that slowly makes its way into a neighboring field, carried by a slight breeze.

Phil and the other men continue to talk. One of the men holds out a large manila envelope for Phil, but he pushes it back. Motioning toward the plane, Phil then hands the man with the envelope our papers.

"This looks like a good time to start praying," Joe says. "We're either home free or dead meat."

I take Joe's advice and say a quick, silent prayer, all the time keeping my eyes on the activities outside.

The man with our papers opens them, glancing in our direction every so often. Finally he hands them to one of the other men who takes them to the larger of the three cars, setting them on the trunk. Getting a briefcase out of the back seat, he pulls out what appears to be a rubber stamp. He presses it on several of our papers and brings them back to Phil.

Then, as quickly as the men in the truck, two of them get into the larger car and one in one of the other cars and they each in turn back around to face the other way, then speed out of the field and down the road, creating another cloud of dust.

Phil is left standing alone by the one remaining car. Probably the smallest of the three, it is also the only one that wasn't black.

I never liked green cars much, but not just because of the color but because I've had two green cars in my lifetime and both of them were lemons. I think that's how superstitions get started. Somebody thousands of years ago had a bunch of bad things happen to him on a Friday the thirteenth, it might have even been Job, and so he tells his kids what happened on that day and they in turn tell their kids, who tell their friends and they all tell their kids, until it's spread all over the world that bad things happen on Friday the thirteenth.

Now I'm not a superstitious person, and a Christian shouldn't be, but to this day I've avoided buying a green car.

Phil points at the plane with one finger then makes a motion to come to him. All of us start to get out of our seats but Steve stops us. "He just wants me, so you guys sit tight for just a little longer. I do think, though, that we're in the clear."

Joe watches to make sure Steve's out of the plane. "Maybe you oughta check the cube again, Bob, just to be sure."

"Good idea. Keep watch for me and let me know if they're coming back."

I get out of my seat, staying low. I don't want Phil to see me 'cause I don't want him to think we don't trust him. Even if we don't.

I take the top off the fire extinguisher and peer inside. Yep, still there. I put the top back on and go back up front.

I look outside in time to see Phil and Steve having a heated discussion that is reminiscent of the one last night at Phil's house. Finally Steve kicks the ground, sending some loose dirt and straw into the air, and begins walking disgustedly back toward the plane.

"I wonder what's wrong now," Joe says.

"I don't know," I reply, "but it looks rather ominous."

"Ominous? Ominous? Where do you get those words? Nobody says ominous. Unless they're trying to impress someone."

"I'm not trying to impress anyone, Joe. I couldn't think of any other word and that one popped into my head and it seemed to fit the situation. If I wanted to impress you I wouldn't use such a small word like ominous. I'd use words like, incongruous, or extraneous, or extraterritoriality, or supercalifragilisticexpealidocious."

"I know that one!" Jim says excitedly.

Joe and I laugh but the good times are cut short by a fuming Steve.

"All right you guys, get your stuff and let's go," he growls.

I figure I should be the one to ask so I do. "What's wrong, Steve?"

"Oh nothing. Just the same as before, sort of. Phil's taking the plane on a couple errands here in France and then he's gonna lay-over in Rome for a few days so if I want to get back home, I'm gonna have to take a commercial flight. So that means I have the honor of escorting you to Paris."

Joe's face brightens. "Does that mean we get to ditch our buddy Phil for the rest of our lives? I hope."

"Seems that way. Only not until he's given us directions to the airport. In the meantime," Steve looks directly at Joe, "don't say or do anything to aggravate him or he could have us going to Spain."

"Don't worry about me, my lips are zipped."

"Okay, then, since that's understood, let's get our stuff and get out of here."

While I'm waiting for everyone else to file through the narrow door I look out the window. Phil is hunched over the hood of that ugly green car writing on a piece of paper.

"Looks like Phil's anxious to get rid of us too, Joe. He's gonna have those directions written down before we get out of the plane."

"Suits me just fine."

"Careful, Joe. The Bible says to love your enemies, and forgive those who do you wrong."

"I will, I will, but not just yet. Maybe in a couple days I'll be in a more loving and forgiving mood. Right now, though, I just want to hate! Hate! HATE!" Joe laughs. "I live to hate."

Steve turns and shakes his head. "There is definitely some-thing wrong with your friend, Bob."

"Yeah, we know, but we put up with Jim anyway."

"No I mean . . . Never mind, you're all nuts."

I get the fire extinguisher down one more time, twist the top off and dump the cube out into the crook of my arm. Everybody else is outside by the time I hang the extinguisher back on the wall. Joe is the only one I can see outside the door and he's surveying his surroundings. I stick the cube in my jacket pocket and poke my head out the door.

"It's pretty country in this part of France," Joe says, still look-ing around. "I always thought it would be rather crowded and dirty with very tiny fields, but this is almost like back in America."

Jim and Steve are already on their way to the car, but Joe seems satisfied to just look around.

I jump out of the plane. "Come on, Joe. Now is not the time to be sight-seeing."

"Yeah, okay, but I think I'd rather just go over and sit under that big tree there for about a week."

"I know what you mean Joe. I know what you mean."

We meet Phil about halfway. As he passes by he says without stopping, "Good luck, you guys. You're gonna need it."

I take a quick look back at Phil climbing into the plane. "Now I wonder what he meant by that?"

"I don't know, but couldn't I just flatten him and then ask God to forgive me?"

"Nah, he's not worth the effort. We'll just let God handle our light work."

"I'd still like to flatten him."

When we get to the car, Steve hands our papers back to us. "Okay, these are all stamped by customs so we're all set until we get to the airport."

Joe looks at the papers in his hand. "How'd Phil manage this? Did he bribe them or something?"

"Don't even ask. I don't think you want to know."

"So what are we gonna do when we get to the airport? Phil isn't going to be there to get us through . . . or is he?"

"No, but don't worry, we'll blow up that bridge when we come to it."

"You mean cross that bridge when we come to it."

"Yeah . . . whatever. I'm just in the mood to blow something up."

"I know what you mean," Joe says.

We put our stuff in the trunk and I sit up front with Steve, who elects himself to drive. We head off down the dusty road in the same direction the other vehicles disappeared.

It seems the field we landed in was one of the larger ones, although the ones we are passing are still bigger than what I expected. A lot of the machinery I see is also quite modern, but I don't seem to see any of the huge four wheel drive tractors that abound on the farms back in the states. I guess I just expected to see the old horse drawn carts filled with produce moving slowly down a tree lined road, driven by an elderly man dressed in ragged clothes. I suppose there are still some of those around and that's what people take snapshots of to bring home and that's probably what perpetuates the stereotypes of France.

It makes me wonder. Since Disney World and Disney Land are the most visited spots for foreigners in the U.S., do they think all Americans look like Mickey, Donald, and Goofy?

As we approach Paris, I notice we are doing a lot of downhill driving and on the sides of the hills there are an increasing number of vineyards.

Jim taps my shoulder. "Are we going to stop somewhere soon? I'm hungry," he whispers.

"I don't know. Let me ask." I turn to the front. "Steve?"

"Yes?"

"It's been quite a while since we've eaten, are there any plans to stop for something to eat?"

"I hadn't thought about it, but now that you mention it I'm kinda hungry myself. Keep an eye out for someplace to eat and we'll stop at the first decent looking place we come to."

It's not until we get well inside Paris that we finally spot something that we know is a restaurant. Of course we probably passed quite a few, but since none of us can read French, we'll have to settle for the golden arches.

"I know what I'm gonna have," I say. "French Fries."

There's nothing like fine French cuisine and I can honestly say that what I'm going to eat is nothing like it. However, after not having had anything to eat after more than twelve hours it's going to be a feast indeed. I order a quarter pounder with cheese, a large order of fries, a large drink, and a chocolate shake. On the other hand, there's Jim. I think he ordered five cheeseburgers and who knows what else. We're going to have to have a separate table just for his empty wrappers.

"Now," Steve says. "Who's paying for all this? I'm willing to pay for mine but I'd have to re-mortgage my house to cover that pile over there," he says pointing to the stack of food on Jim's tray.

"I don't have any money," Joe says.

Jim shrugs his shoulders. "I don't either. Bob has, though."

"Thanks, Jim, but I already figured I'd be stuck paying for the three of us this whole trip." I reach into my back pocket and pull out the wad of folded bills. The envelope that Brother Martin gave me falls out onto the floor and Steve notices it before I can pick it off the floor.

"What's that?"

"Oh, nothing. It's a letter Brother Martin gave me before we left." I stick it back in my pocket.

"Oh yeah? What'd he say?"

"I don't know, I haven't opened it yet."

"Why not?"

"'Cause he told me not to."

"How come?"

"I don't know. I just know I'm not supposed to open it 'till we get to Israel." I hand the cashier a couple of twenties and the cashier gives me a slightly annoyed look as she calculates the exchange rate. I shrug my shoulders apologetically. "So I'm not."

"I don't know what difference it makes."

"I don't either," Joe butts in. "I vote we open it now."

"It's not up for a vote, you guys." The cashier hands me my change in European currency. "So let's just get our food and eat. I'm starving."

"I'll vote for that," Jim mumbles, picking up his tray and heading for a table. He already has several fries hanging halfway out of his mouth.

I look at the new European currency in my hand. I've never seen any but I've read quite a bit about it. The new European currency is the latest major step in the effort to unite the European community economically, eliminating the individual currencies of the member nations.

Most of us are done eating except for Jim, who's working on his second shake. Steve looks at his watch and a sudden look of alarm spreads across his face.

"Oh Lord, we gotta get going!"

"Why?" I ask. "What's the hurry?"

"Don't you remember? You've got a plane to catch. We've gotta be at the airport in forty-five minutes or you will not make your plane in time."

"You heard him, Jim, bring your shake with you and let's go."

We all get up hurriedly and leave our mess on the tables. When we get outside there's a gendarme at the car writing out what looks like a parking ticket. His bicycle is propped against a pole nearby.

"Uh oh," I hear Jim say.

Steve pushes back on my chest. "You guys wait in the doorway out of sight. I'll see if I can't get rid of him or at least move him along a little faster."

The three of us step back into the doorway as Steve walks over to the car. I peek slowly around the corner and Steve is showing the officer his wallet. The officer gives Steve a suspicious look, so Steve puts his wallet back in his pocket and motions with his index finger for the officer to follow him around to the back of the car. Steve points downward in the general area of the license plate and the officer stares at it for a moment, then at Steve and then back at the license plate. Finally the gendarme closes his ticket book, puts it in his pocket, gets on his bike and rides off down the street past us, his eyes darting for just an instant in our direction and then back on the road ahead. He did not look very happy.

We walk slowly out from the doorway onto the sidewalk.

Steve hollers at us, "Come on you guys! Let's move it!"

"Race you guys there," I say as I break into a sprint for the sixty feet to the car.

Jim takes me up on it, but from behind Joe lets us know he's not up to it. "You guys go ahead, I'll just waddle in behind you."

Even before Joe gets his door closed, Steve is pulling away from the curb.

"Hey! You could at least try not running over my foot."

"I'm sorry, but like I said, we are in a hurry."

Steve begins weaving in and out of traffic and Jim taps me on my shoulder. "He drives like you, Bob."

"Not really," Joe says. "If he drove like Bob, we'd already be driving down the . . ."

Suddenly we almost bounce out of our seats as the car hits the curb and we begin weaving through the people walking down the sidewalk.

Jim leans toward Joe. "You were saying?"

"I was saying, where's my seat belt? There's got to be seat belts in this car someplace."

I'm sure we made good time to the airport but when you're

fearing for your life, time seems to move awfully slow and in this case I think it backed up a couple of times.

Except for some minor dents and some fruit and vegetable stains from a street vendor's cart, the car is none the worse for the trip through town.

As soon as the car stops at the curb in front of the airport Joe opens the door and practically falls out. Jim starts to open his door when a loud horn sounds. Jim slams his door shut and a bus goes speeding by.

"I guess I'll get out on the other side."

I climb out and stand next to Joe. I start to close my door but Steve stops me. "Wait Bob, I'm coming out that side, too. The traffic's too heavy on this side."

Steve and Jim emerge from the car, and Steve heads straight for the door of the terminal.

Joe yells to him. "What about our stuff in the trunk?"

Steve stops and turns around looking a bit exasperated as Joe takes several steps toward the back of the car.

"Leave it."

"What?" Joe says.

"I said leave it. Brother Martin's gonna wire some money ahead to you in Israel. You can buy new stuff there. Now come on."

We walk quickly into the terminal, following Steve at a pace that would be less strenuous if we started jogging. We zip past one ticket counter after another until there aren't any more and head straight for the loading gates.

Joe, huffing and puffing, is the first to ask the obvious question. "Don't we have to get tickets?"

"Nope, I already have them."

"When . . ." I start to ask.

"Back in that field where the plane landed."

"See, Joe, I told you Brother Martin is thorough. He's got this planned almost to the minute."

Steve smiles. "It certainly is that."

When we get in line for the metal detector I begin to worry.

"Steve," I whisper. "Won't the cube set off the metal detector?"

"Probably."

"Then how are we going to get it through?"

"Don't worry, we'll figure out something."

"Oh, well that's reassuring."

As we get within several people of the detector, Steve looks around and then at his watch.

"Don't worry, Steve, if we can get past this thing, we'll make the plane in time."

"I'm not worried about that."

Steve looks around again and I look to try and see whatever it is he's looking for, but all I see as a lot of other people waiting for planes.

Steve reaches around me and tugs on Joe's shirt sleeve. "Joe, you and Jim get up here in front of us."

"Why?" Joe asks.

"Just do it."

"Go ahead, Joe. Steve has to figure out a way to get the cube past the metal detector."

We get up to the detector and Joe puts everything he has that's metal into a plastic tray and walks through the small tunnel to the other side without incident.

I'm getting nervous now as Jim begins digging everything and I mean everything out of his pockets.

"Come on, Steve, we gotta do something real soon here."

"I know, just give me a second here." Steve looks at his watch again. "All I need is the right opportunity, a distraction of some kind would be helpful."

The security guard is handing the sunflower seeds back to Jim when from behind us comes the sound of a lot of people screaming and yelling, followed quickly by the sound of firecrackers going off. The four security guards, who are stationed at the two metal detectors, immediately drop everything they're doing and pull out their weapons as they race down the concourse in the direction of the commotion.

At this moment I come to the realization that those are not firecrackers. The reality of all this really hits me hard when a man stumbles around the corner, his face all bloodied, gasping for air and not getting any.

Just as the man drops to the floor, Steve grabs my arm and drags me around the metal detector.

"Come on, Bob! Now's our chance!"

I slap Jim on the shoulder to get his attention as we rush past.

Jim stuffs the rest of his things in his pocket and rushes to catch up with us. I hadn't noticed but Joe must not have even blinked at the first sound of gunfire, because I can see him running farther up ahead of Steve and I.

There's more gunfire and then an explosion that shakes the floor. I dive to the tile floor expecting the ceiling to come crashing down, but Steve, who's still standing, grabs my arm and pulls me to my feet.

"We gotta keep going." We begin running again. "If we don't make it to the plane within the next sixty seconds, we won't be able to get on without a security check."

We catch up to Joe and run with him until we get almost to the passenger waiting area, and then Steve stops us. "Okay, stop and walk quickly to your gate and onto the plane." Steve hands me the tickets. "There you go, you're all set." I start to go when he stops me by the arm. "Oh, and when you get to the airport in Tel Aviv, find the Western Union office and you'll find the money waiting for you. Use the name on your I. D. Now go!"

Steve gives me a small push to urge me on. The three of us walk swiftly across the waiting area to the gate where the passengers are already loading. Evidently the people here are still unaware of what is happening back in the ticket area. That is until a security guard rushes into the waiting area and in fast French, begins informing the staff at the information and departure-arrivals counter.

We show our tickets to the attractive girl at the door. She speaks in broken English with a heavy French accent.

"Have a good flight."

"Thank you," Joe says, taking a little too long to admire her long black hair and big dark eyes.

I push Joe along, nudging him with my knee and kicking at his heels. "Come on Joe, we can't be holding up the plane."

"Okay, okay." Joe waves at the girl but she's already looking over at the information counter where the conversation is becoming more excited and loud.

We hurry through the jetway, the enclosed walkway leading to the door of the plane, where a stewardess is waiting.

"*Bonjour.*"

"Do you think she speaks English?" Jim asks me as I hand her the tickets.

"Ya'll from the U.S.?" Her southern accent is unmistakable."

I reply with a simple, "Yep."

"Good. I think ya'll are the last ones, so let me show you all to your seats." We follow the slim blonde into the plane and down the aisle about halfway back. She looks at one of the tickets in her hand. "Mister Carloni?" Joe doesn't answer right away. "Mister Carrloooniii."

I nudge Joe. "That's you, Mario."

"Oh . . . uh . . . yeah . . . uh sorry, I was daydreaming."

"This is your seat, over by the window."

"Perfect," Joe says with an edge of sarcasm in his voice.

"Is there something wrong, Mister Carloni?"

Fearing a major loss of macho in front of a lovely lady, Joe changes his tune. "Uh no, everything's fine. I like the window seat. In fact, that's where I sat on the trip over here."

Joe starts to move toward his seat when for the first time he notices that sitting in the aisle seat next to his is a rather large woman who's proportions are much the same as Joe's, only in greater abundance. Joe looks at me and gives me a dirty look. I just shrug my shoulders and smile. It's obvious she will have to get out of her seat to allow Joe enough room to get in.

"Excuse me, ma'am. That's my seat." Joe points to the empty seat.

The lady looks up at Joe and smiles the kind of smile that says, "I'd like to get to know you better." She excitedly gets out of her seat, smiling the whole time. Joe slides in, giving me another dirty look as he plops down into his seat. The lady almost instantly is back in her seat. She gives an excited wiggle and lets out a giggle. Joe rolls his eyes and looks out the window.

"Mister Levitt, you have the window seat right in front of Mister Carloni, and Mister Goldbloom, your seat is next to your friend Mister Levitt." The stewardess hands us our tickets.

"Thank you," I say settling into my seat.

"Yeah, thanks," Jim says.

Joe continues to stare out the window.

"If there's anything ya'll need, just let me know. We should be taking off in just a few minutes."

She walks away to attend to the other passengers and I look out the window to see what has Joe's undivided attention. Basically the view consists of the top of the wing, the top edge of the roof of the terminal and a partly cloudy sky.

The lady next to Joe taps him on the shoulder to get his attention, and then speaks to him in slow deliberate English. "Are . . . you . . . A-mer-i-can?" The accent leads me to believe she's Italian.

Politely Joe answers her. "Yes."

"Do you have girl friend?"

At this point Jim and I are shaking with laughter, trying our best not to laugh out loud. Our good time is suddenly cut short though by a male flight attendant who hurries past and meets a couple security guards at the back of the plane. One of them is holding a leash. My guess is there's a bomb sniffing dog at the other end.

I turn and whisper to Joe, "Get ready for a hand-off under the seat."

"Okay."

I take the cube out of my jacket pocket and put it in the seat between my leg and the wall. I sneak a quick look to see what's going on behind me, and then pretend to talk to Joe.

In that split second peek I noticed two more security guards had come on board and they were searching the passengers on both sides of the aisle, one row at a time. This just might work.

I lean over with my left hand still on the cube and look to my right across the aisle to see if anybody is watching. The two men in suits are both turned around watching the search, so I quickly bring the cube down and place it between my feet. When I sit back up I slide my feet with the cube securely between them just under the front of my seat, out of sight. I keep my feet on each side of the cube so I can easily move it forward or back, which ever may become necessary.

I notice that just about everyone has turned around and is watching the search, so in order not to look out of place and thereby draw attention to myself, I turn to look also.

The security guards are four rows back and working quickly, yet meticulously, searching handbags, luggage and anything else that could conceal weapons or explosives. Also, a female security guard has joined the search. Her duties seem to be that of frisking the female passengers.

Finally, a little late for the liking of some passengers, a flight attendant gets on the public address system.

"Please remain calm and stay in your seats. We are currently undergoing a routine search by airport security. Please have all carry-on items ready for inspection and all pockets turned outwards. Hold all objects from your pockets in your hands until the inspection is completed. Thank you."

There's a sudden stirring from about half the passengers as they begin emptying their pockets.

The flight attendant begins to speak again only this time in French.

"*Monsieur?*" A guard is speaking to Joe as the lady next to him is searched by the female guard out in the aisle.

"Yes?"

"American?"

"Yes."

"Stand up, please, and hold out your belongings."

Joe holds out his hands so they can see what's in them. The guard picks up Joe's passport to see what's underneath, then goes about patting him down.

"Don't you want to see my papers?" Joe asks.

"No *Monsieur*, only if you have a Middle Eastern or European passport."

"Oh."

"Do you have any carry-on luggage?"

"No."

"You may replace your possessions now *Monsieur*, we are finished."

The guard takes a quick look under Joe's seat. As he does, I slide the cube forward in case he looks under my seat in the process. He stands back up so I slide the cube back under my seat.

Suddenly, I realize I haven't emptied my pockets yet. I look at Jim as I start checking my pockets, pulling them out as I empty each one. Jim has his own problem. Standing up now, to get ready for the search, he has so much stuff in his hands that he is having trouble holding onto it all. I check the guards positions and wait until they're exactly even with my seat, then push the cube back as far as I can reach.

One guard makes Jim move out into the aisle and another one stands in front of Jim's seat, right over me.

"*Monsieur?*"

It's the same guard who searched Joe.

"Yes?"

"You are American also?"

"Yes."

"Stand up please and hold out your belongings."

I stand up, and at the same time, with the heel of my left foot, I push the cube a few more inches back. I hold out my hands hoping for the same routine as Joe got. If he checks under the seat too soon we're all dead.

The guard looks under my passport and begins to pat me down. He gets down past my waist when he hits something in my right rear pants pocket.

"What is this?"

I'd forgotten about the letter. "It's a letter."

"Remove from pocket, *s'il vous plaît.*"

I pull the folded, curved envelope from my pocket and hold it up for him to see. He pats it on each side with both hands, checking for any irregularities.

"Thank you, *Monsieur*, you . . ."

At that moment Jim drops some change and in the process of trying to catch it, he drops most everything else that was in his hands.

I take advantage of the confusion to glance back at Joe. He gives me a quick thumb's up, and I face back to the guard who is still watching Jim pick up his stuff. I tap him on the shoulder.

"Am I finished?"

"Yes, *Monsieur*, you may replace your things."

He takes a quick look under the seat. "One more thing, *s'il vous plaît*, you have no carry-on luggage?"

"No."

"Very good, you may be seated."

The guard steps over Jim's outstretched arm into the aisle. The other guard is looking a little impatient, his hands on his hips and a scowl on his face. Jim starts to pick up some of the loose pumpkin seeds but is stopped by the guard.

"Leave them and stand that I may search."

Jim obeys and the guard pats him down, looks under his seat and then simply points at Jim's seat, indicating he may sit down. Jim sticks everything into one pocket of his jacket, creating a huge bulge, and then bends over to pick up a few more loose pumpkin seeds. The guard gives him a funny look, shakes his head and turns to the next row in front of us, all the while mumbling something in French.

I suddenly feel my heart pounding with fast, heavy thumps in my chest. I don't know how long it's been beating like this but it probably has for some time. I try taking slow deep breaths and it seems to be working somewhat, but I know it won't get back to normal until we're in the air.

The search continues for about another hour when finally all the guards and the dog file past and out the door.

"This is your captain. The crew and I would like to thank you for your cooperation and your patience." He's speaking over the public address system. "I have been cleared by the authorities to tell you the reason for the search.

"Approximately five minutes before our scheduled departure, there was a terrorist attack inside the terminal. Details are sketchy but a number of people were wounded. Apparently the terrorists themselves are still on the loose. This plane has been searched for weapons, bombs and known terrorists. I am happy to report we are now cleared for our takeoff and we should be departing within ten minutes. Thank you."

Joe taps my shoulder. "I put it back under your seat," he whispers.

I bend over and look between my legs under the seat. Reaching back, I grab the cube, but before I bring it out I look out toward the aisle to make sure nobody is watching. The coast is clear, so I sit up and put the cube back in my jacket pocket.

It slowly dawns on me that the lady next to Joe has been talking to him almost nonstop in the best English she can manage. She again asks Joe the same question she asked before the guards came on to search the plane.

"You have girl?"

I turn around at this question to see how Joe's going to get out of this one. Joe gets a far away look in his eyes.

"Yes," he says quietly.

The smile leaves the lady's face but is replaced by a look of tenderness which is coming from within that gives her a look of beauty that transcends her outward appearance.

"You miss her?"

"Yes"

"I see in your eyes that is true. She must be very beautiful."

"Yes, she is."

I can see tears welling up in Joe's eyes.

"What is her name?"

"Mi-Ling. She's Japanese."

"It is beautiful name. How did you meet?"

"At a friend's house."

"I see that you are much in love. It is good thing to be in love."

Now she's the one with a far away look in her eyes. Jim must have been listening in also because he turns around to talk to the lady.

"Do you have a boyfriend?"

She's taken aback at Jim's question. Probably thinking, who the heck is this guy? She looks to Joe for help.

"Oh, he's okay,. He's with us. Let me introduce you to my friends. This is Jim and next to him is Bob and I'm Joe."

"Nice to meet you. I am Anna, and no I do not have boy-friend." She looks directly at Jim. "Do you have girlfriend?"

"No."

Joe and I look at each other and smile. I know Joe is thinking the same thing I am.

"Uh, Joe, could I talk to you about something?"

"Sure, what is it?"

"It's kinda personal, maybe you should come up here. You don't mind trading seats with Joe do you Jim? Thanks."

Joe's already on his feet and Anna is out in the aisle before Jim even gives a reply.

"I guess it'll be okay."

Everybody settles back into their seats. Joe next to me and Jim next to Anna.

"So what do you want to talk about?" I whisper to Joe.

"I don't care, as long as it's a quiet subject so we can listen in on the two love birds."

"Won't you get jealous?"

"I'll get over it."

"You know though, Joe, she does have a pleasant personality and looking at her, if she lost some of that weight she would be fairly attractive also."

"I wonder how many girls there are out there that, if they took better care of themselves, would be good looking and attract more decent guys."

"Probably quite a few." I look down at Joe's belly. "And I wonder how many guys there are who could use a little shaping up also."

"Okay, okay, point taken. It's too bad the world is so hung-up on the outward appearance. I try to look beyond it at the person's personality, but the physical thing is so indoctrinated into us that it's almost impossible. I mean, it starts right after we're born."

"How do you mean?"

"What's the first thing you hear a bunch of women say when they see a baby? Aww, he's so cute or, aww, what a pretty baby. Right away the emphasis is on the outward appearance. Why don't they say, what a healthy looking baby, or, she seems to have a pleasant disposition, or, what a happy baby. It just starts kids off right from the beginning thinking about themselves and building their egos out of proportion. If people want to exercise to be healthy that's all right, but if they're doing it just to look good, then it's wrong. It's one thing to take good care of your body, which is the temple of God and it's another thing to pump up your muscles just so you can look at yourself in the mirror and say, 'I'm really something, everybody look at me.' Do you understand what I'm saying?"

"Huh? Did you say something?"

"Fine, see if I ever toss my pearls your way again."

"I was just kidding, Joe. I heard every word you said."

"Okay, then, what did I say?"

"Basically what you said was you don't have to exercise because if you do you'll get a big head and you'll get tired, so why bother."

"That's not what I said."

"Maybe not, but it's what you meant, besides, I've heard that speech before. You're gonna have to come up with a new one one of these days."

"Why? It's just as true now as it was before. Why change it?

God doesn't change the Bible. As long as people have pride, what I said will remain true."

The plane begins to move, being pushed backward by a vehicle attached to the front of the plane. After we're backed out, we're towed out to the taxi area where the plane is detached.

Joe is looking nervous again, not as bad as on the other plane, but still not at all at ease.

"I would think you'd feel like a veteran flier by now, Joe."

"I may never get used to this."

"Oh come on, Joe, a couple more times and you won't think anything of it."

"What makes you think there's gonna be anymore next times?"

As we take off at what seems to be about a forty-five degree angle, I notice a significant difference between this 747 and that twin engine job we were on before. Except for the noticeable tilt and being pushed back into my seat, I hardly notice we're off the ground.

After we level off I take a look to see how Jim's doing. I nudge Joe because I want him to see what I'm seeing.

Jim and Anna are laughing and Jim, believe it or not, is doing most of the talking.

Our friendly flight attendant passes by and Joe stops her. "Excuse me. When do we eat?"

"I'm afraid there are no meals on this flight. We'll be landing in less than an hour. I could get some peanuts for you, if you all would like."

"Yeah, I'll have some."

It's no surprise to me that that was Jim. Just the mention of something to eat and you've got his attention.

"I asked first," Joe says. "Yes, I'll have some also."

She looks at me. "Would ya'll like some too, sir?"

"I guess so." I sound, even to myself, like I could take it or leave it.

Joe looks at me. "You don't have to make it sound like we're forcing you to eat them or anything."

"I'm sorry, it's just that we didn't eat all that long ago. I just wasn't sure I wanted some, but I guess I will have a little."

"Very well, gentlemen, three orders of peanuts coming right up.

It seems like we just get finished with our peanuts and the "fasten your seat belts" sign begins to flash.

The flight attendant walks by. "We'll be landing in ten minutes. Please fasten your seat belts."

Joe snaps his seat belt. "Gee, I was going to see what movie they were showing."

"I don't think they show movies on this flight. Only commercials."

"Bob?"

"Yeah?"

"Do you know where we're going?"

"Yeah, to Israel."

"No, I mean where are we going once we land?"

I hesitate before I answer. "You know what? I really don't know. Other than getting the money from Western Union, I have no idea what we do or where we go next."

"You know what else, Bob? We're on this really important mission for God and we don't even know what the mission is. You've got that cube there and all three of us are here but, so what? What are we supposed to do with it? If we have to do anything with it at all." Joe scowls at me. "How'd I let you get me involved in this, anyway?"

"Do the words, 'What an adventure,' ring a bell?"

"Yeah well, I meant what an adventure for you, not me. Anyway, in less than ten minutes we're gonna be landing and we have absolutely no idea what's going on or where we're going, so let's think of something real quick."

I would relieve some of Joe's anxiety by reminding him of Brother Martin's letter, but I don't want the hassle of him bugging me to open it right away and right here on the plane. I'm convinced myself that our next destination is within that letter, and wherever that place is, that's where we're going to have to go.

As we file off the plane we say our farewells to our southern belle flight attendant. Jim and Anna are still talking even as we head down the concourse. That's when I spot our next major obstacle: customs.

"Bob, how are we going to get through this one? We certainly can't count on another terrorist attack."

We move into a line about three people from the front.

"I don't know, Joe, but I think now would be a good time to start praying."

I stick my hands in my jacket pockets to help conceal the lump caused by the cube. Just as it's our turn to be checked, another customs official approaches.

"I'm here to relieve you for your break."

"You're a little early aren't you?"

"I'm just doing what I'm told."

"Are you new here?"

"Yeah, I transferred down here from Jerusalem. This airport's a lot busier than it was there. I like the big planes. Well you're wasting your break and I've got work to do." He whispers, "Besides, the boss is watching me."

"Gotcha."

The other customs official hurries off, pulling a pack of cigarettes from his shirt pocket. The new replacement turns his attention to us, and my heart starts its assault on my rib cage again.

He smiles. "Hi, welcome to Tel Aviv and the great nation of Israel. Do you have anything to declare? Food, animals, or plants?"

I shake my head.

"Enjoy your stay." He stamps my passport and hands it back to me. "Next."

It takes me only a split second to realize I've made it through the customs inspection, and I hurry away to stand by a wall to wait for Joe and Jim. I smile, thanking God for another miracle. I'd like to see Phil call all this just luck or coincidence. God is obviously in control.

Joe walks up to me smiling. "Wow, that was easy. I thought for sure they would have been more thorough than that."

"Let's just count our blessings, Joe."

Jim wanders up and it's time to get going again.

"Now let's go find the Western Union office and get some money so we can go shopping."

Jim smiles. "And get something to eat."

Chapter 11

"Do you have something for Bob . . . I mean Benjamin Levitt?"

The Western Union clerk looks in his log book and then goes to the pigeon holes behind him. He pulls out an envelope and turns back to me. "I need to see some identification please."

I hand him my passport and he studies it for a moment and hands it back.

"Sign here please." He shoves a receipt at me and I sign where he's pointing. The clerk tears a carbon copy off the bottom and hands both it and the envelope to me. "Thank you sir. Enjoy your visit." He says it without smiling, and goes back to what he was doing before I so rudely interrupted him.

"Okay, guys." I hold the envelope up. "Let's go find us a mall."

I notice on the bus trip downtown from the airport that except for the Hebrew language being on everything, Tel Aviv is not much different from any modern city in the United States. I even spot a nice little shopping plaza that looks like it's not going to be too far of a walk from where we'll be getting off the bus. It's a nice little shuttle bus, as shuttle buses go. It just amazes me that this little country is so prosperous so few years after that great influx of not only Soviet Jews, but the Jews that flocked in from all over the world to escape the sudden rise in anti-Semitism. I guess it's just human nature that when things are going bad and people don't want to blame themselves, then they have to go out and find someone they can blame. It doesn't matter if that person had nothing to do with their situation, they simply need to say, 'It's your fault I'm like this.' The sad thing is that after they're finished with one scapegoat, they're still just as bad off as they were before and maybe worse, so they have to find another scapegoat. I guess that's why it's so easy to blame a whole race of people. That way they have an endless supply of scapegoats.

The bus stops and we climb off. Even after the bus pulls away, the three of us are still standing there on the edge of the sidewalk, each facing a different direction.

Jim turns to me. "Where's all the Jews?"

"I'm looking at one right now."

Jim spins around. "Where?"

"No, Jim. I'm talking about you."

"Oh, I know, but I want to see some real Jews."

"We are real Jews, Jim."

"But I want to see the ones that wear the black hats and suits and have the long beards."

Joe is laughing like crazy now and it's drawing some attention from passersby.

"Joe, you're attracting attention, shh."

"Oh, don't worry about it, Bob. People don't know us from Adam here. Most of these people have never even heard of Michigan, let alone know or even care what goes on there. And Jim? You're not gonna see very many Hasidic Jews in this part of Israel. The more conservative Jewish sects are around Jerusalem."

"There, are you happy now, Jim? Now let's go to that shopping plaza I saw back there about four blocks."

We all start walking down the sidewalk looking at all the modern buildings.

"So, Jim," Joe gives Jim a bump that pushes him sideways a couple steps. "What did you and Anna talk about?"

"Not much."

"Not much? Why you and she were talking nonstop the whole plane trip. You could have told her your whole life story in half that time."

"Well, we did talk about our families and what our homes are like. She was really interested in knowing if America is really like what they see on TV."

"What'd you tell her?"

"I told her it was in some ways but not all. It depended on what shows she watched and where you live."

I think about how things have changed in just the last two or three years. "I don't think it matters where you live anymore. I think the violence in the real world is worse than any movie producer could even imagine. In fact, to prove my point, when was the last time you saw a made for TV movie that wasn't based on a true story?"

I wait for an answer but all I hear is the noise of the city and I see only blank looks on Joe's and Jim's faces.

"You're right, Bob. I never really thought about it before, but it's true. It's been a long time." Joe shakes his head slowly. "It's really sad isn't it? Who would'a thought the world would get this bad?"

"God."

"Besides Him."

"Jesus and the Holy Spirit."

"All right, besides those three."

"Beats me."

Joe punches me in the arm. "That's the answer I was waiting for."

Jim laughs and I punch Jim in the arm. "What are you laughing at?"

"You."

"Ooh, he's getting kinda sassy, Bob. What are you gonna do about it?"

"Well I certainly can't let him get away with it or he'll think he can be that way with us all the time. I'm going to have to give this matter some serious thought and come up with a suitable punishment for his lack of respect."

Joe suddenly changes his tone and the conversation. "Let's cross the street."

"Why?" I ask. "The plaza's on this side."

"I want to look in one of those stores over there."

"Why?"

"Okay, I don't really want to look in one of those stores. Actually I think we're being followed."

Jim and I both turn around to look.

"Don't turn around. Sheesh, I'm hanging around a couple of idiots. Let's just go into a couple of stores and cross the street a few times to see if we really are being followed."

"What's he look like, Joe?"

"He's about medium height with a pair of dark sunglasses. He's wearing dark slacks, a light shirt and a dark tie."

"So we're watching for a Mormon."

"I'm serious. If we're being followed it could mean someone's on to us."

"Okay, Joe, let's see if we're being followed."

I personally don't think we are but I guess if it'll make Joe happy it won't hurt us to do a little extra walking.

We stand at the corner and wait for the light to change.

"Is he still back there Joe?"

"I'm not gonna look back every three seconds, Bob. It might scare him off and then we'll never know for sure."

Jim, who's been standing just behind Joe and I, sticks his head between us. "I vote we scare him off."

The light changes and we start across.

"Come on, Jim, let's do it Joe's way like we always do."

"What do you mean, 'like we always do'? Most of the time we're doing it your way. Sometimes I think I could open up a Burger King franchise."

"Well, my way is usually the best way anyway so that's probably why we end up doing it my way."

"No, I think it's because you whine better."

We reach the opposite side of the street and proceed on down the sidewalk. I take up the conversation, such as it is, where we left off.

"I only whine because you can't see the superior logic in my ideas."

"I can't see any logic because there isn't any there to see."

"Then maybe you should invest in a white cane."

"If you keep up with the wisecracks, you'll have to invest in some white crutches."

Jim stops the discussion dead in it's tracks, not that it was going anywhere anyway. "Let's go in here."

I look through the window of the store we're in the process of passing and stop. Joe does the same and then we both look at Jim. It's a bulk food store.

"We shoulda' known it had something to do with food, Bob," Joe says. "But it might not be a bad idea to grab a little snack to tide us over until we're done with our shopping."

"Yeah, okay. Maybe some yummy granola or beef jerky," I say jokingly.

Jim grins a really big grin. "Malted milk balls."

We walk into the store through its modern glass double doors.

In the center, near the front, are four counters arranged in a square. On the counters are four cash registers. Two clerks are standing in the center of the square talking, waiting to serve the customers. There are five aisles going down the length of the store. Three of the five aisles look like they're devoted entirely to candy. It's paradise to Jim.

Jim heads straight to the malted milk balls he saw through the window. I however, was only half joking when I talked about granola and beef jerky. I sort of prefer the dried fruits and nuts, and the fake M&M's with peanuts.

I glance toward the window and although his back is to me, there is a man standing outside the store with a light shirt and dark slacks. He turns his head and I see the dark sunglasses. I turn away quickly so he won't notice me noticing him, and go to find Joe.

I find him digging in the pretzels the next aisle over.

"This is good stuff Bob. Here, try one. They have free samples of each item."

Joe hands me a small piece of a pretzel.

"Uh, thanks, but I need to ask you something. Is that guy standing outside the store the guy you think is following us? Just turn slowly around like your just going to look at the other side of the aisle."

Joe turns and walks over to the bulk items on the other side. I in turn follow him.

"Is that him?"

"Yep, that's him, but we better move on. He might think something's weird if we stand here at the bulk cat food too long."

"Cat food is probably better for us than most of the other stuff in here. At least they put real meat in it."

"We'd better get Jim and see if we can lose this guy."

"Wait, Joe. We still don't know for sure if he's really following us. Let's do a few evasive maneuvers just to make sure. We each should buy something so it won't look funny if we come out without something in our hands. I could use a snack anyway. Go ahead and get yourself some pretzels, Joe. I'm gonna get me some mixed fruit."

"So after you get Jim, are you going to buy something?"

I stop and pick up a quarter pound of dried mixed fruit and go to get Jim, the other mixed fruit. I find him two aisles over with four bags of candy in his hand, each with what looks like a pound in each, and he's in the process of scooping out some mini jelly beans into another bag.

"Jim, do you think you've got enough yet?"

"Almost. I was thinking about getting some of those chocolate covered peanuts over there."

"Uh . . . Jim, I think maybe you've got enough."

"I was going to share."

"That's okay, Jim, I've got my own. Besides, you might have to travel fast and light. Do you remember that guy Joe thought was following us?"

"Yeah."

"Well . . . don't look now, but we spotted him standing outside the store. You might want to put one or two of those back."

Jim holds the bags up and looks at them trying to decide which two to keep.

"Come on, Jim, this is not a life and death decision here, just leave two and let's go."

Jim finally decides on the jawbreakers and the malted milk balls, and we meet Joe at the cash registers.

As we leave the store, I look both ways down the sidewalk and our mystery man is nowhere to be seen.

"It looks like you may have been wrong, Joe."

"I don't know. I have an uneasy feeling about this. I think he's still out there somewhere."

"Well, let's start walking and see if anything comes out of the woodwork."

We walk to the next intersection and cross back to the other side of the street. I can see the parking lot of the shopping plaza just past this next block. I look across the street and slightly behind us, looking at the architecture, when I catch a glimpse of our shadow. I look calmly forward again and without turning toward either Joe or Jim, I inform them of the presence of the uninvited fourth member of our group.

"I'm beginning to think you're right about being followed, Joe."

"Why? Did you spot him again?"

"Yeah, he's following us from across the street."

Jim turns to look.

Joe and I both yell at him through clenched teeth, "Jim!"

"What?"

Joe backhands him on the arm. "Don't look."

"We're gonna have to lose him, Joe."

"Well I'm not going to try outrunning him."

I notice an alley up ahead. "You won't have to, Joe. You'll be able to out walk him."

"And just how am I going to do that?"

"Stop at the corner of this alley here and I'll explain."

We gather at the corner of the alley in a three person circle.

"Okay, what's your idea."

"Joe, you need to back up like you're going to lean against the wall of the building, and Jim and I will move close to the corner to block his view. As soon as we've done that, you take off down the alley and Jim and I will pretend that we're still talking to you. Unless this guy's really into running, Jim and I should be able to lose him. We'll give you two or three minutes."

"Where are we going to meet?"

"Good question. How about if Joe goes down the alley and turns right and just keeps walking straight down the street. Jim and I will lead this guy in circles and when we think we've lost him we'll come back to this alley and just catch up to you Joe."

"Sounds good to me. Just so long as I don't have to do any more running."

"Okay, Joe, take off. See you in about six minutes."

Joe starts off at a fast walk and even starts to jog a couple times, but only for a few steps. Jim and I go through the motions of holding a conversation with Joe.

"Jim, open one of your bags of candy and hold it out like you're offering some to Joe."

"Okay."

Jim holds out his bag of jaw breakers and then puts it away.

"Aren't you going to offer me any? It might look bad if you offer Joe some and not me."

"So that's why you wanted me to do that. You just wanted to mooch some of my candy."

"Well, the thought did cross my mind, but since you're offering . . . thanks, I'll have a red one."

We continue our fake conversation until our jawbreakers are dissolved, figuring that would give Joe the head start he needs.

"Okay, Jim, hang on tight to your candy. Let's go."

We take off at a dead run, weaving in and out of the people on the sidewalk. The cube in my pocket bangs against my hip as I run. I hand my bag of mixed fruit to Jim.

"Here, hold this a second."

I zip up my jacket to keep the cube from swinging as loosely.

"Thanks, Jim."

I take the fruit back from him. I look back when there's nobody ahead of me to run into.

"He's crossing the road to our side, Jim. As soon as you see a good size gap in the traffic, we'll cross the street ourselves."

"Okay."

I split my attention between the people in our way and the traffic in the street. "It looks like we've got a big gap in traffic coming up Jim, get ready."

We run across the drive of the shopping plaza and we're halfway past the plaza when the traffic clears.

"Now, Jim."

We dart across the street but as we do I notice somebody else running down the sidewalk that's on the side of the street where we are going.

"We're gonna have to pour it on, Jim, there's two of them now." I spot an alley up ahead. "Turn right at the alley here, Jim."

I look back and so does Jim. The second guy is hot on our trail.

"He's right behind us, Bob."

"That's good, as long as he's not in front of us."

I should have bit my tongue because from across the street in front of us a third problem comes running toward us. I know Jim's seen him because it makes him slow down a bit.

"It's gonna be close, Jim, but I think we can beat him to the alley."

Just as we reach the corner of the alley the number three guy is about two strides from the opposite corner. We're starting to huff and puff a little and I can tell this guy has barely run half a block. He could conceivably catch us if he has any short term sprinting ability.

I hear something smack against the corner of the building and hear a clattering sound as we turn into the alley.

Jim sounds upset. "Oh, dang it."

"What happened, Jim?"

"My bag of candy ripped open."

I look back and see Jim's multicolored jawbreakers all over the pavement, and problem number three becoming problem number zero as he falls hard onto his rear end.

"Good going, Jim. He slipped on your jawbreakers."

Just before we reach the end of the alley, I take another quick look back at our pursuers. Problem number two has just thrown up his hands and begun walking, while problem number three is limping, looking for a wall to lean against and our original problem is just rounding the corner into the alley at a slow trot.

"Turn right, Jim, and slow down a little. They've given up on us."

"Good, 'cause I'm tired."

Jim slows down to a walk.

"No, Jim! Keep running. We just don't have to run quite so fast. If we start walking they might be able to catch us again."

We run for a few blocks before turning back toward the street we got off the bus on. These don't seem to be as busy as that one, so there is less dodging of people.

We cross that street and go one more block and turn right again. We should be on the same street as Joe now. All we have to do is catch up to him.

We approach an intersection and I make Jim stop. "Wait Jim, we better check down the street on both sides before we go across. If they're down there they might see us run across. In fact, we probably ought to walk across. Running would make us stick out in a crowd. You look on the right and I'll look on the left."

"Okay."

We peek around the corner of the building, looking way down the sidewalk.

"Everything's clear on my side, Jim."

"Mine too."

"Okay, let's go."

We walk out to the curb and wait for the light. There's a small group of about four people there also, so we go across with them, trying to blend in. After we get across and past the corner of the building again we start to run. That little breather helped me catch my breath so I don't feel like I'm about to collapse anymore.

We do the same thing at the next corner, but I find myself wiping sweat off my brow and forehead and when I begin running again, my jeans stick to my legs, making it more difficult to run. I just can't lift my legs as freely as I'd like.

"After this next intersection, let's just walk fast for a while. I'm really working up a sweat."

"I was hoping you'd say that."

We walk for about three blocks before I spot the back of Joe's shirt about three-quarters of a block ahead.

"There he is, Jim. Let's hurry up and catch up to him."

We start running again and sneak up behind him at the crosswalk while he's waiting for the light. I put my hand on his shoulder.

"Mister Maderna!" I say in a deep voice.

Joe almost jumps out into the street and whips his head around to see who it is.

"Don't do that. I could have peed my pants."

"I'm glad you didn't, that'd be real embarrassing for Jim and I to be seen with someone who still needs potty training."

"I take it you guys lost the guy."

"Guys."

The light changes and we start across.

"Guys?"

"Yeah, three of them. Well actually we only outran two of them. Jim got rid of one of them by giving him a bag of his candy."

"I'm wondering which law enforcement branch they were with. I mean if they knew who we were, I would think they could have used more men or approached us earlier with their guns drawn. I was thinking about that while I was walking, waiting for you guys to catch up, and you know what I think?"

"What?"

"I think they were bounty hunters. When we left Michigan there was already a five-thousand dollar reward out on us. There's no telling what it is now. Especially to make it worthwhile to split it between three guys."

"Joe, we gotta find someplace private."

"To hide out for a while, right?"

"No, so we can read Brother Martin's letter and find out where we go from here."

"That's the best idea I've heard yet. Do you have any suggestions?"

"I do," Jim says. "How about over there?" He points across the street and about half a block up at a sidewalk cafe that is situated about five feet higher than the sidewalk. There are some wide steps leading up to it and it is surrounded by a low wall and shrubbery.

"And maybe we could get a small snack too."

I look down at Jim's hand that is still holding a bag of malted milk balls and then back at Jim.

"I thought that was why we got the candy."

"Well, I kinda thought we we're saving it in case we were out wandering in the wilderness somewhere."

"We're not wandering Jews, Jim, so let's just go plant ourselves someplace and read the letter."

"Funny, Bob."

"Thanks, Joe."

"I meant it sarcastically."

"I don't care, you said it and that's all that matters."

"Yeah, well are we going over there to read that letter or not. I think it's as good a place as any."

"Yeah, I guess, and Jim can have his snack."

"And then he won't be hungry again for another fifteen minutes."

"Or less."

We climb the steps and sit at one of the white wrought-iron tables with matching chairs that is as far away from the other clientele as possible. It's not very busy so the moment we sit down a waiter approaches us.

He says something in Hebrew.

"Do you speak English?" Joe asks.

"Vould you gentlemen care to see a menu?" the waiter says with a noticeable German accent.

"Yes, please," Jim replies.

The waiter hands each of us a menu.

"Vould you care for a drink before dinner?"

I'm really thirsty but I have to ask first. "Is your water good to drink here?"

"We haf imported bottled vater. I vould not recommend the local vater."

"I'll have a large glass of water then. How about you guys?"

"I'll have a large coke," Joe says.

Jim looks thoughtful. "Do you have chocolate milk?"

"Whole, two-percent, or half-percent?"

"Two percent."

"Wery good. I vill return for your orders ven I bring your drinks."

The moment he walks away I pull the envelope out of my pocket. I look around carefully for eavesdroppers and then slowly rip the flap open on the envelope.

"Would you hurry up, Bob," Joe says with his usual impatience. "We're not trying to perform surgery here."

"I'm just being careful not to tear the letter."

I pull the letter out and unfold it. It's handwritten on both sides which strikes me as slightly strange because Brother Martin types almost everything.

I flip it over and start reading at the beginning.

> *Gentlemen:*
>
> *Since you are reading this I know you have made it to Israel safely. I have much information to relay to you so I will get right to it.*
>
> *First, the three of you are to take the cube and go to a place on the coast of the Dead Sea called Wady el-Areijeh, it is about two-thirds of the way south on the west coast near Masada. Once you get there, you are to look just north of there to locate the opening to a cave using the cube. I researched the area and could find no reference to a cave of any significance in that area, which is why the cube must be somehow necessary in helping to locate the cave. I was unable, from the photographs, to find any indication as to how you are to accomplish that task. It simply says you are to present it and yourselves before the light of His word. I have no idea what that means. Perhaps you fellows may, or it may be revealed to you at the location in some way. Anyway, that is one item to pray about.*
>
> *Now, once you have found the cave (and I have faith you will) you are to enter in and follow it all the way to the end, (I assume it opens out somewhere) and there, hopefully, you will be at the location where the Garden used to be. What you fellows do then or what happens next, only God knows.*

*That fairly well fills you in on what the cube says, now I
need to inform you of a few things that are going on that you
should be made aware of, and by the time you read this I am
convinced that the situation will have escalated.*

"Bob," Joe interrupts my reading. "The waiter's coming back."

I quickly fold up the letter, slide it back into the envelope and
stick it in my jacket pocket.

"Your drinks, gentlemen."

He places a white napkin down in front of each one of us and
then places our drinks on the napkin. He pulls the menus from
under his arm and after setting his round tray down on a nearby
table, he hands each of us a menu.

"I vill be back zoon to take your orders."

Before he leaves he takes three straws from his tray and places
them in the center of the table. Turning with the tray tucked under
his arm and his other hand on the front edge, he walks off with an
air of dignity.

I pull the envelope back out, pull the letter out again and unfold it.

"Okay, now where was I?"

"You were at the part where . . ."

I find the place where I stopped quickly and interrupt Joe.
"Here it is."

I am convinced the situation will have escalated.

*First, your friendly Detective Taylor has vowed to
search the ends of the earth and to not rest until you three
are apprehended.*

Second, he is building a case trying to implicate all . . .

I flip the letter over to the other side.

*. . . fundamental Baptists in America in the string of
murders, saying we are bankrolling the perpetrators and
protecting them. I think we are seeing the beginning of the
final persecution of the church before the rapture. I will be
contacting the other pastors in the association to make
preparations to go underground.*

*You will also be pleased to know that you are being
blamed for an additional three murders. These people you*

*are dealing with appear to be well organized and extremely
ruthless. Our prayers are with you as we know yours are
with us.*

*Yours in Christ,
Brother Martin Greenhoe*

"That's it guys, what do you think?"

I put the letter in the envelope, fold them both up together
and stick it in my back pocket.

"I think I'll have the fried chicken."

"No, Jim, the letter, what do you think about the letter?"

"Oh that. It was nice."

"Nice? What do you mean 'nice?'"

"I don't know, just nice."

"In other words you weren't listening."

"Yeah I was . . . a little."

"Never mind." I turn to Joe. "So what do you think?"

"I think I'll have a club sandwich."

"Knock it off, Joe, I know you were listening 'cause you've
been dying to know what was in this letter since we left Michigan.
So what do you think?"

"I think it's good to know where we're going next, but it still
bothers me about how vague everything is. I mean, we know where
we're going but we don't know what we do when we get there."

"I guess we just let things happen and we react. Maybe God
wants us to exercise our faith."

"Why not, with all this running around we've been doing I've
exercised everything else."

"How are we gonna get there?" Jim asks, putting his menu
down.

"Oh, you're going to join us now, Jim?" I'm still a bit peeved at
him.

"Yeah."

Joe laughs. "He probably knows what he's gonna order." Joe
stops laughing and gets more serious. "But he does have a good
question. How are we going to get there. Uh, where was it the letter
said we had to go?"

"I don't remember, let me check."

I pull the envelope back out and scan the letter.

"Bob, the waiter's coming."

I stash the letter in my jacket pocket.

"Are you ready to order, gentlemen?"

"I am," Jim says opening up his menu again. "I'll have the fried chicken dinner with baked potato and cole slaw. And for desert I'll have the apple pie ala mode, and could I get another large glass of chocolate milk?"

At this point I realize I haven't even looked at the menu yet. I open it up and it's in Hebrew. How in the world did Jim know what to order? Then it hits me; he ordered items that had their pictures in the menu. Nothing looks good to me so I hazard a guess.

"Do you have pizza?"

"Yes sir."

"I'll have a small pizza with extra cheese and ham."

"I am sorry sir, ve do not serve ham."

"Oh." I feel embarrassed, forgetting that pork in Israel is a no-no. "Then how about hamburger?"

"Ground beef. Wery good sir." He turns to Joe. "Sir?"

"Uh yes, I'll have the same only with everything on my pizza, oh and make mine a medium."

"Ve only haf two sizes sir."

"Oh, well, then give me the bigger one."

"Wery good sir."

The waiter collects the menus and tucking them under his arm in the same manner as he did the tray earlier, he glides back into the restaurant.

"Okay, Bob, he's gone. Now where are we going?"

I pull out the slightly more wrinkled letter and find where our destination is written. "Here it is, it's a place called Wady el-Areijeh. It's about two-thirds of the way down the west coast of the Dead Sea and we're supposed to start looking just north of there."

"So how are we gonna get there?"

"How about by bus? Isn't Masada a tourist attraction? We could find a travel or tourist information center and find out how we can take a tour. That should get us close enough that we can walk the rest of the way."

"Okay, so where do we find a tourist information center? That is without going all the way back to the airport."

"Ask the waiter," Jim says.

"You know," Joe says, "there have been times I've wondered why we let this guy hang around with us and then he opens his mouth and once in a great while he makes sense and almost makes putting up with him worth it."

"I know what you mean, Joe."

I stand up and look out at the sidewalks, scanning both sides and as far each way as I can see.

"What's the matter Bob? See something?"

"No, I'm just nervous about staying in one place too long." I sit back down. "I think as soon as we're done eating we should get out of this city, and the sooner the better. That part in Brother Martin's letter about the bad guys being well organized kinda bothers me."

"The part about ruthless bothers me."

"And nothing in the letter bothers Jim, because he wasn't listening."

"Well if he had been listening, I know what would have bothered him about the letter."

"What's that Joe?"

"The fact that it didn't mention anything about food."

"Okay," Jim says grudgingly. "Let me see the letter and I'll read it."

I hand Jim the letter and he begins to read. That is until he sees the waiter approaching with the food, at which point he hands the letter back to me. "I'll finish it when I'm done eating."

Joe laughs. "Jim, you're never really done eating, you just pause long enough to breath."

After we finish eating, and in between frequent visits from the waiter when Jim finds it necessary to order just one more thing, Joe and I convince Jim to read the rest of the letter while he's still eating. Jim finishes off his second piece of pie and downs his third glass of chocolate milk as the waiter comes back for what amounts to about the seventh or eighth time.

"Vill there be anything else?" He looks directly at Jim.

"Ummm."

"No," Joe and I say short and quick.

I clarify. "Uh, no thank you, we would like the check now, please. Oh, and how might we get transportation to Masada from here?"

"There ist the bus, three streets down," he points in the direction in which we were heading before we stopped to eat, "und vun street to the right."

"Thank you, sir."

I figure that puts us about six or seven blocks down the street from the shopping plaza. Hopefully still out of the range of where our pursuers might be searching.

The waiter sets the check down on the table in the middle using a small round tray just larger than a coaster, and waits.

I read the amount but it's in Israeli currency. I pull out the envelope of money from Western Union and pick out what looks like will be enough to cover the check, and properly put it on the small tray. I wait for a response either way from the waiter.

"How do you vish your change, sir?"

"Keep the change," I say, just gratified that I had given him enough for the food.

His stoic face suddenly brightens. "*Danka, danka-shen.*" He realizes he's speaking German in his excitement. "Thank you wery much, sir. Thank you."

He walks away, not with his usual air of dignity, but almost skipping.

I look at Joe. "Uh . . . do you think maybe we ought to find out how to figure the value of Israeli money?"

"It might save us some money in tips."

We push our chairs away from the table and Jim quickly wipes his mouth with his napkin as he stands up. We check out the street scene for undesirables and head for the steps heading down to the sidewalk. Looking back at the restaurant I see the waiter talking to a busboy with the money in his one hand and pointing toward us with the other.

"I think my little mistake has attracted some attention."

We turn left out at the sidewalk to follow the directions to the bus station as given to us by the waiter.

"Yeah," Joe says. "That tip will make us hard to forget. I just hope none of those guys asks around for us at that restaurant."

"Brother Martin must've sent an awful lot of money. I only gave him one of the bills with the middle amount of zeros. When we get to the bus station and pay for our tickets I'll give the guy one of the same size bills and see what kind of change we get back."

"I think we oughta find another way to get there. Like maybe a cab or hitchhike or something. I just think that even if they don't find out from that waiter, they'll be watching for us at places like bus stations, train stations and airports and so on."

"Yeah, maybe we should find a pay phone and see if we can get us a cab."

"I would suggest one thing though, Bob. Before we pay the cabby, we should find out what our money is worth. They'll never believe you're a Jew if you keep giving out big tips."

"All right Joe, that's enough of the ethnic slurs. You're outnumbered here two to one."

"Oh yeah, I forgot."

Jim points ahead. "There's a phone."

Up ahead against the outside wall of a building just a few steps ahead of us is a pay phone. I dig into my pocket and pull out a handful of assorted change.

"I've got a couple Israeli coins from that bulk food place, Joe. Do you think these will be enough?" I hold out the two coins.

"Only one way to find out."

There's no phone book handy so I dial the operator. It rings six or seven times before a female operator finally answers. She says something in Hebrew.

"I'm sorry, I only speak English."

"Hold please."

I wait only a few seconds and another female operator comes on the phone.

"May I help you?"

"Uh yes, um . . . I'd like to get a taxi, but there's no phone book here. I'm calling from a pay phone."

"Which cab company would you like, sir?"

"I don't know. Which one's closest?"

"Where are you calling from?"

"Uh . . ." I look around for a street sign. ". . . that's a good question. Just a second." I put my hand over the mouthpiece. "Do either of you guys know what street we're on?"

Joe shakes his head and Jim shrugs his shoulder.

"Will you be able to tell if I give you the number on the phone?"

"That may take some time sir."

"Well then, just give me one that's close to downtown."

"One moment please."

Suddenly Joe runs out to the edge of the street waving his arms and a taxi pulls up to the curb next to Joe.

"Uh, operator?"

"Yes?"

"Never mind, my friend just now got one to stop. Thanks anyway."

I hang up and run over to the cab. Joe has his head sticking inside the cab's window talking to the cabby. I turn to Jim who's been standing there for the whole time Joe's been talking to the driver. "Is he getting anywhere with the driver?"

"I don't know, I can't hear them, but I can tell that he doesn't speak English."

"Which one? Joe or the cab driver?"

"Both."

Joe pulls his head out of the cab. "I heard that."

"Well, Joe? Do we have a ride or not?"

"Sure do. I just pointed it out on his map where we had to go and he nodded his head. So let's go."

I climb in first because I don't want to be stuck in the middle between Joe and Jim again. Joe gets in next to me and then Jim climbs in, closing the door after him. The cab driver starts his meter, checks for traffic and does a u-turn to hopefully get us on our way to Masada.

"Hey Joe, you're the religion history expert here, what can you tell me about Masada. I remember seeing a special on TV about it years ago but all I remember is that it was a fort at the top of a mountain where a small group of Jews held out for a long time against a huge Roman force, but they ended up committing suicide rather than give up to the Roman army. Am I right so far?"

"Yep."

"Well tell me some more. I want to hear some details. Give me details."

"I'm not exactly an expert on it but I do have a book about it at home. Masada has a really interesting history. It was the summer palace of King Herod the great. It was at a time when several groups of Jews tried an insurrection against the Roman Empire. About nine-hundred Jews holed up at Masada and were able to hold off a huge Roman force for more than a year before the Romans built a dirt causeway out to it, but the Jews decided they didn't want to die the tortuous death at the hands of the Roman executioners, so they had some of their priests, who were trained in painless animal sacrifices, perform the suicides and then they in turn killed themselves, so when the Romans got there they found only a few survivors who wished not to participate."

"That kind of reminds me of the Alamo, how just a few hundred men were able to hold off thousands of men for the longest time. Just about all of them died, too."

Jim leans around Joe and gives me a strange look.

"What's the matter, Jim?"

"I thought everybody did die at the Alamo."

"Nope. I visited there once and they had a list of survivors there. Shoot, there must have been a half a dozen or more. I can't remember exactly but it surprised me too. I always thought they all died too. I think it was from watching that Walt Disney movie, *Davey Crockett.*"

"I saw that movie," Joe says. "Good movie."

"Yeah, I liked it too," Jim adds.

"Thank you very much Siskel and Ebert. That's two thumbs up for *Davey Crockett.*"

As we get out of Tel Aviv and head east toward Masada the terrain becomes noticeably rougher. Maybe that's an understatement. Perhaps a more apt description would be, if it weren't for the road, traveling through this country would be downright treacherous. The countryside is extremely barren and rocky with numerous valleys that have steep, rough sides. It reminds me somewhat of hundreds of smaller sized Grand Canyons, except the rocks and everything else have been bleached by the sun. It also continues to get warmer, which seems to conflict with the fact that we've been going up hill almost the whole time. The wilderness scene is occasionally broken by a settlement, some older, but most are new and some are just starting to go up.

I don't know how this country has been able to do it but it has somehow been able to take in untold millions of Jewish refugees from around the world and still not have its economy go belly up. I would say that almost every Jewish person in the world has now returned to Israel, at least those that are able to. It wouldn't surprise me any if Jim and I were the last Jews left to come over here, and what with all the widespread anti-Semitism, if anybody had known we were Jewish, we probably would have moved here months ago also, if not sooner.

It's a long, hot, dusty trip to Masada. I personally would have thought that in a climate like this, air conditioning would be standard equipment in all taxi cabs. I see drops of sweat trickling down the side of Joe's face and I wipe the beads of sweat that have formed on my own forehead with the back of my hand. I've already taken my jacket off and rolled it up into a ball with the cube as the center so it won't fall out of the pocket.

"How much farther is it, Joe?"

"I don't know, but if this lasts much longer I'm going to dehydrate. I'm sweatin' like a pig."

"And beginning to smell like one, too. Speaking of pigs, how are you doing Jim?"

"He's snoozin', Bob. I think he could sleep through anything."

"And eat through anything."

I look at Jim and laugh. With each bump in the road, his head bounces off the side window of the taxi and yet he continues to sleep.

"I don't think he's even sweating, Bob. How does he do that? I'm about ready to strip down to my underwear and he's still got his jacket on."

"There's definitely something strange about that guy. Maybe he's an alien. I think we better check for a pulse or poke him with a needle to see if his blood is green."

"Nah, I don't think he's an alien. Aliens would be highly intelligent beings."

"Okay, I guess you've got a point there. So he's not an alien, what is he then?"

"Well . . . if I believed in evolution . . ."

"Knock it off you guys. I heard every word you said." Jim's eyes remain closed and his head continues to bounce off the window.

"I told you he's not human Joe, what real human being would be conscious and let his head bang off a hard window like that?"

Jim sits up. "Okay, you guys happy now? I'm sitting up and I'm taking my jacket off, but I'm not gonna promise I'll work up a sweat any time soon."

Chapter 12

We walk to the wall and look out across a small salt plain below and about two or three miles beyond is the Dead Sea. The air is dry and I can taste the salt in the air. It's either that or it's my own sweat on my lips.

Masada is on a diamond shaped plateau with steep sides. The palace itself is at the corner facing the Sea and is about a half to three-quarters of a mile from the opposite corner of the plateau. I can see why it would be easy for a small group to hold off a huge attacking force.

Of course if the same thing were to happen today, they would just be bombed into oblivion and then helicopters would simply land with forces to clean up the survivors.

About a hundred feet below us on a large ledge is what looks like a huge bowl, probably a cistern for collecting rain water. And another fifty feet below that is another smaller ledge with a building on it. It has the remains of pillars on its top, indicating it may have had another floor to it.

I look around and notice that the three of us are almost the only ones here.

"It must be the off season for tourists here."

Joe wipes his brow. "I can see why with this heat. You didn't happen to notice anyplace where we could get a drink did you?"

"We could ask him," Jim says pointing behind us and to our right.

Walking toward us, between the two-foot high remains of the walls of one of the now long gone buildings, is a man wearing a small rectangular name badge pinned to his shirt just above his pocket.

He says something in Hebrew.

I shrug my shoulders. "English?"

"Oh, good," he says. "I'm still not all that good with my Hebrew. As you can see by my name tag here," he points to his tag, "I'm Norm and I'll be your tour guide. Are there more in your group?"

Joe shakes his head. "Nope, this is it."

"I have to apologize for taking so long, but I didn't see the bus come in and frankly, I thought we were done for the day."

"We came by taxi."

"Okay, that explains it then. It happens every so often. You see, all the tours are arranged in groups and they come by bus, but occasionally a taxi driver, lured by the large fare he'll get, will bring someone out here. It's not your fault, they're supposed to know better. But since you're here and you speak English, thank God, I'll give you a quick tour before it gets dark.

"Well, actually . . ." I look at Joe. ". . . we're not here for the tour. We're trying to get to a place called Wady el-Areijeh." I look back at our tour guide.

"Why do you want to go there? It's nothing but a dry river bed. Well, except when there's a good rain."

"It's kind of an archeological expedition."

"That's cool. I've always wanted to go on one of those digs. It seems like there's one going on just about everywhere you go anymore. How are you guys getting there? I didn't see your cab so it must have left, and the last bus left five minutes ago. Is somebody picking you up?"

"Actually, we were planning on walking the rest of the way there."

"You're kidding aren't you? Where's your supplies?"

Jim holds up his bag of candy. "Right here."

"That's it? A bag of candy?" He chuckles. "Where's your water?"

"Why?" I ask. "It isn't that far is it?"

"As the crow flies, no. You could probably get there in a day, but I don't think you guys can walk on air or water, so given the extra mileage to go over, down and around everything, I imagine it would be a good three days journey."

The three of us look at each other. Joe lets his head drop forward and continues to look at me. If he were wearing glasses he'd be looking over the top of them.

"This was your idea, Bob."

"I know, but on the map it didn't look that far."

"It's not. Israel itself is only about fifty miles wide, but it can take you half a day to cross it by car. I can't believe nobody told you all this before sending you over here. What college are you with?"

I hesitate before I answer. "Actually none. We're sort of a free-lance team."

"Now I don't mean for this to sound like a cut down, but anybody as foolish as you three can't be dangerous, so here's what I'm gonna do. I live over by Engedi which is north and west of here, and you guys can ride with me to my place and spend the night. After that, if you still insist on it, we can get up early and I can drive you out to as close as the roads will take us to Wady el-Areijeh."

"I think that's more than generous." I turn to Joe and Jim. "What do you think, guys?"

"Beats walking in this Godforsaken no man's land." Joe sits on one of the low walls. "My feet are already killing me."

"I vote for riding, too," Jim says with his big grin.

"Good, you can fill me in on what's going on back in the States. I really miss the old U. S. of A. God, I miss English-speaking people."

Norm is a young guy, I would guess about twenty, slim, yet slightly muscular like maybe he works out with weights two or three times a week. His skin is darkly tanned from the desert-like sun. His hair is black and wavy coming just over his ears and neatly combed. By most standards a good-looking guy.

We all pile into Norm's car, a little white Mazda with black interior. With the sun almost down, the interior is still warmer than the outside air. I'd hate to have to be in this car during the hot hours of the day. I sit up front with Norm, and Joe and Jim settle into the back seat.

"I wish I hadn't gotten a car with black interior but when you're out looking for a good deal on a used car you can't be too picky. Thank God I got air conditioning though. Around here you can't live without it."

We head west into the half hidden glowing orange disk that's dropping behind the Judean mountains ahead. When we do turn north, it is already dark enough to make sight-seeing a virtual im-possibility.

"So where you guys from?"

Jim comes to life. "America."

"Oh, I can see this trip is going to be lots of fun. I mean where in America?"

"Michigan."

"Can you be more specific?"

Joe butts in. "The Lansing area."

"Good, that's not too bad of an area. I kinda like Michigan. There's a lot of small towns there and I like that laid back small town atmosphere. I drove through Detroit once and they're all crazy there. Everyone of them. I drove eighty down the freeway and was still gettin' passed like I was standing still, and I swear to God everybody in that town carries a concealed weapon. I don't know if they do it for self protection or if they're on their way to make mincemeat out of a rival drug ring."

I planned on just thinking it but it comes out of my mouth. "Probably both." Now that I've said it, I may as well continue. "I don't know what it was like when you left but it's definitely worse now. And that situation you described in Detroit is now commonplace in even smaller cities than Lansing. I don't know if it's because the problem is too big for the police to handle or if they are part of the problem. Either way, they don't seem to have any effect at all."

"What about the anti-Semitism? It was so bad in Minnesota where I was that it made me move to Pennsylvania, and it wasn't any better there. That's why I decided to move here, plus the fact that most of my family had already moved here."

"I guess if there were any Jews left there to persecute, it would be bad. Last I knew the persecution had begun to concentrate more on conservative Christian groups."

"Well I can understand that more than picking on us Jews. Shoot, we can't help who our parents are, but them Christians, spouting off their crazy theories about a guy coming back from the dead, they chose to be what they are."

Joe clears his throat.

"Oh . . . you guys aren't some of them Christians are you?"

I respond to the question before Joe is able to start what I know would be an endless tirade in defense of the Christian faith.

"As a matter of fact, yes, we are, but don't let it bother you. We're used to it. This doesn't mean you're gonna kick us out of your car and make us walk now does it?"

"No, don't worry. I may not agree with your beliefs but I won't stoop as low as those who have done worse to me just for being a Jew."

"I like that attitude."

"Well, to be honest it's not an attitude that I came by naturally, I had to work at it. Being the target of prejudice makes it all too easy to pick out scapegoats of my own."

"That's basically what happened back home. When the Jews left, they had to find someone else to be their scapegoat, and what better group of people than those who speak against their evil lifestyles."

"I suppose, but you guys tend to bring it on yourselves sometimes."

"How do you mean?"

"Well, like badgering a person by always wanting to talk about your religion and arguing against everyone else's beliefs. I think everyone should be able to believe what they want to believe and not worry about anybody bothering them about it. Does that make sense to you?"

"It sounds good in theory, but it goes entirely against human nature for one thing and for another, not to tell people about Jesus goes completely contrary to what Jesus specifically told us to do. He said that we were to 'Go into all the world and make disciples, baptizing them in the name of the Father, and God the Son, and of the Holy Ghost and teach them all things whatsoever I have commanded you and lo I am with you alway, even unto the end of the world.' Now if your religion gave you such a command, and you knew it would please God to follow it, wouldn't you try to do what God wants?"

"Well yeah, but how does it follow human nature?"

"What is the first thing you do after you've seen a good movie or been to a good restaurant? Don't you go and tell your friends about it?"

"Yeah."

"Okay, now what if you saw a person riding a bicycle down a path and you're riding down the same path with him, and up ahead the path has a fork in it, one fork leads to a bridge that is broken and the other leads to a bridge that is in perfect shape. Now you know for sure which path is the good path but the person next to you believes the other path is the right path, aren't you going to try almost everything to convince him your way is right in order to save his life? To keep him from making a fatal decision?"

"Okay, I'll agree that you have valid reasons for why you do it, but I can't agree with some of the tactics that are used."

"If it makes you feel any better, I don't agree with some of them either. I do, however, believe it's my duty to at least give the Gospel message once to a person, then it's up to them. If they show an interest in learning more I'll pursue it further. But in the time I do have with them, I'll try to be as persuasive as I can."

"I don't mind someone being persuasive, it's the pushy part I don't like."

"Good, then would you consider it being pushy if I ask you why you don't believe Christianity's claims?"

"Nope, I wouldn't consider it pushy. Someone else might but I wouldn't. I just think that the claims made by Christians are based on awfully flimsy evidence."

"Such as?"

I can see Joe's head between us, just behind the back of the front seats. I know he's dying to get into this conversation, but he is showing remarkable restraint.

"Such as the four Gospels. All of them were written by followers of Jesus, hardly impartial, and the prophesies that were supposedly fulfilled could have been self-fulfilled by Jesus because he already had knowledge of what he had to do to fulfill them, and finally, concerning his resurrection, everyone knows his disciples hid his body to make it look like he came back from the dead."

"Do you believe that Jesus was a real person, and that he really existed at about the time the Gospels claim he did?"

"Oh yeah, I have no problem with that. Even Josephus, the Jewish historian of the time recorded something about Jesus, so I'm sure he was a real person. I just don't think he was the Messiah."

"Okay then, let's take the question of fulfilled prophesy. Do you remember Psalms, chapter twenty-two?"

"Not offhand, no."

"I wish I had a Bible with me but it mentions some things that . . ."

From behind me Jim's voice interrupts me.

"My God, my God, why hast thou forsaken me? Why art thou so far from helping me, and from the words of my

*roaring? O my God, I cry in the daytime, but thou hearest
not; and in the night season, and am not silent. But thou art
holy, O thou that inhabitest the praises of Israel. Our fathers
trusted in thee: they trusted, and thou didst deliver them.
They cried unto thee, and were delivered: they trusted in
thee, and were not confounded. But I am a worm, and no
man; a reproach of men, and despised of the people. All they
that see me laugh me to scorn: they shoot out the lip, they
shake the head, saying, He trusted on the Lord that he would
deliver him: let him deliver him, seeing he delighted in him.
But thou art he that took me out of the womb: thou didst
make me hope when I was upon my mother's breasts. I was
cast upon thee from the womb: thou art my God from my
mother's belly. Be not far from me; for trouble is near; for
there is none to help. Many bulls have compassed me: strong
bulls of Bashan have beset me round. They gaped upon me
with their mouths, as a ravening and a roaring lion. I am
poured out like water, and all my bones are out of joint: my
heart is like wax; it is melted in the midst of my bowels. My
strength is dried up like a potsherd; and my tongue cleaveth
to my jaws; and thou hast brought me into the dust of death.
For dogs have compassed me: the assembly of the wicked
have enclosed me: they pierced my hands and my feet. I may
tell all my bones: they look and stare upon me. They part my
garments among them, and cast lots upon my vesture."*

My mouth, somewhere about halfway through, dropped open
and remained that way until Jim finished.

"I'm impressed, Jim. When did you learn that?"

"I don't know, I just remember reading it and it just came to
me."

"Your friend there must have a photographic memory."

"Well if he does," Joe says, "it's always been out of focus and
underdeveloped before. It was very impressive though, Jim. I will
give you that."

"Thanks, guys."

I turn back around and try to remember what Jim just recited.

"Anyway, getting back to the subject. In Psalms twenty-two, as
we just heard, it gives an accurate description of what a crucifixion
would be like, but this was written hundreds of years before it was

even invented. Now do you believe that this chapter is talking about the Messiah?"

"It would have to be because none of that stuff ever happened to David."

"Then we have to assume that the Messiah will come at a time when crucifixions are being done. Which to my knowledge was only done just before and during the first century, and I foresee no plans to begin doing them again here in Israel or anywhere else. Stonings maybe, but no crucifying. So what we have to look for is somebody who was crucified during that period of time that fits all the prophesies given in the Law and the Prophets and the Psalms about the coming Messiah. If we start with Psalm twenty-two you'll see that everything in there also happened to Jesus."

I spend more than half an hour going over every prophesy about the Messiah I can remember and applying it to Jesus' life. We turn onto a road and I see the lights of a small community just a little way up a modest sized hill. Norm interrupts my dissertation.

"We're almost there."

"I hope I didn't bore you."

"Oh no. In fact you've given me a lot of things to think about. I'm going to have to get back into the scriptures and do some studying."

We turn into what looks like the parking lot of an apartment complex. "Kind of looks like the low income housing back in the U.S., doesn't it?"

The buildings are white or light brown stucco, it's hard to tell in the light from the parking lot, and they appear to be groups of town houses. Each door has about fifteen to twenty steps leading up to them with two or three landings depending on the number of steps.

We pull up in front of one of the buildings near the center of the semicircle. Off to our right a man carrying an automatic rifle approaches. Norm gets out of the car and waves. The man waves back and heads off in another direction. Norm leans back into the open door.

"We supply our own security here. It helps save the government a bundle on military costs. Everybody takes a shift patrolling the settlement. Nobody minds doing it because the savings helps to build more of these settlements."

The rest of us get out of the car and Joe steps up on the sidewalk and looks around.

"Where exactly are we anyway?"

"It's a new settlement about five miles south of Engedi. It's so new, in fact, that we still haven't even decided on a name for it yet."

After seeing the guy with the gun I feel a bit uneasy. "I thought you guys signed a peace treaty with all the neighboring countries. Why do you need so much security?"

"Yeah, we signed peace treaties all right but there's still a lot of Arab terrorists out there trying to stir things up. In fact just this morning there was a terrorist attack at an airport in France. They think it was aimed at Israeli passengers, but in this case, they think it was a militant Christian organization that was involved. Kinda like I said before, sometimes you guys ask for it."

Joe doesn't like the insinuation that a violent organization would use the term Christian to describe itself.

"Anybody who uses violence as a means to an end, is not a Christian in my book."

I'm a little taken aback by Joe's blanket statement.

"I don't fully agree, Joe. I think there are times when it's a Christian's duty to use whatever means are at his disposal if the intent is to protect an innocent person from another person. However, I don't think a Christian should ever, under any circumstances, provoke or initiate violence."

"But Jesus . . ."

"This is all very interesting, but do you guys think we could finish this discussion inside my apartment? I've been on my feet all day and I'd like to sit down."

"Sounds good to me," Joe says. "I could use a big glass of nice cold water right about now."

"Water. I've got lots of. Just picked me up several jugs yesterday."

We walk up the steps to the wooden front door of Norm's townhouse. Norm unlocks it and we walk in. Norm flips the light switch next to the door and it reveals an apartment that is as deep as it is wide. All the walls and trim are an off white, not to mention the ceiling. The living room has a low pile carpet on the floor. Straight ahead from the front door are uncarpeted steps leading to the upstairs which, I assume, are the bedrooms or perhaps just one big bedroom. The furniture is sparse and what of it there is, looks well worn. The couch has one corner supported by two short pieces of two-by-fours where a leg should be.

"It ain't much, but it's home. Actually I was lucky to get this place."

I mumble, "No such thing as luck."

"What?"

"You don't want to know," Joe says quickly. "Mind if I ask how much this place sets you back each month?"

"Let me think." Norm counts on his fingers. "About two-fifty to two-sixty. Somewhere in there. I still have some trouble with the exchange rates."

I brighten up. "You know something about how much Israeli money is worth?"

"Yeah."

"Well, here." I stick my jacket under my arm and pull out the envelope of money we picked up from Western Union and pull out a bill, the same as the one I gave the waiter. "Can you tell me what this is worth in American money?" I hand him the bill.

Norm's eyes widen. "Wow."

"I uh . . . gave one of these to a waiter to pay for lunch and told him to keep the change. He got real excited."

"I can see why. I've only seen a couple of these the whole time I've been here."

"So what's it worth?" Joe's impatience begins to show.

"You say you used one of these to pay for lunch? I can see why the waiter got excited all right. I would too if after I gave a tour somebody gave me a tip of over a hundred dollars."

Joe laughs. "A hundred dollars? And you thought I was bad with money. At least I don't go around handing out one-hundred dollar tips."

"So that's worth how much?"

"I'd say somewhere in the neighborhood of a hundred and forty to a hundred and fifty."

"Really? Then how about this one?"

I hand him another bill with a larger denomination on it, and take the other one back from him. Norm's eyes grow wide again and his voice shakes noticeably with his first couple words. "Do you have any more of these?"

"Yeah, I think four or five. Why?"

"Because these are worth over a thousand dollars each. Probably closer to a thou and a half."

"Then my guess is that they won't take this one at a gas station, will they?" I hand him the next bill which is the one that looks like it has the largest denomination on it. Norm seems a bit more composed this time, but still excited.

"I'm not even going to ask you if you have any more of these. Are you guys independently wealthy or rob a bank or some . . ."

Norm takes a step back and eyes us suspiciously. "Look, if you guys are in trouble with the law, I think it would be best for you to leave right now."

"Don't worry, Norm, we're completely harmless. None of us has done anything wrong. Someone would have to frame us in order to get us in trouble."

"Okay, so explain the money. Is it yours?"

"Yes and no. It's ours to use but it was sent to us by our sponsors."

"Can I ask who your sponsors are?"

"An association of Baptist Churches."

I know if I don't answer his questions he's either going to throw us out and make us walk, or call the authorities, or both. I'm going to have to trust him.

"So they're bankrolling your expedition?"

"Yes."

"What is it exactly you expect to find on your expedition?"

"A cave. We're looking for a cave."

"In the wady?"

"No, just north of the wady. On the coast of the Dead Sea."

"I've been up and down there several times in my row boat, and there are caves, but there's nothing in them. Ever since they found the Dead Sea scrolls at Qumran, archaeologists have been over, through and around every cave in Israel with a fine tooth comb. What makes you think you three amateurs are going to find anything."

"Should I show him Joe?"

"I don't know. I don't know if we can trust him."

I turn to Norm. "Can we have some time to discuss this?"

"Yeah, I guess so."

Norm goes to the kitchen and leaves us by the door. The living room and kitchen are separated only by a section of cupboards and a section of counter top that runs out from the wall opposite the stairway. I can see Norm getting a jug of water out of the refrigerator. He's keeping an eye on us, also.

"I think we should show him, Joe."

"But what if he takes it from us while we're sleeping? How would we find the cave? If there is one."

"If we don't show it to him he's probably not going to trust us and that could mean either a long walk to the Dead Sea or a quick ride to the slammer."

"What difference does it make? After we get to wherever we're going, we're still going to be wanted for all those murders."

"Maybe we'll find a secret oasis out there where we can be safe, but right now I vote to show Norm this thing." I pull the rolled up jacket from under my arm. "Jim?"

"I vote yes."

"Are you going to make it unanimous, Joe?"

"Okay, okay, let's do it your way, again."

"You're not gonna start that again are you?"

"No, but it's true."

"Okay, Norm, we've come to a decision. There's something here that we think will convince you."

Norm walks in cautiously. I start to unroll the cube from my jacket and Norm backs away.

"Don't worry, Norm. It's not a weapon or anything. Here, let me put it on the floor."

I put my jacket on the floor and holding a sleeve, I lift upward allowing the jacket to unroll. The cube drops out with a thud.

Norm approaches slowly. "What is it?"

"It's an ancient gold cube. It is supposedly going to help us find the cave we're looking for." I pick it up off the floor and hand it to Norm. "Here, go ahead and take a closer look at it."

Norm hefts it a little. "It's a heavy little sucker. What's all these little carvings on it?"

"It's supposed to be a map."

"It doesn't look like any map I've ever seen."

"Us either, but that's what we've been told it is."

"Okay, let's say I believe it is a map. What's it a map of?"

"This area. I guess basically the Middle East."

Jim, in his excitement blurts, "The Garden of Eden, too."

I turn around and give Jim a dirty look. "Jim," I say sternly. "I'm not exactly sure we should be telling everything."

"Oh, sorry, Bob."

"Now you guys are putting me on, aren't you? Last I heard the Garden of Eden was supposed to have been in either northern Turkey or southern Iraq, not anywhere near the Dead Sea. Now if you were looking for Sodom and Gomorrah there'd be a good chance of finding that in the Dead Sea, but you'd need lots of scuba gear and dredging equipment."

Joe begins to feel like Norm is making fun of us, or at the very least, is unbelieving of our story. "Listen, we didn't ask to come here and in fact we had very little choice in the matter. I'm tired, I'm thirsty and I'm dirty. If I had my way, I'd just pack it all in right now and go home, but I can't, I'm stuck." Joe goes over to the couch and plops himself down. "Now it would be greatly appreciated if you could let us spend the night, eat a little of your food and drop us off near where we need to go, but if you don't, we'll just have to do it on our own. It won't be easy but it won't stop us."

I try for some added incentive.

"We'll reimburse you for any inconveniences we cause you, and maybe even a little extra."

"Okay, I'll tell you what. Give me the whole story from the beginning and then give me a few minutes to give you my decision, agreed?"

"Sounds fair to me. You guys?"

Jim nods his head.

Joe smiles. "As long as I can get some water before you start, Bob."

"Me? Why do I have to tell him?"

"Because you tell it so well, and you're more experienced in public speaking."

"I'll get you all a glass of water," Norm says heading for the kitchen still holding the cube.

"Keep an eye on him, guys," Joe whispers.

Norm places the cube on the counter and fills three glasses with water out of the jug from the refrigerator. He brings the glasses to us, leaving the cube in the kitchen. Norm drags a chair from the other side of the living room next to his entertainment system. He obviously spent most of his interior decorating money on his television and stereo equipment.

"Okay, I'm ready." Norm sits down in front of the three of us, who are sitting on the couch, and folds his arms across his chest. "Let's hear it."

"Are you guys sure this isn't some sort of elaborate hoax?" Norm naturally sounds skeptical. "Somebody could have made that cube, maybe even that professor, and he was going to try to pass it off as the find of the century, and maybe got killed by someone who believed it was the find of the century."

I ask him the question that convinced Brother Martin it was the real thing. "What about the predictions concerning the three of us?"

"Yeah," Joe says. "What do you think of us?"

"The truth? I think you're just three fools on the run. Not dangerous fools, but fools nonetheless. Kinda like that song by Flint Asylum, *Fools on the Run*. You guys remind me of that song."

"'God has chosen the foolish things of this world to confound the wise.'"

We all turn and stare at Jim.

"What? It just came to me. I couldn't help it."

"That's okay, Jim," Joe says. "We're just not used to so much wisdom pouring forth from your mouth."

"'Out of the abundance of the heart the mouth speaks.'"

"Oh no, not you too, Bob."

"That was weird. It just kinda popped into my head so I said it. Is that what happened to you, Jim?"

"Yep."

"Okay, okay, enough of this already. First, anyone can memorize a bunch of Bible verses, so that stuff doesn't impress me. Second, I still think you're victims of a cruel hoax, and because of that I'm inclined to feel sorry for you and therefore I'm considering letting you stay the night and I'll drop you off on the coast of the Dead Sea. I just have one condition."

"I knew it," Joe says. "How much do you want?"

"Oh no, nothing like that. I just want you guys to promise me you won't come back here again. I don't need any trouble from the law. To tell you the truth, the only reason I'm even offering you the ride is to get you guys as far away from here as I can, as fast as I can. Besides, it's too dangerous out there at night to walk and too hot during the day. You'd never make it, and I would feel guilty. So is it a deal?"

"Sounds good to me," Joe says with a grin. "Just so long as I don't have to walk."

"That's okay, Joe, 'they shall run and not be weary, they shall walk and not faint.'"

"Knock it off, Jim," Joe says half joking. "You're starting to drive me nuts."

"Sorry." Jim looks a bit sheepish. "I couldn't help it."

I pat Jim on the shoulder. "That's okay, Jim, I understand."

Norm gets up out of his chair. "Well let's see if CNN has any news about you guys. They should, if you've been accused of what you say you are."

Norm goes over to his entertainment center and picks up his remote control. He steps back a few feet and points it in the general direction of the TV, which appears to be about a twenty-seven inch diagonal and stereo, too.

The television comes on in vivid color and the stereo sound comes from two large speakers at either end of the couch instead of from the TV. Norm switches to another satellite and then flips through the stations until he gets CNN news.

"I've got one of those new little rooftop dishes. It picks up just as good as the big ones at a fifth of the cost."

Norm sits in a recliner in the corner to our left, and we watch ten minutes of uninteresting news. Then a news item comes on about a terrorist attack at the Paris international airport.

"We have an update on the attack and an exclusive video taken by an American on vacation. The death toll now stands at fifty-three. The three gunmen opened fire with automatic weapons at the crowded ticket counters, then as security forces opened fire, they detonated a powerful explosive concealed in a suitcase left at the counter. The explosion allowed them to escape. This video was taken by an American tourist shortly after the explosion just outside the terminal. Notice the three men running away clad in jackets and blue jeans, their faces still covered by their masks. No group has yet claimed responsibility but informed sources say that it is the work of a new militant organization known as The Baptist Crusaders. This group is believed to be responsible for the deaths of more than fifteen people stretching from Michigan, through Canada and Greenland.

We have been supplied with pictures of the three believed to have committed most or all of these murders."

At this point all three of our faces are plastered across the screen. I stare at the screen for a moment, then I look in Norm's direction. He's staring at us.

"Honest, Norm, it wasn't us."

"I know."

"You know?"

"Well I know you didn't do the airport job anyway."

"Just out of curiosity," Joe says, "why are you so sure?"

"That video gave it away. It showed the terrorists running away so I was able to see the size of their calves."

"So?"

"So, I used to run cross-country in high school and I know runner's legs when I see them, and none of those guys do much running, they had skinny calves. On the other hand, I see that two of you do quite a bit of running."

"You're really observant," I say. "I never would have caught that."

"Oh, hey, look at that," Norm says.

Joe perks up. "Turn it up. I wanna hear this."

Norm uses the remote control and the volume gets louder.

I interrupt Joe's listening. "That was quick. Don't they usually take . . ."

"I said I wanted to hear this, now quiet."

"Sor. . . ry."

The camera pans the jubilant crowd in Saint Peter's Square, white handkerchiefs waving in the air.

It comes as no surprise to me as Joe's patience begins to run out. "So show us who it is already."

I question Joe about his sudden interest in the Catholic Church.

"Why are you so interested in what goes on in Catholicism?"

"I'm just wondering if that American Cardinal what's-his-name is the new Pope."

"What is his name anyway? Isn't it something like Lipid or Livid?"

"I don't know but it's a weird name. I do remember that."

The network switches to a different camera to show a balcony high above the square.

The reporter announces, "It looks like someone's coming out."

"How can he tell?" Joe says exasperated. "They're so far away you can hardly see the balcony. Zoom in closer."

Right on cue, as if they had heard Joe, the camera zooms right up to the balcony so that it fills the screen. Almost at the same time a chorus of cheers goes up from the crowd as a man steps out onto the balcony and waves to the crowd.

"There he is," the reporter continues. "The new leader of the Roman Catholic Church, Nain Olyba Blived. The first Pope to come from the western hemisphere. The speed with which he was elected indicates that he has very solid support within the church. At this time we do not know if he will make a statement, perhaps when the crowd quiets down, but it is entirely his prerogative. He seems at this point to be content with simply waving to the crowd. As yet we do not know what Pontifical name he will choose or has chosen, so for now we will simply call him 'The Pope.'

There are several reasons for the Pope's immense popularity, not the least of which was his spearheading the effort that finally brought the Greek Orthodox church back in union with the Roman Catholic church. He has stated many times that his primary objective in life is, 'to see the Church return to the glory and influence it once had before the reformation tore it apart. A spirit of cooperation is essential to bringing this about.' This man is expected to give the church a renewed hope for a more vital and living role in the spiritual lives of all peoples everywhere. It is no wonder this man is loved by so many."

I look at Joe. "Do you think this reporter is just a tad bit biased or what?"

Joe doesn't reply to my statement but Norm does.

"Usually CNN stays neutral in their reporting, but this is almost blatantly one-sided. He must be Catholic himself."

Joe laughs. "I wonder what old Floyd is thinking about this. I can just hear it now. 'The man's got shifty eyes, Millie, yessir, shifty eyes.'"

On the television, the camera has shifted back to the crowd and a reporter, who is standing in the square amongst the throng of people. He is practically yelling to be heard above the noise.

Then something strange happens. Slowly, a wave of silence sweeps through the crowd, from the front to the back, as every one begins to drop to their knees and bow their heads. This continues until the entire crowd is completely silent and the only sound is the wind across the reporter's microphone. The eeriness of it seems to have taken the reporter by surprise as he stands there, speechless for a moment or two. He's the only one still standing.

I nudge Joe with my elbow. "I hope they're all praying to God, because if they're not . . ."

"That's a spooky thought, Bob."

Then the Pontiff yells, loud enough to be picked up on the reporter's microphone.

"Glory and honor to the Church!"

With that the crowd stands to it's feet with cheering, clapping, and whistling. The noise is so loud it distorts the sound coming through the microphone and the new Pope turns and disappears into the building.

"That kind of power over people is really scary, Joe. I hope he doesn't abuse it."

Norm turns the television off and gets up out of his chair. "You guys want a sandwich? We need to eat and then hit the sack. We need to get up extra early if I'm going to give you guys a ride and still make it to work on time."

Norm walks toward the kitchen while we continue sitting on the couch. "This isn't a restaurant and I'm not a waiter so get up and make your own sandwiches."

Chapter 13

I toss and turn most of the night, even though I'm exhausted and the couch is fairly comfortable. I wonder how Joe and Jim liked the floor. I kick the afghan off and sit up when I hear Norm coming down the stairs.

"Light sleeper, eh?"

"I was last night."

"Did my taking a shower wake you?"

"No, that must have been one of the rare moments I was asleep." I blink my eyes and rub the sleep out of the corners. I feel grubby. "Would it be okay if I took a shower?"

"Sure, go ahead. Towels are at the top of the stairs and the bathroom is right next to the linen closet."

"Thanks."

"I hope everybody likes scrambled eggs because that's what I'm making."

"Yeah, that'll be fine."

I step over Joe and then Jim who are still snoozing, Jim being the noisier of the two.

The shower revives me, so for at least for the time being I feel awake. It's a shame I have to put my dirty clothes back on again. I turn off the shower and begin to dry off.

There's a banging on the bathroom door and Joe yells through it, "Hurry up in there! There's other people that's got to use the bathroom too ya know!"

"I'll be out in a minute, I just got done!"

I dry off and get dressed in a hurry, not just because of Joe but because I'm feeling real hungry. I open the door and Joe rushes in closing the door behind him.

"Uh, next?" I say. Jim is standing across the hall, leaning against the wall. "I didn't know I'd created a waiting line. See you downstairs, Jim."

I trot downstairs and walk into the kitchen where Norm is scrambling a large pile of eggs.

"Norm, I would suggest that we not wait for Jim. If we do, someone's not going to get anything to eat and it might be all of us."

"Let me get this straight, Jim is the skinny one isn't he?"

"Yep."

"Huh, I would've guessed Joe to be the bigger eater."

"He does pretty good himself but he doesn't come close to Jim."

"Is there any more?"

"Didn't I tell you, Norm?"

"You were right. And no, there isn't any more."

"Okay." Jim gets up from his chair at the table and goes into the living room. He picks up his jacket and pulls out his bag of candy and begins munching.

"Unbelievable," Norm says shaking his head. "Unbelievable."

"We've known Jim for a few years now," Joe says, "and we still find it unbelievable ourselves sometimes."

"I'm just gonna leave the dishes till I get home tonight. We've gotta hit the road."

The three of us push ourselves away from the table. Norm goes upstairs to get his name tag while I get my jacket and the cube out from under the couch where I'd hid it the night before.

Norm comes back down the stairs. "Okay, everybody ready?"

"I am," Joe says.

"Me too."

Jim sticks his candy back into his jacket pocket. "Me too."

"Good, let's go."

As Norm goes to unlock and open the front door, I slyly slip two of the bills worth about a hundred and sixty dollars each onto the top of one of his speakers. That should cover any inconveniences for Norm.

We walk out the door into the dim light of morning, and Norm closes and locks the door behind us. As we walk down the walk toward Norm's car I see a sentry, different than the one that was on duty last night, standing at the other side of the parking lot. Norm waves to him and he waves back.

"Dan's a good man. He used to be in the armed forces here, but during that intifada thing a few years back he and his patrol got ambushed by about forty Palestinians throwing rocks and molotov cocktails. He barely made it out alive. He got hit on the side of his knee by a rock that they say weighed in excess of six or seven pounds. They would have stoned and burned him to death, and his buddies too, if an Israeli helicopter gunship hadn't happened to be flying over the area at the time. Now he just lives off his retirement and does more than his share of patrol time."

We drive out of the parking lot and I look back at Dan who slowly limps down the small grassy crest that surrounds the parking lot. It's amazing how much pain, suffering and death simple stubborn pride on both sides has caused.

The sun begins to peek over the horizon on my left as we travel south down the road. About half an hour later we're heading straight into the sun. Norm puts his sunglasses on and his visor down but I can tell he's still having trouble seeing.

"The sun seems brighter here than in the U.S., Norm."

"It's because there's so little moisture in the air to help diffuse the light."

"How's the pollution here?"

"Except for the old towns, most of the settlements and factories have the latest technology in filters and recycling so it's really not a factor here."

"How much farther do we have to go?" Joe asks.

"I didn't know we had a little kid along," Norm laughs. "Does anyone have to go to the bathroom, too?"

Quietly Jim says something.

"What, Jim?" I ask.

"I said, 'I do.'"

Norm laughs again. "I was just kidding about the bathroom. Do you think you can wait maybe another ten minutes? When we get there you can find a big rock to hide behind. I hope you don't have to take a dump because not only are there no bathrooms, but there is nothing out there that even grows leaves."

"I'll try."

"You'll do more than try," Joe says. "I don't have a change of pants and neither do you."

A few minutes later Norm stops the car. "Here we are. There's a path leading down to where the wady opens out to the sea, just over to the left there. It's not very wide so watch your step. Also, if you need a boat, there are a couple in an alcove just around to the right after you get to the edge of the sea. Just be sure to bring it back when you're finished. They belong to some of my neighbors at the settlement."

"You go fishing a lot?" Joe asks.

"Don't do any fishing, nobody does. Not here anyway."

"Oh yeah, too salty."

"You got it. We just use them for recreation. I'm afraid you'll have to use the oars though because we keep the outboard motors back at the settlement."

After Jim gets out of the car I slide out and extend my hand to Norm through his window to shake his.

"Thanks for everything, Norm. We really appreciate it. More than words can tell."

"No problem. Just remember our agreement. Don't call me, I'll call you."

"Got it. Thanks again."

I step back from the car and Norm takes off in a cloud of dust, salt dust. I can taste the salt in the air and it makes the air very dry. It's already getting hot, even this early in the morning.

Joe walks up to me. "I hope it doesn't take too long out there. A guy could die of thirst real quick."

"Then let's get started. The sooner we find the cave, the sooner we can get out of this sun."

"If there is a cave."

We start walking toward the edge of the wady.

"Don't be so pessimistic, Joe."

"I can't help it, Bob. You heard Norm, he's been down here and so have countless archaeologist. If they couldn't find anything, how are we?"

"I don't know, but we gotta try."

We reach the edge of the wady and look down its steep slope. The dry river bed itself is about a thousand feet below us. There's a sprinkling of green here and there of plants that have grown up, being watered by the fresh water that comes down the valley after a good rain. Only the hardiest of plants survive the long dry spells and the torrents of water when it does rain enough for the water to make it to the sea.

"Norm lied," Jim says. "There are some leaves."

"It's probably all cactus," Joe says. "I'd like to see you use that for toilet paper."

"If Jim let it dry on he could use the cactus to scrape it off."

"A disgusting thought, Bob."

"Thanks, Joe."

"Okay, so where's this path Norm was talkin' about?"

"Don't know." I move closer to the edge and scan the slope to the left, then to the right. "Aha, there it is Joe, just over to our right. Norm wasn't kidding when he said it wasn't very wide." I follow the path up with my eyes to where it reaches the top. "It starts over there by that group of rocks."

"Let's go." Joe says.

We walk quickly over to the rocks. Behind the rocks there is a four foot drop to where the path starts.

"It looks like they use this rock to climb down to the path. There are some little foot holds and hand holds down the side of it."

"Good, then you go first, Bob."

"No problem, Joey." I climb down fairly quickly. No doubt a result of my tree climbing experience. "Nothing to it guys, come on down."

Joe's a little slower, but neither of them have any trouble climbing down.

"Now all we gotta do is follow this path down. Simple."

I may have underestimated the difficulty, as the widest the path ever gets is where we started. Sometimes the path even disappears for a couple of feet where it's been washed out by past rains. We jump across the short distance but it's a bit unnerving when you have to land on a one foot wide spot on the other side.

About halfway down Joe starts complaining, albeit light-heartedly.

"Simple he says. Just follow the path. Simple, he says."

"So it's a tiny little bit more difficult than I thought."

"Everything we do with you is more difficult than you thought."

"I know a quicker way down, Joe. You could jump."

We reach the bottom, dirty and sweaty, my hands dry from

coming in contact with the salty soil. What I wouldn't give for a bottle of hand lotion and a gallon of water.

We're about a hundred yards from the water's edge of the Dead Sea. The water looks surprisingly blue for the amount of minerals in it. I guess I was expecting a more milky color. The wady is actually quite wide at this point, about two hundred feet, and gets wider as it fans out into the sea.

"Let's go get our boat, guys."

"Where do you get your energy, Bob?" Joe says looking weary from the trip down. "Aren't you tired?"

"'They shall run and not be weary, they shall walk and not faint.'"

"That's easy for you to say, you're not carrying around an extra fifty pounds like I am."

"Well then, Jim and I will go on ahead and get the boat ready and we'll wait for you there."

"Okay, I guess."

"Come on, Jim, it can't be more than a good sprint from here."

I take off running and Jim follows along. The delta narrows as we run around to the right and the cliff gets steeper. The ground is also much more encrusted with the dried minerals that have been washed up on the shore. It actually crunches under our feet. Almost to where we run out of flat ground to run on, there's a shallow cave set into the cliff about six feet above the ground. There are some man-made steps carved out of the rock leading up to it.

"There it is, Jim. It looks like they put some work into those steps."

"Maybe they didn't do it, maybe they've been there for centuries."

"Could be."

We climb the steps and walk into the cave. It's a shallow cave going only about twenty feet into the cliff, and about as wide as it is deep. Lined up side by side are four row boats, three aluminum and one battered wooden one. I grab the front of the first aluminum boat we come to.

"I'll pull and you push, okay, Jim?"

"Yep."

Jim hurries around the boat and stumbles over something, just catching himself by grabbing the back of the boat.

"You okay, Jim?"

"Yeah, I'm okay. I just scraped up my ankle some, but you better come take a look here."

I walk around the side of the boat to the back. Jim is holding a chain wrapped in cloth. The cloth is evidently used to filter the salt out so the chain won't rust. Jim unwraps the cloth from the chain at the top of a metal stake that is pounded into the rock. The chain is padlocked to the stake.

"Now what do we do, Bob?"

"I don't know, let's check the other boats."

We check the other two aluminum boats and they too are chained and locked.

"This ones not," Jim says standing behind the old wooden boat.

"I guess it's better than nothing." I walk over to where Jim is standing. "Not much, though. Now I can see why they didn't bother to chain this one up. Help me turn it on its side so we can see if there's any holes in it."

I get in front and Jim stays at the back and we pull it out to the front of the cave.

"I thought you guys would have had the boat ready to go by now."

"You mean you hoped we'd have the boat ready to go so you wouldn't have to do anything."

"How come you're taking that one? Why don't you take one of those nice, light, aluminum ones?"

"Because they're not so nice and light when they're chained to a fifty million ton solid rock cliff."

"Oh."

Joe stands down below the cave while Jim and I turn the boat sideways to the cave opening and lift it onto its side with the bottom facing outward. I have Jim steady it while I inspect it for any light shining through the bottom.

"It looks okay, guys, only a couple pin holes that I can see. Nothing we can't keep bailed out. Okay, Jim, let's get this bugger down to Joe."

We slide the front of the boat out until the boat is balancing on the edge.

"Hold the boat there a minute, Jim. I'm gonna go down and help Joe." I trot down the steps and under the middle of the boat.

"Okay, Jim, push it out a couple feet and then come on down yourself."

As soon as Jim pushes, Joe grunts under the weight of the boat at the front. I try to help Joe out by moving toward the front a bit more.

"That better, Joe?"

"Yeah. Come on, hurry it up, Jim. This is heavy."

"You want me back here?"

"Yes, Jim," Joe heaves.

"Okay, guys," I say planting my feet more securely. "On the count of three, we lift it up and carry it to the edge of the water. Ready? One . . . two . . . three!"

With all three of us lifting it's not too bad, but holding it so high over our heads makes it somewhat awkward. We somehow manage to wobble our way the whole thirty feet or so to the water's edge.

"I'm gonna get out from underneath here and you guys let it down." I step quickly away. "I'm clear."

Jim is really straining at the wide back end so I go over to help. "Here, I'll get the left corner and you take the other."

We lower the boat to the ground, Joe's end hitting with a bit more force than ours. We all stand up straight and wipe the sweat from our faces. I sit down on the edge of the boat.

"Hey, uh, Joe?"

"What?"

"I noticed you were having some trouble holding up your end of the boat. Are you needing to build up your muscles? Maybe pump some iron?"

"I'm beginning to think so."

As I'm talking I'm untying a rope tied to the front seat. Something clunks to the bottom of the boat.

"Then here, maybe you can start with this." I pick up a small iron anchor encrusted with rust and hold it out to Joe.

"No wonder it was so heavy. How come you didn't take that out before we had to move it?"

"Because I didn't see it. I was only looking for holes, not anchors."

Jim picks up the oars. "Or oars."

"When did you start stuttering Jim?" I say.

Jim looks puzzled. "What?"

"It went right over his head, Joe."

Jim mouths the words again, thinks about it a moment, then his face brightens. "Oh, or oars. I get it."

I set the anchor back in the boat and go around to the back. "Okay, let's get this thing in the water."

We push the boat out until all but a foot of it is in the water. Jim and I hop in and move toward the front to take the weight off the back, making it easier for Joe to push the boat into deeper water. Joe hops in and we're on our way . . . sort of.

"Well, Bob?"

"Well what, Joe?"

"Aren't you going to start rowing?"

"Why me?"

" 'Cause you're sitting in the rower's seat where those doodads are for the oars."

"We'll just have to switch seats then, Joe."

"Why can't you row?"

"Because I'm holding the cube."

"I'm perfectly capable of holding the cube while you row."

"Oh, so now you want to hold the cube. How many days has it been? And now you just happen to want to hold the cube for me? Well forget it. I'm holding the cube and you or Jim are going to have to row."

"Okay, Jim, you didn't paddle the canoe so this time you get to row."

"But I don't know how."

"Now's a good time to learn," I say, getting up and working my way to the front.

"But . . ."

"We'll teach you, Jim. It's not that hard. You use both oars to go straight, the left oar to go right and the right oar to go left. Got it?"

"No."

"Just sit down and we'll tell you what to do."

"Okay." Jim gets out of his seat rather unsteadily and I sit down quickly before Jim can manage to tip me out of the boat. If this were a canoe we'd all be out of the boat. Jim sits down. "Now what?"

"First," Joe says, "you have to face the back of the boat."

"How am I supposed to see where I'm going?"

"Joe will do that for you."

"That sounds dumb."

"Well it's not. You'll see why once you start rowing." Jim turns around and I continue. "Okay, now put the oars into those doodads there on the sides of the boat. Very good, Jim. Now row in a counter clockwise motion so that when your oars are in the water you're pulling the handles toward you."

Jim has a little trouble getting coordinated, but finally catches on. "Hey, this isn't so hard. All you have to do is go in circles with the paddles."

Joe laughs. "Which is what we're doing with the boat, too. We need to turn around and go the other way if we're wanting to head north. Just row with one oar and we'll spin right around."

"Which one?"

"It doesn't matter, either one. It doesn't matter."

Jim gets us turned around and we begin our slow journey northward up the west bank of the Dead Sea.

"Keep us fairly close to shore, Joe."

"Okay. Jim, a little more with your left oar."

The shore isn't much as far as having anyplace where we could stop and get out of the boat. The cliffs go straight up to a height of twelve-hundred to fifteen-hundred feet, and are pockmarked with numerous shallow caves that we can easily see, even from where we are, go only a few feet into the face of the cliff.

I unwrap the cube from my jacket. "Okay, so now how is this supposed to help us find the cave?"

"A little to the right, Jim. Maybe the design on the cube will match the pockmarks on the cliff. Is there anything that looks like the side of a cliff on it?"

I look at each side of the cube carefully, looking for anything that could resemble the face of a cliff. As I turn it, once in a while it catches the sun just right and the reflection is so bright it blinds me for an instant. Evidently I'm not the only one because I get some complaints from Joe.

"How am I supposed to be able to tell Jim which way to go if you keep blinding me with that thing?"

"Sorry, Joe, but it was your idea to check the cube for clues."

"Hey, Bob, there's a promising looking cave."

The cave Joe's talking about is about twenty feet above the water and appears to go back pretty far.

"We need a spotlight to check these caves out."

"Why don't you use the cube like a mirror and reflect the sun's light into it?"

"Very good, Joe. That's the kind of idea I usually come up with."

"Yeah . . . right. Just do it, Bob."

I angle one side of the cube to reflect the sunlight onto the side of the cliff and then move the large square of light across the face of the cliff and into the cave in question.

"Yep," I say, disappointed. "It works really good, Joe. I can see the back of the cave perfectly. Let's move on."

"Well, at least we answered one question. Now we know how the cube is going to help us find the cave."

We travel slowly up the coast and time seems to travel even more slowly. Jim seems to be getting the hang of rowing, but he's also showing signs of fatigue. "Why don't you row for a while, Joe?"

"Why don't you?"

"I told you, because I'm holding the cube."

"Well I think you can put the cube down for a while."

"No, I can't. I have to use it to look at the caves as we go by."

"You won't for about the next fifteen or twenty minutes."

"Why?"

"If you were doing your job, you'd know why. Take a look at the cliff."

I look and the face of the cliff is as smooth and blemish free as a formica countertop. The only exception being a small ledge that extends at an angle from the surface of the water to about one third of the way up the cliff. At that point it stops.

"You see?" Joe says. "Now get back here and row."

"I can't."

"And why not?"

"There might be a tiny cave up there someplace."

"There's nothing there, Bob, now quit stalling."

"Okay, right after I flash the cliff real quick, just to make sure."

"Keep your clothes on, Bob . . . please."

"Funny, Joe, you know what I meant."

"Yeah, but you're still stalling, but if it'll get you back here rowing, hurry up."

I move the square of reflected light quickly back and forth across the face of the smooth grayish cliff in a rather haphazard fashion. Joe's right, I am stalling for time. I figure the less I have to row, the less I'll dehydrate, which I'm doing at a fast enough rate as it is.

I'm only half paying attention to what I'm doing when a dark spot suddenly appears and then disappears on the cliff as the spot of light speeds across.

"Okay, Bob, that's enough."

"Wait! I think I saw something."

"Knock it off, Bob. It's your turn to row. Go ahead, Jim, you can stop."

"I mean it. I thought I saw something." I frantically move the light around in the general area where I thought I saw it. "It was somewhere in . . . here." It appears again, for just an instant as the light passes by. "There, did you guys see it?"

"Yeah," Joe says. "Go back to your right just a little."

"I think it was a little lower," Jim says, pointing.

Now that I've narrowed down the area, I move the light in a slow circular motion. Then it appears, just before where the ledge ends, a cave, and it seems to be quite deep.

"This is really weird, Joe." I move the light on and off the spot several times and each time it disappears and reappears. "It's some sort of false image that's being projected onto the face of the cliff. Like a mirage, and when I put this light on it, it makes it go away."

"Don't get too excited, Bob," Joe says. "It could be the cube putting the image of a dark spot up there. I would think the sun shining on it would be bright enough to make it show up, or even when the sun is at the right angle to reflect off the water."

"Maybe the sunlight and the reflection off the water are the wrong color. Remember the cube is gold and it's going to reflect a shade of gold light."

"I don't buy it."

"Well, I say we should check it out."

"I say you just don't want to row."

"I say you're right, I don't want to row, but that's not important now. I think we should check it out. Tell you what. If this isn't the right cave, I'll do all the rowing until we find the right cave."

"That sounds like a good deal Jim. We'd better take him up on it."

"Good. Let's see if we can get up to it by climbing that ledge there."

"And if we can't?"

"Then I guess we can't and I start rowing."

I try to keep the cube pointed so the light stays on the area that shows the dark spot. As we get closer I'm able to start seeing some detail and depth, making me even more sure that it is a real cave and probably the one we're looking for.

"I know this is it guys. I can feel it."

Jim bumps us up against the cliff fairly gently. There's no place to tie the boat so Joe slowly lets the anchor down. We are afraid to drop it because there may be more water than there is rope, and if that were the case it could flip the boat.

"There's no bottom here guys. Is there any place on that ledge where we could hook the anchor, Bob?"

"Yeah, Joe, I think this little crag here might hold it, as long as the sea stays calm."

"Here, Jim, hand this to Bob."

Joe hands the anchor to Jim, who in turn hands it to me while I hold the front of the boat up against the cliff by holding onto the crag. I hook the anchor onto the crag and Joe takes up the slack in the rope by wrapping it around the seat. The boat swings around so that the right side is now up against the cliff so it'll be easier to climb out and onto the ledge.

I put the cube into my jacket pocket, and even though I'm already sweating like a pig, I slip my jacket on in order to free up the use of both hands for the climb. I climb onto the narrow ledge, which is narrower than the path we took down to the Dead Sea earlier. Looking up in the direction we have to go, I notice that it doesn't get any wider the higher it goes. I turn around with my back to the cliff so I can see how close I am to the edge. My feet stick over the edge about an inch. I move sideways up the twenty degree incline a few feet to give Jim and Joe some room to climb up.

"You're not going to like this, Joe."

"I haven't liked anything yet so why should this be any different?"

"This is worse, Joe, even I don't like it. There is one redeeming factor, however."

"What's that?"

"If we fall, we hit the water and not rocks."

"Well I hate to admit it," Joe says helping Jim up. "But I hope you're right about this being the cave."

"Why's that?"

"Two reasons." Joe pulls himself onto the ledge with a groan and then a grunt. "First, so I can get out of this heat, and second, so I don't have to come back down this . . ." Joe wobbles and catches his balance once more. ". . . again."

Fortunately the ledge's width only varies about an inch either way. As long as we keep our eyes on where we step and our backs to the cliff, we are okay. Joe seems to be having more trouble than Jim or I. I figure it must be the added weight out front causing him to be a little more off balance. The process of working our way along the ledge is slow. Each sideways step covers only about ten inches and they can't be hurried. One wrong move and I take a dip in the sea and then I'd have to start all over again. That is, assuming I survive.

"How much farther, Bob?"

"I don't know, Joe. I can't see the cave without using the cube, but judging by how high we are above the water I'd say we're about a quarter of the way there."

It already looks a long way down and we're only about a hundred feet above the water. The cave looked like it was a good four hundred feet above the water line.

"I'm hungry."

"Shut up, Jim," we both say.

"But I am."

Chapter 14

I feel like I've been going up forever. My legs and especially my calves are tired. My back is sore and all my clothes are sticking to my body and I just plain feel slimy.

I continue to watch my feet as I inch along. "We should be getting close, guys."

Joe's not so sure. "I'm beginning to think I was right about there not being a cave up here."

I look up the smooth face of the cliff ahead. "There's only about fifty more feet to go and the ledge ends, Joe. If we don't find it by . . ."

I suddenly fall backwards and find myself staring up at the jagged roof of a cave. I can hear Jim outside. Evidently he stopped after I fell.

"Bob's gone, Joe."

"Gone where? Did he fall?" Joe's second question had an edge of concern to it.

"I don't think so. I would have seen him if he did. He was just there, I looked away to watch my feet to take another step and when I looked up, he was gone. You don't think it was the rapture, do you?"

"Nah, couldn't be that. We would've been gone, too."

"Well where'd he go?"

"I don't know, but we're not gonna find him standing here."

I stand up and brush myself off in the relative coolness of the cave.

"I'm in here, guys!"

My voice echoes behind me, tapering off until it's barely audible.

"Where?" Comes Joe's answer.

"In the cave!"

"What cave? Come on, Jim, move on up. We can't see any cave, Bob!"

I poke my head around the corner and Jim is just inches from the opening.

"I'm right here," I say calmly.

Jim practically jumps out of his skin and loses his balance. He begins to fall but I grab his arm and jerk him into the cave. We both fall to the floor of the cave. I get up and brush myself off again.

Joe comes around the corner into the cave. "That is really strange, it's like you went right through solid rock, Jim, and Bob's arm was sticking out of it. I kept waiting to bump my head when I came through."

"Yeah, even real close to the entrance you still can't see the cave. I wonder what causes the effect," Jim says brushing some dirt off his elbow.

I ponder Jim's statement. "I think it's an optical illusion made by God, like when the men of Sodom tried to get at the two angels and God struck their eyes so they wearied themselves trying to find the door."

"I thought God made them blind," Jim says.

"If they were blind they could still find the door by feeling for it, but God caused them to see things that weren't there and not see things that were. Kinda like those two disciples on the road to Emaeus. Jesus didn't change his appearance, he was still in his physical body, he simply made them see a different person until he felt it was time for him to let them see. There's one other time, too, when a prophet, whose name I can't remember right now, but anyway, this prophet led a whole army right into the middle of the Sumerian capital to be captured and they were looking for this prophet to kill him and God made it so they didn't recognize him or their surroundings until it was too late and they had to give up. They weren't blind either, God just made them see what he wanted them to see, and I think that's what he did with this cave."

"Nice theory, Bob," Joe says. "But I'm hungry and thirsty and I want to get this done so I can eat, drink, take a shower and go to sleep. So let's get movin' here."

We start walking farther into the cave, but before we go barely a dozen steps it gets so dark we can no longer see where we're going.

"This isn't going to work, Bob," Joe says, his voice echoing back to him several times. "Unless you've got a white cane each of us could use, we're gonna kill ourselves by falling into a hole or something."

"Maybe we could make some torches," Jim suggests.

"Out of what?"

"You know, Joe, out of sticks and cloth or even spider webs."

"There aren't any sticks in here, Jim, and I might ask the all important question, does anybody happen to be carrying any matches since none of us smokes?"

A thought suddenly occurs to me. "I don't have any matches, but do you think this might help?"

I pull my hand out of my jacket pocket and flip on my trusty little penlight.

"Where'd you get that?" Joe sounds indignant.

"From home. I used it when I was running around in the dark getting those pictures of the cube."

"It's not very bright," Jim says.

Joe laughs. "Neither are you but we still keep you around."

"Better than nothing, Jim, but I don't know how long the battery's gonna last or how far we gotta go so we better get moving."

We walk single file with me leading the way. Joe has his hand on my back and Jim has his hand on Joe's. I let them know each time there's something to step over, on, or down.

"Rock, Joe."

"Okay. Rock, Jim."

"Okay."

At first the cave takes us downhill, but after a while we begin an almost steady uphill climb. Not steep, but noticeable.

Joe pats me on the back. "Can we stop and rest? My legs are getting really tired."

"Yeah, we can eat our snacks."

"Good idea, Jim. We could use the extra energy."

I find a couple good size smooth rocks to sit on and turn the flashlight off.

"Hey, I can't see," Jim complains.

"I need to save the battery, Jim."

"Why? Is it under conviction?"

"Just eat your pretzels, Joe."

It's amazing just how dark darkness can be. The blackness seems to be pressing in on me as if it has substance and texture. If I were claustrophobic it would be suffocating.

"Could you turn the flashlight on for just a second, Bob?"

"Why, Jim?"

"So I can see what colors I'm eating. I can't tell what flavor it is unless I see the color."

Joe laughs and it echoes loudly from both directions. "M&M's

don't have flavors. The colors are artificial so they're all going to taste the same."

"They always seemed to taste different before."

"I think it was just your mind playing tricks on you. You thought they should taste different so they did."

"Does that mean you're not going to turn the flashlight on for me, Bob?"

"Just pretend they're all your favorite color, Jim."

I open my mixed fruit and am amazed at how good it tastes. I hadn't realized until now just how hungry I am.

"These pretzels are making me thirsty. I sure wish we'd brought some water along."

"Too bad Moses isn't still around, Joe, maybe he could get us some water out of these rocks."

"No thanks, I don't care to be wandering these caves for another forty years."

I eat most of my fruit before I decide I've had enough.

"You guys ready to get moving again?" I say closing up the bag holding only a small handful of dried fruit that I thought might be good to save for later and stuffing it in my pocket. "Okay, I'm ready." I flip on my flashlight and we once again continue our journey.

"Uh, oh."

"What is it, Bob?"

"We have a decision to make, Joe. There's two ways to go here. There's a large tunnel on the left and a much smaller one to the right."

"How much smaller? If it's too small I could make the decision very easy."

"Not small enough for you not to fit through, Joe."

"The big tunnel will most likely stay large enough for it to be passable, whereas the smaller one, I would think, would be more likely to be a dead end."

"Okay, one vote for the big tunnel. Jim, what do you think? The wide tunnel or the narrow tunnel?"

"'Enter ye in at the straight gate: for wide is the gate, and broad is the way that leadeth to destruction, and many there be which go in threat: Because straight is the gate and narrow is the way which leadeth unto life, and few there be that find it.'"

"Thank you, Mister Bible."

"Wait, Joe, it just might apply to our situation. If we truly are on a mission for God, which I believe we are, then it would make sense for God to put obstacles in the way of those who would not know or understand how to apply scripture to their everyday situations. I was going to vote for the wide tunnel but I've changed my mind. Let's take the narrow way."

"Yeah, sure. You guys just wanna see me get stuck."

"You're not that fat, Joe, especially after these last few days."

"You don't have to butter me up. I was already planning to change my mind the same way as you."

We head into the small tunnel and even though there's less room, it's actually easier going. Because the walls are closer together the flashlight is able to show both walls at the same time.

"Wait guys." I stop and try to listen.

"What is it?"

"Quiet, Joe. I thought I heard some footsteps."

"Prob'ly just our own echoing back."

"Let me make sure first."

I wait for the echoes of our voices to fade away. Then I hear it, and so does Joe, but it's not footsteps.

"That's not footsteps, Bob." Joe perks up and starts pushing on my back to urge me forward. "That's dripping water."

"You don't have to push, Joe, I'm just as thirsty as you are."

As we hurry through the tunnel the sound of dripping water becomes the sound of running water. The floor of the cave becomes noticeably damp and I get dripped on several times. Finally I see a shimmer when the light hits upon a substantial amount of water.

"Here it is guys. Taste it, Joe. See if it's okay to drink."

"Me?"

"Okay . . . Jim you try it."

"Uh, uh, no way."

"Fine, I'll do it myself." I kneel down and stick my finger in the water. I can feel it's coolness flow past my finger. I stick my finger in my mouth trying to taste anything out of the ordinary.

"You're not going to like this, Joe."

"Why? Is it bad?"

"No, you're just not going to like this because it doesn't taste like city water. It's just plain old cool, refreshing, clean, clear, untreated, non-fluoridated, no artificial flavors or colors added, spring water."

"I'll suffer. Let me in there."

Joe squeezes next to me leaving no room for Jim.

"What about me?"

I check to see how wide the water is and then jump the four feet to the other side.

"There you go, Jim." As soon as Joe and Jim begin to drink I turn off the flashlight and quench my own thirst.

The water goes down cool and wet and I can feel it pour through and past my stomach. For a while I just can't get enough and I drink until I feel like I'm going to burst.

I splash the cool water on my arms and face, washing away all the old crusty sweat. It makes me feel clean and refreshed and ready to go again. I wish now we'd brought something to carry water in. Come to think of it, there's a lot of things I would have brought along if I'd thought about it.

"Next time we do this, guys, we're going to have to come better prepared."

Joe gives a grunt. "Next time you're doing this on your own, cause I'm staying home."

"It takes a big man to admit he doesn't have what it takes to make it through the hard times."

"If I could see you, I'd show you who has what it takes."

"Even if you could see me, you wouldn't have what it takes to catch me."

"Maybe not, but one of these days you'll slip and fall and I'll sit on you and squash you flat."

"Yeah, you do have what it takes to do that."

"Okay, enough of this small talk, let's get going. I'm beginning to feel like a mole."

I step back a few feet from the water and shine the flashlight on the water. Joe and Jim each jump across and we continue on.

After several more stops to rest and an unknown number of hours, the cave seems to get wider.

"We might be getting closer to the end, guys. The tunnel's getting bigger."

"I hope so," Joe says. "I think we've walked into tomorrow. I'll bet we've walked thirty or forty miles."

"My guess would be closer to thirty than forty. It just seems longer 'cause most of it was uphill."

My voice seems to echo from all around me. I stop and try to locate a wall, but the light isn't strong enough to shine that far.

"We're in a large open area, guys, I can't find any walls."

"Follow our tracks back and then follow the wall around until we find the way out."

"Good idea, Joe."

I point the flashlight back in the direction we just came and follow our footprints back to where the cave opened up.

"Here it is guys. Shall we go clockwise or counter-clockwise?"

"Clockwise," Joe says. "We should always be going right."

I keep the light on the base of the wall and follow it around, watching for it to go into another cave.

"You know, Joe," I say stepping over a small rock, "as unstable as this area is, I'm surprised these caves haven't collapsed long ago. I haven't even seen very many fallen rocks."

"What are there, Bob? Three or four major faults running through Israel?"

"Four I think. Three for sure, the two on each side of the Dead Sea and the one running through Jerusalem.

"Yep, the one that's gonna split the city in half some day. I think that's what's going to destroy the Dome of the Rock and allow the Jews to rebuild their temple."

"Wasn't it you that showed me that article about how there's a group of Jews who already have all the materials ready for the new temple and are just waiting for the right time?"

"Yeah, that was interesting wasn't it?"

"Aha!" My voice echoes extra loud as I find the tunnel entrance. Just as we're about to enter in I see a light back in the tunnel and it's coming towards us, and fast.

"Somebody's coming," I whisper loudly and start to back up. I bump into Joe.

"What?"

"I said . . ."

There's the sound of rushing air and the cavern room is lit up like daylight. At the same time that I turn to look, I feel the heat coming from the source of the light on the side of my face. Flames flash outward from a white hot interior. I try to look into it to see what's at the center, but it's too bright.

"What is it, Joe?"

"I can't tell just yet. Just a sec." Joe pulls out a pair of sunglasses as we continue to back slowly away from it. The long narrow flames swing back and forth across the entrance, not moving toward us or away. "It looks like there's a big four or five foot sword in there."

"This is it, Joe!" I say excitedly. "This is the entrance to the Garden of Eden!"

"The flaming sword." Joe sounds awestruck, but he quickly comes back to the reality of our situation. "But how are we going to get past it?"

"Maybe if we go at the entrance from three different angles at the same time, it won't be able to get all of us."

"Right, good idea, Bob. Your idea of a good idea is that one or two of us sacrifice themselves so one can make it through. And who here is the slowest? Yours truly. Uh uh, no way. We'll think of another idea, like going back the way we came and forgetting about the whole thing."

"Maybe we just have to ask and it'll let us go through."

"It's worth a shot, Bob. Go ahead, go for it."

"Me? Why me?"

"Because it's your idea."

"All right, Joe, I'll show you who the real man is here." I take a deep breath and step toward the flaming sword. It swings in my direction and stops, pointing straight at me.

"Um . . . excuse me, but could you let us past?"

Nothing happens, then Joe calls to me, "Bob, I think you'd better step back here and see something."

I move backward slowly as if I were confronted with a dangerous animal and any sudden movement might cause it to attack.

"What, Joe?"

"Look." He points out into the cavern room that is now well lighted by the flames.

What has caught Joe's attention and now mine is a scattering of human skeletons. Evidently adventurers and soldiers who have stumbled across the cave down through the centuries. Judging from the positions of some of the bodies, some were trying to escape the way they came, while others look as if they had tried to fight their way through with a variety of weapons. From spears, to swords, to bow and arrow, to guns and even a bazooka. There's the helmet of a World War

II German soldier just feet away from where I'm standing and almost right next to him is the helmet of a U.S. World War I soldier.

"It doesn't look like running is the answer, Joe, and it doesn't look like fighting does any good either."

"Well we can't just stand here! We'll starve to death!"

"You think getting fried is better?"

"It'd be quicker."

"Lord Almighty," I hear Jim say as his arm comes between Joe and I, his finger pointing in the direction of the flaming sword.

I look, and standing on each side of the sword are two large creatures standing about fifteen feet tall with two sets of wings each. One set is stretched outward and up, making them look more awesome than they already are. Possibly a good seven foot wing span, making it about eighteen feet from wing tip to wing tip. The other set is folded partially across their bodies and faces, then as these too are moved and stretched outward they reveal an even stranger sight. At first I only see three faces, but as the human looking face turns toward us, I see a fourth one on the back of the head. Each face is different, the one facing us is human, looking gentle yet stern at the same time. The face to the left of the human one looks like a lion and the one to the right looks like an ox. The one to the back, which seems to fit the body best, is that of an eagle. Then, in a loud voice that easily overpowers the sound coming from the sword, the creature on the right speaks.

"What do you wish with the God of heaven and earth?"

"I think he's talking to you, Jim," Joe says moving around to a position behind Jim.

"I . . . uh . . ." Jim is visibly shaking. "You talk to him, Bob. I can't. I don't know what to say."

"Step forward, one called Benjamin of the tribe of Levi."

"He means you, Bob," Joe says prodding my back.

"I know, Joe, don't push me." I take a step forward. "We're here to find the Garden of Eden."

"By who's authority?"

"God's . . . I guess."

"Which god?"

"The God that created heaven and earth, the Almighty God."

"Then you are prepared to present the vessel, and say the

words." The creature says it in the form of a statement of fact rather than a question.

I turn to Joe and Jim. "What's he mean by vessel, and what words?"

Jim taps my pocket. "Try showing them the cube."

Of course, the cube. In Brother Martin's letter he said we had to present ourselves and the cube. I should have remembered that.

I pull the cube out of my pocket and hold it out in the palm of my hands. Both creatures turn around so that now the eagle faces are looking at us. I guess and eagle's eyes are better able to see the cube, then I notice the other eyes as their movement catches my attention. I don't know why I hadn't seen them before since there are so many of them, thousands in fact, all over the creature's wings. They seem to be looking everywhere, darting one way and then another.

The creatures turn again, back to the human face. "Say the words."

"What words is he talking about, Joe?" I whisper loudly, looking for some help.

"I don't know, just say something."

"What if I'm wrong?"

The creature's voice booms loudly. "Then you may not leave this place!"

This must be the point at which these other guys panicked and made their decision to either fight or run. It seems that both those options appear to have been fatal. Joe must have come to the same conclusion.

"Don't move, you guys. I think if we try to leave this room, we're fricasseed."

"You don't have to tell me, Joe."

We both look at Jim. He looks scared but still in control.

"Say the words!" The creature says insistently.

"What words, Joe? I don't remember anything in Brother Martin's letter about this."

"Maybe it's something from the Bible, like a scripture."

There's an edge of desperation in our voices, as we grasp at any idea that might help.

"Oh, well that really narrows it down to about a few hundred thousand choices."

"Maybe we're trying too hard, maybe we have to let the Holy Spirit work through us."

"I'm too worked up, Joe. I need to calm down."

"Say the words!" This time both creatures say it. Then they turn a quarter turn so the lion's face is toward us and the sword's flames flare.

"I don't like the looks of this, Bob."

"I don't think they're gonna be patient much longer, Joe."

"What was it that Clif said he'd do when he felt trapped? He said it always helped him to allow the Holy Spirit to work through him."

"He said he'd look toward heaven and say 'Jesus is Lord,' but . . ."

The creature on the right booms in an ear-shattering voice, "The time is near!" Then both creatures turn back again to the human face.

"We're doomed," Joe says rather matter-of-factly.

"Wait, Joe. Look!"

The sword fades, then disappears altogether. The creatures both fold one set of their wings across the front of themselves, covering their entire body and faces. Then the one on the right speaks again.

"We must go and prepare, our work here is finished."

With that said, both creatures disappear in a blur that seems to me to be in an upward direction but it happens so quickly I really can't be sure, and it also leaves us totally in the dark once again.

Jim's meek voice comes through the darkness.

"Are we dead?"

Joe and I both laugh, our commotion echoing back.

Time to turn on the little old penlight again. I put the cube back in my pocket and pull out the flashlight. I know this time where the entrance is so I walk straight ahead and into the tunnel, which I am hoping and praying will be the last leg of our journey.

We're all quiet for a while. I guess we're all contemplating everything that's happened. It's not every day a person gets to meet spiritual beings like that face to faces.

"Those were cherubim, weren't they, Joe?"

"Yeah, I guess so. I always imagined them to be a lot smaller though."

"I wish they'd left that sword to help light the way. This trying to find our way using this tiny little flashlight is really getting to be the pits."

"I wish they'd left us something to eat."

"Isn't it amazing, Bob?"

"What's that, Joe?"

"The whole time our lives were on the brink of becoming non-existent Jim doesn't say a word and now, the first thing that comes out of his mouth is something about food. Unbelievable."

"What do you expect. That's the only thing that goes into his mouth. However, a little manna or something wouldn't be bad right about now."

We walk on for a while longer, and I'm beginning to feel the wear of the long, strenuous day on my body, and if I'm getting tired, I can imagine how Joe's feeling right about now. Maybe we should stop and rest.

"You guys wanna take a break and rest for a few minutes?"

"No," Joe says, his answer surprising me. That is until he finishes. "I want to take a break for a few hours."

"Me too," Jim adds.

The tunnel widens out a little making it a good place for all three of us to sit together or even stretch out. "Here's a good spot."

All of us groan to one extent or another as we sit down in the soft soil. I almost turn the flashlight off but it suddenly strikes me as odd that the soil is so soft. I lean over and examine the soil more closely. It's dry, as I would expect it to be since the only water we've seen was that small stream, but it's unusual in it's color and texture.

"Take a look at this, mister future farmer." Joe comes over into the light. "Isn't this about the richest soil you've ever seen? It's almost black."

"Wow, you know with a little water and sunlight, I'll bet I could grow about a bushel of wheat per square foot in this stuff."

"Just think, Joe, this soil has probably been undisturbed since the creation, just the way God originally made it. I'll bet if we took a sample of it to a lab and had it analyzed, we could find out the perfect balance of nutrients God had put there in the beginning, then we could duplicate that balance in the fields and make just about any place a land flowing with milk and honey."

"There's only one flaw to your plan, Bob."

"What's that?"

"You're assuming that the pesticides and other pollutants already in the soil and water aren't going to affect the growth of the plants in any way."

"Okay, that may be true, but at least we'd be closer than what we have now."

"I just thought of another reason it wouldn't work, at least not right now. We don't have anything to put it in that's sterile. Anything we use would change the composition of the soil."

"Then we'll just have to come back later and get samples, now that we know where to find them."

"Who's we? Certainly not me."

"How about you, Jim? It would mean more food at cheaper prices for everybody."

"That's a dirty trick, Bob, you knew the minute you mentioned food Jim would be all for it."

"I was gonna do it anyway," Jim says out of the darkness. "It sounds like a good idea, even if you had to clean and filter the dirt to get out the contaminants, I think it'd be worth it."

"There you go, Joe. We could start out just making potting soil, then expand to selling to greenhouses until we can expand into a process that could clean and mix enough soil to do lawns and fields. Think about it, Joe, think of all the good it could do."

"Aren't you forgetting about one little thing, Bob?"

"What?"

"How are you going to do all this when you're wanted as an international terrorist?"

"I figure when this is over, we'll be cleared of all charges."

"How do you figure?"

"I don't know, I guess I don't believe God would send us on this mission for him and then just leave us hanging."

"You mean like Peter?"

"Okay, poor choice of words. But you're right, God causes it to rain on the just and the unjust alike. I'm still going to plan on coming back here to get samples, God willing." I turn my flashlight off letting the soil filter through my fingers. "I think I'm going to stretch out for a few minutes." I take my jacket off and roll it into a ball and use it as a pillow. "Wake me up if I fall asleep, okay guys?"

I put my head down on my makeshift pillow and close my scratchy eyes.

Chapter 15

I wake up with somebody wiggling my foot.

"Who's foot do I have? Bob's or Joe's?"

"It's mine."

"This is Jim."

"I know, I can tell by your voice."

"Oh."

"How long have I been sleeping, Jim?"

"I don't know, I just woke up myself."

"Where's Joe?"

"I don't know."

"Joe?"

"I think I hear him, Bob."

The sound of heavy breathing comes from just ahead of us and on the opposite side of the tunnel. I turn on the flashlight and spot Joe sound asleep, curled up against the wall.

"Joe! Wake up!" I yell.

Joe startles awake. "What? What?"

"A little tense are we, Joe?"

"How long was I asleep?"

"I don't know. Jim and I both fell asleep too. It could've been minutes or it could've been hours. Hard tellin'."

Joe groans as he gets to his feet. "Judging by the way I feel, I'd say hours."

"I guess we oughta get moving again, eh guys?"

"I'm surprised your flashlight's still working, Bob. What kind of batteries are in there?"

"I don't remember and I don't care, just so long as they keep going and going and going."

We start moving through the tunnel again but we barely go a dozen steps when the tunnel widens out quickly.

"We're heading into another large room, guys, and judging by my echo it's got to be at least twice as big as the other one."

"That's nice, Bob," Joe says, "but are there any signs that we're coming to the end of this thing?"

"You mean, is there a light at the end of the tunnel?"

"Yeah, something like that."

"Not that I can tell."

"I just had a terrible thought, Bob. What if this cave goes on for about fifty miles and then just stops? We'd have to walk all the way back "Even worse, Joe, what if it just circles around and we come back to that large tunnel we passed way back there?"

"I can think of something worse," Jim says, getting into the "what if" contest. "What if this cave just goes on forever, all over the earth?"

Then something cracks and then snaps under my foot. I stop. "What was that?" I point the flashlight down around my foot. "There it is. That's something I haven't seen in a long time, a twig from a tree. Must've gotten carried in here by a bird or something."

"You know, that's something I've noticed," Joe says. "I haven't seen a single animal in this cave. No birds, no bats, not even any bugs."

"Maybe not even they were allowed to pass by the flaming sword, Joe."

"Maybe so, but it's really weird being the only living things down here."

"Except for those cherubim."

"Yeah, except for them, and that kinda makes me nervous too. We might say or do something wrong and they'd sick their sword on us."

"Hey Joe, look here." I put the light on a small patch of dried brown grass. "Now that's weird, Joe. I wonder how grass could grow down here?"

"It's one of life's little mysteries."

"Ouch!"

"What is it, Bob?"

"It felt like I ran into . . ." I reach up and grab hold of it. "It is, it's a branch."

"Well now we know where the twig came from."

I snap the branch off. "This tree's as dead as that grass." I shine the flashlight around a bit and in the faint light I can tell there are two trees in our immediate area, but beyond that it's total blackness. "I only see two trees, guys. They aren't very tall, maybe fifteen to twenty feet is all, and very dead."

"How do you think they got here?"

"I don't know, Joe, maybe there used to be a hole in the roof of the cave that allowed sunlight, rain and a few seeds to fall in here and grow and then a large boulder could have fallen into the opening, sealing it off."

"Good theory, Bob, but what about that sword and them cherubim back there? Why bother guarding that tunnel when anybody could have just dropped down through a hole in the top of the cave?"

"There were two cherubim, Joe, maybe there was one at each opening."

"Then there'd be more bodies here and I haven't seen any."

"So what's your point?"

"My point is that I think this is the Garden of Eden."

"No, no way. It's not big enough. I mean, I can tell by my echo that this room is only maybe a couple hundred feet across."

"Okay, tell you what. If there's no other way out of here except the way we came in, will you agree with me that this is the Garden of Eden?"

"Agreed. If there's no way out . . ."

"There isn't."

"Knock it off, Jim, disguising your voice isn't going to fool us."

"It wasn't me," Jim says defensively.

"It wasn't," the strange voice says. "It was me."

As we turn around the three of us are suddenly hit in our faces by the light from four high intensity flashlights.

"Who is it?" I ask, shading my eyes with my arm and trying to see past the light.

"Light the lantern and put it down halfway between us so they can see what they're up against and then we can talk."

The silhouette of a man holding a lantern walks to within ten feet of us, puts the lantern down and as he begins to light it I notice the gun, probably a 9mm, in his other hand.

I whisper to Joe," He's got a gun."

"I know, I see it."

Jim must have seen it, too, because he's slowly inching his way around to get behind us.

The lantern slowly lights up the cavern. The first person I recognize is the one with the lantern, it's one of the three men who had chased us in Tel Aviv. That means two of the other three are likely to be the others that chased us.

"How'd you find us?" I thought sure they'd still be searching Tel Aviv for us.

"It wasn't too difficult."

Something about the voice is familiar but I can't quite place it. It must be the acoustics in the cavern distorting the sound.

Then it becomes abundantly clear where I'd heard the voice before as the lantern illuminates the face of . . .

"So, Detective Taylor, how did you find us? I thought we left you back in Michigan."

I surprise myself at how calm I am.

"It's not so hard when you have the right resources, and somebody leaves a trail of big bills."

"So what do you want?"

"I want what my boss wants."

"The cube?"

"No, if I wanted the cube I could have gotten it back in Michigan before you got on the plane, but my boss thought it best to just help you on your way and then follow you. Discretion seemed to be the best move for the both of us."

"Then why try to catch us, and what purpose did it serve to murder all those people?"

"My boss is a very impatient man. He simply felt you boys needed a little extra motivation to get your tails in gear."

"Just who is your boss and what is it exactly that he does want if he doesn't want the cube?"

"Who he is is not important, especially since he won't be my boss anymore as soon as I get what he's after. Now back away from those trees."

"What are you going to do with us?"

"Nothing, if I find what I'm after. Now back away . . . slowly." He waves his gun threateningly.

I feel defiant, upset at his lack of regard for human life, but Joe tugs on my shirt.

"Better do what he says, Bob. No use making him shoot us sooner than is necessary."

"Your friend gives good advice, but don't worry. Nothing will happen to you if we find what we're looking for because then neither you or anyone else, for that matter, will be a threat to me. Hanks! McNeal! Cover these three. Grant, you help me check out these trees."

Detective Taylor and the guy named Grant, small in stature compared to his superior, go about shining their flashlights into the two obviously dead trees. For the life of me I don't understand why they're using their flashlights, the lantern supplies more than enough light to see by. Especially since the only thing to see are dead branches.

"Find anything yet, Grant?"

"No sir, not even a leaf."

"Then check in the dirt. They may have dropped off onto the ground."

The last time I saw a man in dress clothes digging in the dirt was on reruns of Green Acres, and now there's two of them.

Fifteen or twenty minutes of this goes by when in frustration Detective Taylor slaps the ground with a handful of dirt.

"This doesn't look good, Bob," Joe whispers.

"Okay, you sorry excuses for human beings, what'd you do with them?"

We all look at each other totally bewildered.

"Do with what?" It seems I've become spokesman for our group by default. What's surprising is that Joe is remaining remarkably subdued.

"Don't play dumb with me. You wouldn't be here if you weren't after the seeds like everyone else."

Joe and I look at each other.

"Bob, the tree of life. He wants the seeds from the tree of life."

"Your friend's a bright fellow. Now hand 'em over."

"Hand what over?"

"Listen here you scrawny little pip-squeak, I'll give you just ten seconds to hand over those seeds or I'll remove them from your stiff little bodies."

"We don't have your precious little seeds."

"Empty your pockets . . . now!"

We start pulling things out of our pockets.

"You! The tall skinny one . . . Jim! Move out where I can see you."

I move to one side and Jim steps slowly forward to stand in between Joe and I. I pull the cube out of my jacket pocket and the money out of my back pocket. I still have my car keys and my wallet. There's also my passport, some change and my little flashlight. It's hard to hold everything in just two hands along with the cube, but I manage to balance it.

Jim is still digging things out of his pockets and just like on the plane, he begins dropping some of them. Of course it doesn't help any when he's shaking like a leaf. I notice the pumpkin seeds as soon as Jim pulls them out, and so does Detective Taylor.

"I knew it! Bring those seeds here you little weasel, and don't try anything smart."

"But . . ." Jim tries to tell him but doesn't get a chance.

"Just shut up and bring them here."

I try this time. "But those aren't . . ."

"Shut up scrawny, or I'll blow that smart mouth right off your face."

I wonder where I heard that before. Maybe it's just as well. He might be satisfied with the pumpkin seeds and let us go.

Jim walks slowly forward and holds out everything to the detective. Detective Taylor snatches out the four or five seeds that have been in Jim's pocket since we stopped in St. Johns, knocking most everything else out onto the ground. Jim starts to bend over to pick them up.

"Uh uh, you can get them later. Get back there with your friends."

Jim moves back between Joe and I.

"Those are only . . ."

"I know, Jim, I know."

"Shut up, you two, or I'll blow away your fat friend there! Grant, come here a minute. I know I can trust you." Detective Taylor holds out the seeds in the palm of his and. "Take one and swallow it."

Grant gives him a strange look, but picks one up between his thumb and index finger.

"You're sure?" he asks.

"You bet. I'll need someone to watch the eastern hemisphere while I take care of the west. You will be my immortal partner."

Grant gives a reluctant smile and lays the seed on his tongue like a pill and swallows it. There's silence for a moment.

"Do you feel anything yet?"

"No. How long do you think it'll take?"

"I don't know for sure, couple minutes maybe. You might not even feel it."

"Then how will we know it's working?"

"Like this."

Detective Taylor raises his gun and fires two quick shots that rip into Grant's chest. Each shot is magnified by the acoustics of the cavern, causing me to cover my ears. Grant falls backward onto the cavern floor, a look of disbelief on his face. The sound of the shots seem to echo endlessly through the tunnels. The only other sound is Grant's gurgling from the blood that is quickly filling both his lungs and suffocating him to death.

"Come on, Grant, get up," Detective Taylor urges. "Get up."

The gurgling stops and Grant lies still.

"All right, I'm through playing games." Detective Taylor turns and fires a shot into the cavern ceiling. "Give me the right seeds or your fat friend there will be the next one to have trouble breathing."

This scenario seems all too familiar, it's like we're acting out the dream I had, only in a different location. Only this time I'm not going to let this guy shoot Joe. Just one problem. I don't have a pillow to swing at the gun.

"We don't have the seeds!" Joe insists. "We showed you everything we have, and we tried to tell you that those were only pumpkin seeds but you wouldn't let us!"

"Then I guess the boss was wrong about this eternal life stuff. It was probably just a myth all along. But you know, it was worth a try. Being invincible would have made me the most powerful man on earth. But since that's not to be, I have no further use for you three."

That line is from my dream also and I know what it means. I

don't have a pillow but I have this. I throw the cube just as Detective Taylor raises his gun. It hits him in the forearm causing the gun to fire once before both it and the cube fly off in different directions. Hanks goes down in a heap onto the ground.

"Are you guys okay?" I ask Joe and Jim.

"Yeah, I'm still here," Joe replies.

Jim nods his head.

"Hanks! McNeal! Where's my gun!"

"I don't know, sir." McNeal looks around. "But I think you got Hanks."

"Keep them covered, McNeal, I'm going to take special pleasure in shooting each one of these three in the head myself."

Joe nudges me and points toward a clump of brown grass about ten feet away. Just barely sticking out is the wood handle of Detective Taylor's gun.

"Well, lookit here. Well, I'll be." Detective Taylor picks up the two halves of the cube which appears to have been broken on the rock it was lying next to. The cube looks like it has a small hollow center. Detective Taylor drops one half and then dumps three peanut sized seeds into his hand. "They were inside the stupid hunk of metal the whole time."

He drops the other half of the cube and holds the seeds out for all to see. "These three little seeds are going to make me the most powerful man in the universe."

I remember reading about someone else who has those same aspirations. His name is Satan, and in Revelation it tells what his ultimate end will be. How can this mere person hope to do better than Satan?

Detective Taylor picks one of the seeds up and just as Grant had done with the pumpkin seed, he pops it in his mouth and swallows it with a total look of self satisfaction on his face.

A shotgun blast rings out and McNeal flies several feet to his right into a crumpled bloody mess. The three of us dive to the ground but Detective Taylor merely turns slowly and confidently to meet the new adversary.

"You're a fool, Mitchell Taylor," the tall man with a long trench coat and hat says. I can't make out any details in his features as he continues to stand in the shadows. "I knew you couldn't be trusted with something this important. You are much too ambitious for your own good."

"It doesn't matter now, you're too late. I've already swallowed one of the seeds and I can already feel it working."

"If you swallowed it whole you're an even bigger fool than I thought."

This voice sounds familiar, too. Why does everybody have to sound like somebody else. I see Joe inching his way toward Detective Taylor's gun.

The stranger in the trench coat moves forward another step, putting more light on his face. I never would have recognized him if it weren't for his cold, black eyes peering out into the scene around him. It's the Pope.

"You don't frighten me anymore. You think those guns will stop me? I'll just rip your arms and head off and there won't be a thing you can do to stop me. I'm in charge here now so you . . ." Detective Taylor suddenly bends over in pain. He straightens up a little, still clutching his midsection. ". . . you . . ." He screams in pain, agonizing screams, as his torso begins to be ripped apart. Quickly, roots shoot downward, weaving in and out of his legs like huge brown worms, tearing the flesh as they go. He continues to scream until a branch grows up his throat and out his mouth. The only sound in the cavern now is the faint echo of his screams, and the tearing of his clothes and an occasional bone breaking. His hand is still closed, clenching the remaining two seeds, that is until a branch grows out just past his elbow causing his arm to straighten out quickly.

The action flings the two seeds into the air and in Jim's direction.

"Catch 'em, Jim!" I yell. This may be our only chance of getting out of this alive.

Jim reaches up and catches one seed and manages to knock the other one down onto the ground near his feet.

"Quick, Joe, stand in front of Jim."

"Why?"

"Just do it!"

Joe and I move over and stand as human shields between Jim and the Pontiff.

I notice the tree that grew out of Detective Taylor is withering and dying as quickly as it grew, having run out of body fluids to thrive on and finding no moisture in the ground.

"Hand over those seeds."

"Jim, if he shoots any of us I want you to destroy those seeds immediately. Now, here's what's going to happen, you're going to let the three of us pass by and through the tunnel and I will leave the seeds on a small rock in the middle of the tunnel somewhere along the way."

I figure the small rock will be one that is about six inches under water in that small stream. Can I help it if the water washes it away?

"I don't think so. I anticipated just such a move by you. My, but you are predictable. So let's up the ante shall we? Steve?"

There's some shuffling of feet in the shadows then a petite woman is pushed forward onto her hands and knees, her long black hair falling all around her face. She lifts her head sobbing and the hair falls away from her face.

"Mi-Ling!" Joe cries out. He takes a step to help her but I grab Joe and hold him.

"Wait, Joe. You go over there and we're all dead, including Mi-Ling."

Joe looks at me and then at Mi-Ling. "Are you okay? They didn't hurt you did they?"

"No, Joe. I am very scared."

"You better not touch her or I'll . . ."

"No more demands, you will give me the seeds or I start killing and I start with her pretty little head." The Pontiff pulls his hand out of his trench coat pocket and places what looks like a 357 magnum at the back of Mi-Ling's head. "Let's have those seeds."

"You better do what he says, Bob."

I hadn't paid much attention to the guy that pushed Mi-Ling to the ground but now I realize who it is. I can't believe it's Steve. The friend I trusted, the church member who led the congregation in *Amazing Grace*. How could he be involved in this?

"He means what he says. He ordered all the murders you three are now accused of. It's also within his power to clear you. All you have to do is cooperate. It's your only hope."

"It's a bluff, Joe." I turn and look at Steve. "It was that Detective Taylor that did it, not him." I stare the Pope in his eyes. "And you're a disgrace to your religion."

He smiles an evil smile. "The only reason I even bother with this charade is because of the power this position holds. I couldn't care less about you or anybody else's religious myths and fables, and as for the late Mitchell Taylor, he had the brains of a flea. The only decision he ever made on his own killed him. Don't you make the same mistake. Give . . . me . . . the seeds."

His gun clicks as he pulls back on the hammer.

Joe panics, he grabs the seeds out of Jim's hands and stops just several feet from Mi-Ling. "Here! Take them, just don't hurt her."

"No, Joe, don't!"

"I have to, Bob, it's Mi-Ling."

"Good boy. Now hand the seeds to the pretty little lady here and go back and join your friends. Then we'll see about rewarding you for your wise decision."

Joe hands the seeds to Mi-Ling, and stands there for a moment looking at Mi-Ling's tear-streaked face.

"Go on, get back to your friends now."

Joe and Mi-Ling touch fingertips and then Joe slowly backs away.

"Okay, pretty lady, hand them up here."

Still holding his gun to Mi-Ling's head the Pontiff leans over and takes the seeds from her hand as she holds them up.

"Okay, you got 'em, now let her go."

"Patience, my fat friend. This is a moment that must be reverenced. You privileged few are about to witness the birth . . . of a god."

"That may be so," I say. "But it will always be spelled with a small 'g.'"

"No!" His voice thunders. "I will be the only god. I will be the new Messiah for the masses to worship! Only I will not be killed like the last one." If his eyes could spew fire I'd be shishkebab. He takes one of the seeds and crushes it between his thumb and index finger. He tilts his head back and lets the fragments of the seed drop into his mouth.

"And now, just to make sure my good reputation cannot be slandered in any way, something must be done about you four. Steve, what kind of gun do you have?"

"A 38 caliber."

"Good, trade me guns."

"Why?"

"Don't cross me, Steve, just do what I say and you'll continue to reap the rewards of my position."

Steve slowly and rather reluctantly hands his gun to the Pontiff who in turn hands his to Steve. Whatever this guy's up to, I don't think I'm gonna like it.

"Now watch and see how problems are taken care of." He turns his attention back to us. "So you won't have any horrible memories going into eternity, I'll be using a much less messy means of public relations."

He points the gun at Mi-Ling's back, and Steve stops him. "No! You said you wouldn't hurt any of them if you got the seeds."

"I knew I left you too many years in that church. You've gone soft on me, Steve. Okay, I won't hurt them."

Steve breaths a sigh of relief. Just as he does the Pontiff swings his free hand around and rips the gun out of Steve's hand.

"There's no room for sentimentality here. Now be a good boy and go join your new-found friends over there."

Steve stares blankly at him, scarcely believing what he's just heard.

"Go now, or I'll kill you where you stand."

Steve walks quickly over to where we're standing.

"Now gentlemen, you're going to see an example of what happens to those who oppose my authority."

I get adamant and scared at the same time. "You said you weren't going to hurt any of us."

"That's right, I did, didn't I. Well . . . I lied."

He begins to raise his gun and I close my eyes, resigning myself to the obvious outcome. Here I come Lord.

With the sound of the first shot I cringe but that shot is quickly followed by a steady stream of automatic gunfire. But nobody here has an automatic weapon. I dive to the ground again and look to see what's going on.

In the darkness, out of the light from the lantern, I see the flashes from the automatic weapon. The Pontiff has turned to face his foe, who seems to have already taken care of the Pope's body guards. Before the Pope can get off a shot he's hit by three or four rounds to his mid section that throw him backwards off his feet and onto the ground with a heavy thud, causing his gun to fly to his right and the one remaining seed to the left. He lies there . . . still, almost spread eagle. The echoes from the gunfire fades as a voice comes out of the darkness.

"You're still all a bunch of fools."

I perk up. "Is that you, Norm?"

"Yep, it's me."

Norm walks into the light sporting a large automatic assault rifle.

"How'd you find us?" I climb to my feet and brush myself off. I can hear the rustling of the others around me.

"I kinda thought something fishy was going on when I drove down a road that on a busy day might get a total of two cars on it, but suddenly had a parade of about ten and one is a limousine. So I decided to turn around and see what all the excitement was about. And I'll tell you, it was a bear carrying this thing up that skinny little ledge. I almost thought about going back to get my little Uzzi. Lucky for you guys I didn't."

I look at Jim.

"Don't say it, Bob," he says.

"I can't help it, Jim, I've got to. There's no such thing as luck."

"So who are these guys?" Norm walks over to where the Pope is lying. While Joe consoles Mi-Ling who's still sniffling a little, Norm stoops over the Pope's body. "What?" He bends to take a closer look then looks at us. "I just killed a priest?"

"He wasn't a priest," I say. "He was the Pope."

"The what?"

"The Pope."

"Oh my God. What's he doing here? And with a gun?"

"It's a long story, Norm, but right now we should get out of . . ."

Suddenly a hand reaches up and grabs Norm's assault rifle and another hand, a closed fist, hits Norm on his jaw, sending him sprawling into the dirt.

The Pontiff stands on his feet, looking as healthy as ever, and pulls the 357 magnum from his belt.

Norm scrambles to his feet and backs away. "Who is this guy?"

"I . . . Am . . . GOD!" he thunders. His voice seems to make the entire cavern vibrate. "I have the power to give life or to take it!"

He swings his gun just a hair to his right and fires one shot that rips through Mi-Ling's body from the back. Mi-Ling slumps forward into Joe's arms, an expression of astonishment on her face.

Joe screams, "No!" He gently lays Mi-Ling on the ground on her back. "I'm gonna send you back to hell where you belong!"

A look of rage comes across Joe's face that I'd never seen before. Joe gets to his feet and before I can say anything he charges the Pontiff, screaming at the top of his lungs. Joe probably outweighs his target by ten pounds, but he's stopped in his tracks by one outstretched arm which lifts him off his feet by the front of his shirt and tosses him halfway back to where he started.

I know what's coming next as the Pontiff raises his gun again. "It is time for you to join your pretty little lady, fat boy."

I can't let this happen. I dive to my left, skidding into the small clump of dry grass where Detective Taylor's gun is still lying. I fumble with it for a moment and take aim in the general direction of the Pope. We both fire at about the same time. A surprised Pope grabs the right front side of his head, dropping his gun in the process and stumbles backward. Joe stands up and with his back to me, just watches as the Pontiff falls forward onto his face, raising a small cloud of dirt around him.

"Are you all right, Joe?"

I get up on my knees, and sit back on my heels. My hands are shaking.

Joe turns slowly. "Yeah, I'm okay, but . . ." He looks down at Mi-Ling. ". . . Mi-Ling." Joe stumbles forward a little.

That's when I notice the blood on the front of his shirt. "Joe, are you bleeding?"

Joe looks down at his shirt. "No, that's . . ." He can't say it.

"Bob," Norm says, "it is his blood. Look, it's still dripping off his shirt."

"Joe, you're hit!"

"No I'm not, it's Mi-Ling, she's hurt. We've got to get her to the hospital."

"Joe, it's too late. You've got to lay down and let us take a look at your wound."

"I am not hurt. It's Mi-Ling."

Joe faints and falls limply to the ground. Jim, Norm, Steve

and I rush to him and Norm rips open his shirt. There's a large gaping wound just below his rib cage on his left side.

"This is really bad." Norm says shaking his head. "There's no way we'll be able to carry him out of here alive."

"Don't say that, we've gotta try." I say it, but in my heart I know he's right.

Joe opens his eyes. "I'm gonna die, aren't I? You don't have to lie to me, guys, I can tell. Good shooting, Bob. You got him good that time." Joe looks over at Mi-Ling. "I want to touch her hand one more time. Help me, would you, Bob?"

"Sure, Joe, whatever you want."

The four of us move Joe close to Mi-Ling and he grasps her hand. "I love you . . . Mi-Ling."

Joe smiles and closes his eyes.

I feel tears well up in my eyes.

"Come on, Bob," Norm says. "I know it's rough, but we need to get out of here."

"Couldn't we bury them first or at least pile stones over them? I don't think we should just leave them here like this."

"Yeah, okay, let's go find some stones."

We all start to get up.

"I told you! You cannot kill me!"

We spin around to see the Pope, with a mortal wound to his head, standing at the spot where he should have been lying, holding his gun. All the other guns are well out of reach, back where Joe had fallen.

Norm can't believe it. "Who is this guy?"

"I AM . . . GOD!" he thunders again.

The cavern vibrates at the sound of his declaration. Then I realize that the vibrations weren't caused by his voice. It's a tremor.

"I have the power . . ."

The ground beneath us actually begins to move as the tremor turns into a full blown earthquake. Rocks begin falling from the ceiling, a couple hitting the dry trees, splintering them into tiny fragments.

"Earthquake!" Jim yells.

Norm's sarcasm comes through the noise. "No kidding. Everybody back near the wall!"

We move back against the furthermost wall from the tunnel entrance and the only way out.

Then it happens, if I had blinked I would have missed it. Both Joe's and Mi-Ling's bodies glow and I swear they're both smiling at me and then, just as quickly, in a blur that seems to be in an upward direction, they both disappear.

I yell over the rumble of the noise. "Did you guys see that?"

"See what?" Norm yells back.

"Joe and Mi-Ling are gone!"

"Of course they are!"

"No! I mean . . ."

Just then the lantern is hit by a rock and we're in total darkness. Then it stops, and the only thing I hear is my own breathing, Jim choking on the dust, and a few loose rocks settling into place.

"Do you guys think he's still alive in here?" I whisper.

"Don't know," Norm whispers back. "Let's see if we can find our way out of here."

We start to make our way to the other side by following the wall. I'd use my flashlight but if he's still out there it would make a perfect target for him. Jim stubs his toe on a rock.

"Ow."

I caution Jim. "Shh."

I hear something zip past my ear followed immediately by the sound of the 357 magnum. I would yell for everybody to get down, but I know they're already headed that way, just as I am.

There's a rumbling, but not the same as it was before with the earthquake. Then the noise becomes deafening and it seems that the entire cavern roof is collapsing around us. I'm not sure which would be worse, to be buried alive under a mass of huge boulders or be shot in the head by a 357 magnum. At the moment though, it doesn't look like I have a choice in the matter.

It stops as quick as it started. I open my eyes and I see a ribbon of light cutting through the thick dust in the air at an almost horizontal angle from behind the huge pile of rock and debris where the cavern room used to be. Norm's already spotted it and is clambering over the boulders just in front of me.

"Come on, what are you waiting for?" Norm says standing atop a square block of stone. "Let's get outta here."

I start climbing, following close behind Norm, and Jim follows close behind me. I don't see Steve. I call for him.

"Steve!"

No answer. I call a couple more times but no use. I continue my climb. Every so often the noise of our climbing is punctuated by one of us choking on the dust. I climb on top of another block of stone when it hits me that these are the remains of a building. We must have been under a town or something.

"What'd you stop for, Bob?" Jim asks, standing in some loose dirt just below me.

"Nothing important, I just think that part of a building collapsed down into the cave."

"Oh . . . well it's hard to breath down here. I'd kinda like to get out of here."

"Okay, Jim, okay."

We climb out through the small opening, after Norm pushes a broken corner of a stone block out of the way, and stand on the flat, cracked courtyard of the place where the Dome of the Rock once stood and before that the Jewish temple. The earthquake has dropped the Dome of the Rock into the cavern.

I hear the noise of sirens rushing through the streets of Jerusalem.

Jim brushes himself off. "Hey, Norm, do you know any good places to eat around here?"

Chapter 16

I sit back on Norm's couch with a huge glass of water, the second one in almost as many minutes.

"Here it is, guys!" I shout into the kitchen, referring to what's on CNN.

Norm and Jim hurry into the living room and Norm picks up the remote control. Spinning around and dropping into his chair, he turns up the volume.

". . . Thank you, Matt. I'm standing where just three hours ago the worldwide moderate earthquake, registering five point one to seven point three on the Richter scale, collapsed an underground cavern on which the second most sacred Moslem holy site, The Dome of the Rock, stood. Virtually the entire building disappeared into the hole. But then, what could only be termed as miraculous, about a half hour after, a mortally wounded Pope dragged himself up out of the hole and related a bizarre story of his kidnapping and attempted murder before dropping off into unconsciousness. Doctors, in this latest report, say the Pontiff is resting comfortably and they expect a complete recovery with no ill effects from the bullet wounds that would have left any normal person dead within minutes.

"Sources report he received three abdominal wounds and a wound to his head just above his right eye. I have a quote here from the Pontiff's hospital bed. He says, 'I attribute my miraculous escape and equally amazing recovery from death to the powers that God had endowed me with while held captive in the cavern by the Christian terrorist group known as 'The Baptist Crusaders.' These powers allowed me to create an earthquake strong enough to collapse the cavern roof. During the earthquake however they made one last attempt to kill me. But the Spirit of

Christ entered into me and I became immortal at that instant.' This is Al Gregor reporting from Jerusalem."

"Thank you, Al. Once again, the latest report from the hospital confirms that the Pope is resting comfortably from his kidnapping and attempted murder earlier today. Reports . . ."

Norm switches the television off. "Who is that guy?"

I lean my chin on my hand and smile at Norm.

"He's a fulfillment of prophecy. Just like Joe and Mi-Ling going up in the rapture during the earthquake."

"How come we didn't go?" Jim asks.

"That bothered me at first, but then I remembered that we are both virgin Jews. Jim . . . I think we're part of the one-hundred and forty-four thousand."

"Wow . . . really?"

"Yeah, and that's why I think we suddenly were able to remember so much scripture."

"Okay," Norm says. "Then how is what's his name, the Pope, a fulfillment of prophecy?"

"Shall I quote the scripture, Jim, or would you like to?"

"Go ahead. I wanna finish this sandwich."

"Okay, in Revelation, chapter thirteen it says, 'And I saw one of his heads as it were wounded to death; and his deadly wound was healed: and all the world wondered after the beast. And they worshiped the dragon which gave power unto the beast: and they worshiped the beast, saying, Who is like unto the beast? Who is able to make war with him? And there was given unto him a mouth speaking great things and blasphemies; and power was given unto him to continue forty and two months. And he opened his mouth in blasphemy against God, to blaspheme his name, and his tabernacle, and them that dwell in heaven. And it was given unto him to make war with the saints, and to overcome them: and power was given him over all kindred, and tongues, and nations. And all that dwell upon the earth shall worship him, whose names are not written in the book of life of the Lamb slain from the foundation of the world.'"

Norm looks thoughtful for a moment, staring at the wall. Then he turns and looks me straight in the eye.

"I want my name in the Book of Life. Can you show me how?"

"Sure . . ."

Jim interrupts. "What happened to Steve?"

"I don't know, Jim, only God and Steve can answer that question, but that's another story. Right now we have to show this poor soul the way to real life."

Epilogue

Steve comes to, finding himself lying face down in the dirt in total blackness and with a very bad headache. He reaches around to feel the bump on his head and cringes at the sharp pain. He's not sure exactly how he got here. All he remembers is that when the cavern started coming down around everyone he ran for the tunnel. He doesn't remember getting hit in the head, just the terrible noise of tons of rock falling all around.

Steve sits up only to discover he can't feel his legs from his knees down.

"I guess I didn't make it after all."

Steve reaches down expecting to find a huge rock has crushed his legs but instead his fingers feel a pile of small rocks and loose dirt. He starts digging with his hands until the pressure on his legs is relieved enough that he is able to drag himself free.

The rush of blood to his legs is at first cool and then painful as his legs begin to tingle unmercifully. He rubs them but that doesn't seem to be doing any good.

Steve remembers that he was the closest to the tunnel, other than the Pontiff, and he was in no shape to move very fast at all when everything came crashing-in.

Steve begins to think about his own responsibility for everything that has happened.

Poor Bob and the others. I didn't want anything bad to happen to them and I don't know why I didn't see it coming sooner. The man was evil, he had people killed as he saw fit. And why did it take something like this for me to finally see it?

"I'll tell you what, Lord, if I ever get out of here I'm going to expose that Pope for what he really was. Nobody's going to erect any monuments to him if I have anything to say about it."

Steve remembers still having his flashlight when the lights went out. Maybe it's still nearby. Now that he can feel his feet again, Steve crawls around on all fours making wide sweeps with his hands until he bumps something metal and cylindrical in shape.

He picks up the flashlight and turns it on. Steve's eyes hurt from the light when it first comes on. "Well at least I know the bump on my head didn't blind me."

Steve slowly stands up. He's sore all over. "A bottle of extra strength aspirin would be nice right about now." Steve limps a little from some bruises and scratches on his legs. It's going to be a long painful journey out of here, but it'll give him plenty of time to sort out everything in his mind.

How did he get in this mess? Was he really brainwashed that much or was it that he simply refused to listen to anything else, being the good soldier. Was Catholicism really meant to be the way Blived said it was supposed to be? He can only hope that with the death of Nain Blived the twisted efforts of his organization will fall into confusion. If it doesn't, then that's something else he's going to have to figure out a way of making right. Maybe if he starts from the beginning, when he first went to the convent, it'll help him figure out where he went wrong and where the weaknesses are in the organization, if there are any. At least with the passing of Blived he won't have to deal with him and maybe he could destroy the organization from the inside out. It certainly would be easier than from the outside in.

"I wish there was something I could have done to help Bob and them earlier. But their deaths will not be in vain, I will do all in my power to defeat the powers that are responsible. I swear it by all that is holy."

Steve sets a determined pace and heads downward back toward the Dead Sea. His desire for putting things right consuming his every thought. Another seed is planted.

THE END

Adult   Fic

Spooner, Robert L.

Seeds of Desire